The whole freight car came hurtling toward her.

Then Talent was throwing Mary down, with the massive car following him. His body, flat against hers, arched and braced.

"Are you hurt?" he snapped out.

"Well enough. You?"

"I've got a freight car on my back," he managed with a grunt. "What do you think?"

"I'm sorry," she offered weakly.

An amused snort left him, and his warm breath gusted over her lips. "As am I." Oddly, it did not sound like a quip but an honest apology.

If they alerted the men nearby to their presence, they'd have to explain how they weren't crushed by the train.

Mary winced. "Thank you, Jack."

He flinched, then stilled. "You're welcome, Mary," he whispered back. The small space between her and Talent grew thick with silence.

Every dull thud of his heart reverberated through her. So closely pressed, they had to adjust their breathing. With each exhale Talent made, so must she inhale. His gaze was unwavering. His mouth was a word away. Deep within her, a shiver began, and her neck ached with the urge to cant her head, tilt her chin just so until his mouth fit to hers. Dear God, she wanted to kiss Jack Talent...

Moonglow

"Action-packed...This richly textured tale of 19th-century London interweaves intricately imagined and historically accurate scenes with red-hot sensual interludes. Like the first, a deeply compelling and imaginative story."
— *Publishers Weekly* (starred review)

"4½ stars! Top pick! Darkest London glows with the light of Callihan's creativity in the second installment of her unforgettable paranormal series. With a strong, sensually charged conflict, intense emotions, chilling suspense and thrilling action, readers will enjoy this haunting tale. Callihan sets the mark for a new style of paranormal historical."
—*RT Book Reviews*

"I really loved this book, very sexy, and tons of adventure."
USA Today's Happy Ever After blog

"A smart, intrepid heroine who is unaware of her own gifts, a tormented, deeply conflicted hero, and welcome characters from the previous series title combine with breathtaking sexual tension, seductive dialogue, and poignant tragedy to propel the complex plot to its intriguing conclusion...Dark, violent, and addictively enthralling, this exceptionally steamy tale is a worthy sequel to Callihan's stunning FIRELIGHT and a perfect lure for WINTERBLAZE, the third sister's tale."
—*Library Journal*

"Simply fantastic...beautifully written...A Perfect 10 is rare for a debut author, probably more rare for the second novel, but MOONGLOW more than deserves the accolade."
—RomRevToday.com

Firelight

"A compelling Victorian paranormal with heart and soul...The compulsively readable tale will leave this new author's fans eager for her next book."

—*Publishers Weekly* (starred review)

"*Beauty and the Beast* meets *Phantom of the Opera* in this gripping, intoxicating story...An exceptional debut and the first of what promises to be a compelling series."

—*Library Journal* (starred review)

"4½ stars! Top pick! Seal of Excellence! Like moths to a flame, readers will be drawn to the flickering FIRELIGHT and get entangled in the first of the Darkest London series...Callihan crafts a taut tale filled with sexual tension. This is one of the finest debuts of the season."

—*RT Book Reviews*

"FIRELIGHT draws readers in...Murder, a secret society, and overwhelming desire keep Archer and Miranda on their toes—and keep readers turning pages."

—*BookPage*

"A perfect 10! FIRELIGHT is a debut novel that will knock your socks off. Readers are not going to be able to casually read this novel. It's a page turner...The growing passion between Archer and Miranda steams up the pages...Excellent secondary characters and an amazing premise...I can't wait for the next book."

—RomRevToday.com

Also by Kristen Callihan

SHADOWDANCE

Kristen Callihan

FOREVER

NEW YORK   BOSTON

Copyright © 2013 by Kristen Callihan

Excerpt from *Firelight* copyright © 2012 by Kristen Callihan

Forever
Hachette Book Group
237 Park Avenue
New York, NY 10017

www.HachetteBookGroup.com

Printed in the United States of America
OPM

First Edition: December 2013

10 9 8 7 6 5 4 3 2 1

Forever is an imprint of Grand Central Publishing.
The Forever name and logo are trademarks of Hachette Book Group, Inc.

The Hachette Speakers Bureau provides a wide range of authors for speaking events. To find out more, go to www.hachettespeakersbureau.com or call (866) 376-6591.

The publisher is not responsible for websites (or their content) that are not owned by the publisher.

ATTENTION CORPORATIONS AND ORGANIZATIONS:
Most HACHETTE BOOK GROUP books are available at quantity discounts with bulk purchase for educational, business, or sales promotional use. For information, please call or write:

Special Markets Department, Hachette Book Group
237 Park Avenue, New York, NY 10017
Telephone: 1-800-222-6747 Fax: 1-800-477-5925

To family. Whether it is the one you are born with or the one that picks you, the support of a good family can make all the difference. I know it has to me.

Acknowledgments

My editor once told me that, to her, working on a book with me was akin to a pregnancy: months of gestation to grow the story, an intense period of hard labor during which one fears the story will never come out, followed by a great reward: the birth of a new book. I suppose she is right. So I thank those who help me along the way: Kristin Nelson, the hardworking staff at Forever, my editor Alex Logan, and my family.

I'd also like to give a huge and heartfelt thanks to the readers, bloggers, and reviewers who have supported this series and helped spread the word about it. First and foremost, I write these books for you.

Thank you!

SHADOWDANCE

Prologue

*I sat down under his shadow with great delight, and his
fruit was sweet to my taste.
He brought me to the banqueting house, and his banner
over me was love.
Stay me with flagons, comfort me with apples: for I am
sick of love.*

—Song of Solomon

London—September 1881

Life was not a long, straight road, but a series of turns.
Moments defined it. A hard choice, a chance meeting, a
bit of bad luck, and everything changed; a new life began.
Even now, at the ripe old age of twenty-one, Jack Talent
had had almost as many lives as a cat. And today? Today,
he felt a new change coming on. It rippled in his bones
and set his teeth on edge as he faced the man before him.
A man who lounged in an ornate mother-of-pearl armchair as if the whole world ought to court him. Jack suppressed a snort; over-puffed peacock was what he was.

"And why should I help Ian Ranulf?" asked Lucien Stone.

Jack maintained his own casual position, leaning back in his seat as if he were perfectly comfortable in this den of iniquity. This was his first assignment, acting not as Ian's valet but as someone he trusted to do the delicate work of social maneuvering. The problem was, however, that Jack was distracted. By a scent.

"Because he will pay you a king's ransom for the service." Jack let one of his brows rise, imitating his employer, as he knew the gesture was quite effective in conveying an air of detached boredom that would irritate Stone. "And we both know you'll do anything for blunt." Just as Jack knew that the way to play a man like Stone was not to appeal to his vanity, but to challenge it.

Stone's lip curled as his ghostly green eyes began to glow. Odd creatures, the GIM. Their eyes could beguile you or haunt your soul. "Quite forward of you, Mr. Talent." He ran a finger along his chair arm. "Ian is teaching you well."

Which was neither here nor there. Jack had an assignment to complete, and he'd do Ian proud by not bungling it. Damn, but that elusive scent had him by the cods. It wasn't Stone; he reeked of the lime cologne popular among London toffs at the moment. No, the scent was feminine, sugar and spice, like oven-fresh butter biscuits, the sticky toffee pudding he'd loved as a child, and woman, musky and...His mouth actually watered.

Stifling a curse, he swallowed hard and braced his forearms on his thighs, keeping his expression unmoved. "Lord and Lady Archer have already been invited to the Blackwoods' ball. Ian saw to that. They are relatives of his. The problem being that we need a female to impersonate Lady Blackwood, as the chit has taken ill. We'd prefer it to be a GIM."

Lucien smiled then, and it was cold. "Because Archer would scent a lycan in a moment, and the 'jig would be up'? Or because GIM are the better spies?"

GIM, otherwise known as Ghosts in the Machine, were the best spies because they had the ability to leave their bodies and roam in spirit form. A human would never notice them. Not many supernaturals could either. As for Lord Archer, the man was a recluse and stubbornly attached to the human world. He only knew of lycans, and would never suspect a GIM watched over his bride.

"Both. Now, will you do it?" Jack pulled out an obscene wad of pound notes and laid them on the table, not missing the way Stone's eyes gleamed once more. "It's a costume ball, so the replacement needs to resemble Lady Blackwood. Archer has never met them, at any rate. Easy work, really."

The money disappeared into Stone's big hand, to be swiftly pocketed. "Ian's a fool to try to part Archer from his bride." The devilish grin returned. "Then again, I understand his fervor. You're too young to know it, but the lady does bear a shocking resemblance to Una."

"So I've heard," Jack said in a bored tone. Personally he agreed with Stone. Ian was being foolish. The way his employer threw himself fully into the pursuit of love and happiness disgusted Jack, if only because he knew the two sentiments to be wholly divergent, despite what the poets claimed. However, he owed Ian his life, his place in the world, so he merely stared down Stone. Besides, he did not like Stone; the man was too pretty, and too easily bought.

Lucien made a noise of amusement as he rang a small bell at his side. Across from him Jack quashed the urge to fidget. That scent. It bloody permeated the room, making him hard, making him hungry. Little fangs dropped in his mouth, a sure sign of his baser nature begging for a shift. Into what, he had no idea, nor was it advisable, nothing like bursting into the form of a werewolf or jungle cat to break up a perfectly civil meeting. Damn. Likely the fragrance belonged to a GIM. There were plenty of them aboard this massive barge anchored on the Thames. He could hear the whirring and clicking of at least six clock-work hearts.

Lusting after a Ghost in the Machine did not sit well with Jack. The whole roaming-about-in-spirit business gave him the creeps. Even so, the light tap of feminine heels coming down the hall had his gut tightening in anticipation. Was it she of the delicious scent?

The door opened, and in walked a woman. Beautiful creature, with black hair and gleaming blue eyes. Fright-eningly, she bore a shocking resemblance to Lady Black-wood. But Jack sagged with disappointment. She smelled of roses and cherries. Perfectly lovely, but not what made him want to bite down on soft, smooth skin, or sink into hot, tight... Clearing his throat, Jack eyed Stone as another, far more important thought hit him. "You knew I'd be coming here."

Lucien's teeth flashed in the lamplight as the woman perched next to him on the chair. "A bit of advice, Mr. Talent, on the GIM. It is useless to try to hide from us." Stone's arm wrapped about the woman, and she gave him an indulgent smile, which he returned as he spoke to Jack. "We'll always find out your secrets."

"I'll keep that in mind," Jack murmured, not amused.

Despite Jack's disquiet, the rest of their meeting went quickly, with Jack giving the woman Annabelle instructions as to how Ian wanted Lady Archer watched at the ball. And then he was alone in Stone's decadent dining room with its saffron-silk-lined walls, ornate Moroccan lamps, and a table laden with rich food that no one had touched. Stone had excused himself for a moment to discuss details with Annabelle. Jack ought to have gone then, but had found himself accepting Lucien's offer of a drink. He couldn't explain the action, only that the bone-deep feeling of anticipation lingered. Why did his instincts clamor for him to stay? And what of that maddening, gorgeous, damned distracting scent? Why did it seem vaguely familiar?

The door opened again and a warm, musical voice danced through the air.

"Lucien, do you know where—" A young lady halted as she spied Jack. Eyes the color of honey in sunlight widened as a small, shy smile lifted the corners of a pink mouth that ought to be named a deadly sin. "Oh, hello. I did not see you there."

Jack sat rooted to his chair, dumbstruck. Jesus, Mary, and Joseph, and saints preserve us. It wasn't merely her scent swirling around him in a dizzying rush and lighting his flesh with the fires of lust. She was the most beautiful, utterly delectable female he'd ever laid eyes on. Claws sprang from his fingertips and sank into the hard wood of the chair arms with a series of sharp cracks.

The young woman frowned at the sound, a small knitting of delicate golden-brown brows. "I'm sorry to intrude. You're here to see Lucien, yes?"

She took a step closer, and his nostrils flared, his body growing harder than oak. God. *Speak, you bloody idiot.*

"Yes." He cleared his throat. "No." *Charming, Talent. Is it any wonder Ian calls you a social clod?* He unclenched his hands and stood. "Rather, we've concluded our business. He ought to be back any moment, if you are looking for him."

She gave a small shake of her head, sending the curling tendrils about her heart-shaped face trembling. "It can wait." Her topaz eyes went to the drink by his hand. "I see he's extended his hospitality. A bit of warning"—her cheeks plumped—"do not try the wine. It is drugged."

"Ought you to be giving away trade secrets?" he asked with a laugh. The gleam in her eyes was infectious, for he was suddenly lighthearted, which wasn't at all common. He felt, well, *right* for lack of a better word. This woman, she was familiar to him in a way that made him breathe easily and yet tighten with a strange sort of dread. Who was she?

She came closer, leaning a hip against the table. Burnished satin lovingly encased her slim form. His hands itched to run along that fabric, feel where she was soft and where she was fragile. But there was nothing fragile about the look she gave him. It was a fleeting thing, a quick assessment that licked along his body as surely as if she'd stroked him, and was gone as she lowered her lashes and sank her teeth into her bottom lip. He wanted to be the one biting her.

"You seem a nice sort," she said softly, and wholly ignorant of the fact that she'd rendered him breathless. "I hate to think of you waking in some alleyway with your trousers around your ankles."

A choked sound left him. "He'd do that?"

Her grin was wide. "Lucien does enjoy his jokes."

"So no drinks then," he muttered, pushing away his brandy glass for good measure.

She laughed. The sound was low, husky, entirely incongruous with her feminine sweetness, and it made him harder than he'd any right to be. "Oh, but the rest of it is all right." She ran a slim finger along the edge of the table, inspecting the bounty of rolls, roasts, potatoes, and cakes. Her fine nose wrinkled at the bridge. "Though nothing that tempts me. Lucien likes his savories. He believes such treats to be more provocative." She sighed. "What I wouldn't give for a sweet pear or a crisp apple."

"'Comfort me with apples, for I am sick of love.'" Jack's face heated the moment the words were out. But again she smiled, her face flushed with pleasure, and that made his heart sing.

"Yes, precisely," she said.

"I'm Talent, by the way." He made a leg. "Mr. Jack Talent, at your service, miss."

Not missing a beat, she curtsied, and quite nicely. "Miss Mary Chase."

Mary Chase. She was a small bit of skirt. He'd be surprised if she weighed more than seven stone. But he had no doubt she'd give any man who wished to pursue her a merry chase. And Jack knew he'd try to catch her. She smiled up at him as though she just might let him. Again came the disconcerting feeling of knowing her, a baffling mix of lust and dread.

Before he could say a thing, ask her for a stroll in the park or simply tell her how utterly lovely he found her, Lucien sauntered in, his queer celadon eyes taking in how close they stood to each other and no doubt the way Jack gazed down on Mary as if thunderstruck, for he was. A lazy smile tilted Stone's mouth as he glided up and, without preamble, wrapped an arm about Mary.

Mary froze, her expression going blank. Then resignation reigned in the golden depths of her eyes, as if she'd been caught out and knew it.

"I see you've met my Mary." Stone's hand slid up and down her narrow waist.

Jack struggled to speak. He did not miss the possessive quality in Lucien's tone, nor the way the man's fingers were creeping up to stroke the underside of Mary's pert breast. The very sight had Jack's hands fisting.

"Yes, I had the pleasure," he said through his teeth.

Lucien gave a short laugh. "Believe me, lad, the pleasure is all mine." And then his blunt-tipped finger ran right over Mary Chase's nipple.

He might as well have pulled the rug out from under Jack's feet. She simply stood there, letting Stone debase her in front of a stranger—a shocking act that only a doxy would allow. Saliva filled Jack's mouth as heat washed over his face.

"I'm certain it is." Disappointment, the sense of wrongness about the whole thing, nearly made his knees buckle. Jack couldn't see her standing there, being fondled as if it were nothing more than a handshake, and keep his sanity.

He reached for his hat and clamped it on his head as Mary Chase stared up at him with wide brown eyes that held what might have been a plea. And then it hit him with the force of a steamer running full throttle, the familiar feel of her, why he thought he knew her. Because he did. Those eyes, that same pleading look. He'd faced those eyes before, just before he'd...Bile surged up his throat on a gag, the ground beneath him swaying. A cold sweat bloomed along his skin. Holy hell. She certainly didn't remember their first meeting or she would be at his throat.

He needed to leave. Now. And he needed to drive a wedge in deep, because he could never look upon Mary Chase again with any sense of honor.

He found his voice, though it was cold and dead, like

his heart. Which was perhaps just as well, for if she ever knew how much she affected him, he'd never regain his pride. And it was the one thing he had left in this world. "It was an entertaining show, at any rate." He forced himself to look down at her breasts. Those lovely breasts that would never be within his reach. Again came the coldness, washing out the pain. "Though not quite to my taste."

Mary Chase's distant expression turned to stone. Her eyes flashed gold before she turned a practiced smile upon Lucien. "I'm afraid we've offended Mr. Talent's delicate sensibilities." That golden gaze flicked back to him, searing his skin, and her smile turned acid. "We rarely have vestal innocents come to visit, you see."

Vestal, was he? The remark hit a bit too close to home, and thus it was easy to give a curt "Good day" and leave.

When he was well clear of Lucien's barge, however, Jack found a dank alleyway and vomited. But it did not purge the guilt and regret that burnt within him, or the sense that he'd lost something precious. But whatever he might do to remedy them ended when a shadow fell over him.

Lucien Stone leaned against the mouth of the alley, his eyes cold and dead as marble. "We have something to discuss, Mr. Talent."

Chapter One

Pulling the hood of her billowing black cloak farther over her head, Mary Chase wove through the mass of humanity that made up London. The November eve was crisp and clear, and her breath left in soft puffs of white. A vermilion-and-gold sky hovered above, a rarity here where fog usually held dominance over everything and everyone. Against the brilliant canopy of dusk, the dome of St. Paul's was bleak and grey, flanked in silhouette by the cathedral's smaller spires.

Traffic became a crush as she made her way along Ludgate Hill, reaching the circus. Omnibuses, carriages, pigs, cattle, and drays fought for space on the road, while hawkers, clerks, newsboys, homemakers, and pickpockets fought for space on the walkways. A perfect place to become lost. At least Mary hoped so. It was essential that she not be followed. Her position within the SOS depended upon stealth and secrecy.

A stew of excitement and anxiety thickened within her. She had a feeling that tonight she would finally get her chance to prove herself. For nearly two years she'd worked as assistant to Poppy Lane, otherwise known as Mother, leader of the Society for the Suppression of Supernaturals, or the SOS. But Mary wanted more. A chance to work on an actual case, to be out in the field with other regulators, agents of the SOS. For, as a certain obnoxious and arrogant regulator had been quick to point out, the ones in the field were at the forefront of danger. And although Mary was trained, she'd yet to be tested.

Mary sidestepped a group of boys hanging on the railing at the base of the Waithman obelisk and then passed a boardman advertising Collingworth's Cigarillos for the Improvement of Asthmatical Ailments. A hollow whistle lowed, and the ground beneath her feet trembled as a great steamer rumbled over the causeway and into the station beyond. Right on time. For once.

Thick black smoke rolled down to the masses, and Mary's mouth filled with the bitter taste of burnt coal. Using the cover of smoke, she rushed toward the overpass, and in the confusion of pedestrians hurrying along, she pulled her cloak off, quickly bunching it up. She emerged on the other side, no longer a young woman wearing a long cloak, but an old grandmother, white-haired and hunched, leaning on a cane for support. Traffic flowed around her as she hobbled along, her massive dress swaying about her small frame. *Slowly now.*

Just before the looming cathedral, Mary joined a cluster of vendors, the scents of meat pies, hot buns, and coffee making her mouth water. She slipped a bob into the hand of one crone selling muffins, then, quick as a cat, ducked behind the wide cart. In a flash she was a lean and spry youth, her step light, her hair out of sight beneath her cap.

Mary chuffed as she skipped along, losing herself in the crowd once again before slipping into a tavern on the heels of a man doing the same. The odor of sweat, spirits, and tallow mingled. Few spoke here, and if so it was to mutter for more drink. Keeping her gaze roving, she headed for the back room. The door opened easily.

"'Bout time you showed," snapped a male voice as she sat down at the small table obscured in shadows.

Mary didn't bother with a reply. An annoyed huff followed, and the man leaned forward, moving out of the darkness. He was handsome, well formed, and well dressed. Quite lovely really. Mary scowled.

"You are foolish, Mercer, to choose that identity." Mary didn't know whose it was, but based on the cut of the suit Mercer wore, she gathered that the poor fellow had been wealthy. It was a tricky business for a demon to take over the life of another. Harder still when the person lived in the public sphere.

Mercer sneered. "I'll have you know that this form gets me into more places than you'll ever creep." An ugly gleam lit his blue eyes. "And more beds."

She swallowed down a shiver of disgust. How many women were lured by this false front, having no notion of what they truly bedded? "And they'll all remember you too. Hard to miss, wearing such a fancy skin. Your vanity will see you dead one day. Which is no concern of mine." She shrugged. "Save when you are dealing with me. You get caught, and it will be my pleasure to strip you of that skin." The demon had been an excellent informant to her over the years, but she didn't have to like him.

Mercer's handsome lips twisted, and for a small

moment his irises flickered mustard yellow. "Mayhaps others will be wanting the information I have. I'm thinking I might sell to the highest—" He yelped as her knife slammed into the table with a thud.

Mercer's gaze drifted down to the sharp point lodged between his pale fingers. Mary looked only at him. "Do you know how a GIM ties a cravat, Mercer?"

He pressed his lips together.

She leaned in a bit, picking up the noxious scent of sulfur and smoke. *Bloody foul raptor demons.* Mary's voice was a blade in the thick air. "We make a nice, deep cut here"—she pointed toward his throat—"so that we might pull your tongue out as far as it will go before we wrap it about your neck."

Sweat pebbled along his noble brow but his yellow eyes glared. "You gonna flap your chaps all night? Or do you want to hear what I have to say?"

Mary sat back with a pleasant smile. "Talk."

His large hand lifted from the table. He made a show of adjusting the lapels of his stolen coat. "I gather you know the Bishop's been busy of late."

The so-called Bishop of Charing Cross was making quite the reputation for himself. First appearing in London in January of 1884, he'd started a sensation by leaving victims with their hearts ripped out, spines severed, and chests branded with a small cross. Their bodies were always found on the plinth of Nelson's Column in Trafalgar Square where it faced Charing Cross. A few eyewitnesses—of dubious credibility—claimed to have seen a man wearing long black robes fleeing the scene.

The newsboys, being the inventive sort, had dubbed the killer the Bishop of Charing Cross on account of the cross brand and the fact that the robes were similar to the cassocks worn by clergy.

So far he'd claimed five victims. Wealthy men, some titled, some not, all of them most thoroughly slaughtered. Only the SOS knew that the victims were, in truth, an assortment of raptor and sanguis demons. It was the duty of the SOS to both protect humans from supernatural harm and hide proof of supernatural involvement in the human world.

"We know," she said. "You'll have to do better than that."

Mercer's grin was evil and cold. "The Bishop made a wee mistake whilst doing his dirty business this last kill."

Mary did not move, but every muscle in her body tensed. "Go on."

Mercer paused, waiting, his expression said, for her to show a bit of good faith. Mary tapped her thigh, and the unmistakable jingle of coin rang out. Satisfied, he looked about for a moment, then leaned in close, bringing with him the scent of rotting onions and perfumed pomade. "I was there when he left his victim out in the open."

Mary stilled. "You saw him?"

One blink.

Mary watched the demon. "Risky of you."

"Don't I know it, love." He paled then. "I'm thinking if the wind were not on my side, I might not be here now to share my good fortune."

Her heart began to whir. "He could scent you?" Most supernaturals had an elevated sense of smell, but some had a more refined sense than others.

Mercer's long finger tapped the scarred table. "The question you ought to be asking, love, is how much does this information mean to you?"

Her smile was slow and thin. She worked it, letting him feel the menace behind it. Two years of training to be a regulator had taught her many things, especially how to wield information like a whip. "Ah, now, Mercer. I already have valuable knowledge, do I not?"

His brows lowered, and she whispered on. "Information that might slip out, carry on the wind where anyone might hear. Such as how you know the identity of the Bishop—"

"Hold your tongue!" He made to grab her hand.

Mary's knife was under the table in an instant. She pressed the blade in deep enough for him to feel. "No, you hold. There are a lot of soft bits here that you might miss, Mercer."

Fangs shot out as he growled. "You don't fight fair no more, Chase."

"More's the pity for you." Mary had wearied of playing it clean. It got her nowhere with the dregs she worked amongst.

"Pay me and I'll tell you."

She didn't move. "If you play me false, I will find you."

"Understood." He raised one brow, prompting her to act. "Now hurry up, I've an assignation with a plump and wealthy widow."

Mary quelled her disgust. A bag of coins hit the table.

Mercer licked his lips. "You won't have to look far for your Bishop, love." He grinned then, his eyes alight with cruel mischief. "He's been right under your nose the whole time. Might even call him an SOS favorite."

Dread pulled at Mary's spine. "Name."

"You know it well." His words seemed to slow, growing more distinct, and suddenly Mary did not want to hear them. But they came regardless, ruining her evening and instantly making her life that much worse. "Mr. Jack Talent."

Later that night, in another part of town—

The moon hung bright over Trafalgar Square, lending the vast space a dreamlike quality in which shadows danced beneath the monuments and fountain pools gleamed with silver effervescence. A soft wind ghosted low over the pavers, kicking up dust and bits of rubbish.

The hour turned and, in the distance, Big Ben chimed. Clean, resonant notes of the Westminster quarters rolled over London, a soothing lullaby, a musical constant that had heralded life, death, and all that came between. With a steady *dong, dong, dong*, the hours rang out. As the last note faded, the night watch strolled along Charing Cross and called the hours.

"One o'clock and all is well!"

Save all was not well.

Scurrying along the dark alleyways where only the desperate or despot dared tread was a raptor demon. A foul creature who fed on misery and pain, the demon had his pick of nourishment in London. Tonight's clear skies and crisp weather promised that plenty of London's populace would be out and about, just waiting to be pulled into the darkness. An excellent night for hunting.

Only he was not the sole hunter out for blood. And as he followed the night-bobby, intent upon making a small meal out of the copper, death followed.

His stalker growled low in his throat, a sound so soft that the demon remained unaware. Ironic, thought the hunter, that serving up death was the only time he truly felt alive. A rage began to boil within his veins and pull his skin tight. So tight that he barely felt the cold November air bite at his exposed cheeks. The very stink of the demon he followed made his nostrils pinch and his insides pitch. How well he knew this one's foul stench.

The bobby stopped, perhaps feeling a thread of danger. After looking about, his handlebar mustache quivering in the breeze, he slipped into a tavern.

Thwarted, but not for long, the raptor turned down a dark corridor, and the hunter followed him. The lively song of a fiddle danced along the cobbles and on its heels came the laughter of men. They were gathered at the very end of the lane, hunched over a fire barrel. The raptor paused and smiled as if savoring the moment. The hunter savored it too, letting the hate within him grow. And then he attacked, slamming into the unsuspecting demon and dragging him into the deepest part of an alley.

Glowing yellow eyes glared back, fangs bared in a hiss. The hunter stalked forward, letting the raptor see him, take a good look at death. And the raptor's eyes went wide, his grey skin going sickly white beneath the moonlight.

"I see you know me." The hunter's voice was whisper-soft and ice-cold, even while his body grew, tearing at the seams of his coat. Fangs slid over his bottom lip, and his fingertips throbbed under the weight of his long claws. The shift was always the same, taking on the form in which death would best be delivered.

A calculating gleam lit the raptor's eyes. "Oh, yes. I'd say I know you well. Tasty blood you have, young lad."

Raptors never were very intelligent. Like a whip, the hunter lashed out. His claws sliced into the demon's gut and shot up, under the ribs, to grasp the hot, beating heart within. The demon screamed, his body bowing, his eyes rolling back.

Holding his prize tight, the hunter hauled his catch up close. "Say my name."

The raptor's bottom lip quivered. Just once before he spoke up. "Talent."

Jack Talent gave the foul heart a squeeze. "Again."

"Talent! Talent!" The demon writhed in his grip, unable to fight back or get away now that Jack held his heart fast.

A cool calm settled over Jack, easing the pain within him, if only for a moment, and he smiled grimly. "Wanted it to be my name on your lips when I sent you to hell." And then he ripped the raptor's heart out.

Washed in blood, Jack leaned down and severed the demon's spine, and the light died in the demon's eyes.

Peace ebbed away before the body even cooled. But Jack knew peace would never truly be his until they all died. Throwing the body over one shoulder, he made his way to Trafalgar Square.

Not a soul stirred as he came upon Nelson's Column. There he would leave the body, just as he had all the others. But as he moved closer, and the moonlight illuminated the spot before the plinth, his breath stopped and his blood stilled. A body already lay there.

Chapter Two

It was inevitable that Jack be called into headquarters. The Bishop of Charing Cross had struck the night before. Murder was nothing new in London. Strange ones of a public nature, however, were another matter. Jack had been the regulator in charge of this particular case for a year now, a blight on his otherwise stellar record. This time a shifter had been murdered. As one of five—make that four now—known shifters living in London, he took it personally. Having intimate knowledge of certain facts, Jack was also unnerved by this new murder. Deeply. And he wanted answers.

Cool shadows slid over him as he strode down the long, echoing corridor that led from the SOS common rooms to the main meeting area. Headquarters was full of regulators updating their intelligence before going out. He did not like being around them, or anyone. Not that he had to worry on that account. The others steered clear of him, their eyes averted and their bodies tense. Fear he could handle, hell welcome, but pity?

One younger agent lowered her lashes when he passed, and a growl rumbled in his throat. She started and hurried off. Rightly so. No telling what sort of beast would break free should he lose his temper. Not even he knew. That was the way of a shifter, not owned by a single monster but possessed by all. He was everything, and he was nothing in particular. In truth, being a regulator was the only certain and good thing in Jack's life.

At the end of the black marble hall, a guard stood beside a massive steel door. He saw Jack coming and swiftly opened it.

"Master Talent," said the guard, "they are waiting for you."

He was precisely on time and the director was already waiting? And what did the guard mean by "they"? His meeting was to be with the director. Who the bloody devil would be here—

Her scent slammed into him like a punch. And what little equanimity he'd maintained flew out the door. Oh, no, no, no...they wouldn't dare. He eyed the inner wood door that blocked him from the meeting room. She was in there.

His muscles clenched tight as he forced himself to enter.

"Ah, Master Talent," said Director Wilde from the head of the table. "Right on time. Excellent. Let us proceed." His clipped voice was unusually animated, as if he knew Jack's displeasure at the unexpected third person in the room and reveled in it. Which wouldn't be surprising. Wilde loved to keep regulators on their toes.

Jack heard every word, but his gaze moved past the director and locked on her. Mary Chase sat at Wilde's right, serene and ethereal as ever. Her face was a perfect replica of Botticelli's Venus, and her body...no, he wouldn't think about that. It was one rule he refused to break. He never, ever, thought too long on Mary Chase.

Mary Chase would have liked to think that, after years of being on the receiving end of Jack Talent's hateful glare, she'd be immune to it by now. Unfortunately it still worked through her flesh like a lure, hooking in tight and tugging at something deep within her. One look and she wanted to jump from her chair and hit him. However, knowing that he found her presence bothersome gave her some small satisfaction.

He stood in the doorway, filling it up, poised for a fight like an avenging angel of Old Testament wrath. Over the last year Talent had reached his physical prime, shooting up well past an already impressive six feet, and adding what looked like twenty pounds of hard-packed muscle to his frame. It was as if nature had given him the outer shell he needed to protect himself from all comers. The change was unnerving, as the man had been intimidating enough before, mainly due to the sheer strength of his stubborn will.

With a sullen pout, Talent dropped his large body into the chair opposite her. She suspected that he sought to convey his displeasure, but the blasted man was too naturally coordinated, and the move ended up appearing effortless. "Director Wilde."

Talent turned back to Mary again. His rough-hewn features might have been carved from stone. "Mistress Chase."

Oh, but the way he said her name, all oil and flame, as if it burned him to utter it.

Mary dug a fingernail into her palm and modulated her voice. "Mr. Talent."

He paused for a moment, his brows raising a touch in reproach. She'd been childish in not giving him the proper form of address, but some things burned for her too.

His quick, irrepressible smirk said he knew as much. "Master," he reminded her.

He loved that she had to call him master. In their first year in training, he'd taken every opportunity to make her use the official title for all male regulators. Their gazes held, and heat rose to her cheeks. Thank God she hadn't the complexion to blush or he'd be all over her. "Master Talent," she ground out.

His annoying smirk deepened, and her nails dug deeper into the flesh of her palms. One day...

"Now that we have our forms of address clear," cut in Wilde, "might we proceed with the actual investigation? Or shall we continue with this little pissing contest?"

"Pray continue. If Chase can manage to refrain from straying off track, that is." Talent adjusted his broad shoulders in the chair and crossed one leg over the other.

Never react. She turned her gaze upon the director. "I was ready to hear the facts of the case twenty minutes ago, Director."

Talent bristled, and she let a small smile escape. He bristled further, but Director Wilde ploughed ahead.

"Good." Setting his hands upon the polished mahogany table, Director Wilde proceeded to give them the facts. Mary had already memorized them, and so she let the director's words drift over her as she studied Talent. The man was good, his strong, blunt features not revealing any hint that he might have personal knowledge of the Bishop of Charing Cross's most recent kill.

One powerful arm rested upon the table, and the fabric of his plain black suit coat bunched along the large swell of his bicep. Talent did not so much as twitch when the director set down a photograph of the last victim.

"Mr. Keating of Park Place," said Director Wilde. "As with the other murders, he has been branded with the Bishop's cross. The sole difference in this victim is that, while the others were demons, this man was a shifter, and by all accounts a law-abiding citizen of London."

Mary glanced at the photo, featuring a young man stripped naked. The cross branding his chest was a raw, ugly wound, but it was his eyes, wide and staring, that made her clockwork heart hurt. It was the expression of an innocent man pleading for mercy.

Talent looked as well. And when he did, she watched him. The ends of his brows lifted a fraction, and she was inclined to believe that he was surprised. Then again, he had always been a fine actor. In the beginning of his association with the SOS, Talent had made a name for himself by successfully tricking a powerful primus demon into believing he was Poppy Lane. Of course being able to shift to look exactly like Poppy had been part of it, but it was his mimicking of her character to the letter that had made the difference between success and catastrophe.

How could a man who had nearly died defending others be a murderer? But Mary feared she understood all too well. Although he was arrogant, obnoxious, and a general ass, he'd survived an ordeal that would break most men. Was he irrevocably broken?

"Do you recognize the victim, Master Talent?"

Wilde's query had Mary focusing once more.

Talent's heavily lidded eyes lifted from the photograph. "Shifters by nature are a solitary lot. No, I did not know Mr. Keating." His long fingers curled into a fist upon the table. "I was under the impression that the SOS kept the identity of shifters secret."

The director's mouth tightened. "We do. There is no indication that the files have been breached."

Talent made a noise that might have been construed as a snort, but it was just soft enough to get by Wilde without earning any reproach. For once, however, Mary agreed with Talent's sentiment.

After researching long into the night, Mary had learned that, in the last hundred years, the SOS had made a concerted effort to locate and document the existence of all shifters living in Europe. A daunting task. However, when the Nex began hunting shifters for their blood—whose properties gave demons the ability to shift into anything—the SOS, realizing its mistake in outing shifters, provided as much protection as it could by offering them new identities and keeping their whereabouts hidden. But it was a constant battle, for the Nex, an organization dedicated to seeing supernaturals rule the world over humans, was resourceful and ruthless.

Talent leaned forward a fraction. "Who was Keating? Before?"

"Johannes Maxum." Wilde pulled a paper from his file and handed it to Talent. "He's an older shifter. Date of birth unknown, but he once worked as an alchemist for Augustus the Strong in the quest to discover the Chinese's secret to making porcelain."

Talent scanned the page, then set it down. Protocol dictated that he hand the paper to Mary, and she might have been insulted at his obvious slight, had she not been expecting it. No matter, she'd read about Maxum as well. Besides, Talent's juvenile tactics would not cow her.

In any event, Director Wilde was now looking at both of them. "Research has been instructed to provide any and all assistance you might require."

"Thank you, Director," Mary said. "We shall keep you informed as the case proceeds."

Talent's jaw snapped up as if he'd been punched. "We?"

The force of his inner agitation was a maelstrom creaking against the walls. Any moment now it would break. Mary remained calm. "We are to be partners now, Master Talent. Or haven't you been paying attention?" *And I will stick to you like a barnacle until I find out the truth.*

The small vein at his temple pulsed. "I work alone. Always have."

Wilde laid a hand over the file. "There is a time to every purpose under the heaven, Master Talent. Which includes knowing when to receive help." The steely look in the director's eyes made it clear that Talent would find no leeway should he protest.

The sound of Talent's teeth grinding filled the room. "I was under the impression Mistress Chase was here in a clerical capacity."

"You hoped," Mary corrected. "Otherwise, I have grave concerns regarding your propensity for jumping to conclusions."

Talent leaned his weight on the table as his gaze bore into her. "Keep baiting me, Chase, and you'll find out what else I have a propensity for."

She leaned in as well, until they faced each other like dogs in a pit ring. "I am quaking in my knickers."

"There you go, mentioning your knickers." His mouth slanted, and his eyes gleamed dark green. "What I cannot discern is if you only do so to me, or if you want the whole of the SOS to be thinking about them."

"Why Master Talent, are you trying to tell me that you think about my knickers?"

His lips pinched so tight that she had to bite back a grin. A low growl rumbled from the vicinity of his chest.

"Children." Director Wilde's expression was stern, but his eyes held a glint of amusement. "The discussion is over. You will work together on this." His good humor fled. "And you will not fail the SOS. Now"—he motioned to the door with his chin—"take your squabble out of here. Perhaps you can pull Mistress Chase's braids in the common room, Master Talent."

On the outside Mary knew she appeared serene as she left the meeting room. On the inside, however, she quivered in anticipation. For years she and Talent had detested each other. He treated her as if she were some low, conniving wretch. Solely because she was a GIM. *Lousy, arrogant bounder.*

The outer hall was cool and quiet. A calm before the inevitable storm. And that storm was right on her heels. Although, in truth, Jack Talent reminded her more of a panther, all dark and brooding, his powerful body so still when at rest, yet capable of instant, violent action.

Mary headed down the corridor, knowing that, while he made no sound, Talent stalked her. The skin at the back of her neck prickled, and her heart whirred away within her breast. With his shifter's senses, he'd hear her spinning heart, she was sure. *Oh, yes, come and get me, and we shall see how well you dance around the truth now, Jack Talent.* It was torture not to quicken her step or turn around.

By the time she reached the shadowed corner that led to another section of headquarters, her breast was rising and falling in agitation. Damn him.

And damn her too, for some small, traitorous part of her liked the chase, reveled in it. Gripping her weapon, she waited until his heavy hand fell upon her shoulder, and then she spun.

He grunted as they both hit the wall. The hard expanse of his chest barely gave under her weight as she pressed against him. For a moment they both panted, then his gaze lowered to the knife she had at his throat.

She had expected his rage, but not his grin, that wide, brilliant grin that lit up his dour features and did strange things to her equilibrium. His cheeky smile grew as he spoke. "Pulling iron on me, Chase? How bloodthirsty." His hot breath fanned her cheeks. "I knew you had it in you."

She did not ease her grip. Training with Mrs. Lane had honed her skills. The slightest move from him and he would be tasting that iron. "Trying to intimidate me, Talent?"

His body tightened, but he kept his hands at his sides. "What the devil are you playing at? You aren't a field agent. You've been hanging on to Mrs. Lane like a limpet, and now you want to partner." He leaned in, not flinching when the tip of her iron blade cut into his skin. "With me."

A rivulet of crimson blood trickled down his throat. She tore her gaze away from it. "This is the most important case the SOS has seen all year. Any regulator would be mad to pass up the opportunity to take it." When he snorted, she gave him a pretty smile. "Who my partner is makes little difference."

His lips pressed into a flat line. "This is my investigation. It always has been."

From the moment she'd asked Poppy to be assigned to the case, she'd known she'd face his rage. But she'd told

Talent the truth: Having the opportunity to move away from her assistant's role into fieldwork was not to be missed. And if he was guilty of murder, she would be the one to take him down. Keeping that little personal victory in mind, it was easy to give him a bland look. "Oh yes, and you've done a bang-up job with the case so far."

His growl seemed to vibrate through her, but Mary ignored it and the way the hairs lifted along the back of her neck. "What gave you reason to believe that it would remain yours alone after all this time, when you have nothing to show for your efforts?"

With an unfortunately easy move, he shrugged free. She let him; bodily contact was not a situation she wanted to prolong, as it was far too unsettling. He loomed over her. "Toss out what insults you will, Mistress Merrily." He poked her shoulder with a hard finger. "But do not for a moment try to undermine me. You think I'm a bastard now, try handling me in a temper."

He turned to storm off when she grabbed his lapel and hauled him back. Taking pleasure in the shock that parted his lips, she smiled. "I've seen your temper, Master Talent. You haven't been privy to mine." With lazy perusal, her gaze took in his heightened color and narrowed eyes. "While you'll be shouting about like a tot who's lost his lolly, I'll be the lash you never saw coming."

It was quite satisfactory to leave him open-mouthed and silent—for once.

Chapter Three

———— ❦ ————

Piss and shit and bloody buggering hell. Ignoring the patrons of the coffeehouse, Jack hunched over his meal of rashers, bangers, eggs, and toast, and shoveled in a bite, even though it tasted like dust at the moment. His mind was a mess. If he thought too long on the fact that Mary Chase, of all people, was now his partner, he'd kick a hole through the floor.

Instead he ran a hand through his shorn hair, knowing the thick, short hanks would now stick up at odd angles. Before, he'd taken care to pomade and comb his hair into an elegant style. Now he just wanted it off his face. He hated anything touching his skin. Fucking demons had taken away his sense of safety. And now Mary bloody Chase was taking away the one refuge found in his work.

Two years earlier Jack had been guarding Inspector Winston Lane due to a threat upon the man's life, when he'd been taken in by a raptor demon disguised as Mary Chase. The humiliating truth was that he'd been so shocked by the notion of Mary Chase, dressed in next to nothing and lounging in his bedroom, that he'd never considered the danger until it was too late. He'd woken up in a cell of a room, naked and crucified to a wall by iron spikes. The hellish days, hours, and minutes that he'd been captive, used and abused to many a demon's delight, was the stuff of his nightmares.

And she'd found him. When he'd been out of his mind with pain and degradation, when he'd wanted to die so he did not have to experience another moment of that hell, Mary Chase had somehow appeared before him, placing her smooth, cool hands upon his fevered skin. She had tracked him down, saved him. And the knowledge burned. Because she knew what had happened to him; there was no explaining away some bruises.

It was bad enough he'd have to hide certain facts from her while trying to figure out just what the bloody hell was going on. But for these many years, he'd had a plan when it came to Mary Chase. Carefully constructed and thoroughly executed. Evade, avoid, and retreat. And, in the event of the rare prolonged interaction, be the biggest rotter possible, so that she never attempted to purposely seek him out.

A lump of food caught in his throat. His plan was now shot to shit. He could not evade, avoid, or retreat. True, he could still act the bugger, but he didn't want to. It hurt to hurt Chase. But over the years, he'd come to realize that it would hurt both Chase and others far more were she to find out why he did it.

"Sod all," he muttered, tossing his fork down and pressing the heel of his hand against his eye.

"You cannot avoid me forever, you know," said a musical voice.

Jack nearly jumped out of his skin. Standing beside his

table with an imperious tilt to her chin was Mary Chase, his golden and glorious nemesis. He did not want to know how she'd found him.

"Christ," he snapped, "I hate the way you GIM slink about." But he loved the way *she* moved, all flowing grace, silently beckoning a man to follow. Even when she was walking away from him. She wasn't doing so now.

Her gloved fists curled tighter. "And I think you are a rude bastard. So we shall both have to grow accustomed to tolerating annoyances." Her gaze slid over him and cooled. "Not hide away in the hopes that the situation will change."

"I am not 'hiding away,'" he lied. "I'm hungry."

Chase's pink lips parted. "It is only half past ten. Why not wait for luncheon?"

"I'm a shifter. Food is energy. And it's bloody good too." He gestured to the chair opposite him. "Sit down, Chase. A proper meal ought to improve your humor."

"Or purge it altogether," she muttered under her breath as she glanced at his half-eaten meal. "I think just tea for me."

The coffeehouse was warm and relatively clean. It was filled with patrons, mainly workers, cabbies, a few students intent on idealistic slumming, and a host of others who wanted a small respite from the cold. In their drab regulators' garb, Jack and Chase blended in. As with most coffeehouses, there were few women, but no one seemed to mind Chase, apart from noticing her lovely features with interest. Jack gave them all a warning glare as Chase settled in her seat. Chase, who'd no doubt seen the whole thing, gave him one of her small smiles.

For Chase a smile meant a slight curving of her lips, a small twinkle of golden light in her eyes. Damn, but her smiles were more rare than his, which was saying something. He wondered what her true smile would look like. But realized he wouldn't be the man to coax one from her.

Across from him she gazed out of the window, and the sunlight kissed the smooth curve of her cheek. Her rosy lips parted with a breath, and he almost lost his mind. His gaze drifted to the velvety swath of skin just visible above her collar, that place on a woman's neck that was fragrant and warm, where she'd be sensitive. He wanted to sink his teeth into that spot, see if she shivered when he did it. And that was no good. But where to look? If not gazing at her neck, he'd be staring at her hair, golden brown and glimmering, or the swell of her breasts, those succulent little apple-sized breasts that begged a man to feast.

Her scent, that rich, sticky toffee scent that had captured him from the first, now filled the small space. Every day in close proximity. Scenting her. Hearing her voice. And knowing that his past made her utterly unattainable.

Hell. He wouldn't survive it.

Since they knew him here, service was quick. Soon enough Chase sipped at her watery-looking tea and watched him with apparent fascination as he finished up his meal. Her gaze was a living thing, making his skin itch and his muscles jump about. He didn't like her, but damn did his body react to her.

"Keep looking at me," he said between bites, not bothering to lift his attention from his food, "and soon I'll have a swelled head." No need to tell her which head he was referring to.

Her honey-warm voice rolled over him like a caress. "I cannot help it. The show is fascinating. Your appetite is the stuff of legend. Even Lucien—"

His knife scraped the crockery with a sharp screech,

and he stabbed another section of sausage with his fork. *Yes, do us both a favor and do not speak of your dear Lucien or his particular appetites.* The sausage tasted of sawdust.

When she spoke again—as he'd known she would— her voice held an air of detachment. "Have you any notion who the Bishop might be?"

He wanted to freeze, but kept eating. Her tone, so carefully light and innocent, had him wondering for a tight moment if she knew it was he. But she couldn't know. He'd been so careful. The muscles along his neck and shoulders protested as he raised his head. He took his time finishing the mouthful of food. "His kills signify rage," he said finally.

Her eyes held his, and there was a calm coolness lying in their bronze depths that had him tensing further. She tilted her head as if she knew of his discomfort. "Until now, rage against raptor and sanguis demons."

Ice spread beneath his skin. He forced his hand to release the fork and knife. They clanked against the plate. Slowly he wiped his mouth with the rough linen napkin. "It appears so."

With brisk efficiency she pulled a file out of the slim valise she wore strapped over her shoulder. "I wanted your opinion on something." She leaned close, her voice dipping low and her scent teasing his nostrils. "About the symbols."

"What symbols?" But he knew, and his food landed with a thud in his gut.

"Unlike the others, Keating did not have a symbol carved upon his wrist." She pushed a photograph of a dead raptor under his nose.

When he did not answer, she pressed on. "A small symbol was carved upon the wrists of all prior victims." Her eyes watched him. "It was in demonish. From the looks of it, either Sanguis or Raptor."

"I've worked this case for over a year now, Chase. I believe I am familiar with the particulars."

Her expression altered from engaged to flat as glass. How well he knew that look, and although it was familiar, he found himself mourning the loss of her animation.

"Do you know what the symbols mean?" Her wide brow furrowed, the merest wrinkling of her clear skin. "I confess, I am not able to read it."

The food in his stomach grew heavy, rolling about as if it might revolt. He'd been found by her. And while he couldn't be sure she remembered the details, the symbols carved upon his flesh had been telling. Should a person know enough about demonology, she would know that the symbols had been those of the raptors. Jack's guts tightened as sweat beaded along his back. He swallowed hard, still held by the power of her searching gaze. He wanted to run from it, from her. Did the scene live in her memory? Haunt her, turn her dreams into nightmares?

No. That was his lot in life. Likely all she felt was pity for the sorry sod she'd rescued two years ago. He fought against the cornered feeling that had his breath stuttering and returned to his food, cutting a banger with care. "Few others bother to learn the culture of Raptors and Sanguis. It isn't as though their kind is well liked."

Raptors were scum who fed off the misery of others. Sanguis demons were not precisely hated, but as they needed the blood of others to survive, they had a certain parasitic quality that made most supernaturals wary.

Chase's lashes swept down then, letting him take an easy breath. She glanced up again, less probing, but unnerving to him just the same. "And what of this shifter? How does he fit?"

The shock of finding the dead shifter in Trafalgar Square still unsettled him. He'd left the scene with due haste, sinking the slimy raptor he'd just killed in the Thames instead. Someone was imitating his crimes, and he wanted to know why.

Jack dug into his pocket, threw a few coins upon the scarred table, and told her the one truth he could. "That is the question of the day, Chase."

In keeping with the mercurial nature of London weather, it was raining when they left the coffeehouse, and while Mary did not mind, Talent insisted upon taking a hack back to headquarters. A silly extravagance that had her protesting and him snarling. They sat, each stewing in silence, the hack bogged down at an intersection, when Mary felt the hum of a spirit. A moment later a familiar form drifted in through the hack window and made herself comfortable on the seat next to Talent.

Hello, Miss Mary. Though she was in spirit form, Tottie's voice was clear as day in Mary's head. Nor did the dingy light of the carriage dampen the bright color of her shining blond hair or the sparkle of her green eyes.

"Hello, Miss Tottie."

Talent perked up at Mary's response and looked as if she were cracked. "Pardon?"

"Mistress Tottie is here. I was saying hello." Tottie, short for Charlotte, was Poppy Lane's newest assistant, handpicked by Mary due to her exceptional memory. That she was whip-smart and irreverent was a boon. Mrs. Lane needed someone to keep her on her toes, after all.

Mmm, said Tottie. *Are you going to say hello, too, you*

exceptionally large wall of man? She leaned into Talent, her shimmering image tiny in comparison to his, and ran her fingers along his neck.

Talent shivered and glared round, his whole frame tensing away from Tottie. "Is she sitting next to me?"

He looked as though he might start swinging, as one swats at a fly, and Mary bit her lip. "She is merely saying hello."

Oh, I am, Tottie agreed. *I've been wanting to say hello to Mr. Jack for an age, personal-like*. Her hand glided over his chest and headed down. *Such a fine cocky fella, ye are. Shall we see if it's all just tall tales, then, me lad*?

"Tottie," Mary snapped as Talent gave a violent start.

The little Irish imp stopped, blinking back with wide, round eyes. *Aye*? She let her hand fall upon Talent's lap.

"Bloody GIM," Talent burst out. "I felt that!" He turned his ire on Mary. "What the hell is she doing?"

"Nothing." Mary kept her expression neutral by sheer will. "Why are you here, Tot?"

The GIM sighed, her small mouth pouting as her diaphanous hand drifted off Talent. *You are no fun at all, Mary Chase.*

"So I've been told."

Talent's gaze snapped between her and a spot above Tottie's head.

"She's a few inches lower," Mary said. "And a bit touchy."

"Hell." Talent practically snarled as he glowered blindly at the spot occupied by Tottie. "Just remember, I can hunt your body down, Mistress O'Brien."

Looking forward to it, Master Talent. Tottie's cheeks plumped before she sobered. *The Bishop's struck again.*

"At Trafalgar Square?" Mary held up her hand to Talent when he made to speak.

Bit of a difference with this one. The man was found in his home, one Mr. Arthur Pierce. He's got the brand upon his chest, an' all the usual hallmarks of the Bishop's work. Wilde's directed the cozzers to secure the scene for your study.

"Lovely." The idea of seeing that horror turned Mary's stomach.

"Damn it, Chase—"

"There's been another murder," Mary said to Talent, lest he keep shouting.

The house is two blocks over, Tottie said, and Mary relayed it directly to Talent as the GIM continued. *Wilde wants you two there now.*

Chapter Four

M<small>r.</small> Pierce had lived in the center of a respectable middle-class suburb of London. Well-clipped lawns led to smart black doors, each graced with the same simple brass door knocker. White lace hung across every shining window.

Talent was ahead of her, his brusque stride so confident that it implied the very air ought to part for him. The rakish tilt of his hat had her longing to knock it off, if only to ruffle his composure and force him to acknowledge her presence.

As if feeling her displeasure, he stopped and turned. "Right then," he said. "You wait here.... What the devil are you doing?"

Mary brushed a gloved hand over his lapel once more. "Clearing a disturbing number of crumbs off your coat. Is that egg?" She flicked a dried crust of his morning meal from his tie. "My, but you look a fright."

Talent swatted her away. "Good God, woman, stop mothering me."

She scoffed. "I am trying to maintain the dignity of our office. You're stomping about as unkempt as a vagabond." In truth his gold SOS pin, depicting the goddess Isis, was the only part of his attire that he appeared to care for. Pinned neatly on his overcoat lapel, it gleamed bright against the dull, unbrushed wool. "The Talent I know and detest would never let his appearance fall into such disrepair."

He showed his teeth in a reaper's grin. "And the Chase I know and detest would not care."

"Of course I care. You represent the SOS, which, by extension, includes me. At the very least, do keep your hat on. Your hair looks as though you've let a goat have a go at it."

Talent's brows nearly met in the center with the ferocity of his scowl. "Are you quite finished?"

Mary looked him over and smoothed one last wrinkle along his shoulder, biting back a smile when a growl rumbled low in his throat. "There."

His cheeks went dull red. "As I was saying, take a look around the grounds. Perhaps you can discover something useful while you wait outside for me."

Mary drew up tight. "Now just a moment, you. I am not waiting out here. I'm your partner, not some lackey." Nor was she letting him out of her sight while they were on this case.

Talent's mouth tilted into a lopsided sneer. "Are you bamming me, Chase? You cannot go with me." He leaned forward, managing to loom even though he was a few feet away. "You go into that house, and you'll have every human there in a snit. Women are not fit to handle death, much less view a murder site. You know that as well as I."

"Not fit to handle death?" she ground out, her arms twitching to do him violence.

But he waved an annoyed hand. "Do not start quoting Wollstonecraft on me. I'm repeating pure social fact. That is what they believe. And that is what they will do, should you"—he pointed at her for emphasis—"waltz in there and expect to be treated like a man."

Mary barely refrained from huffing. He was right. Moreover, it was something every female regulator had to face in the field, always losing out on more interesting cases because of society's ridiculous notions. Confined to playing the spy, the watcher, pushed to the fringes, her female brethren did what they could. It was not enough. Worse, if she waited out here now, not only would she be unsure as to his culpability in this, Talent would assume the role of lead. And he would use it to his advantage at every turn.

Mary steeled her spine and gazed back at him coolly, calmly. "I am going in."

With a curse he dragged a hand over his face. "You are being illogical."

She was. She didn't care. On the other hand, Talent had apparently forgotten about one of her more potent abilities. She gave him a level look. "I'll play the part of your assistant." It hurt to say that, but if he was going to assume she was useless, then she wasn't about to let him in on her plans.

"Investigators do not have female assistants, Chase."

"Fine. I'll be your blind sister who cannot be left on her own." She merely needed to get in the door.

He blinked back at her for a good five seconds. Then a shocked, harsh laugh burst from him. "You object to being my lackey, but you'll be my sister? You, madam, are barmy."

"Lovely to know we've rolled around to the name-calling stage of the conversation," she said sedately.

A string of blue curses filled the air, and then Talent took a deep breath. "Fine. Do not blame me if your stubbornness gets us nowhere in a hurry. And you shall follow my lead. Do not speak until I give you leave."

An unladylike snort left her lips. "Tell me, Talent, do you honestly expect me to listen to the drivel that comes from your mouth? Or do you suffer bouts of delusion?"

His answering grin was serpentine, a viper about to strike. "Hark! She lives." He ambled forward, his head cocked to the side as he studied her. "That's probably the most impassioned tone I've heard from you yet, Chase." Before she could give him another, his expression hardened. "I have seniority, thus I am the lead on this team. You do as I say."

She gave him a false smile guaranteed to annoy him. "I believe I was accepted into the SOS before you were, thus I am the one with seniority."

He stepped closer, surrounding her with the vibrant energy of his body and the appealing scent of him. By rights he ought to have an irritating scent, like lye soap. But no, Jack Talent's scent was instantly recognizable, yet drifting off before she could properly dissect it. Which made her want to lean closer and inhale deeply. Most annoying. And quite dangerous.

Mary tilted her head back and met his gaze. They glared at each other for a long moment before Talent's clipped response broke their standoff. "You joined as Poppy Lane's assistant. Should we be in need of secretarial work, Mistress Chase, I'll be happy to let you lead."

The dirty rotter.

He nodded as if she'd finally come to her senses. "Know your place, Chase, and we will not have a problem."

Mary set her fists on her hips. "I am not doing as you say."

"Yes, you are."

"No, I am *not*."

"Oh, yes, you are—" Talent broke off with a curse. Close as they were, the dark stubble around his mouth was visible in the morning sun. "Christ almighty, we are not in the nursery."

"I agree. Kindly desist in behaving like an infant."

His jaw clenched, red washing over his cheekbones. "So help me, Chase—"

Mary turned away from him, loving the way he snarled at her departure. "We have interviews to conduct, and the day is waning with all this posturing." Her skirts swished about her ankles as she put a bit more sway into her walk. "Come along, Master Talent." This time she used his title as a headmaster might and was rewarded with another blue curse from behind her.

Confident that he'd stomp along after her, she jumped only a little when his voice suddenly buzzed at her ear, the heat of his breath raising gooseflesh upon her skin. "It will take more than the sway of your arse to distract me, Chase." Then he was ahead of her, once more leading the way and whistling a familiar tune.

Mary halted in the act of following him. "Are you whistling 'Row Your Boat'?" Incredulity had her choking out the question. She detested the nickname he pinned on her, because he thought of her as a "merry bit of fluff."

Talent's happy little tune broke off mid-note, and his sly gaze slid over her for a moment. "Why, I do believe I am." He turned his head back around, and his step grew lively. His pitch-perfect baritone lilted over the quiet street. " 'Merrily, merrily, merrily, merrily, life is but a dream."

Mary was contemplating murder by cranial bludgeoning when Talent gave her a look over his shoulder. A strange gleam sparkled in his eyes, but before she could question it, the light around him distorted, and his features blurred. Quick as a blink, he shifted.

"What do you think?" His voice was more gravelly now, an older man's. "Am I the picture of a non-threatening yet authoritative inspector?"

Longer of face, wrinkled, bushy-browed, and sporting an impressive handlebar mustache of grizzled brown, Talent appeared a man of fifty years. He'd kept his height and basic form, for he could not alter his clothing, but a bit of a paunch stretched out his grey waistcoat.

"To the letter," she admitted. "But why?"

The crow's feet around his now-blue eyes deepened. "I have a suspicion that this household will be more accommodating to respectable old John Talent than scowling, yet undeniably charming, young Jack Talent." His true grin on another's face was a strange sight indeed. "With a blind *niece* in tow. God help me."

Charming, was he? Mary barely refrained from rolling her eyes, but then paused. "Is your given name truly John?"

He touched the brim of his hat with a deferential nod to her, but the humor had dimmed in his eyes. "John Michael Talent, at your service, miss." He glanced back at the door they were to knock on. "For all of one hour. Then back into the shadows he goes."

Something dark and ugly rode in the undercurrents of his tone.

"Do you not like your given name?" She really ought to curb her curiosity in regard to him, but could not seem to do so.

"I hate it." Then he stalked forward, leaving her to catch up.

The housekeeper answered the door. "The house is not receiving visitors at this time." She moved to close the door when Talent stuck his boot in.

"We are not visitors, madam. We are investigators here to discuss the crime."

The housekeeper's thin face paled. "The both of you?" Her gaze landed flat on Mary, and she balked again.

Hubris was the damnedest thing, Mary reflected bitterly while refusing to look at Talent.

To his credit, he leveled the housekeeper with a stern, unyielding look. "The crime scene, if you please, madam."

Her gaze darted about the empty street, then back to Talent. "Come."

She led them into the front parlor. When Mrs. White had left, a man entered the room and frowned. "I am Mr. Rush, a longtime friend of Mr. Pierce. I am here to assist in closing up the house." Rush was a man of about thirty, well groomed and so stiff-backed that it was a wonder he did not have a poker stuffed up his arse. "How may I help you?"

"I am Inspector John Talent, and my partner Miss Chase." He flashed his credentials. Official-looking documents designed to impress and quell inquiry.

Rush's gaze flicked to Mary, and his expression darkened. "Partner?"

Frankly, Mary was now as surprised as Rush. What had happened to "blind niece"?

"I'd rather you had not arrived so close to calling hours," Rush said. "It is most indelicate. But I suppose there is no help for it now."

"You plan to receive callers on such a day?" Talent asked.

"Well, no." Rush frowned. "It is merely the principle of you being here during an hour in which callers might be driving past the house."

"Can't see how they'd know we are here," Talent muttered as he pulled out a small notebook and pencil. Likely he didn't need them, but he'd clearly decided to act the part of a proper investigator. "Who discovered Mr. Pierce?"

Rush clearly wanted acknowledgment for his little chastisement, but he answered. "That would be Mrs. White."

Talent scribbled something down, and Mary glanced at his pad, stifling a laugh as she read the words: *Look into the prat's background—Mrs. White's too.* He pocketed the notebook. "We'll need to speak with her, then. And view the crime scene."

Again, Rush's gaze darted to Mary. "Of course, Inspector." Then he gave her the condescending look one employs with an ignorant child. "If you'll wait here, miss. I'll have tea sent in."

"Miss Chase shall be accompanying me."

Rush's thin nostrils flared, then pinched. "A crime scene is no place for a lady."

"Try not to view me as such at the moment, Mr. Rush." She moved nearer and caught his gaze. Only a moment more, and he'd be hers. But he broke the connection.

"Believe me, miss"—cool grey eyes traveled up and down her form in a way that made her skin prickle—"that shall not be hard. Regardless—"

And that is when Talent's temper broke. He stepped closer to her, his body not quite shielding, but aligning itself as if he would, given further provocation. Dark clouds of irritation twisted his features, a gesture familiar to her, even though he wore the face of another man.

"Here is what shall happen." Talent's tone was iron. "You shall turn around, walk out of this room, and collect Mrs. White, who shall answer any and all of our questions. And then we shall view the body." His gaze bore into Rush. Though he was now older and softer about the middle, Talent's physical presence was undeniable. "Or I shall haul your arse down to the magistrate so that you can explain why you have interfered with an official investigation."

All color fled Rush's face, and his thin mustache quivered with outrage. He made no move to answer. Talent's setdown had rendered him frozen.

Talent's expression turned bland. "One foot in front of the other, Rush."

Really, Mary thought, as she laid a hand upon the irate Mr. Rush, Talent had no sense of delicacy whatsoever. Upon feeling her touch, Rush glowered down at her, and Mary locked eyes with him and let her full power go. The effect was instant, and the man's body went lax and warm. She gave him a little smile. "You will do as the inspector says, then you shall go find yourself a nice cup of tea."

"Tea sounds lovely," Rush murmured, gazing down at her with something akin to adoration.

"Yes, doesn't it now?" She gave him a gentle pat. "And

when you have finished your tea, you shall have no memory of me."

"No memory." He nodded in an absent-minded way.

"Lovely." Mary gestured to the door. "Now off you go, Mr. Rush."

Rush ambled off as though in a fog. Perhaps it was because GIM were not as physically strong as other supernaturals that Adam had sought to give them other methods of defense, but whatever the reason, a GIM had the power to beguile a person into doing her bidding by simply locking gazes and willing it so.

The moment the door closed behind Rush, Talent sneered. "I swear to all that's unholy, Chase, if you ever come after me with those GIM eyes, I'll..." He faltered there, and she laughed lightly.

"You'll what? You wouldn't even remember." Mary would never use her ability on Talent; it wouldn't be sporting to best him in that manner. But he needn't know that.

Talent's skin flushed dark. "Oh, I'll remember. Somehow I'll remember, and you won't like my retaliation, Chase." In a shimmer of light, he shifted back to his true form—so as to properly glare at her, she supposed. He pinned her with a threatening look. "It shall be long and creative."

"What are you doing?" Mary hissed with a glance at the door. "Get back into character before someone sees you."

He waved a hand. "Takes but a second. And the bloody mustache itches."

"You ought to have thought of that before."

Talent ignored her in favor of scowling at the door Rush had closed. "Besides, if they do, you can work your little witchcraft upon them, now can't you?" He laughed shortly and without real humor. "Hell, I cannot believe I forgot that particular trick. An utter waste of breath on my part, wasn't it?"

"I must admit that I am surprised you defended me," Mary said. "I was under the impression you felt the same as he."

He made a rude noise through his lips. "Bother, Chase, did you not hear a word that I said? Sex has nothing to do with proficiency. Our head director is a woman." His expression grew smug. "Any objection pertaining to your role here is due to you being a pain in my arse."

"Oh, well, that is a much nicer sentiment." Though in a perverse way, it was.

"Of course it is." Oblivious as ever, he went back to glaring at the door. "What I object to in that prat is he's a bloody middle-class fool." His upper lips curled. "A more priggish bunch I have yet to meet."

In many ways Talent was correct. The middle class, in their drive to mimic their betters, tried to live beyond reproach. "They do set a rather high standard to live by."

"Bloody England. I ought to decamp to the States and be done with this land. Only the bloody Yanks are just as grasping."

"Perhaps you should travel there. Just to be certain." Mary bit back her smile. Really, the man was so readily worked up, it was almost too easy to needle him. "They might appreciate a man of such revolutionary ideals."

Talent rounded on her, his fierce frown shifting into an expression of wry admonishment when he caught sight of her expression. "It won't be that easy to be rid of me, Chase."

"Pity." She sighed. "I suppose I'll have to try harder."

Mary cleared her throat and touched the lace doily on the back of the couch with an idle hand. What was she doing, bantering with Jack Talent? And why was she enjoying it? Unconscionable. She felt like a traitor to herself. She turned to face him again, and her skirts swished against the couch. "Do try to contain yourself with the housekeeper."

He gave her a long look, all flaring nostrils and sneering lips. "I do not have time to shilly-shally with social niceties."

A strangled laugh caught in her throat. "You said it yourself, Talent. Social niceties are unavoidable. But you? You have all the tact of a Bedlamite ranter."

He made a rude noise. "Are we finished with the deportment session? May we kindly return to our case?"

"My word, you phrased that so nicely. I am quite astonished."

His scowl was truly aggrieved. But then he suddenly grinned bright and crafty. Without warning he reached over and tweaked her ear in a move worthy of a five-year-old. "Lest you think I'm learning anything," he said with his evil grin still in place.

"Pinch me again and lose a finger." She meant for it to be a threat, but her voice came out oddly husky, his touch having made her pulse quicken.

As if he'd picked up on her tone, his lids lowered a fraction, setting her off balance, for heat lit his eyes. An illusion surely. Her breath sharpened as Talent's voice turned sultry. "Is that a dare, Chase?"

Their gazes clashed, and Mary had the disorienting sense of the world's having suddenly turned upside down on her. Her lips parted, and he studied them, his looming form tilted toward her as if drawn. *Impossible.* The door opened, and they sprang apart. Which was ridiculous, given that they'd been standing at a respectable distance.

Mary, for one, was glad of the intrusion. With an unsteady hand, she smoothed back a lock of hair that hung heavy at her temple, and was shocked to find it damp.

True to his word, Talent was now back in form and raising an imperious, bushy brow. "Well then," he snapped to the housekeeper, "Let us proceed."

Chapter Five

Jack's steps were slow as the housekeeper led them into the bedroom where Mr. Pierce had been found. Sunlight brightened the room, the heavy brocade drapes having been thrown back. Thankfully the housekeeper had not thought to open the windows. Despite the rank stink of death and decay that made his stomach roll, Jack needed to inhale each scent, his shifter's sense of smell giving him the ability to find clues within the muck. He let it flow over him, and then it hit him. He knew this victim. The knowledge turned over in his gut, and it took everything he had not to react before going to the bed in which the departed Mr. Pierce still lay.

The housekeeper's pale lips pinched tighter than a lockbox, her thin body stiff as a post. "It isn't decent, letting him lie there."

He shot the woman a look. "And it isn't decent to let the murderer get away with taking his life."

Some days Jack hated his job. Give him a good chase, something to fight, anything but trying to cajole information out of prats. He finished the rest of his oft-said speech. "By leaving him as he was, we might find some clue as to who did it."

The woman nodded sharply. "Aside from the drapes, nothing's been touched, sir."

He studied the dead man. His eyes were open wide, terrified, his mouth gaping in the way of death. He was lying on his back, and his hands were up by his head as if they'd been held there while he died. Blood matted his dark hair and soaked the bed, turning the fine linen sheets into a macabre splatter of black and crimson. In the center of his bloodied nightshirt, just over his left breast, a cross had been branded, burning through the fabric and into his flesh. The smell of char and roasted flesh was a thick note amongst the rot of death. But there again was Pierce's natural scent, and Jack knew it well. It had permeated his skin on a long-ago day when this very bastard had sunk his teeth into Jack's neck.

"And how did you find the drapes, Mrs. White?" He glanced at the housekeeper. "Shut tight? Slightly open?"

Her long, sharp nose wrinkled. "Shut tight."

Which did not mean the killer hadn't come through the window. Jack walked over to them, but found the sashes locked tight. No forced entry of any kind. Which did not mean much when dealing with the supernatural. Down below, black-topped carriages ambled by, and a pair of ladies strolled along the walkway, their blue and yellow parasols up to protect them from the rare London sunlight. Yet a few clusters of gawkers were hovering on the street corners and idling by the low, wrought-iron gate across the way.

Jack let the drape fall and turned, only to notice Chase hovering by the door. Jesus, but the woman was grey.

Sweat beaded her brow, and her mouth hung slightly open. As a GIM, she ought to have seen plenty of death, but she acted as if today were her first experience with studying corpses. Something within him softened.

"If you'll excuse us, Mrs. White," he said to the house-keeper. Unsurprisingly, the woman fled the room. Once she was gone, he set his attention back on Mary.

"Chase." He said it quietly but she flinched. Her brown eyes were round and glassy as she looked up, and he fought the urge to move closer. "Why don't you question the staff?" Hell, he needed to be alone for a few minutes at any rate.

She did not like being told what to do, that was bleeding obvious. Her eyes narrowed, and he suppressed a sigh. "Look, there is nothing wrong with admitting you find a task distasteful. I bloody hate talking to witnesses, as you have pointed out my distinct lack of tact. It is quite obvious you are one breath away from vomiting."

She stiffened. "I am not." A shaking breath left her. "Not one breath, anyway," she finished with a petulant mutter that made him want to smile.

He kept his voice gruff, lest she catch on. "There ought to be some benefit to having a partner. Sharing disagreeable duties tops my list."

With lips as pinched as Mrs. White's had been, she studied his face as if looking for some sign of foul play or sarcasm. He let her do it, knowing that he had her. When she let out another quick breath, he relaxed.

"All right," she said. "I'll see to the staff." She hesitated for a moment, her gaze cutting to Mr. Pierce. "He wasn't a shifter, was he?"

His head jerked. "How did you know?"

Chase's soft mouth quirked. "He does not smell of shifter. And Pierce was a registered shifter."

Jack paused. "And what does a shifter smell like?" He believed her, only his curiosity now ran rampant. How would she describe it? Did she like the scent? Did she like *his* scent? *Bloody pathetic idiot, he was.*

Her firm little chin rose a notch as she stared him down, clearly seeing this as a challenge. "Well, I only know your..." Her mouth snapped shut, and he almost grinned. *Only his scent. She knew it and none other.*

Chase's eyes narrowed as if the look could stop him from reaching that conclusion. When she spoke again, her voice was snappish and resentful. "Like earth and stone." There was an abrupt pause. And his breath caught. Her eyes grew lighter, glimmering gold as her words slowed. "Warm yet strong. Like granite baking in the hot sun."

"Very astute, Chase." His voice was too thick and rough for his liking. He looked away. "Now get to it."

Thankfully, she fled the room with as much haste as Mrs. White.

Once alone he crouched down and put his head in his hands. "Shit," he muttered.

Jack glared up at the corpse, its white foot listing at an awkward angle over the bed. Ever since he'd been freed and able, he'd been looking for those who had tormented him in the dank, iron-lined room. He remembered every fiend's scent, so that he would know them when he killed them. Finding them was the hard part. The Nex hid their own well. And now someone had beaten Jack to this kill.

Starting to rise, Jack froze as he spied a tiny triangle of white peeking out from under the apex of the man's arm. It was a piece of paper. Jack swallowed hard and opened the tightly folded paper. Lines of blood ink came into view: "Luke 15:29–30."

It had been years since Jack had thought about the

Bible, much less read it. But every word was burned into his memory. His parents had made certain of that. He said the words now by rote, not even pausing to think. " 'And he answering said to his father, Lo, these many years do I serve thee, neither transgressed I at any time thy commandment: and yet thou never gavest me a kid, that I might make merry with my friends: But as soon as this thy son was come, which hath devoured thy living with harlots, thou hast killed for him the fatted calf.' "

Jack rubbed a hand over his eyes. "Bloody hell but I hate riddles."

It wasn't until Mary closed the door to Pierce's bedroom and walked a ways down the hall that she could take a proper breath. God, the stench. The mangled body. Mary swallowed hard, even as she cursed herself blue. It appeared that she would never get past her inability to stand death. Worse still, Talent had noticed her weakness.

Frowning, she paused by a little hall table poised beneath a gilded mirror. The woman frowning back at her through the glass appeared pale and drawn. Sweet Lord, but she looked a fright. That in itself did not bother Mary. No, what perplexed her was Talent's reaction to her obvious distress. He'd been kind, gentle with her. When she'd expected sarcasm, sneering, ridicule. He had the perfect excuse to see her off the case. If she could not confront death, study the victims, she could not do her duties. Perhaps he'd taunt her later, but she still could not account for the way he'd helped her now.

The jangle of the housekeeper's keys, accompanied by the starchy march of crinolines, pulled Mary's attention away from the mirror and the quagmire of her thoughts.

"Mrs. White," she said as the woman drew near, "I

should like to ask you a—" She sucked in a sharp breath, for Mrs. White had moved into the shadows and Mary caught a glimmer of spirit about her physical form. It was a flicker of light but enough, and quite distinctive. She hadn't paid proper attention to the housekeeper. She did now and heard the steady click and whir of a clockwork heart.

As for Mrs. White, she halted, her frame tensing. Her dull blue eyes began to glow as her gaze darted about for an exit.

"Why didn't you identify yourself as a GIM?" Mary asked, slipping the baton strapped to her forearm down into her grasp.

"None of your business, is it?" Mrs. White snapped.

"I am SOS," Mary said. "Any supernatural lingering around the scene of a crime is my business."

A bead of sweat trickled down the woman's temple, and the sound of her working heart grew louder.

"Why are you nervous?" Mary did not move, but she was ready, her body poised for a fight. She considered calling for Talent, but rejected the idea. The woman might bolt, and Mary could manage one GIM.

"What do you want with me?" Mrs. White's fingers clenched and unclenched. Fight or flight. Which one would the GIM pick?

"Tell me about the body in Pierce's room," Mary said. "You had to know he was a demon. Where is the real Pierce?"

At that moment the door to Mr. Pierce's bedroom opened, and Talent came into the hall. He took one look at Mary and Mrs. White facing off. In an instant his demeanor moved from an investigator's to a predator's, and the very air seemed to crackle about him.

Like an animal cornered, Mrs. White launched forward, her arm raised. Talent leapt toward them, trying to intervene, but Mary was closer, and the GIM was coming at her. She sidestepped the woman and swung her baton deftly against Mrs. White's wrist. The bone snapped, and Mrs. White screeched but she didn't stop and fight as Mary had expected; she ran.

Narrowly missing Talent's grasping hand, Mrs. White threw a potted palm at them as she darted into the servant's stairwell, slamming the door behind her. Talent was a beat behind. With a mighty kick he smashed the door inward and stepped through the wreckage.

Mary was on his heels. The stairwell was empty. A GIM could move on silent feet if needed, and not a sound came from the dark corridor.

A wild light lit Talent's eyes, and small fangs grew in his mouth. "Up or down?"

"You go up, I'll go down," Mary said.

His heavy tread boomed up the stairs as Mary flew down them. A glimpse of black skirts on the ground floor landing had her shouting, "Talent! She went down!"

Not waiting for her partner, Mary picked up her skirts and ran faster, her feet barely touching the treads as she descended into the humid air of the subterranean kitchens.

Startled cries and the crash of dishes rang out as Mrs. White scattered servants in her wake.

Mary leapt over a toppled breakfast tray and burst into the kitchen. In the next instant a shadow flickered in the periphery of her vision, and she ducked as something whizzed by her cheek. Baton in hand, Mary straightened and found Mrs. White poised between the stoves and the massive butcher-block table in the center of the kitchen.

A side of beef lay upon the table and, before it, a row of gleaming knives.

Bloody hell.

Mrs. White's eyes lit with evil intent. And then she reached for the next knife.

One, two, three, the knives hissed through the air in a blur. Mary swung, using her baton like a bat. With a clink, clank, clunk, she knocked the knives down. Her arm vibrated, her hand sore from the force of the hits. When the last knife clattered to the kitchen floor, she glared at the irate GIM. "Finished?"

Mrs. White snarled, the cry echoing against the stone. She grabbed the remaining cleaver and rushed forward. Mary braced, baton at the ready. But from out of nowhere Talent smashed into the GIM, blindsiding her and taking her down with a grunt. They tumbled in a twist of legs and crinoline, Talent landing on top and the cleaver skidding across the stone floor.

Nose to nose, Talent grasped the woman's bodice with a massive fist, and that wild light in his eyes grew more unhinged. "You dare pull a knife on her?"

The GIM merely laughed. "Aye. An' I'd have sunk it into her pretty neck too. What shall you do about that, Regulator?" Her eyes began to glow. "Rip my heart out? I hear you like the kill better than the hunt."

Fangs snapped down with an audible click, and Talent grew an alarming shade of red.

"Talent, I had it in hand." Mary moved close, touching his arm, but he ignored her.

"Did you kill Pierce?" he demanded.

Inches from Talent's fangs, the GIM glared back in defiance. "The Bishop did that, didn't he? Or don't you know?"

Talent gave her a hard shake. "Who do you work for?"

Mrs. White did not answer. She went grey, her eyes rolling back in her head. And then Mary heard it, Mrs. White's clockwork heart grinding to a halt. The GIM began to convulse, spit foaming at the sides of her mouth.

"Hell. Talent, let her go." Mary tugged on his arm and tried to wrench the woman free. "She's stopping her heart."

On a curse, Talent dropped the woman to the floor. "She can do that?"

"Yes. It is a closely held secret, however. For if someone has control over her soul, it is the simplest way to destroy a GIM." Helpless to do anything other than watch, Mary knelt next to the cold GIM. "It isn't Adam or Lucien. They do not allow suicide, nor do they kill in that manner." Adam created every GIM, but Lucien managed all those who lived in London. Unless the GIM had earned her freedom, she would be under their control.

"Piss and shit." Talent briskly slapped the woman's cheek. But she was gone. Dull blue eyes stared up at the yellowed ceiling. "Who the bloody hell would have control over a GIM if not Adam or Lucien?"

A glimmer of grey about the woman's neck caught Mary's eye. She leaned in close and pulled down the edge of Mrs. White's collar. Tattooed into the dead woman's skin was a chain collar. A slave. At some point Mrs. White had given her free will to another. Mary met Talent's annoyed gaze. "Her new master, apparently."

Few things could dissuade Jack from working. But tonight was Daisy Ranulf's birthday ball. Daisy was the only woman of his acquaintance who would demand a ball to celebrate. As if knowing he would find a way to back out of going, his boss Poppy Lane had cornered him early this morning and told him to get his "dodgy arse" to the ball tonight or she'd tack him to the common room wall by his cods. Lovely woman. Truly.

So he'd gone, and was now surrounded by his adopted kith and kin in the Ranulf House ballroom, which had been festooned with so many candles that the air had turned hot and hazy, smelling of melting wax and hot-house flowers. Despite the slaps on the shoulder and shouts of welcome he received as he made his way through the room, he felt as he always did, alone, apart. Because a part of him never eased, never shed the feeling that any good fortune to fall into his life could just as quickly be snatched away.

Leaning against one of the onyx pillars that held up the gilded ceiling, Jack watched the dancers. Most were familiar, but there was no one with whom he wanted to engage. The lines of the Bible verse repeated in Jack's head as they had all day. The story of the Prodigal Son. Was the killer sending a message to Jack? Or referring to himself?

Across the way was Ian Ranulf, decked out in the Ranulf kilt, a fine black dress coat, and a white lace jabot at his neck. Antiquated attire, but expected of the lycan king, and certainly put together well enough, though his shoes could do with a bit more glossing.

There were days when Jack missed being Ian's valet, and the simplicity of it. He knew most people wouldn't understand, but the work had been soothing. By happenstance or fate, Jack—a half-starved lad, battered and beaten to within an inch of his life for daring to defy his crime bosses—had fallen on Ian Ranulf's doorstep, unable to go any farther. And Ian had taken him in. It had been Jack's pleasure to take care of the man who'd given him a home, and it had been the only way he could think of to properly repay Ian.

But Ian understood Jack better than he realized and had set him free; rather, he had ejected him from the nest. A blessing, really, for whether or not Jack had wanted to admit it, he had grown restless and bored. His adventure with Inspector Lane had been the start of something that fired his blood and gave him true purpose. Then it had all gone to shit.

Jack's throat closed, the smoky air smothering him. He stretched his neck, and a series of small pops cracked along his spine.

"You came," said a feminine voice at his side.

Daisy. He hadn't even noticed her approach. Jack straightened. "It was either that or become an exhibit in headquarters' main hall." He leaned down and gave Daisy a light kiss upon her smooth cheek. "Happy birthday, Madam Ranulf."

Her cheek plumped. "Poppy got to you, did she?" Daisy's eyes scanned the dancers and paused upon the woman in question, who was presently dancing with her husband Inspector Lane.

Dressed in grass-green taffeta, Poppy did not appear to be the warrior woman capable of leading an entire organization, but a goddess sprung from the earth. The married couple executed a turn, and Poppy's sharp gaze clashed with his. She gave Jack a short nod of acknowledgement.

"I believe her words were," he murmured, returning the nod, " 'If I have to suffer, then so do you.' "

Beside him Daisy snorted. "I am overwhelmed by the love and affection bestowed upon me by my family." She sounded more amused than put out.

Jack turned to look down at her. She was lovely tonight, resplendent in a primrose gown and little white hothouse daisies tucked into her golden curls. Her blue eyes glowed with the power of a GIM and the light of a woman content.

His tone softened. "I'd say our grievances are with parties in general, not you."

"Pish. You and Poppy are peas in a pod, reticent homebodies I have to goad into doing anything remotely carefree." She glanced at him askance. "Though you are rude to boot. At least my sister has retained a modicum of tact."

"Speak your mind, why don't you?"

Her mouth pursed. "My apologies. But I am cross with you."

"What have I done?" But Jack had a fairly good idea. And he had it coming. His face burned with the truth.

Daisy's gaze went back to the ballroom, and to her husband. "He misses you."

The burning rose up to his ears as guilt loomed to the fore. Jack crossed his arms over his chest and leaned against the pillar once more. His heart thudded against the cage of his ribs. "I haven't gone anywhere."

Her skirts hissed over the black marble floor as she turned to fully face him. "Do not play that game with me. You've shut him out, all of us out, and..." She drew herself up with a deep breath and, when she spoke again, it was with a forced lightness as if she were trying to spare him pain, despite her ire, which made Jack feel all the worse. Her words skipped over him like stones across a frozen lake. "Do what you must. I will not crowd you. Ian says we mustn't."

Perfect. He might as well have been two inches tall then.

"But know that we are here for you, Jack."

Jack grunted. She ignored him, a wicked and irate gleam turning her eyes crystal blue. "And I had better not hear that you are being rude to Miss Chase. I love that girl, quiet thing though she is."

Jack wouldn't have defined Chase as quiet. Though, in retrospect, she was not particularly animated; unless, of course, she was goading him.

Where was Chase anyway? Daisy would have sent her an invitation.

"I have not been rude to her," he muttered, trying not to chafe at the lie he'd just told.

Daisy harrumphed. "Are you behaving in your usual manner?"

"Don't see how else I'd behave." God save him from loose-lipped, well-meaning females.

She made the noise again. "Then you are being rude."

Jack glared, and she had the temerity to buss his cheek. "Well, of course, *we* love you as you are."

"Who loves whom?" Ian strolled up and wrapped himself around his wife like ivy, but his attention locked onto Jack. His expression was wary, as if he expected Jack to bolt and sought a way to prevent it.

Jack cursed. God save him from his whole family. Being near Ian set Jack's nerves on end. He hated the disconnect between them but nothing seemed to ease it. Jack watched the dancers instead of meeting Ian's eyes. Piss and shit.

"We are discussing why Jack feels the need to be rude—pardon," she gave Jack an exaggerated nod of deference, "*excessively* rude to Miss Chase."

Ian's grin was all teeth, and most of them sharp. "That is simple. Because he wants to tup her."

"Bloody hell," Jack snapped, "is there a moment in which you do not think of tupping?"

Ian laughed. "And Jack the Prude returns. It might do you well to think of tupping now and then, *mo mhac*." He'd spoken with lightness, a typical Ian jest, but the moment the words were out, he paled. Jack froze too, ugly, thick feelings sliding like sludge through his chest. There was too much knowledge in Ian's eyes.

Jack whipped about, needing to get away, but not before seeing Ian's expression fall.

"Jack..." Ian began. His disappointment and regret, and the soft plea in his voice, worked a shaft of pain into Jack's chest. He knew he was hurting Ian and Daisy by keeping his distance. Especially Ian. But he could not stand to look upon him for too long. Not when it was Ian who first comforted him when he'd been rescued. Not when the man knew what had been done to him. The familiar tight, suffocating feeling stole over him.

"No worries," he said over his shoulder, even as his abdomen tightened in regret. "I'm late for work."

It was another lie, and they all knew as much. But they let him flee.

Chapter Six

‑‑‑‑‑‑‑‑‑‑‑‑‑‑‑‑‑‑‑‑‑‑‑‑‑‑‑‑‑‑‑‑ ❧❧ ‑‑‑‑‑‑‑‑‑‑‑‑‑‑‑‑‑‑‑‑‑‑‑‑‑‑‑‑‑‑‑‑

Book in hand, curled upon the couch with a soft cashmere rug tucked about her, was a delightful way to end the day. Mary did not want to think about Jack Talent, or the case, or anything at all. What she wanted now was to immerse herself in another world until she drifted off into a dreamless sleep.

Yet she found herself not reading but floating from her body. With detached calm she hovered above herself. So still, eyes open wide but glassy. Precisely how she would look in true death. The thought no longer bothered her. If death came, it came.

Not wanting to dwell on morbid thoughts, she let her gaze roam listlessly about her small parlor. She loved her flat. Assembling it for comfort, she'd picked big, padded armchairs and covered the floors in plush carpets. Robin's-egg blue lacquered the walls, the high gloss reflecting the light of her lamps and candles when it grew dark. Cream-colored velvet drapes kept the chill from creeping through the windows, and her couch was, in truth, a large, wrought iron campaign bed of some long-dead general's and was piled high with plump pillows for lounging. Quite satisfactory. And nothing like the homes in which she had been raised.

Though the location changed from time to time, her childhood homes had all looked the same within—pink silk damask walls, dainty gilded furniture, and numerous mirrors to reflect Maman. Everything glittering and feminine. And Mary most of all. Always resplendent in frothy petticoats, rich satins, and lacy pinafores. Hateful, really, that Mary still loved to wear high fashion. Back then, however, she had loved it all. Loved playing with the battalion of French dolls provided for her, loved waiting for Maman to grace her with a morning visit. They'd sip rich chocolate and eat buttered crumpets, and Maman would tell her stories of lovely men. It wasn't until later, when Mary fully understood just who and what those men were and why they provided the riches around her, that a sick, twisted dismay would weigh down her chest upon Maman's arrival.

Maman. Ha. They weren't even French. It had taken Mary ridiculously long to figure that out as well. But Maman was long dead, and that part of Mary's life over.

She had friends. Tonight she might have gone out, might have danced and laughed. Yet she had stayed home. For she did not know how to be at ease with others. She'd never learned, growing up as that girl in the ivory tower. Mary sighed and sank back into her body. The sensation was akin to slipping under a warm blanket. It took her but a moment to orient, pick up her book, and turn toward the warmth of her heating stove. The cream enamel Swedish stove was more efficient and used fragrant wood instead of muddy coal. Behind the grate the flames danced.

Self-pity never helped a thing. And she was better off than most. Being alone was perfectly fine. Perfectly.

A creak sounded upon her landing. Tensing, she glanced over the high back of her couch. Her hall was dark, only the small reading lamp at her side hissing away. Which made the sliver of light shining along the base of her front door perfectly visible, as was the shadow of someone standing behind the door. Mary's hand slid to the revolver she kept by her side. Even in her home, she never let herself be without a weapon.

When she wanted to, Mary could move with speed and silence. In a blink she lightly vaulted over the couch, ripped open the door, and had her gun cocked and aimed. At Jack Talent's broad chest.

"Put it away," he said in a bored tone.

She allowed herself the pleasure of ignoring his request for a long moment. Then she lowered the gun and took stock of him. He stood, feet braced, hands at his side, in a manner that ought to have conveyed trust, but with his rippling strength, he appeared ready to pounce. Mist glittered at the tips of his cropped hair and on the weave of his black wool overcoat. He towered over her, all bunching muscle and boiling energy, and he had to tilt his head down to meet her gaze.

"I thought you were at Daisy's birthday ball," she said.

A deep furrow ran between his brows, brows that, when he smiled, tilted upward at the tips like the leaves of a bascule bridge. The feature ought to have given him an open, almost boyish look of expectancy, but his sour nature fought that appearance, twisting it into a near-permanent glower of disappointment. Even so, the very idea that nature had given him a face more inclined to joy made her fight a smile. Served him right for being so prickly.

"I thought you were invited too." He gave a pointed look at her simple housedress. Mary kept her focus on his chin, now covered in a fine stubble of evening growth. It made his mouth appear softer, defining the bow of his upper lip. She flicked her gaze back up to his eyes.

"I didn't fancy going out to a party." Or seeing him there, if she were honest. Mingling with Jack Talent in a social setting was more than she could tolerate at the moment. Yet here he was, at her home. Her skin prickled.

His voice grew flinty. "I didn't fancy staying."

Before she could ask why he was here, or how he'd even found her home, he brushed past, his upper arm grazing the tips of her breasts as he went. Mary crossed her arms over them as she pivoted to face him. "Oh, do come in."

"Thank you." He made himself at home on the parlor chair, which, unfortunately, was big enough to accommodate his large frame. The sight made her want to stamp her foot, or bolt. This was her refuge, and he was filling it up with his scent, his energy. She'd be surrounded by it for days now, unable to scrub it from her furniture.

Lamplight shone over his blunt profile as he glanced about her room, taking it all in. "Cozy flat." The high bridge of his nose wrinkled. "Small, though."

Resigned to the fact that he wasn't leaving, Mary closed the door and set her gun upon the hall table. "Yes, well, I had a larger place but I kept getting lost." Actually, she owned the building, but he needn't know that.

His quick grin returned before he took it upon himself to pick up the book she'd discarded and leaf through it. "I always thought Mr. Rochester was a melodramatic prat." He tossed the book back down.

"I like Jane."

"Everyone likes Jane." He picked up an apple from the

glass bowl she had placed in the center of her tea table. Mary loved apples, and every fortnight she found a basketful of them sitting on her doorstep. A gift from Lucien that she'd always appreciated. Talent stared down at the green-and-red-marbled fruit engulfed by his big hand. He contemplated it for a moment, a strange look ghosting over his features before he appeared to pull himself free from whatever thought haunted him and took a hearty bite. Mouth full of crisp apple, he munched away, a bit of juice making his firm lips wet. And all the while, he watched her.

Mary gave herself a mental shake and focused on the situation at hand. "How did you find my home?"

The flat was located on the top floor of the building. Only three persons knew of its location: Lucien, Poppy, and Daisy. And she doubted any of them would tell Talent. Or that he would ask them.

Talent's gaze grew hooded. "Followed your scent."

"What?" Gods, but she did not want to know what her scent entailed. Nor did she like the idea of Talent knowing it so well that he could track her down by it.

That grin of his flashed bright. "Don't fancy that either, do you?"

"Do you mean to tell me, Mr. Talent, that through the whole miasma of London, you were able to track me down based on scent alone?"

Talent's hard mouth slanted as he looked her over in a way that she felt to her bones. "We're in each other's pocket now, Chase. Most hours, you're all I smell."

Gracious. Heat flooded in unfortunate places, and to her horror, Talent's gaze narrowed, his nostrils flaring as if he scented that reaction too.

An uncomfortable, stifling silence fell over the room. Mary swallowed down the urge to twitch.

"What are you doing here—"

"Do you want to work—"

They paused, their clashing questions falling into an awkward silence. Then Talent set down his half-eaten apple and sprang to his feet, a graceful move so fast she almost missed it. Her heart jumped but he merely regarded her with his usual scowl.

"Well? Shall we go out?" His hard features were once again implacable.

Mary cleared her throat. "Let me get my cloak."

They did not speak as they headed into the frigid night. Londoners fought back against the cold by heaping on the coals. Great billows of smoke rose from a profusion of chimney pots. What was too heavy to dissipate fell in black flecks that danced about them like the devil's snow.

Due to the late hour, few were out, most human traffic being shepherded by coach now. A hack rattled past, horse hooves clipping over the cobbles.

Walking next to Talent, she felt the singular, cozy comfort that steals upon one who is with a good friend. That Talent gave rise to such equanimity instantly shattered it, and her stomach clenched. She ought not trust him any further than she could toss him. Perhaps it was not his presence, but the predictability of all his actions that she took comfort in. Well, one could hope. "Where are we going?" she asked to break her muddled thoughts.

His attention stayed on the walk before them, but his pace, which he had slowed to match hers, faltered for just a step. A wry grimace twisted his mouth. "You know, Chase, I don't believe I thought that far ahead."

"And you are admitting this?" She made a noise of astonishment. "I shall have to make note of the day."

He looked at her sidelong, and the brackets framing his mouth deepened. "You better. It doesn't happen often."

Mary ducked her head to hide her smile. "Well," she said after a step, "we might consider going to Trafalgar Square. Perhaps we can learn something from it."

Talent grunted. "Perhaps."

Taking that as an agreement, Mary headed down Charing Cross road. They soon entered the square, a wide-open public space that featured tranquil fountains and a Corinthian column rising 170 feet into the air. The monument was in honor of Admiral Nelson and was guarded by four large bronze lions, one at each corner of the massive base. Half walls flanked three sides of the square, creating a sense of place despite the openness of the area.

Far off, keeping to the edge of the square, a group of women idled about. A lone man, wearing a horrid lime-green bowler—its color so vivid that it was discernible even in the low light—lounged against the wall, close enough to keep an eye on the women but not so close as to interfere should they be approached.

And approached they were. Two fellows strolled by, eyeing the flesh for sale, before one broke away. An agreement was clearly reached, and the man guided two women off to a shadowed corner.

"Perhaps the fellow in the hideous hat might have seen something. It appears as if he might be here nightly."

"And if he had, you'd be the last person he'd tell," Talent retorted. "He might be a sinner but he isn't stupid. The ones who stay alive never are."

Mary caught Talent's expression. "My, the way you are sneering, Talent, one would think you've never partaken in that particular exchange." Most males she knew had at one time or another.

Talent's brows lifted just a touch. "Once, when I was too young and ignorant to know any better."

It was her fault for broaching the subject, but the sudden image of Talent bedding a strange woman was entirely unpalatable. "And you do not approve of it now?" she asked, as if untroubled. "Odd, seeing as your former master used to be quite infamous in regards to his bedding of prostitutes." She would not call them whores. Despite what society thought, she knew too well how human they were beneath their protective veneer.

The corner of Talent's mouth twitched. "Ian and I do not see eye to eye on everything." He resumed his glaring. "Point of fact, I cannot fault the women for seeking coin. I know how desperation feels. The men who use them are what makes me ill." The scowl upon his face grew. "It's disgusting."

"Because they are not treating the woman as people?" She almost smiled at him. But he brusquely shook his head, killing her sudden goodwill.

"Those women make their choice to be treated as such." His lips curled. "But by procuring, those men are degrading the act into something meaningless."

He shocked a laugh out of her with that. "Goodness, you are a prude."

Talent snorted. "Prude? Because I object to the buying and selling of women? How very hackneyed of you, and everyone else," he muttered before leaning forward to crowd her with his body and pin her with an intense look. "Believe me, angel, I am *not* a prude. Just because the very idea of lying with a woman who doesn't truly want me turns my stomach doesn't mean I don't want to tup one. I'd simply rather have some regard for my partner."

Mary blinked and tried to ignore the flush of warmth his words wrought in her. "But you're a man."

He cocked his head. "What the bloody devil does that have to do with anything?"

"Men do not differentiate between the physical act and love." Not any she knew. As for her opinion in the matter, she found the endeavor noisy, awkward, and undignified. Indeed nothing in her personal experience would lead her to recommend it.

"First off, I'm not talking about love, merely mutual respect and desire."

"What is to say that the prostitute and the procurer do not mutually respect their arrangement?" She was half goading, but enjoying it nonetheless. "How very short-sighted of you, Talent."

Again his mouth twitched, but it wasn't a happy smile he fought, not if the annoyance in his eyes was anything to go by. "Secondly," he went on in an imperious manner, "I don't know why I'm bothering to discuss this with you, as women are notoriously weak of will and flesh, especially when it comes to carnal matters. You are far too innocent to be hearing such things." A sneering laugh drifted into his tone. "By rights you shall be soon swooning."

Blood rushed through her veins. "Why you arrogant, ignorant bast—" She stopped short, catching his pointed and eloquent look. Inwardly she winced.

Talent's voice was smooth silk, tinged with the smallest hint of censure. "Do not pigeonhole me, Chase, and I won't do so with you."

Despite her having been outmaneuvered, a smile pulled at her cheeks. Talent's gaze went to her mouth, and he drew an audible breath, leaving Mary feeling a bit breathless herself. "Point to you, Talent."

His grin was quick, devastating, then gone. But he did not crow over his victory. Instead silence fell between them again. It wasn't exactly comfortable, but certainly a truce. "I wish the rest of your sex felt similarly," she said after a time.

"Do not hold your breath, Mistress Chase."

She made a noise of agreement. But her curiosity would not let go. "So, then, if not with prostitutes..." *Shut up, you imbecile.* "That is, there are certainly other means...." Gads, but she couldn't say the words and survive the humiliation. She bit down on her lip to stop.

He peered down at her. "My, my, Mistress Chase, you do have quite the interest in my sexual activities."

She picked up her pace, heading for Nelson's Column. "Do not give yourself airs. I merely asked out of banal curiosity. I've never met a man who eschews casual exchanges, and I wanted to understand more."

His laughter reached her just before he did, easily catching up to her with his long legs. Without warning he grabbed her, the quick move forcing her to swing round and face him. "Little liar." Talent's eyes danced with annoying glee, the brackets along his mouth deepening with his amusement. "Ask it," he demanded in a husky voice. "How many women have I had?"

Impishness ought not be so beguiling. Nor should he smell so good, nor the heat of his body be so compelling. His lips, when he wasn't pressing them together in his angry way, were well-formed and appeared surprisingly soft just then. Mary edged back. Those lips had spewed forth far too much verbal vitriol for her to be admiring them.

She focused on a point over his shoulder. "I don't care."

He dipped his head, and his lips came close enough

to steal her air. "I'll tell you my number if you tell me yours."

Mary ignored Jack and concentrated on the moonlight glimmering off the fountain pools and the rush of falling water mingling with the sounds of light traffic passing around Charing Cross. Calmed by the gentle rain of falling water, Mary turned to the business at hand. "Why did he leave his victims here?"

Energy radiated from Talent, a violent vortex, one that felt as though it might crash into her, but it didn't. Talent's answer was flat, controlled. "Because it's public."

"There are many public places in London. Why this place? What does it mean to him?" She kept her gaze away from him. His voice and the tone he used would tell her more, at any rate.

Again came the surge of aggression, anger, and control. Always that tight rein on his temper. Many of her colleagues believed Jack Talent didn't feel a thing. She had never thought that to be true. Talent had always been a seething cauldron of emotion, ready to overflow. His capture and torture by the demons had merely served to draw that rage inward, pulling him into deeper darkness. After his torture, she'd feared he would do himself harm. She'd been wrong. The SOS gave direction to his rage. Or so she had thought. Now she worried that he'd turned to murder instead.

The scuff of his boot told Mary he'd taken a step closer, and she tensed, but he sounded quite calm. "The square is considered the official center of London, from which the distance of all roads leading in are measured."

"It is also the preferred location for political protests and national celebrations," Mary said thoughtfully. "Perhaps you are correct in stating that the square does make for a rather public spectacle." Standing at the base of Nelson's Column, where the victims had been left, they faced Whitehall, which sloped down toward the Palace of Westminster. From over the treetops in the foreground, the great eye of Big Ben's clock tower peered down at them.

"So then," she said, "the question is, what public statement is the Bishop trying to make?"

Before Talent could answer, she spied a glimmer of black on the relief depicting the death of Nelson at Trafalgar. A soft breeze kicked up, and the object broke free and drifted down to the ground. It was a large, glossy black feather. Reaching out with caution, she picked it up.

"A raven's feather," Talent said. "Must have fallen from the sky."

"And landed perfectly arranged in this fellow's hat?" She gave a pointed look at the figure of a man holding up the felled Nelson. "Besides which, there are no wild ravens in London. And the Tower ravens cannot fly." Gently she ran a finger along the feather's edge.

A shock of sensation bolted down her arm and straight into her heart, causing her to catch her breath. Power—strong, clean, yet tainted with a malevolent darkness—resided in the feather. Power that burned. So much so that Mary looked at her finger to see if it was cut.

"What is it?" Talent made a move to snatch the feather away from her, but a set of footfalls sounded.

They turned as one and faced the man walking toward them. Talent stood with his shoulder nearly touching hers, so close that she felt him stiffen and heard the small, surprised intake of his breath when the man came into view. He was a tall man, lean and rangy. He was dressed as they were, in a long, fitted overcoat and heavy boots.

But his coat and top hat were of an uncommon blood-red hue. Silky white hair flowed to his shoulders, and Mary expected him to be old, but he came closer and revealed the firm, smooth skin of a young man. A smile played over his lips, and a glimmer of fangs flashed in the moonlight. He'd let her see those fangs, a warning perhaps.

The male was a Western sanguis demon, if Mary had to guess. With that white hair and those fangs. Aside from elementals, all supernaturals had the ability to grow fangs, and often did when roused, but the sanguis's were longer and thinner, designed to puncture, not tear.

"Hello, Jack," he said. "I thought I recognized your sullen hunch from across the Square."

No menace there, only familiarity. It did not stop Mary from wanting to grip Talent's elbow, though she wasn't certain if the desire was to hold him back or provide support.

Talent's expression remained unmoved. "Will. I thought you were dead." He didn't sound as if he had been particularly put out by the notion.

Will's lips curled further. "Close enough to it." He lifted his chin a touch, and his eyes appeared beneath his hat brim. Cold, beautiful, haunted. Ice-blue surrounded by an outer ring of deeper blue. "I've not been as obvious about my activities as you, my friend." His icy gaze slid over Mary, and she fought a shiver. "Nor do I keep as lovely company."

Talent didn't move but it suddenly felt as though he'd separated himself from her. "Appearances can be deceiving. There is nothing lovely about Miss Chase. She'd just as soon gut you as look at you, mate."

If she hadn't been used to his insults, the pain would have cut. As it was, it merely landed with a dull thud upon her chest.

Sympathy filled Will's eyes, which irked further. "Jack never did appreciate women as he should." He tossed a quick grin toward Talent. A true smile returned as he looked back to Mary. "As I doubt my old friend here will perform introductions, allow me." He touched his hat and bowed. The man's manner and accent spoke of good breeding, but there was a bit of street rat about him, just as with Talent. He might have been raised in a proper home, but it was doubtful that he still lived a proper life. "Mr. William Thorne at your service, Miss . . . ?"

"Mary Chase," was all she got out before Talent cut in with a brusque "What do you want, Will?"

Thorne frowned. "You injure me, Jack. Fifteen years since we last spoke and this is the reception I receive?"

Talent's brows lowered. "What do you want?"

His words were a thick fog in the air. For a moment Mary wondered if Thorne would speak at all, he'd gone so stiff, but then she realized that he was restraining himself, just as Talent was.

Thorne's sudden response cut through the night like a whip. "Perhaps I am not here for you, Jack." Eerie blue eyes sought Mary out. "Do you know, Miss Chase, that a shifter doesn't have a particular scent? But one of many?"

Beside her, Talent went rigid, his shoulder touching her arm as he moved perceptibly closer.

"I'm not sure I follow, Mr. Thorne." Despite herself, Mary wanted to know more about Talent's breed. Shifters were rare, and if they were anything like other supernaturals, they must have kept a few secrets close to the bone. "I fear my sense of smell is not developed enough to note a difference in scents." Talent had always smelled the same to her, and familiar enough now that she'd recognize him in a crowd.

Thorne's weight shifted, bringing him an inch closer. It was enough to send a low rumble through Talent's chest, and he glared at Thorne as though he was imagining ripping his throat out. As for Thorne, he appeared relaxed, his long body loose of limb, even as his eyes twinkled with evil intent.

"Perhaps you fail to notice a change because Jack here always feels the same emotion when in your presence. You see, Miss Chase, deep emotion changes a shifter's basic scent." His smile was a taunt he lobbed at Talent. "Very subtly, mind you, but each emotion gives it a different taint, hate, fear"—Thorne eyed Mary again—"love—"

"Enough." Talent took one step in Thorne's direction, putting his shoulder in front of Mary's so that she was partially blocked. "Enough games. Talk or we are going."

Mary did not particularly like the way Talent lumped them together, but she agreed that Thorne was merely baiting him at her expense.

"Games amuse me," Thorne complained before his demeanor grew serious. "I am here to offer a partnership. Between my organization and yours."

"The Nex?" Mary snapped.

A touch on her hand stilled Mary. She'd had her baton out and had taken a step in Thorne's direction without realizing it. Only Talent's hand upon hers had stopped her.

Thorne's gaze focused on their hands when he answered. "The very one. But we are not at odds here." His jaw clenched. "Someone has killed our own."

Mary let her hand fall away from Talent's. "The shifters?"

"No. The demons." Thorne's gaze moved from Mary to Talent. "They were slaughtered first, were they not? Or has the SOS chosen to forget about them?"

Talent hadn't spoken in so long that his sharp reply made Mary's skin twitch. "The SOS forgets little," he said. "Nor do I."

"What do you propose, Mr. Thorne?" Mary asked.

"It does not matter," said Talent, his ire gathering like a storm. "We have nothing to say to the Nex."

"Call me Will, Miss Chase," Thorne offered as though Talent hadn't spoken. "And I merely suggest a mutual exchange of information."

"No." Talent was more emphatic now. He grabbed Mary's elbow as if to pull her away. "We do not work with the Nex." When Mary hesitated, he turned his wrath on her, leaning down so that they were nose to nose. "Ever."

It was in her to protest and raise a holy ruckus against his high-handedness. Save for one thing—he was in the right. It was an implacable SOS rule. Wrenching her gaze away from Talent's, she addressed Thorne, not missing that he'd followed their exchange with ill-concealed delight. "My partner is correct, Mr. Thorne. We do not negotiate with the Nex."

Thorne did not appear crestfallen. He merely smiled and tipped his hat to her. "Should you change your mind, I will find you."

Chapter Seven

———— ❧ ————

Talent insisted on walking Mary back home. Unnecessary, but the stubborn man would not be dissuaded. And so they traversed the lonely streets in a strained silence.

"You and Mr. Thorne appeared quite familiar with one another," Mary said after a time.

"I don't care to discuss Thorne."

What a shock. Mary decided to refrain from speaking at all.

The sound of their footsteps echoed off the cobbles and the brick buildings leaning in on them. A vortex of yellow-green fog obscured their surroundings, and the hissing gas lamps did little more than brighten the fog and make it appear thicker. Talent's gaze roamed and remained vigilant. Mary knew his eyesight was better than hers, but the fog was hindering him too, for he edged closer to her side and tensed as if preparing to spring into action.

"Something smells off," he murmured.

"Could you be more specific, Mr. Talent? Everything smells off in London."

He glanced at her, and the corner of his mouth twitched. "Don't be daft, *Mistress* Chase." Reminding her yet again that she ought to be calling him *Master.* "There are familiar foul scents, and there are odd ones."

"Well then, let us say that my sense of smell is not as developed as yours. Fortunately." He snorted wryly, and she went on. "What is it that you smell?"

His nose lifted slightly, and his mouth opened to the night. "Don't precisely know. It smells a bit like oil. Not lamp oil, but the sort you scent down by the factories. Sharp, sulfuric."

His description tickled the edges of her memory, but she couldn't catch a hold of the proper recollection. They were silent. Both of them searching the night. *Click, click* went Mary's heels. Her breath sounded over-loud in her ears. And then she realized. There were no other sounds. No city sounds, no scurrying of little rodent feet.

Convulsively, she clutched Talent's arm. "Oil." A discordant grating sounded in the night.

Talent stopped short. "What the bleeding hell?" Around them shadows darkened, becoming thicker, taking on shapes.

Mary backed up, and her shoulder met his. "It can't be..." But she rather feared it might. "Shadow crawlers," Mary whispered, her hand slipping underneath her cloak to her hip, where her weapons belt lay. She grabbed the small bullwhip.

"What?" Talent glanced wildly around. He could see the shadows, that was certain. He just didn't know what they were.

The grinding of gears, a hiss of steam, and a clank, clank, clank rang out.

Bother. "Mechanical men." She braced her feet as the

shadows surrounded them. "They live in the shadows and draw power from them. I've never seen one, but have heard stories. They're called Adam's first experiment. A nightmare version of the GIM."

"Hell."

Precisely. And then they appeared. Two lurching, hulking men making their way down the street. Vile experiments, partially flesh, mostly metal. Red eyes gleamed in the dark as one of them advanced, a blackened thing oozing oil, with steam billowing from the open iron rib cage in which its black heart pumped. The other crawler was more gold than flesh and appeared vaguely familiar.

"Piss and shit," Talent uttered with wide eyes.

"Be creative in your shifting, Master Talent!"

Mary leapt back as one lunged, and then let her whip fly. It snapped around the thing's massive iron leg, and she pulled hard. Gods, but it was heavy. The crawler wobbled. A hard kick to its chest had it toppling. It crashed to the ground. But before she could free herself, it caught hold of the whip and tugged. Mary went flying into it, stopped only by a metal fist smashing into her face. White spots exploded before her eyes as her cheekbone cracked and blood poured into her mouth.

Dimly she heard a roar of fury and saw the blur of Talent launching into the golden crawler. His claws swiped, and sparks flew as he connected with raw metal. But then another hard tug dragged her roughly over the cobbles. The whip had become tangled about her wrist, and the crawler was hauling her back to him. Hands shaking from pain, she got her knife out, sliced through the whip, and fell back. A second later, fire burst hot and bright from the crawler's mouth. Mary flung her arm up against the blistering heat, but something fell upon her, trapping her against a brick wall. Through a haze, Jack Talent's eyes, gleaming in fury, stared down at her as flames roared behind him.

He hissed, and she saw them—thick, leathery wings of onyx arched over his head, forming a barrier between them and the crawler's fire. Before she could say a word, the fire died, and he reared around, his fist smashing into a crawler's jaw. It barely made an impact, and the crawler lunged forward, punching a hole through one of the strange wings that had sprouted from Talent's back.

Talent snarled. With whippet-fast speed, he caught hold of the crawler's arm and simply ripped it off. Metal gears and springs pinged to the ground, and fresh, hot oil splattered. It did little good. The crawlers advanced, pinning her and Talent against the wall.

Another blast of fire hit, leaving Talent barely enough time to cover Mary with his enormous wings. But it wasn't enough to protect her from the heat and pain of fire nipping through the hole in his wing. She ground her teeth against it as she clutched Talent's massive shoulders.

Above her he panted, sweat dripping down from his temples.

"Talent." Blood bubbled through her lips, and agony burst through her shattered cheek. He winced as he looked over her face. With effort she kept speaking. "When I fade, rip out the hearts." The crawlers would guard them with their lives, but if Mary was successful, they wouldn't have a chance to. "Watch their eyes. Attack when they dim."

Talent's brows snapped together. "Fade?" His voice was a rasp of pain, and he appeared on the cusp of protesting.

They didn't have time to waste. Surprising herself, she touched his cheek. The contact made them both flinch.

"Do it," she said. Then left her body.

It was fast. And more forceful than she'd ever attempted. Mary's spirit shot straight through Talent, and she felt the warm glow of his soul and his lurch of shock as she passed. Then she slammed straight into the golden crawler. Its body was a dense mass of misery, the soul trapped within screaming for release. Pity made her heavy. The crawler fought as she wrapped herself around it and tugged the soul free. Out of the body they went, Mary and the pitiful soul of the crawler.

Below her, Talent whirled about and tore straight into the now-empty shell of the crawler's body. Teeth bared on a snarl, Talent yanked out the clockwork heart, and the body toppled.

As soon as the body fell, the soul in Mary's arms eased and stretched up toward the night. Like a shooting star, it trailed across the sky then disappeared.

Bloody, buggering hell. Jack's teeth ground as the remaining crawler leapt upon his back and its iron fingers tore through his flesh. He smashed a fist into the crawler's gut but hit a gate of metal ribs for his efforts. *Bad hit. Learn from your mistakes, mate.* Nearly all of the crawler's body was metal, a thick shell that withstood Jack's blows. Over the grinding of gears and the whistle of steam came the ominous whoosh of fires being stoked within the thing's lungs, and Jack braced for another blast. The massive wings on his back, the ones that had popped out as if by instinct, throbbed in pain, but they could apparently withstand fire. But if the dull ache coming from them meant anything, there was a limit to their strength. And unfortunately the crawler had him by the shoulder, leaving him no way to turn. The fire was going to come at him full on.

Shit and piss, this was going to hurt.

But then a shroud of blessed cold surrounded him, then passed through him. *Chase*. He'd felt her slide through him before, a second after her eyes went dim and her body fell limp. If he lived a hundred years more, he'd never grow accustomed to the sight of her simply vacating. It unnerved him to the core. But now, when the crawler's red eyes suddenly went black and its body slackened, he might have kissed Chase in gratitude. Somehow she'd drawn the crawler's soul out, leaving Jack free to make the kill.

He didn't waste time. Skin ripped from his knuckles as he punched past the metal rib cage and grasped the clockwork heart. Hot oil and solid iron filled his palm before he tore the device free. The crawler didn't even flinch as it crashed to the ground with earthshaking force.

For a long moment, Jack panted as blood dripped from various wounds. Then he turned and knelt by Chase's prone form, close enough to feel the residual warmth of her body and bask in her cinnamon-and-spice scent. "Chase?"

Christ, but her body did not look good. A massive bruise colored her right temple and her eye was swollen shut. Blood crusted her lips. But it was her cheek that worried him. The crawler's hit had crushed the bone, caving in the side of her face. So delicate, Mary Chase was. Illusions, for she'd heal soon enough. But the thought of someone hitting her, damaging that fragile beauty, made his breath catch.

She came back into her body with a jolt and inhaled sharply, her body stiff as starch. Her wide golden eyes shimmered with pain. And it was bad. Her body twitched, her lips pressed tight as if she held in a cry. Before he could think, he cupped her good cheek with infinite care. He'd never touched her in tenderness. And he cursed himself for doing it now. Even so, his thumb caressed the silk of her skin.

"Hold still." With his free hand, he dipped his fingers into the open wound on his shoulder. Fingers coated in his blood, he held them up to her soft lips. Understandably, Chase drew back, not harshly, but away from him just the same, and her nostrils pinched as if discovering something foul. He held her steady. The small movement she'd taken had made her wince. Black blood bloomed along her sunken cheek.

"Can you trust me, Chase?" He said it as softly as he could.

Her eyes narrowed. It was clear that she did not want to talk. A shard of helplessness speared his chest. And he sounded gruffer than he wanted as he eased his bloody fingers past her parted lips. "Let me in."

Her little gasp and the moist touch of her mouth lit through him. "It will heal you," he managed. His gut tightened, and he swallowed hard. "My blood." Shit, shit, shit, what the hell was he doing?

Shock and hesitation were clear in the gleaming depths of her eyes. But her lips parted farther, and he slipped inside. Hell's bells, he hadn't thought this out properly. The tentative flick of her tongue at the tip of his finger sent a lick of heat straight down to his cock. It leapt to life with a reflexive jerk, and Jack took a steadying breath.

"Suck it."

Her eyes widened, and Jack grimaced. "Lick it—damn it." Heat rose over his face. "I meant, the blood. Take the blood."

Thankfully she understood and, God help him, her

lips closed around his two fingers, and the wet, warm flat of her tongue stroked along the base of them. He barely stayed the groan that wanted to rip free or the way his body yearned to sway closer to hers. Somehow, though, his hand had cupped the back of her head, and he held her close. He didn't have it in him to draw away. Not yet.

Her lashes lowered, as if looking at him was too much to bear. But the effects of his blood, fresh as it was from his body, were immediate. Healthy color bloomed along her skin, and the bruising around her temple and eyes faded. Her cheek, however, was still crushed, the bones knitting too slowly for his liking. Nor did he fancy the winces of pain she made with each small move.

Breathing through his nose, he pulled his fingers free of the torture that was her mouth. Chase's plump lips opened to speak, and he laid a finger on the soft bottom curve stained crimson from his blood. "It's not enough," he said, and then, because he was part idiot and because he couldn't stand seeing her like this, he eased her head up to his shoulder.

The warm puff of her breath brushed the bared skin at his shoulder. And Jack shivered. Glancing down, he saw that his wound had already knitted closed. With an impatient sound, he grew a pair of claws and tore it open once more. Pain lanced down his arm, and hot blood pumped from the wound with every hard beat of his heart, but his mind was already on the woman half in his embrace. Warm, soft, fragrant. Holding her was an alien experience with which he had no practice. He did not hold women. Nor offer them his greatest gift and secret. Yet here he was.

She stared at him, quiet and thoughtful, and look-ing just a bit shocked. He knew she understood what he wanted. Yet he found himself speaking, low and too urgently for his own good. "Take more, Chase."

Mary knew she'd received a hard hit, but the pain hadn't truly registered until the fight was over. It consumed her now. Yet the moment she'd taken his blood, relief had flooded her veins. Her cheek tingled and itched as it struggled to mend. Now his solid arm was wrapped around her back, and his hand held her head to him with surprising care. He wanted her to take his blood straight from the wound. A shocking intimacy.

Later, when the pain passed and she could think clearly, Mary could cringe at the memory. But now she stared at the rich, dark blood flowing from his shoulder and acted without thought. His body stiffened at the touch of her tongue to his flesh, and his sharp, indrawn breath had her heart speeding up.

Mary closed her eyes and ignored everything around her. Nothing but his blood. Experience told her it ought to taste metallic and flat. Instead it held the flavor of bittersweet chocolate and fortified wine. Again came the surge of well-being and the sharp tingle as her blood quickened. Her lips closed over hard muscle and warm skin. Talent grunted, his fingers gripping her hair and his heart pounding hard enough for her to hear. Her breasts pressed against his chest, and her nipples tightened. Heat flooded her limbs, swirling low in her belly as she lapped at his blood. What was she doing? She ought to be repulsed, yet the flavor of him teased her tongue, delicious, then fading away an instant later. She wanted more. Was this why they'd kept him? Taken his blood, one after the other? The thought slammed into her, cold and sharp. She froze, her lips just touching his skin.

Against her Talent shivered, his hard body tensing as his breathing increased. Agitated. Holding it back by force.

This was wrong. She should not be using him in this way. And yet he'd offered. Mary couldn't account for it. Regardless, she eased back, her lips brushing his shoulder in a manner that was far too close to a kiss for her comfort. He resisted for a moment, as though he thought she needed more. But then he let her go.

Mary felt no pain as she sat up and lowered her gaze to her lap. No pain, but a thick, hot press of embarrassment. Silence descended between them, smothering and unnerving. Then he cleared his throat, and his deep voice swept over her. "Better?"

Yes. And no. She'd healed. But she'd been in his arms, had taken sustenance. So very intimate. And with *him*.

She risked a glance and found Talent stone-faced as usual. Only his eyes held any curiosity.

"I've never heard of blood being able to heal," she said.

Talent blinked. "It isn't usual." He looked away, and the weak alleyway light cast his face in shadows. "In truth, I don't know of another's blood that can."

"How long have you known?"

His massive shoulder, now healed, lifted. "Long enough." The corner of his mouth curled a touch, a secretive sort of smile. "You've heard of Ian Ranulf's salve?"

Mary had. The ointment, made by Ian's houskeeper, had extraordinary healing properties. Daisy went on and on about how it mended serious injuries so well. They'd used it on Winston Lane after a werewolf had attacked him.

At her nod, Talent's smile twitched. "My blood is in it. Ian thinks Tuttle makes it. But I do. Tuttle won't say a thing because the household reveres her for the skill."

"Why haven't you told Ian?"

Again his shoulder lifted. "Didn't trust him in the beginning."

Mary remembered her first days with Lucien. She'd feared letting anyone in. Feared that her good fortune would end, simply from the act of accepting another person's care. She didn't know what Talent's early life had been like, but it could not have been any better than hers.

Talent's voice grew flat and impersonal, his eyes on the cobbles beneath them. "Later...Well, I didn't want to explain why I'd kept it a secret."

She knew Jack Talent hated the idea of disappointing Ian Ranulf.

"And it's not something I want anyone to know..." Talent stiffened, his expression hardening, and Mary realized that he hadn't meant to voice that particular thought.

"By Adam's touch, I swear that I won't tell a soul." As a GIM, it was the most sacred oath she could make.

He nodded awkwardly, then his attention abruptly turned to the corpses strewn about the narrow space. Mary hadn't forgotten about them, precisely, but was glad to study them now. On shaking limbs she stood, and was almost up when Talent hauled her the rest of the way with a firm grasp at her elbow. He let her go immediately, brusque once more as he stepped closer to a crawler.

"Looks familiar, does he not?"

She glanced down at the crawler. "It's Mr. Pierce."

"Mmm." Talent peered closely. "The real one. Or what's bloody left of him."

Pierce's limbs were composed of both gold and flesh. The flesh was rotting and falling away in places, giving off a horrible stench.

"I understand shifters have an exceptional rate of

regeneration, Master Talent; do you not find it odd that, although he was a shifter, Mr. Pierce is in such an advanced state of decay?"

"Yes," said Talent grimly. "Something has been done to him. A shifter's body ought to reject the application of false limbs. We can regrow ours, after all."

"Curious."

Talent turned toward the other crawler. "Now this fellow I don't know."

His body had been mutilated. Crude metal legs, an iron-forged false fist—which was what had smashed her face—an iron clockwork heart that looked wrong when compared with the GIM's elegant devices. His flesh was grey and decaying about the edges of his limbs.

His torso was made entirely from iron, and coals glowed dimly at the bottom of his rib cage. He'd been the one to breathe fire upon them. The memory had Mary looking Talent over again. "What happened to your... wings?" The huge wings had been leathery like a bat's but had the graceful shape of an angel's.

Talent gave a small start. "Went away." He attempted a lighthearted look but it didn't quite work. Bemusement flickered in his eyes, as if he hadn't expected wings to sprout from his back either.

"The only beings I know of with wings," Mary said, "are primus demons and fallens."

Primus were said to be the first demons created, born from the collective thoughts of mankind. Fallens were angels who had chosen to live among men, and thus were cast out of heaven. They were rare as a diamond in the sand; no one in recent memory had seen a fallen in the flesh.

Talent's green eyes looked straight at her then, and a

wry smile tugged at his mouth. "Where do you think a shifter comes from, Mistress Chase?"

He had her there. Onus, the offspring of primus and human beings, included weaker demons and shifters. Most onus were many times removed from their primus forefathers. Mary pursed her lips. And his grin grew. "Your father must have been an exceptionally strong onus."

The light in his eyes dimmed. "My father, whoever he was, was pure primus."

At her shocked look, he shook his head slightly. "The ignorance, really..." Talent leaned slightly into her space. "The reason there are so few shifters in the world is that we are the direct get of a primus."

Primus themselves being rare and not inclined to mingle with others.

"You... you don't know who your natural father is?"

His jaw hardened. "Nor do I want to. Now"—he bent down, and with impressive strength hauled one crawler over his shoulder before grabbing hold of the other—"let's stop flapping chaps and get these back to headquarters. Grab the hearts, will you."

Hefting both unwieldy crawlers like sacks of grain, Talent strolled out of the alleyway, leaving Mary to follow.

Chapter Eight

The devil often hid in plain sight. No one knew this better than Jack. After he dropped the shadow crawlers' bodies off at headquarters the next morning, he headed out. Time was short—Chase would be meeting him soon—but he could not put off this particular task. Nor did he want to.

Blood boiling and teeth set, he took the stairs leading up to the *honorable* Mr. William Cavendish's Belgravia town house two at a time. The black lacquered door was little impediment to his rage. One swift kick and it flew open, the sound of splintering wood and the clanging brass knocker giving him a short satisfaction.

A footman yelped, jumping to attention after his delayed shock. "Hold! Stop—"

One punch to the man's jaw and he fell like a sack. Jack shook out his hand and kept going, heading past the vivid display of red hothouse roses and toward the sound of titters. Female and slightly alarmed. Behind him other servants scurried, the hushed plea of "Ring for the constable" coming from one of them. They needn't bother. He would not be here by the time the bobbies arrived.

Wrenching open the tall double doors that led to the parlor, Jack took in the sight. A gaggle of women, feathered in silk ruffles and plumes of satin bustles. They scattered upon his entrance, squawking and flapping their arms in fright. One proper miss swooned. But the eldest stayed seated, her eyes alight with impotent rage. He grinned at her, showing his teeth, a promise that fangs would soon descend. Her iron-grey curls and the soft wattle of flesh at her neck trembled.

She tilted her chin when he bent over her. "Mrs. Cavendish." His hand clasped her neck, claws digging in enough to hurt, if not draw blood, and a chorus of feminine screams erupted once more. Jack leaned in and spoke against her ear. "Take me to him now or I'll snap your neck and smear your fetid blood over this white silk davenport."

Their eyes met, and a flash of yellow sparked across her irises. He'd expected that, but not the powdery scent of gardenias that choked his nose. That particular cloying scent, mixed with stale demon, was familiar. His insides went ice-cold before raging to hot. Over the years many demons had pretended to be the elder Mrs. Cavendish. Most of them had been harmless. But not this one. It was all he could do to refrain from acting on his threat. He gave a squeeze to convey the direction of his thoughts, and she gurgled before wrenching away with a strength no human would ever possess.

"Ladies, do be calm." The old hen clapped her hands like a governess calling for order. "This is a simple misunderstanding. Go on with your tea. I shall only be a moment."

None of the women believed her, but, for the English, order was more important than logic, and so they quieted as Jack and Mrs. Cavendish left the room.

Out in the hall, scurrying servants halted when they spied their mistress walking with Jack. "Close that door," she snapped at a gaping footman. "And go about your business."

"Mum," began the butler.

"It is nothing," she hissed through yellowed teeth. "Do you understand?"

Her small frame vibrated with fury as she led Jack farther into the house. Once in the library, she went to a set of tall bookshelves and yanked out a frayed copy of *Pride and Prejudice*. With a creaking groan, the floorboards just before the shelves lowered, revealing a set of stairs descending into darkness. Jack had to laugh. "Doesn't someone always want to read that book?"

She practically snarled at him, her eyes now full-on yellow. "Not in this house."

They spoke no more as they went down the stairs, but Jack was at the ready should the crone decide to attack.

"They will kill you for this," she said.

At times, he'd rather they did. But now was not one of them. Not until he got his pound of flesh. Jack said nothing, but followed her deeper through the maze of small tunnels, lit here and there by hissing lamps. The weak light sent his shadow dancing against the rough stone walls, and the foul scent of kerosene and mildew filled his lungs.

She stopped at a wood door riveted with golden bolts and, after knocking once, punched a key code into the lock—one quite similar to those the SOS employed—and opened the door to reveal a cheery, bright room. Peach silk damask lined the walls, and heavy mahogany furniture supported the weight of three females and one male sitting around a dining table, illuminated by a brace of candles. The scent of cigar mingled with peat smoke. All eyes turned to Jack.

"Mr. Jack Talent to see you, sir," Cavendish all but snapped. She turned to go, long nose in the air and prim lips pressed, when Jack caught her by the throat and hauled her close. She gaped at him, her fingers clawing at his hand as he pressed against her windpipe.

"You were there." He never forgot their eyes, not a one. Or their stench.

Wrinkled flesh mottled, showing patches of grey against pasty white. "I never touched you."

She hadn't. They hadn't let her because she was just a servant, the one who collected the pans before they overflowed with his blood. Jack's sight went red, and he slammed her against the iron doorframe. Her head connected with a thwack before she went limp. He let her fall, a crumple of rose silk skirts and sprawled demon limbs. Rendered senseless, the form of Mrs. Cavendish disappeared and, in its place, a raptor demon lay. Jack stepped past it and into the room.

"You certainly make an entrance," said Will Thorne, his arm draped across the back of his chair, his fanged smile curling in slight mockery.

Jack paused long enough to look the bastard in the eye, then let his knife fly. It embedded itself in Thorne's shoulder with a thud, and the man flinched.

"Fuck all, Jack," Thorne hissed as he wrenched the knife free. "You're in a pisser of a mood."

His playmates hadn't moved, but the three women eyed Jack appreciatively. Will glanced at them. "Leave us."

They obeyed without hesitation, walking past Jack as if he weren't there. Their scent was pure human. Collecting the fallen demon as they went, the women quietly closed the door behind them.

Once they were gone, Jack rounded on Will. "You were to stay far away from me. Not stroll out and make a bloody introduction to my partner."

"Your partner?" The evil little smile of his grew. "Come now, we both know she's much more than that." A speculative look gleamed in Thorne's eyes. "I thought you vowed to keep away from Miss Chase. Make it your life's work to antagonize her, whatnot." He waved a hand for emphasis.

Jack tamped down a growl. "I've been forced to work with her. You, on the other hand, have no excuse."

"What can I say?" Thorne shrugged, halting the movement with a wince as if he'd forgotten his injured shoulder. "I wanted to meet her. She appears in good health. For now."

Hell. "She's of no importance."

"I cannot even begin to measure the magnitude of that lie, my brother."

"I'm not your brother."

"We were once as close as." Will's pale fists pressed into the arms of his chair as his icy eyes grew pure black. "And don't you forget it."

"How could I?" Even in the unlikely event that Jack managed to forget his past, William Thorne would be there to remind him.

"What do you want, Jack? You've interrupted my breakfast. And after the greeting I've just received, I'm not keen on inviting you to join me."

Jack didn't want to spend another moment in this place,

or with Will. He could barely stand to look at the man, not after he'd seen the bruising along the necks of the women who'd been sitting there. Blood partners: willing donors who enjoyed being fed upon. Jack's throat convulsed. The day he sat idle as another demon feasted on his blood fresh from the flesh was the day he severed his own spine.

Coals glowed red behind the heating stove's black grate. "Give me the names of those who still live," he said. "I want the ones who did the most damage. I want the bastard who took me."

Because there had been one, the sick fuck who had first sunk his teeth into Jack's neck. A dirty bastard who took the most, who decided who could have a turn and for how long. Jack almost doubled over at the memory, and it was all he could do not to retch.

Will studied the bone goblet before him with undue interest.

A lurching, cold feeling shivered through Jack's veins, and he laughed without humor. "God, I am a fool." He gripped the short hairs at the back of his head. "You're never going to let those names go, are you?"

On a sigh Will stood, his lean face almost pure white as he moved into the shadowed space where candlelight did not reach. "If the Nex—"

"I don't want to hear it," Jack shouted.

"Well you are going to!" Will volleyed hotly. "I've risked my arse to help you. Bad enough that you return the favor by leaving the bodies of our agents on our bloody doorstep."

That had rather been the point, Jack thought bitterly. What he had not been able to tell Chase last night was that the plinth of Nelson's Column hid a favored entrance to the Nex lair. Jack took perverse pleasure in knowing that.

Jack shook his head. "I cannot fathom why you continue to work for an organization that thrives on misery."

Will rounded the table. "We deserve the right to live outside of the shadows. Or have you forgotten those hours forced upon you, hours praying for forgiveness from a God who never showed?"

"I forget nothing. Nor will I kill innocents because I am stronger than they are. That makes me no better than the man who put me on my knees."

"Says the one who has killed nearly ten supernaturals in cold blood."

Jack hauled Will close. "Those were no innocents." His teeth snapped together with an audible click. "They drank *my* blood." It burned to say it, to even think it, but the truth could not be denied. And though each kill had destroyed a bit more of his soul, Jack would have done it all over again.

The heat left Will's light eyes. "Aye. And they deserved to die for it."

"And the ones who took more than my blood, they do not?" Jack could barely say the words through the hot constriction in his throat. "The Nex let them do it to me. You and yours kept me there."

"I didn't even know," Will snapped back. "And when I learned of their debauchery, I agreed to help you, did I not?"

Jack had to believe that, had he truly known, Will would have taken him out of that hell. But there were times when he wondered if he knew his old friend and partner at all.

"Then give me the rest, damn you," he said.

"Most of them are our top agents. I cannot reveal their names. If anyone finds out what I am doing, I'm dead. I'm risking my arse for you, but it only goes so far, mate."

Jack cursed and raked his fingers along his skull, if only to alleviate the pressure building beneath his bones. "Did the Nex kill that shifter?"

Will's nostrils flared. "Why the devil would we do that?" He snorted in disgust. "He was our biggest supplier. Hell, if you only knew how tasty his blood—"

Jack smashed his fist into Will's nose. The bony protuberance crunched against his knuckles.

"Shit!" Will's hand flew up to his face. "Stop fucking attacking me, or I will hit back." Giving Jack a baleful glare, the bastard wiped at the blood with the back of his sleeve, and the crimson blood became a macabre beard.

"I keep waiting for you to." Jack would welcome a good knockdown fight with him. "But we both know I can take you apart with one hand."

"Only because I took a blood oath not to hurt you," Will said bitterly. An oath Jack had talked him into when they were both ignorant lads of fourteen.

"Pity those oaths don't bind shifters in the same way they do sanguis." Jack almost grinned because, when he'd first imparted that small fact to Will, the demon had been bloody brassed off. The thought of them as children sobered Jack. He reached into his greatcoat and tossed Will a linen handkerchief. "I never thought you'd stoop to taking shifter blood."

Wiping at his face, Will still managed to roll his eyes. "He offered it up, and gladly, you arse." Will spit upon the ground, then eyed Jack. "We want supernaturals to rule this world. We don't abuse them." Jack snorted in sheer incredulity, and Will spoke over him. "That business with you was personal, and you know it."

"Revenge against Ian, was it?" Jack sneered. "Or was it that I tried to stop Isley from taking over?"

"Take your pick. You made enemies when you chose to side with the SOS. It was bloody stupid not to properly protect yourself against retaliation."

Yet another regret that filled Jack's mouth with a foul taste.

Will's shoulders wilted. "Look, I don't know who is killing the shifters but he's bad for business."

The impostor Bishop had destroyed the Nex's best shifter blood source.

"Given that he's mimicking your crimes," Will added, "I think it safe to assume he's taken umbrage with you, not the Nex."

Jack watched Will carefully. "Last night, after we left you, Chase and I were attacked by beings that were half man, half machine. She called them shadow crawlers."

The interest in Will's eyes was evident, but they held no hint of guilt. "What happened?"

Jack told him, and Will whistled long and low. "Hell of a thing. Would have liked to see that, actually."

"I bet you would." Jack snorted. "You've never heard of them?"

"No." A wry smile pulled at Will's mouth. "Though my specialty is extermination, not research."

"I'm done playing," Jack said in a low voice. "You don't want to give me the names. Fine. I understand that. I'll find another way."

Will glanced at him. "The other way is staring you right in the face. Join us. Your blood is incredibly valuable now. Bargain with them."

"No." Jack slashed the air with his hand. "I will not sink that low." He'd fallen enough because Will was Nex, and that made Jack guilty by association.

"Ah, now, Jack, do not waste an opportunity over

righteous indignation. You're already as good as one of us, at any rate. Once in, it is for life. You've always known that." Will's hand lashed out and grabbed Jack's arm, shoving up his sleeve to expose his wrist. "Look at that. Smooth, clear skin." Eyes flashed with dark humor and too much pity. "Why am I not surprised that you hide it?"

Because it was a shame that he could not bear to look upon. And Will knew it. When Jack tore free, Will lifted his own arm, revealing the mark of the Nex tattooed upon his skin, holding it out like a taunt. "They saved us. Me, you, and Nicky."

Jack didn't need reminding. As if he'd forget the rag-tag group of orphans collected and trained by the Nex to haunt the streets for funds and information. The sanguis, the shifter, and the half-breed. They'd formed their own little gang of terror, stealing from weaker human gangs before the fools even knew what had hit them. Nicky had been their leader. Following him had been the greatest mistake of Jack's life.

Leave her. She's dead anyway, and the bobbies are coming.

Jack pulled himself out of his crippling thoughts. Not that Will had noticed, for he was still sermonizing. "When you couldn't breathe through the fucking hole shot in your chest, they brought you in."

Jack shook him off. "And when I wanted out, they beat me until I could not walk, see, or think. Just me and the pain. Who took me in then, Will?"

Will's upper lip curled. "And what will your new little family do when they find out? When Ian Ranulf realizes his precious adoptive son is no better than the brother he'd been forced to overthrow?" Because Ian's late brother had sympathized with the Nex's cause, and Ian most certainly did not.

Deep inside himself, where it did not show, Jack trembled. The air grew thin. There was not enough of it to draw into his compressed lungs. His world was crumbling, and it was of his own making.

Will laughed, short and ugly. "And what of your sweet Mary?"

She is not mine. Never will be. Shit. The shaking within spread outward. Through clenched teeth, Jack got the words out. "Leave her out of this."

God, but the urge to run and seek her out, protect her from all of this, had his bones aching. But who would protect her from him? The constant knot in his stomach grew larger, harder.

"Or you'll kill me?" Will offered.

Jack searched his smirking face, the smothering, airless feeling pressing down on his chest. They both knew Jack could not do it. They were bonded by blood and circumstance. Neither of them could betray the other, because they both had too much to lose. Even so, Jack slowly shook his heavy head. "I'll simply make you wish you were dead."

Will's eyes grew cold. "I already do, mate. And the pisser is you know that if Mary should find out what you've done, she'll wish you were dead too."

Chapter Nine

I do not know how much I can tell you. This"—Poole waved a hand in the direction of the crawler lying upon his dissecting table—"being far beyond my purview." He harrumphed and bent closer to the body. "At least the other beings you've brought me were made of flesh and bone, not like this mechanical nightmare." The crawler that had breathed fire was about 80 percent metal, though his eyes, glassy and staring up at the ceiling, were far too tortured for Jack's comfort.

After a long night being beaten black and blue and having to spar with Will this morning, Jack was tired, irritable, and hungry. He moved closer to the table and the portly little surgeon. "Perhaps concentrating on the fleshy bits instead of grousing might help."

Poole narrowed his eyes at Jack. "Very amusing, Master Talent. Worse than Ranulf, you are. Certainly more of a pain in my—" He cut himself off with a quick apologetic look at Mary Chase, who stood as far away from the table as she could without actually leaving the room.

Wan and silent Chase, who, if Jack had to guess, was trying desperately not to cast up her accounts. She was going a bit green around the mouth.

Jack quirked a brow at her, wondering if he ought to find an excuse to get her out of the room, but upon receiving a defensive frown turned back to Poole. "You can say *arse* in front of Chase, Mr. Poole. She's quite familiar with the word, I can assure you."

"You being the greatest arse," Chase retorted blandly.

Poole snorted. "Walked into that one, my boy."

Yes, hadn't he? Why the devil in him wanted to provoke, he couldn't say. He'd been twitchy since setting eyes upon her this morning. Why it pleased him that she had the wherewithal to snipe back at him was a mystery as well.

Chase stepped close, bringing the faintest scent of spice with her. The work lights caught the tiny gold earrings in the shape of the goddess Isis that she wore, and when she moved they glimmered, pulling his gaze to the delicate hollow just beneath her ear. Jack's entire body seized up, his awareness of her humming along his veins. Which was damned annoying.

"The decomposition is quite advanced," she remarked, and Poole, of course, beamed.

"Quite. What interests me, Mistress Chase, is that the deterioration only went so far, then halted."

Beneath the harsh electric light of Poole's surgery, Chase's skin held a greenish cast, which may or not have been due to her aversion to death, but the smooth curve of her cheek and the lovely turn of her lower lip held Talent's attention. She was whole and well. A spot on his shoulder tingled, and the memory of her mouth there, licking and sucking, lingered.

Suppressing a grunt of irritation, Jack adjusted his

stance. "So he was the walking dead. Or is there another point you're both alluding to?"

Both Poole and Chase peered back at him as if he'd said something rude, and Jack glared. "Were we to spend endless minutes getting around to the fact that these things are part zombie and part machine?"

With exaggerated patience Poole drew the thick examining spectacles he favored from his breast pocket and put them on. "Don't know why anyone need speak, seeing as you know all," he muttered, as he picked up a scalpel and bent very close to the crawler. Using the tip of the blade, he peeled back a flap of skin from a cut he'd previously made along the crawler's thigh. Beside Jack, Chase swayed a bit before steadying. He resisted offering her a hand. She would hate that, and he did not want to touch her, not after last night's exchange; that had been hard enough to walk away from.

"What I can tell you," Poole went on in a crisp voice, "if you care to learn anything, is that this fellow was likely dead before these limbs were applied."

"How can you tell?" Chase's question was weak, and her gaze darted to the foot of the table.

Poole's blue eyes were big as moons behind his glasses as he glanced up. "Well, note the way the blood has collected along—"

He broke off when Chase abruptly turned and left the room with haste. Jack watched her go and then forced his attention back to the bodies upon the table. "I'd advise simply stating the facts with Chase next go-round."

Poole nodded grimly. "Hides it better than Inspector Lane." There was no judgment in Poole's voice. Rare was the soul who did not become ill after, or during, a visit to his surgery.

Jack pressed a knuckle to the underside of his chin as he studied the crawler that used to be Mr. Pierce. "And this one?"

Poole assumed his brusque stance. "I do not believe this one was dead before the change. However, look here." He pointed with his scalpel. "He did not have artificial limbs applied. More like he was becoming metal. It's as if the gold melded with his flesh."

Upon close inspection, gold seemed to blend like little gleaming fingers into his decomposing flesh. "Reminds me of ivy," Jack murmured. "You know, how it will attach to a house and encompass it."

"Yes, exactly." Poole shook his head. "Strange business." He looked particularly gleeful about the notion. Regulators did not call him Poole the Ghoul for no reason.

Jack straightened as Poole sighed. "In all honesty, Master Talent, I suggest you have Mistress Evernight take a look at them. She's the mechanical expert, after all."

Mary braced her hand upon the cool plaster wall in a dark corridor off Poole's gruesome surgery and took another deep breath. Blast it, she could do better than this! How galling that she should lose her composure in front of Talent.

"Are you ready?"

Mary bolted upright at the sound of his deep, smooth voice. Damn that man, but he crept about on cat feet. And damn her for not quite being able to meet his eyes. "Yes."

Smoothing her skirts, she stood before him. She would not make excuses, but she could not quite find the strength to talk to him either.

Oddly, Talent filled the silence for her. "Here." He reached out, and she flinched, but with a perfunctory flick of his fingers, he merely tucked in a lock of hair that had dangled over her temple. His expression was grim, almost angry, as if she'd put him out. Another brusque touch at her sleeve straightened her gown where it had bunched. Mary could only gape up at him. And his frown grew. Without a word he turned and crisply walked away.

Mary found herself following.

After a moment he spoke. "We're headed to Evernight's laboratory."

She could feel his gaze running over her.

"I thought she might be able to tell us about the mechanics," he added, as if chastising her for not asking.

"Yes." Mary took another breath, hating her embarrassment. "That is a good idea."

Talent halted with a curse, and Mary stopped too. His eyes narrowed on her. "So help me, Chase, if you grow meek-mouthed on me, I'll lock you up in the infirmary and have them examine you for madness." He lifted his large hand in annoyance. "So you have an aversion to dead bodies? Why shouldn't you? They are foul. *Murder* is a foul business. If any one of us were in our right minds, we'd be as far away from all this as possible."

His hard features darkened as he worked himself up. "If you ask me, the ones who are immune to it all are already half dead. Don't lose what bit of humanity you have, Chase. It makes you better, not weaker. End of discussion. So just...let go of this useless embarrassment, accept this about yourself, and get on with the damn case."

He stopped there, apparently out of steam from his lecture. And, having no more to say, he crossed his arms in front of him and simply glared.

Mary's lip twitched. "Lock me in the infirmary. Not

bloody likely, Talent. I'd cut your knees out from under you before you took two steps."

That haughty look he'd perfected grew in intensity. "I wouldn't lay down a challenge if I were you, Chase. I might just take it up."

With a sniff she turned on her heel, her step light and brisk, and he followed easily.

"I'm all aquiver."

His pace missed a beat before he muttered, "I wouldn't be offering up that information either."

Holly Evernight's laboratory was massive, bright and open with a grid of floor-to-ceiling windows. However, as it was also the work place for a host of inventors, the bodies were brought into another room for privacy.

"I've secured an area out of the way," Holly explained as she pushed back a pair of massive oak doors to reveal a cavernous room at the top of the building. Constructed like a greenhouse, the room was comprised entirely of glass-and-iron panels. Sunlight flooded the space, but since it was London, the light was grey and weak. A set of levers, linked to a network of large chains, made it possible to slide the roof open. Mary needn't wonder for what. She drew to a halt and gaped.

"Is that—?"

Holly stopped beside her and beamed. "A dirigible. Yes."

Talent whistled long and low as he too took in the sight. "Never seen a model such as that."

The dirigible was nothing new. In 1883, Mary, along with the rest of London, had read about the Frenchman Gaston Tissandier and the first electric-powered airship. A marvel of modern ingenuity. A year later *La France*, the first fully controllable airship, made its maiden voyage. Heady times, yet Talent was correct. Those ships had been, in essence, hot-air balloons attached to a motor and pilot's basket.

What loomed over them was different.

Shaped like an elongated cylinder, the balloon was about one hundred feet long and painted in cloud-like patches of grey and white, much like London's typical sky. A web of wires hugged the stiff frame of the balloon and attached it to an enclosed pilot's cabin, also painted shades of grey. Two enormous propellers hung off the back. The whole thing was suspended halfway off the floor by a network of steel girders.

"I've always wondered what it would be like to fly," Mary said before she could think to stop the words.

Talent glanced at her. "Do you not fly in spirit form?"

"Yes," she said, keeping her eyes upon the airship. "But there is no physical sensation to it. I have my doubts as to whether it would be the same." She turned to him. "You've shifted into a bird before, yes? Is it lovely? To fly?"

His expression was so blank that she knew she'd surprised him. He took a moment before answering. "Yes," he answered with a breath, "it is lovely."

She'd thought as much.

Talent turned his attention back to the dirigible. "That is quite an airship, Evernight."

"It is a semirigid construction," said Holly proudly, "which allows for strength and lightness of weight. The frame is a steel skeleton under a canvas skin. Not only is it fully maneuverable, but it reaches a top speed of fourteen knots."

Holly smiled up at the conveyance. "However, that is not what makes it special." She walked over to a large wooden cabinet fitted with numerous brass dials and knobs. Taking a key from around her neck, Holly slipped it into a slot upon the panel and turned it. Instantly the great airship began to hum, the floor beneath Mary's booted feet vibrating. And then the very skin of the airship seemed to shimmer before dis appearing altogether.

"No need having Londoners see us up in the sky." Holly gave a nod that spoke of self-satisfaction. "I would explain how the process works, but it would likely bore you to tears."

This much was true. Shortly after joining the SOS, Mary had become friends with Holly, finding a kinship in their shared social awkwardness. And while Mary enjoyed Holly's company, hearing her wax on in scientific terms often had Mary's mind drifting.

"You, Mistress Evernight," Talent said with one of his rare grins, "are bloody brilliant. Have I ever said?"

Mary could only blink in shock at his effusiveness. Holly, however, appeared accustomed to such praise from him, for she merely nodded, then added briskly, "Despite what you may think, Master Talent, flattery will not get your hands on all my toys."

That grin stretched, and it twisted something in Mary's chest. "We shall see, Evernight."

"If you are through?" Mary snapped.

When they both looked at her in mild surprise, she made a vicious inward curse and modulated her voice. "There is business to attend to." Which did not include Talent flirting with Holly. They could do that on their own time.

"Of course," said Holly. "This way."

In uncomfortable silence they entered a small chamber to the side. Mary braced herself for the inevitable nausea and light-headedness, but was pleased to see that the bodies were tucked inside an alcove where Mary did not have to look at them.

Talent took it upon himself to assist, and, donning thick rubber gloves and a heavy smock, had the grim task of retrieving mechanical devices for Holly to inspect. Grudgingly Mary accepted Talent's advice and simply waited as far away from the bodies as possible.

"Let's see now," said Holly, when they'd finally cleaned off poor Mr. Pierce's gold heart. "This device is, as far as I can determine, a GIM heart." Midnight-blue eyes, framed by thick black lashes, turned to look at Mary. "Quite elegant hardware you GIM possess, dearest." She started to smile, but glanced at Talent, as if just remembering he was there, and a wash of pink touched her cheeks.

Discussion of a GIM's heart was akin to asking another supernatural what sort of knickers she wore, and everyone in the room understood as much. As for Mary, she refused to look at Talent. True, it was simply her heart Holly had referred to, but it did not quell the feeling that part of her had been mercilessly exposed.

"That is to say," Holly began awkwardly, "I merely meant..."

"Let us not try to step around the elephant in the room," Mary said with a small smile in her voice. "Say what you need to say and do not worry about my tender sensibilities."

Talent moved near, his big body sending a shadow over her as he blocked out one of the electric lights. "Get on with it, Evernight."

Holly went back to her examination. "This one here"— she pointed to the heart taken from the massive crawler whose identity remained unknown—"is quite interesting.

It is close in design to those of the GIM in that one cannot detect a single weld mark and the gears are of a similar style."

Mary did not want to know how or when Holly had had the chance to inspect GIM hearts.

"However," said Holly, "unlike the golden heart of the GIM, the material used is an outdated blend of iron." She picked up a scalpel and scraped along the outer edge of the heart. With her free hand, she pulled on a pair of massive goggles and peered at the fillings. "Yes, you can see it quite well here."

Talent gave Mary a look clearly stating he'd take Holly's word on that account. Mary bit the bottom of her lip to keep from smiling back.

Holly lifted her goggles and frowned a bit as she studied the hearts lying side by side.

"Go on, Mistress Evernight," Talent said, knowing, as most regulators who consulted with Holly did, that she had a propensity for drifting off in mid-thought. "In broad terms, if you please."

A reluctant amusement glinted in Holly's eyes. "Very well. The older heart is not as efficient. It is bigger, the gears clumsy and not well designed." She gestured to the hearts upon her table. "Just look at them side by side. Even a novice should be able to see the difference."

Mary studied the hearts. "I wonder.... Hmm."

"Out with it, Chase." Talent's hard features were even more so than usual, and she knew suddenly that he wanted to be out and about, searching. A restless soul.

"It simply struck me that, while the older crawler very well could be one of Adam's early experiments, Mr. Pierce is not. He possesses a GIM heart, yes, but if he were a true GIM, he would not be ... well, a veritable physical mess."

Holly grinned wide. "My thoughts as well. See there." Her thin, pale finger pointed to the golden GIM heart that had found its way into Mr. Pierce. A thick weld mark ran down the curve along what would be the left ventricle. "It has been repaired."

A jolt of understanding, and dark dread, went through Mary. "There is a saying, that one must possess a GIM's soul to possess a GIM's heart." She glanced at both Talent and Holly. "If you try to take our heart without earning our soul, our heart will break."

"Pretty words," murmured Talent. "But it sounds as though you are suggesting this is more than a bit of poetic fluff."

"That is exactly what I am suggesting, Master Talent." She studied the broken heart. "To my knowledge, no one has ever tried to steal a GIM heart until now. Perhaps the heart truly did crack upon theft. In some ways it makes sense. Adam gave us a clockwork heart so that he might control us. I can well imagine him placing that sort of proprietary restriction upon the device." Mary looked at Holly. "Would the break, and subsequent weld, affect function?"

Holly bent close to the heart, gingerly turning it this way and that. "Given the precision of the design, I should think it highly likely that the break would hinder performance."

Talent grunted, then tapped his chin with one long finger. "Tell me more about Adam and these crawlers, Chase."

"There isn't much in the way of hard facts. These are stories. Before now, I cannot recall anyone having actually seen a crawler. But it is said that they were the very first beings Adam created. Unlike with the GIM, there were no souls waiting to find a new home or for extended life." Her lips pressed together as a bitter taste flooded her mouth. "It is said that he simply found a dead body and tried to revive it."

She glance at a horrified Holly and a grim-faced Talent. "Of course the results were disastrous, as the body was nothing more than a mindless machine." Mary stared at the hearts. "So he found souls to place in them. That too was a failure because the damage was already done to the body." She grimaced. "If the brain has started to decay, then the body is not a good candidate."

In the silence she risked a look, not at Talent, but toward Holly. "Now, I do not know if part of his failure was also because the bodies he used for the first ones were demonic, not human. Lore says that demons, shifters, and lycans cannot be turned into GIM as their bodies do not accept the invasion of metal within their systems."

Holly glanced in the direction of where the bodies lay covered with a shroud. "Pierce was a shifter. And the other one, his eyes appear black now. A demon?"

"Looks like it." Talent turned to Mary. "So Adam turned his focus on fresh human bodies. Irreverent bloke, isn't he? I'm surprised his primus brethren didn't come after him for such offenses."

"Perhaps they tried. All I know is that eventually Adam learned to use more of his magic. Now when he creates a GIM, the heart, our revived health, all of it, occurs with a touch of his hand."

Talent stared down at the two clockwork hearts. "At the risk of jumping to conclusions, someone else appears to be trying their hand at creation."

Chapter Ten

———— ❦ ❦ ————

Poppy Lane listened to their report without moving. The past two days' discoveries had pushed their case up to the top of Mother's priorities, and Poppy called them into her office as soon as they'd finished with Holly. She reclined in her desk chair, her booted feet propped upon the desk, her pale fingers tented beneath her chin. Two years ago, before going off to battle a demon, she'd hacked off her hair. An act that, Mary knew, had left Inspector Lane nearly in tears. Now Mrs. Lane's growing hair was swept back in a severe, if sparse, bun, leaving her clean profile stark against the dark walls of her office.

"I heard from Lucien this morning," Mary said. "He remembers releasing one Eugenia White from her contract with the GIM in 1844. She's had ample opportunity to make a slave pact with someone." Mary glanced at Talent. He'd been relatively quiet, forgoing even his usual snide remarks. "I gather you found nothing further, Master Talent?"

He stirred, as if the whole business bored him. "No.

The only significant difference in the crime is the obvious: it was not Pierce but a raptor demon posing as Pierce."

"Why turn Pierce into a crawler?" Mary asked. "If his blood is so valuable? Why kill the raptor disguised as Pierce, for that matter? When all it served to do was alert us to the abduction?"

Talent's eyes narrowed as if he was annoyed at her question. "We cannot yet say with any authority that whoever killed the raptor also made Pierce a crawler." The muscle along his jaw bunched. "You do realize that Pierce might have been sold on the black market for experiments."

On that pleasant thought, the room fell silent.

"I do not know if it is of any significance," said Mary, "but we found this at the scene in Trafalgar Square." She pulled the feather out of her pocket and handed it to Mrs. Lane. Even that small contact sent a zing of power down her fingers.

Mrs. Lane's straight brows lifted. "An angel's feather." She held the thing with care, touching only the very base with her fingertips. "Extraordinary."

"Angel?" Mary took back the proffered feather and carefully tucked it away. "Are you quite sure?" An angel hadn't been sighted in London since 1666, during the Great Fire of London. That catastrophe had apparently occurred when a fallen angel decided to set London ablaze in an attempt to cripple England during its war with the Dutch.

"Quite," Mrs. Lane said smartly. "Can you not feel the power in it?" Her pale lips flattened. "Dark and disturbed. I would guess that particular plumage belongs to a fallen."

"Christ," said Talent. "That is just what we need, an incalculably strong, and likely mad, immortal to add to the mix."

"Why do you assume mad?" Mary asked.

His expression turned cold. "The older ones usually are. And fallen are older than dirt."

Poppy nodded in an absent sort of way. "Sometimes they are mad. And there will be times when a fallen will be standing right in front of you, and you will never know it because they appear so human." She gave a brief, small smile. "They aren't inclined to reveal their true nature to anyone other than one of their own kind. Nor are they inclined to mix with other immortals."

"Someone would have seen a fallen flying about," said Talent. "Can't mistake something that big for a bloody bird."

Mary almost laughed but caught herself at the last moment. "Yes, but how many people ever look up? And there is our lovely London fog to hide in, is there not?"

Poppy shook her head. "Perhaps you two are unaware of this, but a fallen can shift his appearance as well as you can. Likely even better. A person might very well see a bird when one flies overhead." With a sigh Mrs. Lane sat back once more and idly tapped her lip with her forefinger. "So, we have an identity stolen, dead shifters and raptors, shadow crawlers running amok, and now possibly a fallen interfering. What a bloody mess." She turned then, her dark gaze sharp and waiting. "What is the connection?"

The real question was, how was it all linked to Jack Talent? Mary might have considered him guilty of killing raptors, but to kidnap a fellow shifter? Make a shadow crawler? She couldn't fathom it. Mercer had to have been lying to her. But why?

"It is impossible to tell," Talent answered before Mary could. "With this shift in his pattern, it will be difficult to track the killer at the moment."

"Not entirely," Mrs. Lane said. "As it appears he has a new taste for shifters, we'll have to find a way to catch him in the act." Her legs swung down as she sat upright and pulled a sheet of paper from a file. "The list of remaining shifters," she said, handing it to Mary. "One of whom is in America at the moment, visiting relatives."

Mary read over the list, aware that Talent hadn't moved to take it from her or even read the thing. "That leaves a Jonathan Deermont, tenth Earl of Darby and…" Mary trailed off as she read the name.

Mrs. Lane's hard gaze flashed to Talent just as Mary's did. "Master Talent," said Mrs. Lane, finishing for her.

Mary's blood ran cold. Was he a target? Or simply making himself the last shifter left in London? Her head throbbed.

Talent's sneer was chilling, but a certain dark humor dwelled within his gaze. "Perhaps I should just offer myself up at Trafalgar Square and be done with it." He did not appear to mind the prospect.

A wry smile tilted Mrs. Lane's lips. "My sources tell me Lord Darby has arrived from Hampshire this afternoon. We shall make arrangements to watch him. After that, we'll see if you need to be offered up for bait."

Holly Evernight loved her job. It was what she'd been born to do. Inventing was in her blood: from her grandfather Eamon to her cousins, the Evernights viewed the world differently. Possibility. Potential. Life was filled with them. One did not look at a gun and ask, How do I refine it? One looked at a gun and asked, How do I make it extraordinary? A thing was not defined by its limits, but by its potential to reach beyond them. Holly often thought people would do well to subscribe to the same practice and reach beyond society's expectations. Which was precisely why she loved the SOS, for it never set limits.

Yet even the most dedicated worker must at some point rest. A fact Holly could concede a few hours after her meeting with Mary and Talent. She rubbed her dry eyes and set down her propelling pencil. The design she worked on wavered before her, a sure sign to call it a day. Or night rather. The lofty space of her workshop was quiet and still, wide shafts of blue moonlight pouring in clean lines through the big windows. For a moment she simply stared at the geometric grid the moonbeams made upon the marble floor, then shook herself out of the trance.

Cleanup took but a moment. Locking away her drafts, Holly moved on limbs that had gone as stiff as cooled India rubber. Outside, in the main halls of the SOS, regulators drifted around. Their natural, free-flowing conversations pinged like brittle tin against Holly's ears. She was not accustomed to social interaction. Indeed, it drained her and took time away from better things, such as the next invention. But she tried to offer a smile in return for the ones given her.

Heading toward the tunnels and the way out, Holly came to a halt when the massive iron doors swung open, and a pair of fellows came in pushing a trolley between them. Beneath a black pall was the lumpy form of a body. One man caught her gaze, and his hooded eyes lowered as if he hadn't the right to look at her. It was a ridiculous notion but one that baggers tended to stick to, for few of their colleagues wanted anything to do with them.

Baggers had the inglorious job of prowling the streets for bodies. Should they find any of a supernatural nature, they picked them up and brought them in for inspection and disposal. A grim bunch. Regardless, Holly understood death as a natural progression of life. And so she gave the man a decided nod. "Good morning, Mr. Kane. Or evening rather." Her smile felt awkward. "I tend to muddle the time."

His black brows lifted a fraction, but he nodded back. "Mistress Evernight." His voice was a deep burr, rough as broken glass, but welcoming enough. Not that he paused. He and his partner, a stocky fellow whose name eluded her at the moment, walked on, his partner giving her the side eye as if he wondered over her sanity because she had talked to them. But he nodded as well and gave a curt "Miss."

Holly, however, caught the distinct acrid scent of an electrical fire. That it was mixed with the unfortunate aroma of roasted flesh did not stop her from stepping forward. "A moment, gentlemen."

They paused, the large Mr. Kane lifting those thick brows of his once again. But he did not speak.

"Has this poor person been burned by electrical shock?"

Now his partner joined him in raised brows. "It isn't anything you'll be wanting to see, miss."

"I gather not," she agreed. "However, as my current specialty is electrical devices, I may be asked to give my opinion regardless." She motioned to the body. "If I could take a look."

The man bristled but Kane lifted back the pall. The sight was gruesome. Melted flesh, black singed clothes, and a gaping hole where the fellow's chest ought to be. Most definitely death by electrical shock. Holly swallowed sharply, then leaned closer. There in that bloody, gory cavity were the remnants of metal. "He was a GIM," she said, peering at the network of finely wrought valves that were attached to the various arteries and veins.

The sheet flicked back over the body, and Holly gave a start. Coal-black eyes met hers. "As you say, miss," Kane murmured before pushing off without so much as a by-your-leave. Holly stared after the silent pair, the squeaking wheels of the trolley echoing in the dim space. With a suppressed sigh, she left for the tunnels.

Outside, the air was icy and sharp, and she sucked in a good lungful, trying to refresh her sluggish brain. To her right lay the Palace of Westminster, looming so high and proud that it blocked the moon. Coaches rattled by, and the sounds of the city filled the void. Holly moved toward the hack stand where an SOS guard stood in disguise, his job to keep watch over all comings and goings from this particularly busy entrance. But before she could take another step, something slammed into her, and a hard hand clamped over her mouth.

Holly had no time to swing a fist before she was dragged back into the shadows. She thought she heard someone shout her name, but the sound was muffled. From the periphery came a glimpse of pale hair and the flashing of green eyes. The hand pressed so hard that tears prickled her eyes, just as a pinch at her neck sent a jolt of pain and the welcoming oblivion of darkness.

Chapter Eleven

〜〜〜〜〜

"How is it that an earl is a shifter?" Mary asked as she and Talent danced around the earl's elegant ballroom. Conversation was necessary. Having been dispatched to watch over the Earl of Darby, the last remaining shifter in London—aside from Talent—they'd been obliged to dance, as the activity brought them closer to their mark. It also brought them into close contact with each other. A notion that had glared like scorching sunlight upon Mary when Talent gruffly took her hand and led her out to the dance floor.

The first touch of his hand upon her waist had brought her into stiff resistance. And for the first few notes of the waltz, they'd stumbled around the floor in awkward, mutual reluctance, any sense of grace destroyed by their attempts to remain at a distance.

But now Talent leaned in a touch, and his warmth enveloped her. "It runs in his family. He is one of the few who chose not to hide himself in another life."

"I suppose the fact that he holds a title is a good motive to remain as he is," Mary murmured.

In the golden, hazy candlelight of the ballroom, Talent's eyes glinted as he scanned the crowd, his features arranged in a scowl of concentration and vague disapproval. Dressed in fine evening kit, his hair tamed for once and his cheeks clean-shaven, Talent certainly appeared the part of an entitled gentleman, if one overlooked the frenetic strength emanating from him. He stood a head taller than she, his large body buffering her from the writhing sea of people who ebbed and flowed in the swirling turns of the dance.

"You being the other shifter who lives out in the open." Mary spoke her mind without forethought, but instantly cursed herself for her words.

His perusal of the room halted, and he lowered his gaze to her. "And me." Darkness flickered in his eyes, and she knew that he was thinking the same thing she was, of the demons who had held him because of his blood. And because Jack Talent had never hidden who he was, they'd known to take him.

Cursing inwardly once more, Mary resumed studying their mark. Lord Darby was a well-made piece, glossy and fine-featured, save for the bump along the thin blade of his nose. A flaw that only served to enhance his devil-may-care facade. Brightly handsome in the way of Lucien Stone, he seemed to reflect the light about him, drawing ladies and gentlemen toward him to flutter like moths about his luminescence. The man turned to greet yet another coyly smiling lady, and the candlelight caught the bronze highlights in his hair.

In some ways the Earl of Darby made an ideal mark. Wealthy and known for his libidinous ways, he was constantly in the public eye and was thus easy to follow without drawing much notice. Should he be cut down, however, it would cause an uproar in London.

Without warning, Talent's low voice was at her ear, a pleasant, flinty vibration along her bones. "Do you find him pretty, Chase? Perhaps we ought to consider a close-contact assignment." She needn't look to know he studied Darby as she did. His voice grew colder, harder. "A willing bed partner who could watch him day and night."

Anger coursed along her spine like a bolt of electricity, but she merely turned her head slightly, causing her hair to brush along Talent's face. But she smiled—her pretty, false, party smile—and set her eyes on the room while she set him down. "Do not attempt to whore me, Talent. That would make you a panderer. Roles that give neither of us the credit we deserve."

She expected a harsh rebuttal, but he lowered his lashes, his cheeks going ruddy. "You are correct. I apologize." His fingers pressed into her back, a light touch but one that she felt far too keenly for comfort. "I shall rephrase," he said, as he guided them around the perimeter of the room. "Perhaps a dance with Darby might bring us some clue as to what he does or does not know." For Darby could be either prey or the predator they sought.

"A good plan," she admitted, "but I am not the one to entice Darby." Years of watching her mother work had given Mary insight into men's preferences. She'd been taught to calculate them at a glance.

Talent snorted. "Then you must suffer delusions, madam."

The absolute certainty of his tone had her nearly bumbling a step. "A woman is not going to charm secrets from him." She focused her attention back to the spectacle of Darby and his women. "He's surrounded by them all the time. Thus he is accustomed to their wiles."

Talent frowned slightly as he looked to her and then Darby. "I think you're blind to your charms, Chase.

Perhaps you are correct, but Darby just might be fickle enough if you gave him a good challenge."

She laughed shortly and kept her gaze resolutely just beyond Talent's broad shoulder. "All men want a challenge, Talent. That much I do know."

They executed a sweeping turn, Talent's wide palm pressing firmly against the small of her back, guiding her, supporting her, and a tingle of warmth spread along that spot. "Perhaps they do. But I'll let you in on a secret." He leaned infinitesimally closer. "We also need to know that there is some hope of getting what we want."

She glanced at his face. He hadn't expected her to look up at him—it was clear in the way he flinched slightly, as though caught—and she realized he'd been staring. At her. She was not foolish enough to think he wanted her, not when anger and resentment colored nearly all of their encounters. But she found herself wondering, what was it Jack Talent wanted and could not have? She looked away, unaccountably flustered.

They grew silent, deferring to the music and the light sounds of their not-so-steady breathing. It was far too easy to let her thoughts slip to the fact that he was holding her, not in anger or strife, but carefully and with skill. Too easy to soak in the warmth of his mouth near her temple and the crisp scent of his skin. A heavy stillness fell between them, as if he too became overly aware. His movements grew more deliberate, a gentle glide, an arcing turn that seemed to hang in time, forcing her to feel the strength in his large body and what it was capable of doing.

"You dance well," she murmured, desperate for something to say, if only to break the spell he wove.

Talent let the words drift off before answering, his

voice sun-warmed slate now. "There are many things I do well."

He could not possibly be flirting. Mary turned her head toward him. A mistake, for his blunt chin brushed against her temple, and a sizzle of sensation licked along her skin. His warm breath touched her ear, a teasing lilt in his voice. "A four-in-hand knot, the one-punch knockout, ham-and-mustard sandwiches..."

Mary found herself smiling, and the crest of her cheek grazed his lower lip. A hitch caught in her chest. "I do not believe that last one can be counted. How difficult can it be for one to excel at sandwich-making?"

A soft rumble vibrated along his frame and into hers. Talent chuckling. She could barely fathom it, and then his lips were a hairsbreadth away from the sensitive spot just before her earlobe. "Shows what you know, Chase. A multitude of catastrophes can occur when constructing a sandwich. Too much mustard"—he spun her around, making her dizzy—"uneven bread. Not enough ham. No, Chase, you cannot approach the task willy-nilly."

Despite the confusing heat that thrummed through her limbs, a light laugh left her. "*Willy-nilly, shilly-shally,* your vocabulary veers toward shocking frivolity, Master Talent."

He paused a beat, and then she could feel him smile. "Mmm," he murmured warmly, "and yet why do I suspect that pleases you, Mistress Chase?"

His hand upon her back eased up an inch, a smooth, subtle move, and her lids fluttered closed, her fingertips sliding just beneath his silk lapel. And all the delicious muscles along his shoulders tensed.

"Does it?" she whispered. Her voice betrayed her, for God help her, she did like this version of Jack Talent.

And as if he'd realized this startling fact as well, he drew back, just enough to look down at her. "Does it?"

Heartbeat thundering in her breast, she slowly raised her gaze to his face. He'd said it lightly, a quip, and yet a certain wistfulness tainted his words. The moment drew close. Long enough for her to count the light scattering of freckles at the edges of his bottle-green eyes. Four on the left. Six on the right. A honey dust that was only noticeable up close. As if unable to bear her study, he lowered his lids, and his gaze settled on her mouth. A mistake too, for now she felt the throb inside her lips, as though they needed to be touched.

"Chase..." The rough, almost awkward intensity of his voice had her breath stopping altogether, but then his gaze flickered up as if some movement beyond caught his eye, and his expression hardened, even as he slowed and took a step back. Then he let go.

A man stepped before them, his pale jade eyes gleaming in amusement. Lucien.

"Ah, *chère*"—Lucien caught up Mary's limp hand and kissed it—"you shine like the sun in the night sky of this room." His gaze wandered over her, warm and melancholy, and guilt expanded within her belly and had her lavender silk gown feeling too tight. His smile grew. "You humble me as always, my dove."

Unfortunately aware of the man glowering at her side, Mary answered Lucien pleasantly nevertheless. "Hello, Lucien." She gave each of his cheeks a buss. "And what are you doing here?" She had missed him, even if she'd rather have seen him without Talent.

"Charming the knickers off unsuspecting ladies, one hopes." Lucien's grin was unrepentant until he let his attention slide to Talent, then all humor fled. "If it isn't the happy-go-lucky Mr. Talent. You know, I could all but feel you sucking the joy out of the room from across the way."

Mary cringed. Lucien was well aware of Talent's attitude toward her, and he'd often offered to "kick the young pup's arse." Not that she hadn't appreciated his concern now and then. But at the moment, she would really rather kick Lucien.

Next to Lucien, Talent's form was so large and muscular that he appeared a dockhand. One quite ready to take a swing. His mouth drew in a tight smile. "Mr. Stone. Out prowling for new prey? Odd. I didn't think you could catch any flies without your particular brand of honey." The smile grew into a sneer. "Or do you carry your drugs in one of those gaudy baubles you're wearing?"

Ice crept over Lucien's eyes but he answered easily. "Admire my rings, do you?" He ran a thumb over the enormous ruby he wore on his middle finger. "Play nice, and perhaps we can come to an arrangement. You know, I'm open to all sorts of experiences."

Mary fought not to close her eyes and wish herself elsewhere. There would be no living with Talent now.

"I'm certain you are." Talent did not look at her, but she felt his judgment all the same. His square jaw bunched as he glared at Lucien. "I'm tempted to offer a rejoinder about you experiencing my foot up your arse, but you aren't worth the bother." He walked away, never looking back.

"Such a pleasant fellow," Lucien mused. "I envy you working with him."

"Oh, yes," Mary said lightly. "And it shall be a delight now." She snapped open her fan and waved it hard, as if that might somehow blow him away too. "Why do you needle him so?"

Lucien's flawless face glowed beneath the lights. "Because I can."

With a flick of her wrist, she let the fan snap shut. "I knew the answer, Lucien. I merely wondered if you might think for once on how your selfishness reflects upon me."

High color stained his cheeks. "I do not like you partnering with that man."

"Lucien, I am not, nor was I ever, your property. I thought myself your friend, but perhaps I was wrong."

His mouth fell open, the color draining from his cheeks. "*Chère*—"

"Do not bother. I am working and would appreciate it if you stayed out of my and Talent's way." She left, annoyed at him for starting up, at Talent for taking the bait, and at herself for feeling guilty about all of it. Men, she thought, could go bugger themselves.

Jack hated losing his temper. Which was hilarious, really, given how often he lost it now. Piss and shit, but he ought to have kept his damn mouth shut. The last thing in the bloody world he wanted was to give Chase and Stone the satisfaction of letting them know how much it bothered him to see them together. Stone he simply wanted to kill every time he saw the man. The smug triumph that lit Stone's eyes, and the knowledge that he'd had Jack by the bollocks all these years, made Jack want to punch something.

Jack ground his teeth. He'd kept his word to Stone. And done a thorough job of it. Hell, Chase had detested him for the past four years. The fact that the bloody man felt the need to taunt Jack regardless was the last straw. But his anger deflated with his next breath. It was for the best. He'd been outright flirting with Chase. Shocking.

And stupid. He could not get close to her. Because he'd continue to maintain his pact with Stone, and with himself. Even if it killed Jack.

Hell, this whole night was an exercise in futility. Jack's gut told him this wasn't about shifters, not with the murder mirroring the Bishop's earlier kills of demons. Whatever the motive, Jack feared he was being set up and it would lead directly back to him. But he couldn't very well tell Poppy and Chase, "Sorry, loves, you're both barking up the wrong tree."

The crowd tightened around him. Laughter flowed, raking over his skin. And the scent of ripe bodies, doused in flowery perfumes, plucked at his nostrils. Humans in silks and satins. Worm threads. The odd visual stuck until all he could see was bodies wrapped in colorful, wriggling cocoons.

Devil take all, he needed air.

He wasn't going to get it, though. Not when Lord Darby stepped in front of him, the shine of his golden hair almost blinding in the light of a thousand candles. Jack repressed the urge to squint. Another bloody peacock.

"Master Talent." White teeth flashed. "I gathered the SOS would come crawling about soon enough."

"I expect Director Wilde's note explaining the situation would have been your first clue." It had been delivered to Darby posthaste, and an invitation to this accursed ball had arrived at headquarters soon thereafter.

Jack gleaned some small enjoyment from watching Darby's simper fall to irritation. With a clipped toss of his chin, the earl bade him to follow. As it was his duty to discuss certain things with Darby, Jack acquiesced.

Darby led him to a small parlor where lamps had been lit and a merry fire crackled in the grate. The ready room, far from the ball, led Jack to believe that Darby had words for him as well.

"I'm so glad they sent one of my kind," Darby said as he closed the door. "It makes me feel quite protected."

Etiquette was a bizarre business. Supernaturals' warren of rules was no exception. In general, one did not discuss one's genus upon first meeting. It was akin to asking what color knickers someone wore. Or, as in this case, it was an attempt to put Jack in his place by conveying that he was unworthy of basic privacy. Unfortunately, Jack had long ago ceased to care about manners.

"Good," Jack deadpanned. "Then I needn't worry about explaining how you ought not do anything foolish like running about on your own."

"I see you are working with Lucien's little bird," Darby said lightly. "Lovely creature." The mockery in Darby's eyes made it clear he'd aimed to hit Jack's underbelly with that volley. And while it irked, what bothered Jack more was the way Darby spoke of Chase. She'd left Stone two years ago, and still all of London's underworld thought of her as his property. As though she hadn't ownership of her own life.

"I'm working with SOS Regulator Mistress Chase," Jack corrected patiently, as if instructing a slow-witted student. "And though we shall be shadowing you for the foreseeable future, neither of us has any intention of getting in your way." He gave the man a magnanimous smile. "Pretend we aren't even here."

Darby's lip twitched in obvious annoyance. Though Jack had been the one to tweak Darby's temper, Jack did not hold the sentiment against the man; he'd be damned furious if the SOS put two shadows on his arse. Not that he would admit as much, not after Darby had run Chase through the mud.

As if he were closing a curtain, Darby's temper ended with a pivot toward a spindly-legged drinks cart. With undue care he poured two glasses of port before turning back to hand one to Jack.

The cool crystal stem felt as fragile as ice between Jack's big fingers. He held it steady and watched Darby take a contemplative sip of his drink. Despite their sparring, the earl appeared relaxed. His shifter scent was light, masked by expensive cologne and a liberal application of pomade. There was no indication as to how strong a shifter Darby was. Physical size meant little; it was quick thinking and the ability to shift into something unexpected that won battles.

Darby studied him with equal intensity. "I heard about what they did to you."

Jack tensed so quickly that his skin tingled. He stared back at Darby, willing himself not to react, not to fucking blink. Only his family and one other knew the details of what had truly happened to Jack—bad enough, that—but nearly every supernatural knew he'd been held and his blood forcibly stolen. An utter humiliation. Darby's half-smile was annoyingly sympathetic. "We shifters have never received the proper respect. The Nex and their minions disgust me."

Jack didn't want sympathy. And he didn't want a bloody friend. "Have you noticed anything unusual of late?" he tossed out, just to see how Darby would react.

"Aside from regulators skulking about?" Darby gave a tight smile. "No." He cocked his head, and his carefully combed and shellacked hair shone bright. "Why is it, do you theorize, that the Bishop has turned his attention to shifters? Jealousy perhaps? Hate?"

"I couldn't wager a guess at this time."

"Cannot? Or will not?"

Jack did not know why Darby's questions sounded like a taunt, but he didn't like it. "Have you a theory?"

Darby shrugged. "I'd say he was trying to send a message." Jack's gaze sharpened, but Darby merely took a casual sip of his drink before finishing. "But that's your burden to discover, not mine."

"Hence my presence here."

That ugly thing, a strange emotion Jack couldn't quite pinpoint, pushed along the edges of Darby's fallacious smile. Yet when he spoke, it was all lightness and lordly boredom. "I'm going to take two up to my bed when this party is over. And I'm going to fuck them. Rigorously." He quirked a golden brow, his gaze measuring. "Are you and your lovely little partner up for watching?"

Jack set his untouched glass down. "We'll be watching your house. If you need an audience to perform, then fuck in your ballroom for all I care."

Darby laughed. "An interesting idea. However, I find I rather like the idea of regulators watching. Perhaps Mistress Chase can give me a little rap on the knuckles if I fail to perform to satisfaction." His smile grew dark, luxuriant. "Are you certain I cannot persuade you? Or perhaps you'd care to join in?"

"Do these taunts ever work?" Jack asked idly. "For I confess, they bore me."

"What would it take to shock you then, Mr. Talent?"

"I understand it chafes to be guarded. Unfortunately, you have two choices. Leave the country and go into hiding until this is over"—an option Jack would greatly prefer—"or bear the inconvenience."

High color blazed across Darby's cheeks just before a snarl rent through his clenched teeth. "Unless this Bishop is the bloody Prince of Darkness himself, I will tear his head off before he gets within two feet of me."

"So confident. And yet he's killed two shifters."

Darby waved a hand. "Weaklings who never saw him coming." He laughed lightly. "Believe me, the bastard doesn't stand a chance."

"Then I don't have to worry about saving your arse. My partner and I will instead focus on capturing him." Jack adjusted one of his cuffs, and the gesture, one that he hadn't bothered with in ages, felt good. "Thank you for being our bait."

Chapter Twelve

⟞⟋⟍⟋⟍⟞

I don't believe I'll ever get over how tedious it is to do a watch." Talent's voice, though lower than a whisper, was crystal-clear in the sharp morning air. It was a quip, given the situation, and one much appreciated by Mary just then. Since he'd returned, he hadn't spoken more than necessary, except to proclaim Darby a peacock nitwit of the first order.

Mary, who stood scant inches away from him on the rooftop facing Darby's open bedroom window, huddled down farther in her thick cloak. She'd changed into thick woolen trousers, a heavy tunic, and fur-lined boots, all the easier to move quickly and efficiently should the need arise. Even so, her feet were numb, her fingertips and nose too, but she wouldn't complain. "The waiting is much more comfortable in the astral plane, I can tell you." Though impossible now, since she needed to be prepared for a physical confrontation should the killer show. God give her the strength, for her spirits were flagging.

The ball had lasted until three in the morning, but Talent and Mary still had watch over Darby for hours more. Regulators Honeychurch and Evans would take over the next evening.

But until then they'd had to suffer. Just their luck that Darby had left his curtains open and proceeded to have intercourse with both a man and a woman until the sun came up and rode high in the sky. Now it was afternoon, and the bloody shifter was still going at it, with another couple. When working for Lucien, Mary had seen all manner of sexual acts, from the profane to the mundane. It meant nothing to her. In truth, the more she saw of the act, the less she was inclined to partake in it. But to watch while forced to stand next to Talent was another matter. So she did what she'd done her entire life and sank deep into herself where such things ceased to matter, where it was nothing more than moving shapes and flashes of color.

Strangely, Talent seemed as unaffected as she. As though the whole business were no different from observing London's street traffic on the Strand. Given Talent's views on swiving, Mary would have assumed he'd be fairly blushing by now. But nothing about Talent or this case made sense to her. While she could readily imagine him killing raptor and sanguis demons, she could not fathom why he'd hurt shifters, or make crawlers. She'd seen his face when the shadow crawlers attacked: he'd been gobsmacked.

He could not be the Bishop, she decided. He simply could not. Mary only wished the tense bands along her neck would ease with that thought.

Next to her Talent stirred, and she felt his attention upon her like a touch. "How does it feel?" he asked after a moment. "To roam about as a spirit?"

A start of surprise tugged at her chest. He'd always acted as though the very nature of a GIM was repulsive to him. The bloody man constantly set her off balance, and she wondered if he did so purposefully. She licked her dry lips before answering. "It feels...wonderful. Limitless. Freeing." Her breath hit the high collar of her cloak before bouncing back warm against her cheeks. "You'd be surprised what burdens we carry within our flesh."

"No," he said low and dark, "I wouldn't."

She risked a glance and found him glaring down at Darby's house. He caught her looking, and the corners of his eyes crinkled. "I envy you the ability to escape it." When she didn't reply, for really she couldn't speak just then, he asked another question. "Do you miss being with them?"

The GIM. In many ways her job with the SOS was the same, but there was one crucial difference. Whereas once she had worked for hire, regardless of circumstance, now she worked to keep peace and order. It was a balm to the soul. "No," she said.

He was silent. They stood, unmoving, the cold air surrounding them, save where their shoulders nearly touched and their body heat mingled. Neither of them was foolish enough to forgo that small comfort. A long day lay ahead of them, and they needed to keep what strength they could. Mary fought the urge to move closer still. She hated that she craved his warmth. She hated touching others. Yet not him. Why? Why, when he'd been her enemy for so long?

"Are you happy?" His abrupt question had her turning. Talent's hands were stuffed deep into his pockets, marring the lines of his simple working overcoat. His brow furrowed. "That you became a GIM, I mean."

Talent had the particular knack for making the term

"GIM" sound like something profane. Perhaps they were. Perhaps all supernaturals were a mistake of nature. Then again, she did not feel any different than she had when she was fully human. Perversely, she wanted to smile, but did not. "You mean, would I rather have died than become what I am?"

The furrow of his brow deepened. "No. That is not what I meant. Nor do I care for your tone."

"Oh no?" She ran an idle hand along the rough edge of the roof balustrade. "Come now, Talent. You've been quite vocal in your distaste for the GIM. Do not profess outrage when I come to the natural conclusion that you believe I'd be better off dead."

His nostrils pinched on a sharply drawn breath. In the weak light of a London sun, his features were harsh, a marble statue of an irate man. Then, as if someone had turned down a lamp, his gaze dropped. "GIM are immortal made, not immortal born. It was a choice for you. The rest of us, we're trapped in this endless life whether we wanted it or not." A ghost of a sigh whispered from him, and his lashes cast shadows over his skin as he tilted his head back and stared into nothingness. "I never understood why, is all. Why choose this?"

"Because I want to know what comes next."

"What comes next?" Bafflement clouded his eyes, and the corners of his mouth dipped down.

"What happens the next day, and the next. Life is not a straight road, you realize. There are all sorts of bends and forks. I like wondering what will happen should I choose one road over another."

He blinked, a little recoil of shock licking over his features. The gesture was so quick and small that she almost missed it. But on Talent, it was like a shout.

Mary took a hesitant breath. "You wouldn't choose life? Over death?"

"With no hope of reprieve from this misery?" The wide curve of his lower lip thinned. "Despair hangs over this city like a shroud, suffocating all of us. And the monotony of facing day after day?" Slowly, he shook his head. "Are you not afraid that you'll go mad? Most of us do."

She knew this. The elders, who'd seen their family and friends wither and die, had a haunted look in their eyes now and then. Ian Ranulf had carried that look until he'd met his Daisy. Lucien carried it still. Mary understood that loneliness might one day become a crippling thing. Certainly, on occasion, loneliness, bitter and sharp, would pain her. It crept closer as the years rolled on.

"You would choose death, then?" she asked. Was he truly so unhappy? But she knew the answer. It was written in the very lines around his hard mouth and deep-set eyes.

Talent sighed, a heavy lift and fall of his chest, and then ran a hand through his hair. His hand stayed at the back of his neck, squeezing it. "I merely wanted to know if you were happy."

Why did he care? She could not ask, for she feared hearing the answer.

"For now, I believe that my life is a gift. The moment Adam raised me up from the pavement, my body was whole and strong in a way it had never been before. I am in possession of more than most women could hope for. Freedom, self-sufficiency, and the ability to protect myself physically. I'll never grow old, never die, and yes, I realize that particular gift might not be welcome one day."

She shrugged. "As do I realize that I'm still in my natural youth. I've not lived through the death of all that is recognizable and true about my human life. But I am well enough at the moment. I've friends, a position that makes me proud, and a home that is solely my own."

Oddly, Talent appeared less and less pleased as she spoke. Did he want her to be miserable? Or was it that he found her views unbelievable?

Mary straightened and faced him head on. "Satisfaction, Mr. Talent. That is the prevailing emotion I feel when I consider the choices I've made." She *was* satisfied with her life. Save for one thing. Jack Talent. The ever-present burr in her side.

He looked at her for a long moment, his expression giving no hint of his thoughts. And then turned away. When he spoke, his dark, smooth voice was thoughtful. "And the freedom you had to exchange for your life? Your arrangement with Lucien?"

Talent's attention did not move from the window, yet she knew he was aware of her every move by the way his side tensed, as if waiting for a blow. He despised touch as well. Perhaps more than she, but he did not shy away from contact with her either. Before she could reconsider, she found herself speaking.

"It was an act between Lucien and me. From the very start."

A change rippled over Talent, hardening his features into something resembling marble. Still he did not turn his head to look at her. "I have no interest in what lies between you and Stone, Chase."

"Yes you do."

His head whipped about then, his glare ferocious. She did not flinch. "Lie to yourself, if you like, Talent. But you cannot lie to me. You would not take every opportunity to get in a snide remark about my relationship with Lucien if it did not factor."

Talent's nostrils flared on a sharply drawn breath. "You speak of lies." Suddenly he was closer, his broad chest nearly touching her. "Do not forget, Chase, I've seen your little show. Many times." Mary wanted to wince then but held firm as his harsh words scraped along her skin. "You appeared to enjoy yourself..." His gaze wandered over her breasts. They were well hidden by her bulky cloak, but even so, her nipples tightened. "...Quite well."

"Appearances can be deceiving. You ought to know that firsthand."

Talent's head tilted as he continued to watch her. "Oh, I know. And yet I still find it hard to believe, having been witness to your breathy little sighs."

Her cheeks turned tight and hot, yet she stood her ground. "I felt nothing. Feel nothing when it comes to carnal acts." The sad truth was that Mary was broken in her own way. She did not yearn for a man, or even a woman for that matter. Lucien had quite despaired for her in that regard.

His gaze narrowed. "Then you are quite an accomplished actress."

"Why would I lie?" That she kept her voice neutral was a miracle.

"Good question." His lip curled in a sneer. "Better yet, why would you let Stone fondle you in front of the world if it was all an act? What could possibly be worth that sort of debasement?"

"Call it payment of a debt."

He snorted at that. "Let it go, Chase. Your story doesn't hold water. While I personally think the man is a useless ponce, I have eyes in my head. No man blessed with his looks need employ a false mistress. It makes no sense."

And here is where it grew complicated. "That is Lucien's secret to keep."

"Ah, of course." He stepped away, leaving her in the cold. "How wonderfully convenient." His hand grasped the ledge of the roof. "And how very loyal of you to keep it."

"He deserves my loyalty," she snapped. "He saved me, after all."

Talent went quietly still. His grip on the wall was bone-white. "Did he?" He didn't sound surprised, or particularly interested.

"Yes." It was she who came closer. "Do you know how I died?"

He swallowed hard but did not answer, his face going pale as if he didn't want to know. How unfortunate for him, because he was going to know. She'd had enough.

"My mother was a courtesan. A poor Irish beauty who made the world believe she was an exotic French opera singer. Only she forgot that money fades along with beauty." Mary glared up at his blank expression. "And when that happened, she offered me up for a neat sale to the highest bidder."

Talent seemed to step back, but he hadn't moved, barely breathing as she let her past out. "I ran from that room and into a pack of thugs who raped me in a back alley." Even now, all these years later, the memory turned her stomach, made her blood ice-cold. "After the third one had me, I got away. I ran. Straight into a bloody gin wagon that crushed me into the pavement and left me where I lay." Mary took a deep, cleansing breath. It wasn't as simple as that. A world of regret lay between one action and its inevitable conclusion. She still remembered the pain of that regret with sharp clarity.

Sweat bloomed over Talent's brow. Did her tale disgust him? Upset his narrow view of her world? She didn't care. Not anymore.

"Despite...well, despite what they'd done to me, I found myself wanting to live." She laughed shortly and without humor. "Devil of a thing to realize once one is already dead." Mary held Talent's gaze. "Lucien Stone offered me life anew. A home. A way to live as few women are allowed to do, with autonomy. Do you think I'd find the small act of being his mistress for show so much of a sacrifice?" It hadn't been. Not in the beginning. Not even now did she regret it. Only in regards to the way this man thought of her. A man who hated her, and who, for some reason, she could not let go of. "So, yes, I am loyal."

His eyes searched her face. "What do you want from me? Why do you tell me this?" It was a harsh plea, as if he'd like nothing more than to leave her, but stayed out of pride.

"I do not like working in strife! I go about, walking on pins and needles for fear of upsetting your tender feelings, but I'm rather tired of it all now. If you do not approve of my choices, that is your misfortune. But I suggest you buck up or get your arse off this case, because I am not going away."

His expression was murderous, his teeth bared, his eyes flaring bright green. Then he looked away, his shoulders so tense that they visibly bunched beneath his coat.

Mary sighed, her anger deflating as she glanced back at Darby's window. "I liked you. When we first met," she clarified when he turned sharply. "You seemed a good sort. Until you began to look at me as though I were something found under your boot."

Talent cursed beneath his breath. "I liked you too, when we met. Enough to believe that you did not deserve such treatment. But you let it happen. You say it was an act? Fine. Then either you liked the attention or you have no understanding of your own worth. Loyalty ought not come at the price of your reputation, Chase."

A shiver started at the base of her spine and worked its way violently upward. Her throat hurt, and her head pounded. He didn't understand. And yet he'd just voiced the very reasons why she had left the GIM and found her own way. She was prepared to sweep by him in a grand gesture, but he ruined it by brushing past her instead, his expression fierce and on the street below. Mary stopped. "What is it?"

"There." He pointed to a shadowy figure slinking across Darby's back lawn. And then Jack Talent leapt off the roof.

"Damn it!" Mary shouted. She was his partner, which meant she had to follow him.

Jack hit the ground running, his booted feet flying across the pavement and his coattails flapping. Ahead, the bastard in a similar coat raced off. He was a fast fucker. As if he knew it, the fiend threw a taunting glance over his shoulder at Jack.

With a growl of annoyance, Jack increased his speed. At the periphery of his vision, he saw Chase launch from the rooftop, her graceful arms windmilling as she arced through the air, suspended for a flicker of time. His heart stilled, his pace faltering just enough for him to take note of her landing safely and racing after them, her hair loose and streaming like a bronze banner.

Then he let himself go. The man had pulled ahead, weaving through the light pedestrian traffic as if it weren't even there. Jack cursed as a strolling couple got in his way; a shoulder bump and spin around a rotund matron slowed him down further. Jack leapt over an apple cart and almost missed the man darting across Grosvenor Place. Jack kicked an overturned basket to the side, lest Chase run into it, and the peddler shouted at him.

Jack focused on the man running away. Whoever he was, he carried the scent of something acrid like ozone or burning chemicals and the sickly taint of rot, not a recognizable scent for a supernatural, but he was certainly not human. Not with that speed or agility. He was a black blur as he headed for Victoria Station. Jack dug in and, with a burst of will, drew nearly close enough to reach the man's coattails. But the fiend jerked right, crossing into the rail yard.

Both men leapt over one set of tracks and then another. Devil take it if a foot got stuck between the ties. The man glanced back again and grinned. "Come on, then," he shouted.

The strange friendliness of it, as if they were playing a game, had Jack seeing red. And when the little bastard vaulted a parked strand of freight cars, Jack did too. And then skidded to a halt when he came face-to-face with his quarry. For a moment they simply faced off, each lightly panting from the chase. Tendrils of smoky fog snaked over the gravelly ground, coiling as if searching for prey. The cold air permeated Jack's clothes and snapped him to attention.

The man before him was of a similar height and build. A long, fitted black topcoat covered his body, and was a bit too similar to Jack's regulator coat for comfort. His features were indistinct, plain and forgettable. The strands of hair that peeked from beneath a black bowler were a watery color between brown and blond, his eyes an even brown. Whether it was his true appearance or not, Jack could not tell.

"Who are you?" Jack asked.

The man's smile was a slow curl. "A friend."

A cold, ill feeling crept down Jack's spine. The man was unbalanced. Surely. "Friends don't usually run away," he said, as if any of this behavior were normal.

"You were the one chasing me," the man pointed out idly.

"True. What is your name? What were you doing at Lord Darby's home?"

"Looking for you."

In the distance a set of light footsteps grew closer. Chase. With all his being, Jack didn't want her anywhere near this man. "What do you want?"

The man's eyes darted toward the sound of Chase coming close. "A bit of privacy is in order."

As if doing his bidding, the fog about them grew. Colder, thicker, smelling of gravestones, the preternatural mist swarmed in, obscuring the yard. A low growl rumbled in the back of Jack's throat, and a set of razor-sharp claws tore from the tips of his fingers. The man before him drifted in and out of view—a pair of glittering dark eyes and a smiling mouth.

"I want to help." It appeared as if his irises flickered silver like a shaft of sunlight hitting a mirror just before the curtains are drawn. Or perhaps it was an effect of the fog, for he moved his head slightly and the irises were simply brown. "Vengeance."

Jack's heart gave a leap as he slowly circled the man, keeping him in his sight. "I don't know what you're talking about—"

"Yes you do." The man glanced toward the car, barely visible in the consuming grey, and his grin grew off-center. "Discuss it with Miss Chase as well, shall we?"

No. "I don't need your help," Jack snapped. His heart raced now. Who the hell was this devil?

"Oh, I think you do. When you let yourself relax, it all comes back, doesn't it? Hanging helpless as the blood is sucked from your body—"

"Shut up," Jack snarled, his skin crawling with revulsion and shame.

But the man paid no heed. "You feel their touch every night, don't you?"

"Shut your fucking mouth!"

"I have the list. You want vengeance."

Jack balked. He had the names? Temptation, cold and clammy, coiled around his heart, "Why would you want to help me?" His words bounced around in the air, brittle and thin.

"We live by the blood. We die by the blood." It was the Nex motto. But it also was one of the things they'd said when they had stolen Jack's blood.

A shiver of disgust lit through him. "You're Nex?" Shit and piss but he hated their fucking round-robin ways. None of them ever followed a straight thought.

"Didn't say that." The man's eyes grew cold and opaque.

"And if I did want this list?" The Nex had strung him along far enough. If this was the only way, then so be it. He would finish this, and perhaps, just perhaps, he'd feel some sense of peace.

The man chuckled slowly. "Blood for information."

"No."

The man shrugged. "Then you don't get your revenge."

A cold wind blew down the tracks, swirling the thick fog and lifting the ends of the man's hair.

Impotent rage held Jack in place, but he knew it could

also send him over the line into true damnation. "You're copying the Bishop's kills. Why?"

"Your kills, you mean."

It took all Jack had not to flinch. This man knew far too much about him.

"Needed to get your attention," the man said when Jack remained silent and waiting.

Jack let out a harsh sound of annoyance. "A knock on my door would have done the trick, mate."

"Yes," the man agreed with a laugh. "But it also got the attention of the SOS. And one cannot forget the nice supply of delicious shifter blood."

Jack could smell it on him now, the shifter blood running through the fiend's veins.

"If you have shifter blood, then you don't need mine."

"But yours isn't quite like theirs. Is it, Jack Talent?"

Jack growled low. One leap and he could tear out the bastard's throat, rip his heart free. But if he missed, he'd be no closer to the end of this. Did the man really have the list?

Another hot wash of shame coated his skin at that desperate thought. "Are you the one responsible for making those crawlers?"

"You killed my pets." The accusation was petulant. "They were merely trying to bring you to me."

Jack snorted. "Then they ought to have been more polite about it. Instead of trying to burn me and my partner to a bloody crisp."

A cold sigh escaped the man. "It was a failure. The shifter blood I have is unfortunately weak. Didn't control the change properly. But yours? 'Whoso eateth my flesh, and drinketh my blood, hath eternal life.' "

More Bible verses. Lovely.

Fangs showed when the man smiled. "And I want a taste."

Jack laughed without humor. "You think I'll give you mine after a statement like that?"

A calculating gleam filled the man's eyes. "I think you want revenge so badly, your teeth ache."

Piss and shit. Jack should not listen. He strained against the words. But that dark, haunted place that lived and breathed within his shattered soul soaked it in and cried out for more. To feel peace. Could it ever happen? The man had the list.

Swallowing against temptation, Jack took a step back. "Not interested."

"Liar."

Again came the nearly vibrating need to hunt. "I won't give you my blood."

"Oh, I think you will." So very assured. A slow smile spread over the man's face, and a glimmer of fangs appeared behind his lips. "It would be a pity if your secrets came out in the open, would it not?"

Hell. Bloody, bloody hell.

"I suggest you think hard on that before you refuse me. I'm quite comfortable continuing on, exposing your underbelly as I go. I'll have that blood. One vial. In return, you can have the list of names."

"That's all you want?" Jack did not believe that for a moment.

"One hour," was the answer. "Paddington Station. Look behind the Pears baby, and you'll have your names." He stared at Jack with something akin to mad pride. A strange look that had Jack turning cold.

Jack gritted his teeth. "If you think—"

"Talent?" Chase's worried voice rang out from the other side of the freight car.

Shit. Jack glanced between the man and the direction of Chase's voice. A mistake.

The crunch of gravel echoed. Everything in him screamed to go to her and draw her close. It was too late. An evil gleam lit the man's eyes.

"The lovely Miss Chase," said the man. "Shall we say hello?"

Before Jack could move, the man gave a great push to the side of the freight car. It rocked toward Chase and then started to fall.

It all happened too quickly. Mary had been standing beside the train, walking toward the sound of Talent's voice, when the whole car came hurtling toward her. Then he was there. She made a grab for Talent, and he for her. Their hands collided, a messy tangle, then he was throwing her down, with the massive freight car following him. Her head cracked into the rough gravel, and his face smashed into hers. An instant later another blow came, so hard and swift that it knocked the air from her lungs. Talent grunted, his breath whooshing too, but then his body, flat against hers, arched and braced, as if forming a human cage around her.

And then it all stopped.

Mary blinked, taking stock of her bruised body and the fact that Talent was lying flush against her, grinding her into the ground. The rough, green-painted boards of the freight car loomed behind him. On him. She tried to catch a breath and failed. The bloody thing was on top of them.

From beyond came the shouts of men. "Cor! Did you see that?"

"What made it crash?"

"Dunno. It just seemed to fall over. Thought I saw a couple of people for a moment. Don't see 'em now."

A hard snort. "If they're under there, they's flat as a fritter by now."

Mary's focus narrowed back to Talent, just visible in the dim light. They were nose to nose, his chest, belly, and hips crushed against hers. From what she could feel, his thighs straddled hers. Mary took light breaths, trying to ignore the sensation of his large, male body all around her.

His arms, bracketing her, shook with strain. Dear God, but he was holding the worst weight of the car off of her. A bead of sweat trickled down his temple. "Are you all right?" he asked.

"Well enough. You?"

"I've got a freight car on my back," he managed with a grunt. "What do you think?"

"I'm sorry," she offered weakly. For, really, what did one say in such a situation?

An amused snort left him, and his warm breath gusted over her lips. "As am I." Oddly, it did not sound like a quip but an honest apology. The ghost of their earlier argument whispered between them once more.

When their gazes met, his mouth canted. "If I move, the car will topple back on the men." His voice was barely a sound.

"Hell," she whispered, then glanced toward the sliver of light beyond. And if they alerted the men to their presence, they'd have to explain how the train hadn't crushed them.

Mary licked her dry lips. "What happened?" She hadn't been able to see a thing in the sudden fog that had rolled in. Sounds had been distorted, and for a moment she'd been quite vexingly lost.

Talent's voice turned flat. "He ran, I almost had him, he tipped the car over onto you, and so forth."

Lovely. So their current predicament was her fault. Mary winced. "Thank you, Jack."

He flinched, then stilled. "You're welcome, Mary," he whispered back. Only then did she realize she'd used his given name, and he hers.

As the two fellows beyond nattered on about how to right the overturned car, the small space between her and Talent grew thick with quiet. And all the sharp words and anger that lay between them had no place to grow here.

The wide expanse of his chest mashed her breasts against her rib cage. An uncomfortable sensation. And yet awareness of his chest, so solid and strong, had her nipples pebbling. Did he feel it? Did he know? Or did he choose to ignore it, just as she tried to ignore the thick length of cock pressed impossibly hard against her belly?

Mary wasn't so ignorant as not to know that a man might have a cockstand merely because he was in close contact with a woman. It did not stop the empty space between her legs from growing warm, or a soft, insistent throb from developing there. The sensation was so unexpected, so unfamiliar to her, that Mary didn't know what to do with herself. For lack of a better place to go, her hands settled on the sides of his trim waist, and a tremor lit through him. She let her hands fall, but it didn't seem to help. Every dull thud of his heart reverberated through her.

So closely pressed, they had to adjust their breathing. With each exhale Talent made, so must she inhale. Back and forth, in and out. Sharing the same air, building a soft, slow rhythm. She had no escape, nowhere to look but at him, into his eyes. His gaze was unwavering, studying her as though he saw her soul. And perhaps he could, for she felt splayed open. His mouth was a word away, close enough to feel every breath he took.

Deep within her a shiver began, and her neck ached with the urge to cant her head, tilt her chin just so until his mouth fit to hers. Dear God, she wanted to kiss Jack Talent. Perhaps he saw the knowledge dawn in her eyes, for his gaze narrowed, his breath coming faster.

"Christ, Chase, close your eyes or something." As if leading by example, he closed his own, turning his head slightly.

It was a two-shot knockdown to her heart, and her breath hitched, the action pressing her farther into him. A strangled sound wrenched from deep within his chest.

"Why?" she managed to ask.

His throat moved on an audible swallow. "Because the sight of you is causing me pain. And even if I do not look, I can feel your gaze on me." The confession was raw, agonized, and angry.

It destroyed what was left of her pride. Mary closed her eyes. It hurt to look at him too. His head moved an inch, bringing his cheek flush with hers, and the stubble of his beard scratched her skin. She squeezed her eyes tight, fighting to ignore the feel of him, and his earthy scent made her mind a muddle.

"Admit it," he whispered wryly. "I am the last person you'd want pressed into you in this manner."

She stilled. Was he? Rocks gouged her from head to foot. A particularly sharp one had her shoulder blade screeching for relief. Nothing was comfortable about the situation. And yet where his hips ground against hers had grown unbearably hot. She wanted to move, if only to grind back. Her cheeks flared with the knowledge.

Good God, would those blasted men ever leave? She could not breathe anymore. She needed out. Her chest sawed as she tried to get more air. But there was only Talent, surrounding her, making her think things she shouldn't.

He did not miss her distress. A ragged sound broke from his lips, and he adjusted his position, the action making her squeak.

"Toss it, I'm going to shift," he said against her skin. "It will be sudden, and hopefully it will knock the car clear of those chatterboxes." His breath tickled her ear. "The moment I do, run. Don't look back. Run all the way home."

"I am not going to run away. I can help you." She wanted to run, but she couldn't leave him.

She felt him smile against her. "I am going to be quite nude when I shift back." He paused. A beat that pulsed through her. "Do you truly want to be around when that occurs?" He was laughing at himself.

But she couldn't. Not when the very image filled her with disquiet. How horrible, when he couldn't even look at her. "No," she admitted. "I'll go."

"Good thinking. Besides, I'm running too. I will see you again tomorrow, little fritter."

Something soft brushed her cheek. His lips. It was so light and fleeting she couldn't be sure if he'd truly kissed her or simply moved his head. And then she couldn't think at all.

A violent swirl of energy and movement licked over her, disturbing the air. A hard limb struck her elbow, another her knee, and Talent was a blur above her. Then the freight car was flying to the side. Cool air hit her face as men shouted. Mary leapt to her feet, running despite the screaming pain in her limbs from the sudden action. She dashed over the tracks as cries rang out. Only when she was nearly clear did she look back. And a laugh burst from her as she saw one man faint and a great black horse race across the yard.

Chapter Thirteen

━━━━━━━━━◆∞◆━━━━━━━━━

Darkness greeted Jack when he returned home. He lived alone now. Ian, that thickheaded, stubborn Scot, had insisted that Jack was his heir apparent. As such, Jack was entitled to a third of the vast Ranulf fortune. When Jack had tried to return the funds, Ian flatly told him to "either take it or throw it into the Thames, but give another word of protest and I'll stuff it down your bloody throat."

So Jack bought himself a modest home and let Ian's man of business take care of the rest.

He had more than enough money to employ a full staff, but it felt wrong. He wasn't a lord, or even upper-crust gentry. Acting the part wouldn't make it so. He had a housekeeper come round to clean and launder, and see that his pantry was stocked, but that was the extent of it. Hell, he'd been a valet long enough to look after his own wardrobe, and he could cook when needed.

He was grateful for the solitude as he stood in the cold, dim hallway with the memory of his discussion in the rail yard playing in his head, and with it came temptation. To find his tormentors. To end it all.

Bare-arsed naked and shivering from the cold, he made his way up the stairs and into his room. But just at the threshold, he tensed and paused. Every muscle in his body quivered as he inched his way in, claws extended and at the ready. Stupid that he'd come this far into his home without taking proper precautions. And fucking miserable that he still worried about being ambushed.

Nothing stirred. No scent of something off. He was safe. Relatively.

Jack bolted the door to his room, then made his way to the bathing chamber. Heedless of the cold porcelain, he sat his bare arse in the tub and let the water fill up around him. The rush of water and the still hollowness of the bathing room calmed him as he stared up at the medallion on the ceiling. He'd lit one lamp, and a golden halo of light kept the shadows at bay. But it was too quiet. He used to love silence. Now it only allowed thoughts to creep in.

Hot water lapped at his chest, stroking his skin like a tongue. Jack's throat constricted on a gag, and he lurched up, grabbed the soap, and scrubbed it over his flesh. Lather foamed, his skin stinging as he used his nails. And still a sticky film of muck seemed to cover his skin, sinking into his guts and churning them.

They were out there. And Jack could have their names. If he wanted them.

"No. Let it go." It was too dangerous to go out now. And he'd have to face *her*. With blood on his hands. He rocked in the tub, need and vengeance crawling through him. "Let it go."

Scrubbing, scrubbing. Not enough. The soap dissolved, and his fingers swept over his skin like a caress.

Sly caresses, hard hits. He never knew how they would touch him next. A sob broke from him. He sank beneath the water, and it folded over him and burned his eyes. His world was silent and warm. Suffocating. A second later he burst from the watery womb on a snarl, his body trembling and tight.

They were out there. And Jack could not live while they did.

By the time Mary limped home, the sun was close to setting. She was bruised, battered, and exhausted. Nothing else mattered save stripping off her dirty clothes and sinking into a hot bath with a cup of tea and a good book to keep her company. Decadent. And necessary. Limbs aching, she climbed the steps that led into her building, only to stop when a cloaked figure stepped in front of her.

In an instant Mary had one knife pinned to her visitor's throat and the other poised to sink into the person's gut.

A breathless feminine laugh filled the cold air. "Bleeding hell, Mary," said Tottie. "I thought you were more hospitable than this."

Mary studied the GIM's eyes and listened for the telltale sound of her whirring heart. Satisfied that it was truly Tottie, she slipped her knives back into their hidden wrist holsters and moved back. "One cannot afford hospitality in our line of work, Tot. Something you ought to know."

Tottie gave a curt nod. "It was careless of me." She scanned the area around them, taking in the shadows that grew along the stairwells and fenced front walks. "Especially now."

Mary's back tensed, a trickle of forewarning creeping along her spine with cold feet. "Has there been another murder?"

"Can't be telling you what I don't know." Tottie gave a brusque shake of her head, her GIM eyes going cold and worried. "Director Lane wants to see you immediately."

There were moments when Jack wondered how he got out of bed. He knew why, however. In bed, he'd sleep. With sleep came dreams. Rather, memories. Because before—and he always thought of life in terms of Before and After the torture—Jack had not had the imagination required to think up such horrors. Early on, in those dark days of raw healing, he'd tried an opiate to sleep. Instead of giving him welcome insensibility, it made his dreams more vivid: the hands holding him down felt real, as did the sick pain. He woke screaming. And couldn't seem to stop. Best to sleep as little as possible.

Tonight, however, there was no need to sleep. The devil's offer lay heavy on his shoulders. Tonight, lying in wait was a list of names. Not the ones who'd merely stolen his blood. But the others. The pain and rage brought forth by seeing that bastard today had only made things worse.

In the grey shades of night, Jack wove around muck-filled puddles as he made his way down Bishop's Bridge Road. All was quiet, still in that small slice of time when the great city slept. Such a small rest London gave itself. But when it did, the world seemed to stop. The soft hiss of rain filled the echoing void around him. Raindrops pelted his face and tasted bitter as they trickled over his lips. He walked on ghost feet, keeping to the shadows like a slinking cat.

Ahead, Paddington Station sat waiting for him, its ubiquitous Greek revival architecture giving no hint of the splendor that lay within. Jack made quick work of getting there. Once inside he stopped, rubbed a hand over his wet face, and raked his fingers through his dripping hair. The enormous space soared above him, a lofty latticework of iron and glittering glass, stretching out in three great arching spans. He felt at once tiny yet infinite, comforted yet free. So still in here. So very still. The steady tap of rain upon the vaulted glass roof merely highlighted the quiet. A man could let go of his tension in such a space.

Slowly he walked, the vastness surrounding him. Jack loved rail stations. Cathedrals to transit, they offered a chance for escape. Stopping before tracks that pointed the way out of London, Jack took a deep breath, tasting the coal and the metallic bite of brake dust.

In a few hours, trains would arrive. He could go. Leave everything and everyone. He let himself imagine it, climbing into a car, the gentle rock and sway of the carriage as it sped out of the city. No one would know who he was, what had happened to him.

Heat and pressure prickled behind his lids, and he swallowed convulsively. A man could run, but he couldn't hide from himself.

With a heavy tread, he found the advert panel, promising smooth and youthful skin. A plump, rosy-cheeked tot having a bath smiled down at him as he slid his hand along the wood frame and lifted the hidden latch. The smooth coolness of paper touched his fingertips, and he grasped it, even as his entire body recoiled at the idea. A year ago, even a few nights ago, he would not have hesitated, so great was his rage, his need. Now luminous brown eyes, the precise color of topaz backlit by the sun, hovered in his mind's eye.

Chase's condemnation would be the swiftest, the most foul. Others, the ones who loved him, would be more hurt, but the mere thought of facing her disappointment sent a wave of disgust through his flesh. Shame was a sticky tar that coated and burned. Jack gritted his teeth against the sensation and closed his eyes against the sight of the small square of paper he held between his fingertips. He kept his eyes closed as he pocketed the missive. And he squeezed them tighter still as he reached inside his great-coat and pulled out the vial of blood within.

His hand shook, his shame growing thicker, hotter. *Do not do this.* Regret and despair rolled down his throat like slime. His hand shook harder, sweat pebbling his brow. Hissing a breath out between his teeth, he shoved the vial into the hidden compartment. Another two breaths and he was staggering to the nearest rubbish bin. His evening meal came up in a violent wave. Empty and battered, he slid to the floor, wiping his mouth with a shaking hand.

The flutter of the doves among the iron rafters and a distant whistle told him it was time to go. But he stayed a moment longer, pulling out the paper. The first name leapt from the page: Mercer Dawn.

Mercer. A shudder went though Jack. He remembered. *"Mercer, finish off, will you? There's others who have need." "Just one more taste."* Gleaming yellow eyes look-ing him over, cold hands on his fevered skin. *"Such tasty blood, he has."*

Relief and despair mingled. Jack now had the means to kill those who had hurt him. But deep in his heart, he feared that was not what would heal him.

Chapter Fourteen

~~~~≈≈≈~~~~

Mary had been the assistant to Poppy Lane for quite some time. Certainly long enough to be well acquainted with being called into Poppy's office at odd hours on a moment's notice. This was what Mary told herself as she gave a nod to Poppy's secretary, Mr. Smythe, who sat just before the large iron-and-brass office door. But Mary had her doubts.

Outwardly she gave the impression of calm. Mary was known for her unflappable demeanor. She'd overhead enough SOS gossip to know that she and Poppy were often called the Stone and the Icicle. They'd had a laugh over that, fostered the image even, for theirs was a hard life and having a formidable facade was yet another layer of protection.

What worried Mary now was that inwardly she was an utter mess. Instinct told her that this meeting was not to be a friendly chat to see how Mary was getting along in her first case. Worse, Poppy Lane knew Mary well enough to see past Mary's well-crafted social mask.

Slowly Mary turned the doorknob and went inside.

Poppy smiled when Mary entered. More trouble, Mary thought grimly. Poppy only smiled when she was about to pounce.

"Mistress Chase. Sit." She gestured to the empty chair placed before the nice little heat stove.

Mary settled in, and Poppy moved to pour the tea. "You look a little worse for wear."

Mary hadn't had time to change her gown or re-coil her hair before coming to see Poppy, and she was dusty and unkempt. "I work alongside Jack Talent," she said wryly. "We thought we'd found a suspect today, but we lost him in the train yard."

"Pity." Poppy handed her a cup. "Speaking of Talent. What is your impression of him?"

Calling on every bit of training she'd amassed, Mary held Poppy's piercing gaze without flinching. "He is cagey, suspicious, quick to anger, and quite arrogant."

"Well, yes," said Poppy with a touch of asperity, "but we all know that much already." She cleared her throat. "I ought to have been more specific. How do you find his handling of the case?"

Just the question Mary had feared, for suspicion lurked in Poppy's dark eyes.

Mary's heart worked so fast now it hurt. The compulsion to tell all was thick on her tongue. Poppy Lane was not merely her employer. She was her mentor, her friend. And what did she owe Jack Talent? He lied, perhaps murdered, he . . . She swallowed down a sigh. He suffered. She knew that with a bone-deep conviction.

"Mistress Chase?" Poppy prompted. "Has the cat got your tongue?"

"He has little patience for questioning." Best to stick as

close to the truth as possible. "But he is also quite percep-
tive. And quite determined to catch this killer."

Sweat trickled down her spine as Poppy studied her.
"You haven't noticed anything...unusual?"

Mary allowed herself a smile, as if her insides weren't
quaking. "I have never before had a partner, Mrs. Lane. If
you want me to speak ill of him, perhaps you'd better tell
me why."

Poppy did not move, but it seemed as though her
narrow frame leaned closer. "All right then. Let us cut
through the muck. Jack Talent has had control of this
case for far too long without his usual results. In agreeing
to assign you to the case, I had hoped you might give us
insight into this anomaly."

The cold shaking within Mary grew. Poppy had
wanted her to keep watch over Jack. Yet again, Mary had
been maneuvered. "If you had intended for me to spy on
my partner, you might have said when I began."

"Come now, Mary," Poppy snapped. "You and I both
know you had reasons for picking this particular case. I
did not bother to ask, because I trust you. But surely now
you can confide in me as to what those reasons were?"

Good God, what did Poppy know? It had to be damn-
ing for her to turn against Talent. "Forgive me, mum, but
Jack Talent has been more than loyal to you and yours.
According to the Ranulf, he is your family."

"Of course he is!" Poppy's slim shoulders slumped,
and she pressed her fingers to her eyes. "Last night, about
an hour before Lord Darby's ball, Mistress Evernight was
abducted in front of the SOS offices."

Mary's hands clenched convulsively. "What can I do?
How can I help?"

Grimly, Poppy bent to retrieve a strip of vellum pressed

between two sheets of paraffin paper. "This was found near the spot where Mistress Evernight was taken. I do not know if it pertains to Evernight or not, but we kept it regardless. Mr. Lane is going to have a look at it under a microscope to see if it yields any clues to its origin."

Taking care not to damage or over-handle the note, Mary put on her gloves and peeled back the paraffin paper. " 'Be not forgetful to entertain strangers: for thereby some have entertained angels unawares.' " Mary glanced up at Poppy. "My mother used to quote that verse to me." Unfortunately, those whom Maman considered angels were not quite benevolent, winged beings.

"Bible verses," Poppy muttered. "I do hate it when they resort to using quotes. It smacks of an overdeveloped sense of one's own cleverness."

Mary fought a smile. Many a criminal liked to taunt, and Poppy Lane hated taunts. Mary handed Poppy the papers. "While most attribute the quote to a basic Christian duty to be hospitable, given that we know angels are real, I wonder if this message is trying to tell us something more."

"Mmm." Poppy tapped her fingers upon her lap. "Do you suppose someone has entertained angels unawares?"

"Perhaps so. Or perhaps it is all nonsense. I can tell you that, to my knowledge, the Bishop of Charing Cross has never before left a message behind. Perhaps this incident is not linked to the case."

"Perhaps." Poppy smiled vaguely. "A bit too much 'perhaps' for my liking, Mistress Chase."

"Mum, forgive me, I do not see how this involves Talent."

But Poppy's pale lips pursed in negation. "A witness has come forward," she said. "She claims she saw a man greatly resembling Jack Talent grab Mistress Evernight."

Bloody hell. The precise time Mary had been getting ready for Darby's ball. She'd assumed Talent had been doing the same. Now she could not be sure.

Poppy took a slow sip of tea, and her hand shook. The porcelain cup landed on the saucer with a delicate clink. "No one knows of this but you and me."

"And his accuser. Who is it, if I may ask?"

"Tottie." Poppy tapped her nails upon her thigh. "As she is my assistant now, she came directly to me." Poppy frowned a bit, and her tone became almost sorrowful. "Jack is not the same. Not after…" She took a bracing breath. "You must understand how it would grieve me were it true, but I cannot ignore this. So I am asking you, do you have any suspicions that Jack Talent has turned against the SOS?"

For years Mary had entertained herself with little fantasies of being the one to bring Talent down. She'd imagined herself in this very office, telling Poppy that she had finally found proof of his perfidy. Now Poppy stared at her, those keen brown eyes searching. The perfect opening. And yet Mary paused.

Despite the iron-hard will and resolve in Poppy's countenance, there was a plea in her voice. It was well hidden and slight, but there just the same. Jack's downfall would do more than grieve Poppy; it would devastate her and her family.

For that alone, Mary could only pray that Talent was innocent. Even though she feared he was far from it.

"I need to know," Poppy said in a low voice. "Is Jack the Bishop of Charing Cross?"

Mary stared straight at Poppy as she consigned her honor to the devil. "I do not know, mum. But I shall find out who it is."

*   *   *

He whispered through the night, black ink spilling over ebony wood. Unnoticed, unheard. But alive, so alive and waiting for the moment. The moment when he could breathe without that sick, choking feeling taking hold. His prey slithered in the darkness as well, comfortably ensconced in a stolen coach and not quite as silent, for he was too sure of himself and his role as predator, never realizing that there was a bigger predator in town now.

Jack followed along, leaping with ease from rooftop to rooftop, watching, waiting. And listening.

The woman's laugh drifted up first, a high, tittering sound, designed, he supposed, to entice a man to continue with his attentions. "I shouldn't, my lord." There was a breathy little catch to her voice.

"You really should, my love. Just give me a little taste. Yes, like that."

A moan, then grunting. Far above the rocking coach, Jack's innards rolled. Memories threatened. Hands upon him, the laughter, the jeers. That voice: *just a little taste.* Teeth sinking in deep, and the slick tongue sliding over his flesh, sucking. Jack's skin crawled, leaving him with the desire to rip it from his bones. Disgust, humiliation, shame. And hate. So powerful that he shook with it. Hate transmuted into rage. He held on to it, channeled it into power and control. Moving along the edges of the Pall Mall, the coach finally turned onto a smaller lane, the rider sitting straight as if he couldn't hear the slapping of flesh against flesh. Perhaps he couldn't, perhaps he'd grown immune.

Jack had not. Ideally he would have waited until he and his prey were alone, but not tonight. Not with those sounds filling his head. Teeth grinding, his body vibrating with the need to maim, he jumped, landing upon the coach roof with light feet. The driver turned. One punch and the man slumped. A startled noise came from within. Jack gave them no more time. His claws tore through the roof as if it were paper. The woman inside screamed. Glimpses of her pale, bared thighs filtered through the red rage, but he had little care for her. No, it was the insect crawling away from her, desperate to flee the carriage.

Jack reached down and grabbed him, heedless of the blows the little bastard rained upon him. He hadn't shifted. He wanted this scum to see who was going to end his life. Holding his prey secure, he leapt high, the weight in his hand making the launch awkward. His prey screamed, his flailing legs hitting the edge of the coach roof hard. A snap rang out, followed by another scream, this one of pain. Jack held fast, using the strength in his legs to jump again, a great bound that took him to the end of the lane. He dragged his catch along until they were deep in an alley where no soul would dare follow.

There he tossed his prey down. The demon scrambled, one limb twisted at an odd angle. "I've no quarrel with you, Bishop!" His skin was turning from human ivory to demonic grey, the stolen visage of a handsome lord melting into an ugly mug. Jack squashed down his chest with one booted foot.

"Just a taste," Jack growled, his sight going hazy. "Isn't that what you said?"

The demon's wild eyes flared. "What? No! I never—"

Jack hauled him up, his claws sinking deep into the demon's belly. "Just a taste of me! Isn't that right, Mercer Dawn?"

Black blood trickled from Mercer's lips. "I didn't make it hurt. Not like the others. I could have."

On a roar Jack raked his claws upward, gouging through the demon's flesh, making the rotter convulse. "Do not speak!" Fangs elongated in his mouth, his body began to grow, muscles swelling, and leathery black wings once again sprang from his back.

The demon gaped with terror. "You're no shifter. What in hell's name are you?"

He towered now, a being over nine feet, and the surge of clean, hot power running through him was unfamiliar yet welcome. The demon dangled in his grip. One good swipe and he'd easily sever his prey's spine. He craved that death. He would kill everyone who had ever touched him. "Revenge," he growled.

Mercer cried now. Vile tears tinged with blood. "Please. Have mercy. I didn't…" Yellow eyes stared up at him.

Golden-brown eyes filled his mind's eye. Shining up at him as he bracketed her body to protect her. Jack paused. Bile coated his throat. Memories threatened. Mary Chase dancing in his arms. Taking a life. Hanging from that wall.

I liked you. When we first met. Mary. Hell, focus. His claws sank deeper into the demon.

"Please," Mercer babbled, "I'll give you anything. Anything you want."

Anything? Jack's list of wants had grown. He wanted his sense of control back. Damn it, he wanted his life back. He wanted…. Jack's body trembled as the roar built up in his chest, pushing, choking, until it burst free.

Chapter Fifteen

Holly shivered and huddled closer to the rough stone walls that lined her cell. Across the way was a cell made of thick glass panels and a grid of gold bars. Inside sat a diminutive woman. Nothing by way of features to see but a pair of dark, glittering eyes that peered out from behind hanks of thick black hair. The woman had taken to bashing her head upon the bars as she recited a man's name over and over until it became a mad song.

Holly looked away, not knowing who this man was, but rather fearing he'd be in for trouble should the woman escape, because the way she uttered his name was not kind. Those eyes were insane and made Holly feel as though her soul would be sucked away should she gaze upon them for too long.

Refusing to cry, she began to rest her head upon her raised knees, but stopped and flinched. Her face was on fire with pain, her jaw and cheek throbbing where the female guard had punched her. At the very least she had refrained from blackening Holly's eyes.

"She needs to properly see," her cohort had said, another woman with beautiful light-green eyes. Dead eyes. "Her hands are not to be harmed either."

Oh, but her stomach? Her legs? They could be pummeled.

Clutching herself tighter, she rocked a little, trying to create some warmth. There were others down here. She could hear them moaning. And smell the stench of their uncollected waste.

At the sound of clattering keys, her heart leapt in terror. The lock of the far-off cellar door turned with a groan, and everyone went alarmingly silent. Footsteps rang out, a slow, horrific *click, click*. Holly dug her nails into her palms. She would not beg; she would not scream.

But the shadowy shape of a man grew closer. And then he was there before her. Watching. Waiting.

Holly lifted her head, for she knew it would only get worse if she did not acknowledge him. A shock jolted through her body. The man before her was Jack Talent. She'd heard many stories about Talent—that he was mad, soulless, a killer—but she hadn't wanted to believe them. They stared at each other, and his eyes began to glow with a manic light.

"It is time to go to work, little girl." Talent's voice was not his usual one, but cold and flat.

"You'll have to kill me, for I won't help you." Brave words, for even now her stomach revolted with a hard lurch that she barely kept down. She rather doubted she could withstand the torture that would inevitably come before said killing.

Talent's teeth flashed in the light as a disjointed laugh broke from him. Then he shifted, growing and becoming a thing of nightmares, his jaw elongating, fur erupting over his skin, claws and fangs shining in the low light. A lycan. His words came out oddly muffled as he talked with that long snout. "Properly terrifying?"

Mutely she shook her head, not to disagree but in terror.

He laughed again. "Not to worry. I won't hurt you." He turned his misshapen head in the direction of the other cells. "I'll just let you watch as I tear them apart. Perhaps I'll start with the proud Lord Darby." He gestured to the shifter who had been brought in the morning after she'd arrived in this hell. The poor golden-haired fellow strained against the iron chains punched through his shoulders and looped around his body. Embedded deep in the stone wall, those chains held fast no matter how much he struggled. Blood poured through the shifter's open wounds, and Talent leaned down to lap one rivulet up with his tongue as the shifter roared behind the gag in his mouth.

This time she could not restrain herself. Holly turned and retched, the acrid burn of vomit scorching her throat and nostrils as Talent laughed. "Ever had a taste of shifter blood? No? It is quite delicious. And potent." He paused, his brow furrowing as if he pondered the effect. Then his frown grew. "But not as powerful as this, I think."

In his hand he held a glass vial filled with blood. It ought to have repulsed her, but there was a glow to the deep-ruby liquid, a richness of color that held her in thrall until she blinked hard. Talent turned to address one of the thugs in the room with them. "Help yourself to Darby, and then take his place quickly." He laughed. "We shall need to keep the SOS distracted for a while yet. Then you may do what you want to the agents guarding him.

"As for you, Miss Evernight," he said to her. "We'll get you cleaned up and ready to work."

Holly's limbs trembled as she rose. God forgive her, because she was going to do as she was told.

Spying on a supernatural was a tricky business. In general, most could not see a GIM in spirit form. Save for the lycans. The wolf in them could see spirits. However, strengths and weaknesses were as varied as people. Mary knew of some lycans so out of touch with their inner wolf that her spirit could dance naked in front of them and they wouldn't bat an eye. Demons, on the whole, were too obsessed with the flesh to see the spirit, and elementals were too human, which meant they didn't trust what was not corporeal. Then there were the shifters. Despite what many believed, shifters were not animals hiding in human skins. True, they might shift into an animal, but that was through force of will. It was not setting an animal free, as lycans did. No, shifters were more demon than anything else. Thus trailing a shifter ought to be an easy business. But Jack Talent was an unknown threat. Because getting caught by him would not only be disastrous and humiliating; if certain facts were to be believed, it could get her killed.

The very idea of Talent being the Bishop made her ill to the core. Was he a killer? Who was it they'd chased earlier? It occurred to Mary, rather belatedly, that Talent had been alone with the strange man for enough time to converse, and yet he hadn't made mention of any revelations. Perhaps Talent was working with this man.

Mary did not know what to think. She had, however, seen the worry in Talent's dark-green eyes when he had realized that she'd be working alongside him. Just a flash of it before he'd smothered it away. And Mary now wondered, was it because he had intended to sabotage the case from the inside? Had he taken Holly because she'd discovered something about the clockwork hearts?

Damn it, but this was Jack Talent, the man utterly loyal to Ian Ranulf, the man who had risked his life to help Poppy and Winston Lane. Talent lived and breathed the SOS. Since he'd joined up, no other regulator had solved more cases than he. She ought to know, as she'd been the one tasked to record every regulator victory.

Divergent thoughts muddled Mary's mind as she trudged back to her flat. Once there, she hid her body within the secret compartment specifically designed for the task, and went on the hunt.

Outside, Mary spread her spirit wide, losing all sense of shape. In spirit form she could be vast. It was a strange experience, to let go of one's physical form. Even as a spirit, one tended to need that connection to life. Letting go took great faith in the knowledge that, no matter what the form, the essence of oneself was not in the physical but in the spiritual. And so Mary dissipated, melding with the fog that hung in the night air. Odd as it felt, odder still was the lingering feeling of having a heart, having lungs. Those organs she'd left behind, and yet it seemed as though her breath came on fast and her heart whirred within her breast. Mind was not matter, but will. And it did not easily give up the sensation of being flesh.

In the blue of twilight, the city's souls were a map of stars laid out over London, so profuse that it took effort to sort out each individual. Oh, but it was the worst sort of invasion, looking at the light of a person's soul. As a GIM, Mary could see every soul's light, but she'd been trained to turn that power off until necessary, for it was too personal a thing. Necessity trumped manners tonight. It was the light of Talent's soul that Mary sought. Having connected to him before, she need only relax and let the link join them once more. Talent, she thought. *Jack.*

A recognizable vibration brushed up against her, the touch of his soul to hers. Far below, a gleaming, silver-blue light emanated from his form. Gone was the sickly mustard-yellow of pain that had tainted it when she'd tracked him down years ago. His physical pain might be gone, but his inner turmoil was strong, a brilliant flame fragmenting like sunlight hitting the edge of a diamond.

Like a bird of prey, she swooped down low, following the glow of his soul toward Portman Square, then onto Baker Street. Once there she stopped and gazed up at the town house in which Talent's soul lay. The house was quite lovely, a stately Georgian, with a front colonnade, black brick facade, and cream trim. Almost all the windows were dark, save for a lonely light coming from the third floor.

Mary drifted close to the house, where the sharp scent of coal smoke mingled with the crisp cold night. Was this his home? Another victim's? What was Talent doing now? To go inside was a must. Even so, the urge to stay outside was strong. Cursing inwardly, Mary went through the keyhole, as unnerving an experience as any.

She did not linger in the dark halls—nothing alive was on the ground floor. What she did see, however, were fine furnishings, if somewhat sparse. The house felt unused and forlorn. Beneath the emptiness, however, a glimmer of Jack Talent hummed. Faint echoes of his essence ran from the door and up the stairs, as if he frequently took this path, never lingering in the public rooms but always going into the private areas of the house. Mary followed the trail. Too soon, the door from which the sole light shone was before her.

Had she a heart, it would have been working at top speed. She had to enter, had to believe that he would not see her. Had to believe that he was innocent. Only one way to find out.

The room was a bedroom. A sense of familiarity struck her, as if she'd been here before. Then she realized that it was filled with Talent's furniture from his old room at Ranulf House. The sound of water tinkling caught her attention. Rising into the upper reaches of the ceiling, Mary drifted with caution. Most people never looked up. Certainly not in their own homes. But then, Jack Talent was not most people.

All thought ended as she entered the bathing room and found him. Happy Christmas, but he was a sight. One that had her spirit swelling, then tightening, with a surge of emotion. Hunched before the washbasin, Talent's bare back was to her. She'd never given much thought to the aesthetic qualities of the male back. Perhaps because she hadn't seen a truly beautiful one in the flesh until now, and thus hadn't had a chance to appreciate how elegant the lines could be.

The mellow glow of lamplight caressed Talent's smooth skin, highlighting the clean symmetry of his broad, straight shoulders and the tight slabs of muscled flesh that flanked the valley of his spine. Pale linen drawers hung loosely on his narrow hips, low enough to expose where his spine met the indented globes of his arse. Happy Christmas, indeed.

Talent ought to look vulnerable, undressed as he was.

In all their years of acquaintance, she'd never seen him in anything less than full and proper attire. She did not count the dark day when she'd found him hanging nude and bloodied in that torture chamber. Honor demanded that she keep that image separate from the man she knew as Jack Talent. It had been merely a tormented body, not him, not his soul. Now the impact of seeing him struck her like a fist. The corded strength of his neck and the tight swells of his shoulders alone could hold her in thrall.

His reflection in the tall vanity mirror was clear, and the front of him was as glorious as the back. His naked chest was brutish in its musculature. Flat, wide pectorals, small brown nipples, abdominals like tightly packed cobbles, and smooth, taut skin. The image of it all burned into her memory with just one glance. Dear God. It should not affect her so, his animalistic strength. She'd never favored such physiques, and yet her attention was riveted.

She ought to go. Talent was merely undressing. Nothing untoward. Unless she counted her own actions. Guilt swamped her. This was unconscionable. She really ought to...

He dipped a hand into the basin, swirling the water with his fingers, and the network of muscles along his torso rippled, a breathtaking display of power in motion.

She found herself sinking down, her spirit reforming into the shape of her physical body as her defenses weakened. She wasn't flesh, she ought not feel a thing, yet unbearable heat flooded her being.

His fingers swayed back and forth, a meditative movement, as he stared at the water, his expression somber and his big, strong body stooped forward. Atlas holding up the world.

It hurt to witness. More so when he stopped and looked at himself in the mirror. And kept looking, as if he couldn't quite recognize his reflection. Or perhaps he didn't like what he saw.

It was that lost, almost hopeless darkness in his eyes that made her want to go to him, despite the numerous rejections he'd volleyed her way over the years, and despite the very real possibility that, if she did, he'd be furious. But he wouldn't see her at any rate. She was invisible to him. Sorrow held her there, heavy and painful. She ought to go. She couldn't leave.

The pure, tinkling notes of dripping water broke the silence as he lifted a rag to his chest and began to wipe it. The movements were perfunctory, a swipe up his neck and down the other side, the hard scrub under his arms, then over his chest and stomach.

The heat surrounding her became a pulsing thing. It was as if she were the one holding the rag, drawing it along that dense flesh, feeling his warmth, wiping him clean.

Crystalline beads of water trickled over his skin, found the valleys between his muscles, coalescing and traveling down to the dark thatch of hair just peeking out above the line of his drawers. Linen drawers that were growing wet from his bath, growing transparent against his long, large...

Talent stopped, the rag in his hand spilling water in a steady *drip, drip, drip.* Fear tingled through her. Had he sensed something amiss? But he did not look up. The wide column of his neck shone wet as he kept his head bent. And though the fan of his lashes hid his eyes, the direction of his gaze was unmistakable. As was the growing bulge beneath his drawers. The shaft thickened and rose, curving in a painful looking bend as it met with the resistance of the fabric. Idly, he scratched the skin of his taut belly, his fingers drifting nearer to his burgeoning cock.

Mary's being went utterly still. Surely not. Surely he wouldn't....

But he did. The rag fell back into the basin with a loud plop as his hand went to the ties of his drawers. The linen snagged on his cock before he eased the fabric away. And then, good God, but his member rose up, proud, ruddy, and straight, so lovingly displayed between a dark nest of hair and his heavy cods.

She almost fled, dissipated right then and there, save she could not look away. Not from that glorious, rude cock, nor his firm arse and powerful thighs. He was extraordinary.

Ignorant of being watched, Talent gave himself a slow stroke, skimming it really, as if contemplating further intimacies. He caressed it again, up and down, clutching the wide shaft in the circle of his fingers with absolute authority, going slowly as if letting his pleasure build. Up. Down. A chuff of breath left his parted lips, and his eyes fluttered closed, his thick brows furrowing. His speed increased, the tendons on his forearms shifting and straining as he moved.

Mary stayed. Transfixed. Yearning. *I want to be the one doing that.* She coalesced further, until she could feel her ghostly palms pressing against phantom skirts. It made no sense. He was horrid. She didn't care. She wanted to fondle Jack Talent's cock.

The soft slap of flesh working against flesh, and Talent's

light pants, filled the air. One arm came down to the
basin, bracing, his muscles flexing. His expression was
one of near agony, his lips parted.

His hips were working now, rocking and thrusting
his cock into his clenched fist, and he grunted, small,
helpless sounds. He undid her with his magnificence
and the unfettered passion he let loose. It felt strangely
intimate, as though she were locked in the battle with
him, sharing the moment in some small way. Equally, she
was utterly apart from him, watching without touching,
spying without his knowledge. The divergence rattled her
soul.

The massive muscles of his thighs twitched and
bunched, and his heavy cods swayed with the force of
each tug. The knuckles bracing him up turned white with
strain. And that cock, so engorged now that the fat head
was nearly purple. As if it were weeping for release, a
gleaming drop of moisture welled from the tip and rolled
down like a tear. Talent's thumb swept over it, spreading it around, making the head gleam. Mary's soul flared
white-hot. Had she a mouth, she would be crying out,
begging for mercy.

It was too much. And not enough, because she wanted
to touch him. Her whole being strained closer, watching
as his buttocks clenched and his calves lifted. A series
of guttural, helpless groans broke from his lips, his fist
positively slamming over his poor, abused cock. Then he
came, all those glorious muscles bunching hard and tight.
Her mind went blank.

A pregnant stillness settled over the room. Jack leaned
forward, shaking and hunched over the basin as if his
legs might give out. His chest heaved, his abdomen taut
and quivering with each breath. And then his dark eyes,

glittering in the reflection of the mirror, looked right at her. As if she were flesh.

Sheer terror, tinged with hot humiliation, prickled through her being as his husky voice lit over the room. "Was it good for you, too?"

Chapter Sixteen

———⚜———

Dread was an emotion well known to Mary. But not like this. It permeated her bones, made her movements lax. Every step she took was an exercise of will. Her gown weighed a ton, and the heavy fabric tangled about her limbs as if trying to hold her back. She appreciated the favor. Yet she walked on, aware of the very air about her and the fact that, with each step, she was closer to facing Jack Talent.

Like a rank coward, she'd stayed home far past the hour at which she was to meet him. Now it was going on luncheon time, and headquarters was all but deserted. Perhaps he wouldn't be there. Perhaps he'd gone out on his own. She could report in and go out on her own as well. But she knew better than to hope. His presence changed the vibrations of the building. The strong souls could do that. And he was waiting.

Ye gods. Her face positively burned. Every moment of the night before was etched in her memory, as sharp as a blade. She did not have to close her eyes to see his molded torso, or the water trickling in glistening drops along that honed flesh. She could not stop the vivid, heat-inducing image of his cock, thick, hard, angry red at the tip.

Her step bobbled, her knees weakening. Mary fisted her skirt. She could not face him. Last night she'd fled so hard and fast that she'd slammed back into her body with enough force to make it buck.

The tendons straining at his neck, the sounds of his pants and the slap of flesh against flesh. Her breath grew agitated once more. Pressing a hand to a nearby wall, she stopped. Beneath her closed lids, illicit images played out before her. A strangled sound left her lips before she gathered her courage and pushed off the wall.

Her heels clicked along the marble corridor, and then she halted so abruptly that her skirts swayed forward. Talent leaned against the doorframe that led to the main offices. His big body appeared at ease, yet when his dark eyes homed in on her, they narrowed with tight focus, and his jaw tensed. Color flooded his face as his lips pressed together. He'd flushed when he reached completion as well.

Mary's head swam, her lips going numb. Gods, she was going to swoon. Sucking in a breath, she turned and fled, but not before seeing Talent launch forward, his expression twisted with outrage.

"Chase!" His deep voice cracked out like a shot. "Get your arse back here and face me!"

She could not. Her steps quickened. And so did his, hard and loud behind her. She could all but feel him bearing down on her, a wildcat running her to ground. Her throat burned raw.

"Stop." His voice was too close, a rumble laced with

equal parts anger and annoyance. "Now. Or I'll be forced to stop you."

The very idea of his physically restraining her made Mary balk. Cursing inwardly, she halted halfway down the dark, unused corridor that led to the archives. Where had she been going? She'd been running blind. Talent stopped as soon as she did. He was just behind her, close enough to feel his energy and heat.

Ahead of her lay a long stretch of floor, and escape. But he'd only follow. Her breasts heaved against the tight structure of her bodice as she waited. Oddly, she had the fleeting notion that perhaps he did not know what to say either.

A theory crushed when he spoke directly at her ear. "Did you wonder if it was you I thought of when I took myself in hand?"

The gears of her heart ground to a halt as her mouth went dry and her sex grew wet. Staring blindly ahead, she could not formulate a reply. She hadn't thought...Had he been?

Talent's smooth voice turned to a gravel-laden purr. "That it was your plump lips I imagined stretching over the head of my cock? Sucking it in deep."

Her knees buckled. She held fast to her skirts, closing her eyes as if it would drown him out.

"Drawing back out..." His hot breath buffeted her cheek. "Tormenting me to completion."

"Stop." She could not think of it. Her breasts swelled against the edge of her bodice, her nipples throbbing points of pain.

The tips of his fingers touched her side, and her body jerked. "Have I offended your delicate sensibilities?" He traced the seam of her bodice, a light glide. Beneath the silk, her skin tightened.

"Your…" She drew in air. "Your anger is deserved." It irked her to say, but she could give him that much.

A small, wry laugh left in a burst of breath. "Anger?" he repeated lightly, his lips tickling the outer shell of her ear, though they didn't truly touch her. "Is that what I'm feeling?"

Irritation bloomed under her skin. "I have no notion of what it is you feel, Mr. Talent."

"Hmm." The sound buzzed against her flesh, and suddenly he seemed closer, as if his body might meet hers should she breathe deeply. "Perhaps I am merely curious if you'd prefer to do more than watch."

Mary ground her teeth together. "Do not mock me."

"Why?" Talent's grip tightened along her waist for a quick moment. "When you seek out my home and watch me as a woman starved."

Mortification prickled along her cheeks. "What you observed was horror, not starvation."

Strange how she could sense his body tensing.

"Oh, yes," he said after a moment. "You have no interest in the carnal."

Mary winced, hearing the disbelief there. The heat of his palm against her waist burned through the layers of dress, corset, and chemise. Then his hand moved, gliding upward, leaving her flesh shivering in his wake.

"A man's touch doesn't affect you." His hand drifted higher, toward her breast. He touched her as Lucien had often done, mocking that show, seeking to recreate it now. But there was a proprietary perusal in his hold that Lucien never employed. His mockery turned her blood to ice, yet, horribly, her sex clenched and her breasts grew heavy and waiting for the inevitable moment when he would fondle her.

But he paused. Indecision coloring the move. Together they stood, waiting, their breathing matched in quick, light draws. Mary found herself fighting the urge to move, to beg of him to travel that small distance and cup her. She wanted that touch with a ferocity that frightened her.

"Do not do this," she whispered, raw and desperate. *Not like this.*

His hand tensed, and his thumb pressed against the underside of her breast with enough pressure that she almost whimpered. His voice was but a breath. "Why? When you violated my privacy so thoroughly."

She had, and it shamed her to the core. Even so. "I have not given you leave."

"As I gave you last night?"

"I—I was in the wrong. Do not make the same mistake and ruin whatever remains of our relationship."

"A relationship?" He laughed shortly, bitterly. "Is that what we have?"

What else could she call it? They were part of each other's lives, indelibly, even if they did not want it so. If Talent used her as a toy, something within her would break. He had to know this. "I will not forgive you for it, Talent."

A beat of silence stood between them. Then he spun her around. Before she could draw a breath, her shoulders met with the cold, stone wall. His large hand framed her ribs, and the other hand went to her jaw, a firm, warm touch that had her stilling. Dark brows slanted over gleaming eyes, a fierce glare, and one that gave her enough time to know what he would do. One that spoke of possession and retribution. The scowl settled on his lips, and he swooped down, the movement stiff and angry.

Cold fear had her jerking her head to the side. Awkwardly he followed, but when she wrenched her head the other way he stilled. A ribald curse broke from him before he stopped and pressed his forehead against the wall beside her. A second later his fist smashed into the stone. Mary twitched, but held steady. He was all around her, his big body boxing her in, no longer touching her but an effective cage nonetheless. Every heavy breath he took sent his chest brushing against hers as they stood, neither of them willing to move.

"So only he can touch you." Beneath the sharp lash of his anger was the sound of frustration, perhaps disappointment. It shocked her but not enough to stay her bitter response.

"He did not seek to mock me with his touch. You do."

Talent leaned back. His expression was a hard mask. But his grip claimed her waist once more, steady and calm. "You have no notion what I seek."

She turned, her cheek meeting the cool stone. She could not face him. Not so close on the heels of her humiliation. And she knew damn well that he'd sought to put her in her place now. The knowledge made her final shot cold. "No," she snapped. "Because you trust no one, do you?"

"No."

Not one second of hesitation. Mary scoffed. "And yet you'd take all my secrets if you could. Would you not, Master Talent?"

Jack squeezed his eyes shut and swallowed down the urge to tug Chase back to him. The scent of her arousal surrounded him, darkly sweet like hot syrup. A miracle and a torment. God, he wanted to lick her up, drown in her rich fragrance. But he was not a fool. She made it clear his kiss was not welcome. Jack knew perfectly well that arousal could occur without consent. And he would never take what wasn't offered.

Damn it, but the memory of what he'd done last night burned so hot within that his aching cods drew up tight, begging for release. Jesus, he'd been a fool. Thought he'd teach her a lesson, had he? When all he'd done was engage in the most erotic act of his life, with her. Yet she hadn't touched him. He wanted that touch. Did he want her secrets as well?

"Yes." He leaned a shoulder against the wall, settling directly behind her. "I'd take them from you." His lips skimmed along the crown of her head, and a shiver worked deep within his belly.

She shivered too. It should have been a triumph, but it wasn't. Not when he feared it just might be from disgust. She knew what had been done to him, after all. Did she think him less of a man now? Today she had run from him as if she might never look him in the eye again. It had set off a boiling rage. Because he knew that day would soon come. They were too close now. Eventually he'd have to tell her everything, of what he'd done to her and why.

"I deserve something," he murmured, distracted by the scent of her. *Mary.* Mary Chase. The one woman he couldn't have. Not when she finally learned the full truth about him.

Her quick breath sounded in the silence, and she responded with clipped anger. "What do you want?"

Everything. To be another man. A better man.

She'd watched him take his pleasure, her ghostly form hovering close, her eyes wide, her lips parted softly as if she wondered what it would feel like to touch him. Or perhaps it truly was horror she'd felt. He hadn't held back as a gentleman might. He'd been raw, unfettered, when he took himself in hand and thought of her. Those lips taking over the job of his hand, sweetly sucking him off. God, he wished it had been so, and not simply a fancy of his desperate imagination.

Jack struggled to regain control of his breathing, to regain control of himself. The pads of his fingers burned hot against the satin hugging her waist. "How—" His voice broke, weak and hungry. He hated the sound. He tried again, stronger this time. "How did you find me?"

The intricate knot of her coiffure brushed his lips as she turned her head slightly, and another heady rush of her scent filled his senses. Jack gritted his teeth. *Control. Control.*

"You won't like it," she said.

So soft, that voice of hers. Would her skin be thus? Would it be hot silk? Or cool satin?

"No," he agreed. "I won't." His fingers twitched along her bodice, grasping, then resisting. "Tell me anyway."

Her sides lifted on a sigh. "You know my scent. Well, I know your soul."

Everything in him went still and quiet. "Know it?" His heart began to beat again, a hard, insistent thud.

She faced forward, but being taller, he could see the smooth curve of her cheek and the gilded tips of her thick lashes. "When you were lost to us before..."

Us. As if he was connected to her.

"...I needed a way to find you. I thought of you, sank into the chair you favored, and found the essence of you." Another deep breath. "I connected with a link to your soul. It brought me to you."

All the frozen muscles in his body contracted with a painful clench, and his heart stopped for one raw moment.

"That connection," she said softly, "can never be broken." Her slender throat worked on a swallow. "I can always find you now."

His shoulders trembled with the force of restraint. Even so, his head fell forward. Her hair was cool, soft, and held the fragrance of ambergris and figs. "You're right," he said as his palm smoothed along her waist, noting the way she shivered, making him shiver in return. "I don't like it."

Control.

His hips touched her bustle. So much fabric he couldn't feel her. And she couldn't feel the strain of his erection against his trousers. "I hate it," he whispered. *Liar.*

She shuddered, her arm twitching. But she said nothing, nor did she move away.

"Can you see—" His breath hitched with rage over his vulnerability. "What do you see?"

The way she tensed told him she understood the question perfectly. When she did not speak, he clenched her waist and pressed his mouth into the tender skin of her temple. Warm, she felt warm. Sweat dampened her hair.

"Tell me," he said.

Her cheek moved as she licked her lower lip. He nearly groaned but did not waver. "What do you see?"

"Pain." The word shot from her lips. "Rage, fear." She gasped. Jack eased his hold but wouldn't let go. Her back touched his chest as she breathed. "And hurt." Her voice was so small then. As if she didn't want him to hear it. But he did. When she spoke again, the sound rang in the pained silence. "But the greatest component, the one that has never changed, is obstinacy." Her silken hair dragged across his face as she turned her head slightly, not looking at him but making sure she was heard. "Your will is the strongest I've ever seen."

He closed his eyes to fight the burn there. He needed to tell her everything. And then she'd be gone forever. Neither of them moved until he forced himself to speak. "Yes," he said. "It is."

And then he fled. It wasn't until later that he even wondered why she'd been spying on him.

Chapter Seventeen

Crisp air kissed Jack's cheeks as he walked down a wide avenue that led into Mayfair. Darkness did not live here, but light. Clean houses lined up in a row, each black iron gate protecting a manicured front garden from unwanted visitors. Walking cleared Jack's head and slowed his pulse.

Upon reflection, he was grateful that Chase had discovered him *en déshabillé*, as it were, instead of a quarter hour before. Likely she'd never have looked him in the eye again if she'd witnessed him tearing into Mercer Dawn. Jack scowled down at his dusty boots. It wasn't Chase's, or anyone else's, business how he dealt with his pain. "Whatever you want to tell yourself, mate," he muttered.

"Talking to yourself, Mr. Talent?" Lucien Stone stepped in front of him, blocking the narrow walkway.

Ever the dandy, Stone wore a dove-grey cashmere overcoat trimmed in ermine, and a grey silk top hat that would have better served as evening wear. Not that Jack would tell him so.

"What the devil do you want?" Jack was in no mood to trade quips with the sod.

Stone's jewel-covered fingers tightened on his walking stick. "Mary Chase was nearly crushed by a freight car last night."

Tell him something that he didn't know. "You know, Stone, it occurs to me that you're privy to everything that goes on in this city."

Stone gave him a magnanimous nod.

"Which makes me wonder," Jack went on, "why the bloody hell you don't help out more? Oh, but I forgot, you let others do the dirty work while you hide away on your little boat."

A sneer twisted Stone's perfect features. "Careful, boy. I could kill you as easy as breathing."

"Then do it," Jack said. "Or sod off." He moved to push past when Stone stepped forward.

It was the last straw. He slammed Stone into a garden wall. Stone's teeth clacked, though he did not fight back, only glared with his glowing jade eyes. Jack pinned him, his forearm crushing the GIM's windpipe. "Get the fuck out of my way."

Stone grabbed hold of Jack's wrist. Instantly, agonizing pain shot through his arm and down his side. Jack gritted his teeth as Stone pushed him off and leaned in close. "No."

They stared at each other, each breathing hard in agitation. Jack stood a few inches taller, but Stone didn't back down.

"Now that you are unfortunately partnered with Mary," Lucien said, as he adjusted his lapels, "do not think to go back on your word."

Jack clenched his fists to keep from pummeling Stone. "Wouldn't cast you in a flattering light, would it?"

"Nor you." Stone smoothed back a lock of his dark hair. "If you have an ounce of care for that woman, you'll keep your mouth shut. For if she should learn—"

"She'd hate you too," Jack interjected through his locked jaw.

"Not as much as she'd hate you." Stone's pitiless gaze held. "I'll not have her unnecessarily hurt."

"You ought to have thought of that before you laid out our little agreement." Fucking bastard. Blackmail was more like it. Jack had had enough of it. Of everything.

Stone read this well, for he narrowed his gaze. "And should your family learn that you were with the Nex, have been for all these years?"

"Shut your fucking GIM mouth." Hate coursed through Jack like hellfire. "You have no idea who or what I am—"

"And yet you've kept your *fucking* shifter mouth shut all these years, no?" Stone's smile was tight. "So I'm thinking there is more than a kernel of truth to what I know."

Jack's shoulders met the rough wall behind him with a thud. Stone had him. For years he'd had his number. When Jack could speak, the wrong words emerged. "You have her. Always have. What more do you want?"

A wrinkle formed between Stone's brows. "I want her safe."

Jack laughed, hard and ugly. "Too late for that, mate."

"Because of you." Stone punched the center of Jack's chest, where it felt hollow. The hollow feeling spread, and he couldn't bring himself to punch back. Stone took the advantage. "You want to protect her, as I do? Then stay away from her as I told you to do." He took a step, and they were nose to nose. "Before you destroy her just as you do everything around you."

For Mary, a Sunday roast was a lovely event that she, the only child of a woman who liked nothing better than to sleep away that particular day, would never experience. She wasn't even certain when or where she'd heard of this mythical moment during which families got together to eat a grand feast and simply enjoy each other's company. Perhaps she'd followed the scent of roast beef and pudding in the air one crisp autumn day to press her nose against a window. Or perhaps her nanny had espoused its glories. She didn't remember. It was simply a clear picture left in her mind, one of happiness, warmth, and light.

Whatever the case, when Inspector Lane sought her out after Talent left her, and extended an invitation for Sunday lunch, Mary accepted. More out of shock than anything else.

"Excellent." Lane's eyes crinkled kindly at the corners. He touched her arm, a solicitous gesture that spoke of friendship and camaraderie, and yet Mary stiffened. Lane curbed the move but the damage was done. He'd noticed and was clearly chagrined. Mary cursed herself. She hadn't meant to react; she was very fond of Inspector Lane. But the unexpected touch of a man's hand had set off the immediate instinct of defense.

The air grew thick and awkward between them. More so when Inspector Lane merely gave her a soft smile. "I consider this visit progress, Mistress Chase." He spoke so affably that one might never have known she'd insulted him. Mary inwardly cringed as they began to walk down the hall, and he continued speaking as though nothing odd had occurred. "Soon we shall have you attending every Sunday."

"Let us not be hasty, Inspector." She wanted to smile, though, for his desire to include her in his family warmed that small, cold place that always felt like an outsider.

"Now, now, Mistress Chase," Lane admonished, "I shall not be dissuaded. Mrs. Lane considers you one of us, and quite rightly." He opened the outer doors for her and ushered her through, careful not to actually touch her. "Without your assistance, I might have lost my family." Lane's handsome and scarred face darkened for but a brief moment. He brightened again. "So as you can see," he went on as if she understood him perfectly, which she did, "your presence is quite important."

"Inspector, you do not have to feel obliged to—"

"And let us not forget Mrs. Ranulf," interrupted Lane. "She's been most vocal in her desire to see you at the family roast." Lane glanced down at her, and his mouth twitched. "I needn't tell you how persistent that woman can be once she has a bee in her bonnet."

"No." Mary's own mouth twitched. "I am quite familiar, Inspector."

Despite her gaffe, they shared a companionable trip to Lane's home. When little Ellis Lane was born, the Lanes had moved from their small flat above their bookshop and into Mayfair, close to Poppy's sisters. The house was not a mansion by any means, but cozy and lovely, with well-proportioned rooms and light-filled spaces. The kind of home Mary would pick for herself should she have a family.

Commotion ensued the moment she stepped inside the warm home, with Poppy coming up to buss her husband's cheek before putting a fond hand upon Mary's

arm in welcome. Daisy was far more boisterous, kissing all and sundry, and Ian Ranulf much the same, pulling Mary into a quick hug of hello before she could
protest. It struck Mary anew how these people did not
behave like *ton*, or even new gentry, but more like simple
countryfolk. Laughter and affection ruled, as did the free
discourse.

Mary bounced along the periphery of it all. The loveliness both repelled and charmed her. How could they be
so happy and carefree? How could she not? She knew it
wasn't all roses for them. Only it felt as though it were,
and she were the weed infiltrating their garden.

Nonsense really, yet she couldn't shake the feeling of
being out of her element. Mary pasted a tight half-smile
upon her face as Daisy hooked her arm through hers and
led Mary into the family parlor. The tight, queer feeling
intensified within her. The house smelled of roasting beef
and crackling fires. Everything glowed with golden lamplight, and nothing felt familiar.

A pair of dark-green eyes clashed with hers, and the
world about her whooshed to silence.

She would have liked to tell herself she'd forgotten that
Jack Talent was part of Lane's family too. But it would
have been a lie.

He sat hunched on a large sofa, his arms resting upon
his bent knees. He looked up at her, his expression as
impassive as ever, save for that hooded gaze, shining
brightly by the light of the fire. Nature had painted him
in bold, simple strokes. And he was immense. Simply sitting there, he felt too big for the space he occupied. As
though a wrong move might crush the furniture beneath
him. And he was glorious. To her.

Mary's breath left in a shivery hiss. Heat and agitation stroked the cage of her breast. As if he scented it, his gaze grew hazy, his mouth parting slightly as if to draw in more air, draw in more of her. Mary dug her nails deep into the flesh of her palms to remain still.

The strained silence between them grew, until Daisy let out a little huff. "Jack Talent, don't just sit there like a clod. Get up and greet Miss Chase like a proper gentleman."

His gaze flicked to Daisy and then back to Mary. And then he stood, a fluid motion that brought him up, up, up. So tall. And all that spectacular strength hidden beneath staid black suits. She could not take this. She needed to leave.

"You do realize, Daisy Ranulf, that I am only five years younger than you," he said. "That you are not, in fact, my mother." Talent turned his attention to Mary, and his smooth cream voice had a soft bite to it. "Roped you into it too, did they, Chase?"

Something within her eased. "I fear so, Talent."

"Cheer up, angel." The corners of his eyes creased and then came that grin, the one that made her knees wobble and her heart seize. "Sunday roast only comes once a week."

As if she'd be there every Sunday. As if he'd accepted that fact. She found herself smiling back even as Daisy nattered on about cheeky ingrates.

It was all right then. It would be all right.

Hours later, filled and sated, the family drifted back into the large parlor to lounge about and talk of this and that. Mary found herself a comfortable chair and was content to simply watch. Better still, they left her to it.

"Ian, darling," called Daisy, "Archer sends you his

regards." Curled up on the overstuffed sofa, her feet tucked beneath her skirts, Daisy smiled as she read through the latest letter from Lord and Lady Archer. The couple was in Ireland, visiting a young man they'd learned was the Ellis women's brother. Miranda had grown particularly close to him, as she and the youth shared the deadly ability to manipulate fire.

Ian strolled over, smiling a bit as he bent down to kiss the top of his wife's head. "And what does the old stiff say?"

Daisy's lips curled. "Mmm. Well, he says that Ireland is great sheep country, and that he has rounded up a nice bunch of fatted lambs for you to frolic with should the London fare become too bland."

Inspector Lane gave out a great laugh. "Perhaps Daisy ought to knit you a fuzzy woolen jumper so that you might hide amongst them."

"Now, darling," Poppy said reproachfully, "be kind. You know very well Daisy detests knitting."

"'Tis true," Daisy agreed with a plump-cheeked grin. "But I am certain we could scrounge up a lambskin for Ian to use."

"Cheeky arses the lot of you," Ian muttered, then grinned. "Would serve Archer right if I did hightail it up there and pounce on his flock."

Smiling, Mary left her cozy chair and wandered out of the room. A flash of dark coat sleeve had caught her eye. She found him sitting alone in the half-darkened conservatory built at the back of the house. Made almost entirely of glass, the room was cooler than the parlor and bathed in the blue light of the full moon. Potted palms graced the corners, leaving the center of the room open for a grouping of lacy white iron tables and chairs.

She wasn't surprised that he'd drifted off on his own. All through luncheon she'd watched him from the corner of her eye, noting the way he had deliberately distanced himself from the rest. The others had glanced at him as well, their gazes ranging from worried, such as Ian's, to penetrating, such as Poppy's. They all wanted to know what thoughts ran through Talent's head. As for Mary, although what she might discover terrified her, she too wanted inside that thick head of his.

This time, when she entered the room, he stood. "Care to sit?" his voice was soft as he gestured to one of the chairs.

The chair was cold, the iron pressing into the backs of her thighs. Mary was grateful for the discomfort. It took her mind away from the slow burn within her. Talent resumed his seat, and they sat in silence, letting the sounds of the house party drift over the still air.

"You might as well come out with it, Chase." Weariness weighted his voice, but there was also wry amusement there. She risked a glance, and the corner of his mouth kicked up. "You think I do not know you well enough by now? That you aren't squirming over there, trying to find a way to broach the subject?"

"I do not squirm." That he knew what she was about annoyed her. That he knew precisely what she wanted to discuss made her want to hit him.

Talent merely stared at her, his brows winging up in that way of his that appeared at once expectant yet reproachful.

"Very well," she snapped. "You asked me how I found you…" Mary licked her dry lips and pressed her palms closer together. "I should like to know how you saw me." Pray God the heat in her cheeks did not show.

His body was unmoving, his rough-hewn face expressionless. Only his eyes were alive, glittering with dark intent as his gaze roved. The air about them seemed to still and grow heavy, as they both relived those moments. And though her skin scorched now with that heat and her dress became oppressive, she refused to lower her eyes in deference.

The moment swelled, then he moved. A simple adjustment in his seat, but enough to make her heart stutter. "It appears," he said in a bland tone, "that this connection you forged works both ways." Again, his unwavering attention bore into her. "You can see my soul, and I can see yours."

Mary swallowed thickly before nodding once. "It happens at times." When the connection was deep, or the ties between persons were binding. She had suspected but didn't want it to be true. Rubbing a finger along the brocade of her overskirt, Mary aimed for a bit of levity. "So then you knew—"

Talent leaned forward then, the movement of his powerful body setting off little frissons throughout hers. The deep glide of his voice crept along her skin, licking over sensitive spots and making her twitch. "The entire time, Chase."

God. The admission horrified her. And it twisted something dark and aching deep within her. She fidgeted, her hands running along the hidden throwing knives strapped to her thighs.

"If you knew I was there, then why did you…" Her words died on a flush. Bloody Talent.

"Pleasure myself?" he offered helpfully.

She was not amused, but deserved his teasing. "Yes, that."

Talent's green eyes grew darker, wicked. "Because I knew you were there." The pink tip of his tongue peeked out from between his teeth, taunting her. The gesture was perverse, a little flickering come-hither.

Her heart pounded against her throat, but she would not give him the satisfaction of seeing her disquiet. She set her attention on the wall of windows, and the ghostly reflections of them sitting close wavered back at her. "Fine. Don't answer me."

"But I just did." He sounded so reasonable, save for the laughter tickling the edges of his voice.

Mary pressed her lips together, her grip upon her skirts tightening. "You're being evasive."

"And apparently, you are being obtuse."

"Bother." Her skirts rustled as she stood.

He struck like an asp, catching her wrist with his long fingers. Instantly she froze. It wasn't a hard grip, but his warm touch rendered her unable to move.

"Don't go." His eyes, framed by thick lashes, looked up at her. Talent's calm voice coiled along her body. "I confess, I don't understand you at times, Chase." The blunt tip of his thumb brushed her sensitive skin, and the contact licked over her flesh. "You open a line of conversation, then become angry with me when I oblige by answering truthfully."

"I admit," she said, "it baffles me that you didn't fly into a rage the moment you realized I was there. You were unclothed, for pity's sake." Fierce heat filled her cheeks. She needed to stop talking altogether.

Talent's mouth trembled at the corner, his eyes alight with utter glee. "Chase, the idea of a woman watching is in no way a deterrent for a man. It adds a level of excitement."

She would die now. Surely fate could be kind to her for once.

He looked her over, shaking his head as if in disgust. "And to think you lived with Lucien Stone, debaucher of innocents, and didn't know as much."

"Sorry to disappoint you."

"Disappoint?" His voice turned smoky then, surrounding and obscuring her mental clarity. "On the contrary, I find myself wholly enlightened. I hadn't thought you'd be so virtuous." The soft touch of his thumb returned, agitating and seductive. "In the future, I shall endeavor to subdue my frankness."

Mary tensed, her gaze searching his and finding no hint of guile. Gods, he *was* being truthful. Which meant he'd been having a laugh at her when he took himself in hand. The smarmy, rutting bastard. She couldn't speak past the lump of rage gathering in her throat. When she looked away, his thumb swept across her inner arm once again, so whisper-quick and soft she wondered if he was aware of doing it. More curious still, regardless of her ire, she didn't want him to stop.

"What is it, then?" he asked. "What's got your skirts in a twist?" A smile lightened his eyes. "Other than my usual charm, that is."

I want to kill you. I want you to pull me down into your lap so that I might feel those long hard muscles I've seen flex and thrust. "You have yet to ask me the most damning question, Master Talent." Gods, but this was rash. Stupid to wave a red flag in front of a bull, but she needed the distance between them to return. If only for her sanity. She leaned in, close enough to feel his rumbling energy. "Why was I spying on you?"

A pulse of tension traveled down his arm and into his

fingers, where they tightened on her wrist. He could snap her bones in a second, yet he immediately lessened his hold, but still did not let go. Hooded dark eyes studied her. "Why were you spying on me, Mistress Chase?"

The evenness of his tone sent a skein of warning over her skin. She ignored it. "Because I do not trust you."

She might as well have slapped him. His lips parted, soft on a breathy exhalation, even as his brows snapped together. It was a look of hurt, horror, and then growing anger. Only there was a flash of guilt that made her grow colder still.

His words came out clipped and controlled. "And you thought watching me stroke my cock would disabuse you of this distrust?"

Heat flared along her cheeks. "A joke instead of an answer, is it?"

The grip on her wrist tightened. Enough to make her fingers thrum. His jaw bunched, and his gaze burned her. *Answer me. Tell me I am wrong.* Her fingertips throbbed in time with her pumping heart. *Tell me you are innocent.*

But she knew he would never protest his innocence. Even if he was innocent. Jack Talent would never beg for understanding.

"Holly Evernight was abducted outside of headquarters last night," she said.

His nostrils flared as he took a harsh breath. "You believe I would harm Evernight?"

"No, but there are some who might. And the SOS is beginning to wonder why it has taken you so long to solve this case. Poppy . . . She is worried about you."

"So you are to be my watchdog, is that it?"

"If I must." She tried again to break free of him, but

could not. "You know more than you let on, Talent. But I do not think you so broken that you would hurt one of our own."

Talent's green eyes dulled. "Now there is where you are wrong. You would do well not to trust me, Chase. Whatever deeds I have or have not done, the essential truth remains that I *am* broken."

Chapter Eighteen

———⟡~⟡———

Mary ought to be afraid. Or, at the very least, unnerved by what she'd revealed to Talent. Instead her mind acted like a dogcart stuck on a track, constantly driving back around to the image of him coming undone.

Blast him. She did not feel like herself anymore, didn't recognize this woman she'd become. An invader had taken over her skin. Logic had fled like a frightened spirit. Instead she felt. Everywhere. Everything. Her bones thrummed. She was at once too heavy yet oddly buoyant. Her breasts ached and tingled, as though the flesh there had been asleep and now needed to be rubbed fully back to life. A horrid thought, and yet the very idea of big, rough hands rubbing over her tender flesh... God almighty, she quivered. Intolerable.

It was endless, this *feeling*. When she walked, she felt the length of her own legs and the curve of her bottom, where the fabric of her drawers moved and teased. And she felt her own slickness between her legs, a strange slip-slide that sent little judders of sensation over her, an uncomfortably hot syrup that coated her inside and out.

How was she to live like this? The shift from stasis to this shivering, heated...*bloom* of feeling was most unwelcome.

The worst part was that it was *his* fault. And hers. Hers, because she'd spied on him, watched as he handled that big, hardened length of flesh, and now she could not get past the horrid feeling of want. And his because he'd deliberately done it to taunt her.

She hated him. Lousy, dirty bounder. Devil incarnate. Possible murderer to boot. God above, she was feeling this way for a man who might be guilty of horrendous acts.

"Are you going to brood during the whole of our walk?"

Daisy's voice snapped Mary out of her *brooding*. Devil take it, she had utterly forgotten the woman was next to her. Shortly after Mary had confessed that she would continue to spy on Talent if necessary, Daisy had waltzed into the room. "Take a walk with me, old girl?" was all she'd said, and Mary had been grateful for the escape.

Now heat flooded her cheeks. Daisy couldn't read her thoughts, but the mere idea that she'd been having them was bad enough. Because it was a bothersome truth that GIM felt each other's emotions keenly. Even when they did not want to.

Daisy's breath floated away in a ghostly puff as it hit the crisp evening air, and she continued as if their walk had just begun. "Such a lovely night. I confess, I quite needed it after that heavy meal."

"Is that why we're out here?" Mary had her doubts, crafty as the Ellis sisters were.

"Well, that, and the irritation blasting off you was giving me the twitches." Daisy looked at her wryly. "I thought you might need some air as well, pet."

Mary could only muster an inward sigh.

Daisy's bright blue gaze traveled over her, taking stock of all that Mary sought to hide. "How goes it with Mr. Talent?"

Likely Mary would never meet another soul more astute at ferreting out sexual agitation in others. She tucked her hands farther into her cloak pockets and set her concentration on the road before them. "Do you want to know about the case? Or if we've done each other grievous bodily harm?"

Blue eyes looked at her askance. "You aren't limping, so he hasn't yet tupped you." When Mary stumbled, Daisy caught her arm and laughed.

"I was referring to giving him a swift kick in the bollocks," Mary muttered, before wrenching away as Daisy merely laughed more.

"However the two of you like to play is entirely your business, Miss Mary."

The back of Mary's neck stiffened. "You are unconscionable. Has anyone ever told you?"

"Plenty of times, dearest." Daisy caught her arm again and huddled close in the way Mary had seen female friends do. The touch, while warm, made Mary's skin tighten. She wondered if she'd ever get accustomed to contact with others. Daisy, however, did not appear to notice and prattled on. "Look, Jack Talent is an ass. We all know it." Daisy shrugged. "Why he feels it necessary to be a particular ass to you, I cannot say. But he cares with his whole heart. And his loyalty is not to be matched. For heaven's sake, he lost an arm defending me."

"An arm?" Alarm shot down Mary's spine.

"Mm-hmm, that mad werewolf intent on getting me tore it clean off when Jack tried to stop him. Right from the elbow." Daisy blanched as if remembering the sight.

"Extraordinary," Mary murmured.

Daisy winced. "He lost an eye as well. But did he convalesce like he ought? No. He came to sit with me for fear that I'd be distraught." Her blue eyes went soft and glowing. "He hates to hear it, but I do love that man."

Mary frowned down at her shoes. "I can hardly imagine him doting." But she could. He was loyal. And fiercely protective. Mary wondered what sort of defect she had that made him dislike her so.

Daisy's gentle voice broke the silence. "You must learn to trust him, Mary."

Accusations rose and clogged in Mary's throat. Why not tell Daisy the truth? She was a fellow GIM and more of a confidant than Mrs. Lane, who, despite their mutual regard, was her superior. And yet she could not do it. Without true proof of Talent's guilt, she could not sully his name with suspicion. Not after the trials he'd endured trying to keep those he loved safe. She picked her words carefully. "He is much changed. I fear that what occurred might have altered him irrevocably."

Daisy's lively gait slowed, and since she still clutching Mary's arm, Mary's did as well. "He's stopped visiting Ian. Which hurts my husband more than he will admit. I believe Jack merely needs time..." She trailed off with a morose frown.

"If—" Mary pressed her lips together, then tried again. "What would the Ranulf do should Mr. Talent lose himself to darkness?"

Daisy halted and turned to face Mary. The wavering light of a town house lantern sent shadows sliding over Daisy's plump cheeks, but her eyes glowed with the incandescence of a GIM's. "What are you saying?" But they both knew. Would Ian be able to put Talent down, should it come to that? The thought seemed to swirl between them, and they both outwardly shivered.

Mary tried to speak, but a feminine screech cut through the quiet. Another scream followed, this one laden with pain and terror. Cold sweat bloomed along Mary's skin. Her throat closed, the sensation of a cord wrapping around her neck making her gag. For an instant she was not on the street with Daisy, but in a dank back alley, the broken, wet cobbles grinding into her bare back, and foul male flesh slamming down on her. *You like that, toffer? Listen to her moan. Bet she's loving it.*

Head spinning, she clutched Daisy's arm just for a moment before pulling in a draught of cold air. The taste of sulfur and coal grounded her, and she stiffened, her arm snapping down to release the baton hidden up her sleeve. Cool steel filled her palm, and then she ran.

Daisy was at her heels, her parasol clutched in her hand. They both had weapons of preference, and Daisy's was the small sword tucked into each of her pretty parasols. Miranda had taught Daisy, and Mary could only hope the lessons had stuck as she heard male laughter.

Rounding the corner of an apothecary shop, they clamored into a dark alleyway. Three men crouched over the crumpled form of a woman, her brown dress no more than a stain on the filthy ground. Ice flowed through Mary's veins. Oh God. It was too similar. Too much. She could not breathe. And yet the sight made her shout.

The men jumped as one and turned. Mary heard their sneers and taunts, but they did not penetrate the fog of rage that had overtaken her. Her baton met with the first man's head, and he slumped to the pavement. Blows buffeted her, yet she did not feel them. Strike, slash, duck, punish. These were the thoughts that ran through her head. Vaguely she was aware of Daisy dispatching a man in short order, slicing his forearm and jabbing his thigh. He howled and ran off. One left.

The thug looked at the wild women who had no fear of him and then fled as well. Mary clutched her baton, fighting the urge to chase him down. Panting with rage not yet abated, she stood over the fallen woman until Daisy lightly touched her arm. Mary flinched, her hand half lifting in defense, but the fog cleared, and she let Daisy aside.

Thick blood seeped into Daisy's yellow skirts as she knelt before the woman. Mary's knees grew weak, and she followed Daisy down.

The woman's appearance told its own story. Sensible brown homespun dress, clear complexion that was now grey, and wide, unseeing brown eyes that stared up at Mary in supplication. A large pool of dark, glistening blood spread out in front of the woman's small waist, and yet another at the base of her throat. A gruesome wound that barely trickled now.

Mary swallowed thickly and averted her eyes.

"No pulse," Daisy murmured, pressing her fingers against the woman's pale throat. "They gutted her. Poor dear."

"No!" The silvery form of the woman stood beside them. She glared down in outrage, and her light-blond hair seemed to swirl in the wind. Her dark eyes flashed as she caught them looking. "I cannot be dead. I refuse to go. Not like this. Not from the likes of them." Again came that flash of ire and need. The need to live.

Daisy glanced at Mary, and hesitation rose high in her eyes. But her voice was calm as she addressed the spirit. "I'm afraid you are dead. I am very sorry we did not arrive sooner."

The woman fisted her hips. "If I am dead, then how is it that you both see me?" Her eyes narrowed. "And why do you both glow?"

"You are seeing our spirits," Mary said. "Just as we see yours." Around them the breeze began to stir, and with it the soft moans of other spirits. They hovered still in the shadows, but soon they would come out for a look. Ghosts were always attracted to a new one. Mary sighed. Although sorrow weighed down her breast, she'd been around death for so long that she was all but numb to the plight of the newly dead. "There is still a chance to move on. You must feel it. I suggest you take it, lest you be stuck here just as they are." She didn't need to explain who "they" were. The woman surely felt them creeping in, just as Mary and Daisy did.

Indeed, she looked over her shoulder before rubbing her arms in an agitated fashion. "I feel it. Like someone is plucking on my sleeve." She shuddered. "I...I can't! I don't want to die."

"Well, who does?" Daisy mused. However, her head tilted as she eyed the spirit thoughtfully. "Would you really rather stay? Even if it meant you never died?"

"Is this a true question?" Her accent, now that Mary turned her attention to it, was flat and hard. An American. Likely fresh off the boat.

"She has spirit," Daisy said to Mary.

"She's a strange one." Most newly dead sobbed or went into hysterics over their destroyed bodies. Mary had. Best not to think about those memories.

The woman quirked a brow at Mary. "Says the woman who rushed in like a crazed banshee and beat down three full-grown men."

"She's in shock," Daisy said to Mary with a smile.

Mary could not help but smile too. "Likely you're right."

The strange woman nodded. "I agree. Likely I'll soon..." She wavered, and her throat bobbed on a swallow. "Can we move on, please?"

Mary could not fault her. The mere fact that she knelt next to a dead body threatened to make her sight go black. She kept her eyes firmly upon Daisy. "We could..."

Daisy's eyes widened. "We could," she agreed.

Mary's gaze snapped to the hovering spirit, who seemed about to attempt jumping back into her old body. "You'd be a slave. For however long he deems."

The woman blinked. "Who is 'he'?"

"The man who can give you back your life," Daisy said simply.

"Will it involve..." The spirit's nose scrunched up. Being women, none of them had to say more.

"No," said Mary emphatically. "You will have to find other willing spirits for him."

"For what reason?"

"Well, there is the rub," said Daisy a bit sadly. "Only he knows. Some he allows to return to their bodies and live life out as we are now. Others he takes with him. Though he promises no harm will come to them, no one here knows what happens to those souls." Her blue eyes grew solemn. "You will not know until it is your turn."

It was a devil's bargain to be sure. Yet Mary had never regretted her decision. She supposed that was the unifying factor for all GIM: they simply loved life too much to lose theirs, even if their circumstances were less than pleasant. Did it make them selfish? Wrong somehow? She wondered every time another was offered the choice, every time she speculated on where the others went.

"Fine." The spirit drew herself up and set her hands upon her hips once more. "I accept."

No hesitation. Mary had to admit, the woman had more will to live than most. Adam would love that about her. Which would also put the woman in a dubious position.

"Well, then," said Daisy. Yet her hand fluttered in the vicinity of her heart, not quite able to press it there.

Mary understood and rested a hand on Daisy's limp one. "You know how?"

"Of course." Daisy grimaced. "You sure?" she asked the spirit.

The woman's form gained strength, glowing bright in the darkened alley. She wouldn't look at her body, but only at Daisy and Mary. "Ought we not hurry?"

"Your body is safe for now," Daisy murmured, but her gaze stayed resolutely away from it.

Mary knew why Daisy hesitated. The process of becoming a GIM was not pretty, or clean. And meeting their maker was always disconcerting. On a variety of levels.

With a sigh, Daisy pressed her hand against her clock-work heart and murmured the words that would call Adam forth. Instantly the air about them grew hot and florid with the smoky scent of myrrh and something darkly cloying. The effect of that fragrance upon Mary was instantaneous. Heat washed over her, tightening her nipples and making her sex throb. It was most unfortunate, and not a sensation she enjoyed, given what caused it. By the look of Daisy's pinched lips, she too was affected and not happy either. Then again, their creator's scent had that effect on men as well as women, so they could hardly be shamed.

On the heels of the scent came the darkness, black and

endless as it coalesced on a spot just next to them until it formed the shape of a doorway.

The spirit at Mary's side fluttered, her eyes wide. "What is it?"

"Hush."

The echoing of footsteps, as if coming from far off, sounded. And the scent grew thicker, richer, making sweat bloom upon Mary's skin and her clockwork heart go just a bit faster. She took a steadying breath and tried to ignore the shiver working through her body.

Through the darkness he came, his step jaunty and arrogant. Mary swallowed. Gracious, but the demon was sin incarnate. Tall and lean, black hair tousled about without care, and light-amber eyes beneath thick, stern brows. His aquiline nose would be considered too big on a lesser face, his mouth an angry slash, yet somehow plump and inviting. Such intense masculine beauty was dizzying.

Oftentimes Mary wondered if Adam was an incubus. Especially when he smiled as if he knew exactly how he stirred their emotions, and his deep, rich voice rumbled over them like heated cream.

"My delicious daughters," he said fondly. "My most lovely creations. How may I be of service?"

Daisy cleared her throat, a high blush warring with eyes flashing in annoyance. "My lord Adam, we have one who desires to join."

His gaze was a palpable caress. It slid warm and sticky over Mary to rest on the silent spirit. Adam's nostrils flared as he drew in a deep, sharp breath. Odd, as he was never anything other than nonchalant or flirty.

"Your name?" His lazy tone had gone clipped. The loose-limbed way in which he normally carried himself tensed.

The spirit narrowed her eyes, her gaze sliding up and down Adam's form as though inspecting something distasteful. "Eliza May."

"Mmm." It came out as a dubious rumble. Adam flicked his attention to Mary. "I'll have a word with you, sweet Mary Chase—"

"And you are?" Eliza May cut in, her translucent hands upon her hips.

"Not to be interrupted, treats." Adam's expression was hard and cold.

Eliza lifted her chin. "I've a right to know your name, sir."

With a smile that chilled the bone, Adam sauntered over to the hovering spirit. When he reached out to trace the line of her cheek, his finger did not drift through her, but made contact, as though she were flesh still. "My Lord and Master, My Irresistible Liege," he murmured in his rich purr. "Pick whichever one you want. Then shut up. I am speaking, and not to you."

His gaze moved to Mary but stopped as he spied Eliza's body lying bloodied and battered upon the cobbles, her skirts still rucked up, a pool of blackening blood widening about her head like a macabre halo. His lips flattened as his eyes glowed so brightly that the area about them was illuminated with golden light. Mary had seen the reaction before, and it never failed to unnerve. But she understood. Violence against women was something he could not abide.

Eliza, seeing the direction of the demon's gaze, swished over her body as though she might hide it. "Don't look at me, it." Her teeth bared in a snarl. "At my body."

"Why?" he asked, mildly. "It's dead. And if you want to keep it, it's also mine."

Eliza flinched, her mouth gaping before snapping shut. "I thought...they said that you wouldn't want..."

The glow in Adam's eyes returned, not as bright, but quite fierce. "Devil take it. I quite literally have beings knocking against each other for the opportunity to have me." Indeed, ghosts stuck between worlds had gathered, bumping against the periphery of the alleyway as though held back by an invisible wall. The silent, wraiths twisted and undulated in unmistakable entreaty. "I've no interest in unwilling, prissy misses."

Eliza's mouth curled in distaste. "Oh, how the other ghouls must envy you."

The air about them trembled and heated. Adam took a step in Eliza's direction. "Let us get this over with. Will you swear fealty to me?"

"What would I have to—"

"Yes or no. Right now, Miss May."

Eliza May glanced between Mary and Daisy, her expression unsure and pained. They could not speak now, nor assuage her. It was forbidden. But Mary tried to convey that it would be all right with a soft look.

"Tick-tock, Eliza."

"All right." She drew herself up. "I swear it."

The triumph in Adam's expression was absolute, and not what Mary was accustomed to seeing. "Excellent." With a flick of his wrist he conjured a thin golden chain. Lightning-fast, it coiled around Eliza's spirit and her body. Adam gave the chain a lazy tug, and Eliza flew into her body. A great gasp broke from her lips as her body arched off the ground, then flopped back, struggling against the golden bonds like a fish in a net.

Mary and Daisy looked on in horror. This was nothing like their times. Nor were the ones taken bound in gold.

Before they could say a word, Eliza May disappeared, and they were left alone with Adam.

"Good Lord, Adam," Daisy said, her eyes beginning to glow. "What have you done to her?"

He waved an idle hand. "Nothing you need worry over." His expression brooked no argument. "Now, then, doves, as neither of you is indebted to me for souls, I consider this a personal boon." Something wicked and altogether unsettling flickered in his gaze. "Therefore"—he reached out, and the hot, dry tips of his fingers touched their foreheads—"a gift." An electric buzz shimmered through Mary, delicious and heady before ending in a warm glow.

"What was that?" she asked.

His smile was brief. "Motherhood."

As if she had been pinched, Daisy let out a garbled squawk. "Did you…" She colored furiously. "Did you just impregnate us?"

Adam's full-throated laughter echoed along the brick walls. "Hell's bells, no." His eyes watered as he tried to calm himself, and Daisy huffed. Clearing his throat, he tried again. "You do not need me for that, sweets. Unless you'd like to?" He waggled his dark brows, and Daisy huffed again.

"But we are…" Daisy waved a helpless arm. "You know…" She stopped there, her face flaming, which Mary had to admit was rather amusing, seeing as Daisy could wax lyrical about sexual topics without care.

Adam eyed her with a mixture of wry caution and good humor. "If I may be so bold, darling, but do you experience your courses?" His mouth twitched. "I shall take the shade of crimson on your cheeks as a yes. Which means there is nothing stopping you."

His gaze slid over both of them. "You aren't corpses,

for pity's sake. You are life anew, better and more precious because you asked for it with eyes wide open." He sniffed in annoyance. "I swear, do none of my flock pay attention when I tell you the rules upon creation?"

Mary was rather glad to hear she was not expecting and had to smile at his chastisement. She'd known, but hadn't realized Daisy was ignorant of that particular part of her nature. "My lord, would you explain what you meant by 'motherhood'?"

His smile was beatific. "Simply that you may choose to create another. Only one, mind. No need for us to get carried away."

Mary and Daisy blinked. Shock coursed through Mary's bones. She could create a GIM? The notion was at once horrid and fascinating. "I..." Mary took a breath and curtsied. "You honor us, my lord."

"I know. Choose wisely, my doves. Creation is the most intimate act one can do. That soul will be bound to you, helpless as a babe until you choose to set it free. Even after, you will always feel a connection."

"But how do we—" Daisy's question was cut off with a wave of Adam's hand.

"I cannot dally all night. Do as I do, and the rest will follow." His attention turned to Mary. "Miss Chase. As I was trying to say before, I suggest you keep an eye on that man of yours."

"Why?" Mary would not contradict the demon by protesting that Jack was not *hers*, but his words left her tight and cold.

Adam's mouth curled, revealing small but sharp fangs. "I do not take threats against my children lightly. I do believe that Jack Talent will soon find himself in the thick of a great one. Some beings were never meant to be GIM."

"You mean the shadow crawlers."

His expression grew pained. "Mix any sort of demon flesh with metal, and you will find yourself with a disaster on your hands." His gaze leveled on her, and she felt the immense power he held within him. "Do not let it happen, Miss Chase."

Dawn was slow in coming for Mary. She was being watched. She knew it with the same certainty with which she knew her name was Mary Chase. The sensation whispered over her skin like spider silk and crept along her spine to nip at her neck. An unnerving distraction that robbed her of peace and kept her awake.

It was not a new sensation. It had come and gone for some time. Too long. So long that she was almost used to the feeling. Almost, but not quite. Had she not the ability to see spirits, Mary would have wondered if her house was haunted, for the sensation of eyes upon her nearly always occurred when she was in her home.

"Nonsense," she muttered, and tossed back her bedcovers. The white light of morning was shining through her curtains as she crossed the cool floors and headed for her front room. Still she could not shake the sticky feeling. For someone accustomed to doing the watching, it was not only unnerving but an affront.

Two tall windows dominated her parlor. Framed by cream velvet curtains, the windows gleamed like a pair of bright eyes, watching. The desire to draw the curtains fully closed prompted Mary to do the opposite. She stalked right up to them, yanked them wide, and pressed her nose to the icy glass.

She spotted him immediately, the sight giving her a start. Crouched on the corner of the opposite roof like some gargoyle of old, his black-cloaked shape formed a hulking silhouette against the lemon-yellow sky.

The gears in her heart nearly stopped, then sped up. But she knew that body, and the distinct shape of that head. Jack Talent.

Her palm spread wide upon the window, the heat of her body emitting waves of condensation along the glass. The light was in her eyes, and he merely a black outline. But then a cloud scuttled over the sun, and his eyes gleamed, looking straight at her. And she felt that gaze as if it were a living, breathing beast upon her. Slowly he stood, his tall form perfectly balanced upon the jutting roof edge. And simply watched her.

Her body tightened. Had he always watched her? It couldn't be so. But for a moment, she felt certain that he had.

As if he'd been waiting to see her reaction, he raised his arm then and gave her a graceful salute. The next moment he was gone, leaving with inhuman speed.

Mary stared at the spot where he had stood. The salute ought to have been a mockery. Only it felt like an acknowledgement, and a message. Stranger still, his actions did not feel like revenge. Nor did it feel as if she were being watched, as much as watched over. As she put the kettle on and prepared for the day ahead, she realized that the idea of Talent doing the watching made her feel safe. And wasn't that the most unnerving sensation of all?

Chapter Nineteen

─────────────❧ ❧─────────────

Today would be a late day. Because the Bishop of Charing Cross appeared to do his work at night, so must they. Which was fine by Mary. She needed a bit of space between her and Talent and was happy to wait until luncheon to meet him. Then again, dining with Talent had its own pitfalls.

"Do you ever stop eating, Mr. Talent?" Mary pursed her lips at the spectacle that was Jack Talent gorging on his fifth meat pie.

He paused as though surprised she was speaking to him, then his dark eyes looked at her sidelong. "Stay with me long enough, and you might find out." He popped the last golden bite into his mouth, then licked his lips with a flick of his pink tongue. Somehow he managed to grin while chewing. His throat worked on a swallow, and that grin grew teeth. "Besides, I told you I like eating."

How he was able to make the statement both carnal and irritating, she'd never know. Mary set her attention on the report spread open on the table in front of her. Talent, adamantly eschewing the quiet containment of headquarters, had dragged them out to yet another tavern, this one being loud, smoky, and crowded. It did, however, serve an excellent supper, as Talent was quick to point out when she'd voiced her annoyance.

Unfortunately she had to admit to herself that the tavern afforded a level of anonymity they would not receive at headquarters. Too many regulators took it upon themselves to make a study of Talent and Mary. She feared there might even be a betting pool going on about just when and how they'd kill each other.

Lousy, busybody rotters. True, tempers between her and Talent were strained. But they were partners, like it or not, and she intended to behave in a sensible manner from here on out. She would not think of breathless, voyeuristic pleasures, or near kisses, or nighttime vigils.

It did not help matters when Talent suddenly gave her a slow perusal, lingering along the length of her bodice where the satin lay smooth and tight over her torso. Heat prickled along her skin, and she bristled. He could not look at her in this manner. Not if she wanted to get through the day.

As if he was annoyed, his mouth turned down at one corner. "You're looking rather turned out today, Mistress Chase." His low voice turned into a drawl. "Why do I suspect I will not like the reason?"

"I could not fathom." Mary ordered her papers into a neat stack and was quite proud that her hands did not shake.

"Do not tell me you're dressing to impress that popinjay Darby." Talent's scowl grew sour, his nostrils flaring.

They were slated to watch Darby later this evening. A

prospect Mary did not find remotely appealing. Even so, she could only shake her head slightly at Talent's absurd accusation. "Perhaps I dressed for you."

She said it to unnerve, and his open mouth and flushed cheeks had her fighting a grin, but she hid it and stuck to the business at hand. "I took a look at Mr. Pierce's financial situation—"

Her plate of barely touched fish pie was pushed in front of her. "Eat," said Talent, who had clearly recovered from her parry.

"I'm not hungry. Now about Pierce—"

"I'll be damned if I have to hold back because you've made yourself weak due to stubbornness." His blunt chin lifted. "You eat. I'll read." Taking the report from her, he gave the plate an encouraging nudge farther in her direction.

Mary narrowed her eyes but he merely stared back. Unmovable. Grumbling, she picked up her spoon. Warm, creamy sauce and tender morsels of fish filled her mouth. Immediately she wanted another bite.

Talent gave a grunt of satisfaction, then ignored her as he read over her notes. "This is new information on Pierce." When he glanced up again, creases deepened around his mouth. "You do not sleep enough."

Well, he ought to know, since he'd been watching her house all night. She refrained from saying so, only because bringing the fact out in the open would lead to questions she wasn't sure she wanted answers to. "I don't need much sleep, and the report needed to be done."

"You'll be no good without sleep either," he snapped before his gaze dropped once more. "Keep eating."

Glaring, she took an exaggerated bite, which was lost

on him, as he did not look up. Worse, a sense of well-being filled her with each blasted bite. Blasted Talent. "Did you know Mr. Pierce was a clockmaker?"

"No." Talent scanned the pages. "I assume it's important."

"Well, it's rather odd, when one considers his main employer."

His brow furrowed as his big body hunched over the papers. Talent's reading expression, it seemed. So very serious. Mary could not fathom why it made her want to smile.

"Worked for the Archbishop of Canterbury, did he?" Talent's head lifted so quickly he almost caught her smile. He, however, was far from amused. His golden complexion ebbed to pasty white. "Can't imagine why the archbishop would need a clockmaker in his employ."

"Do you . . ." Mary was about ask if he knew the archbishop, but that would be a stretch. The clergyman took tea with the Queen. "As you can see," she said instead, "Pierce received regular payments from Lambeth Palace. I believe it would do us well to speak to the archbishop. In that vein—"

"We don't need to question him." Talent's big hands crumpled the pages.

"Of course we do." Mary pried the papers from his clenched hands and smoothed them out before organizing them into a neat stack. "I've already made the arrangements."

"What?" His chair screeched as he lurched to his feet. "When?"

Mary stood as well. "We had a bit of luck there. I sent a note of inquiry to the palace—"

"You contacted Lambeth Palace?" Ire snapped in his

eyes, his lips forming a flat line as though he was trying not to shout.

Mary tucked the report into her working bag. "If you'd let me finish—"

"There isn't anything to finish, Chase." Talent's hard, masculine jaw clenched. "You do not decide who we interview. I do. This is my case. You are assisting me."

Was there any answer for that nonsense? Mary rather thought not. "Calm yourself. You're drawing unwanted attention."

Conversation had petered out, with more than a few patrons giving them a speculative glance. Talent only had eyes for her. His shoulders bunched beneath his dingy coat.

"Look here, Chase." He pointed a finger in her general direction. "You do not manage me." He took a step closer, looming, his breath sawing. "Am I understood?"

Yes. At the very least, this Talent she understood well. She had to tilt her neck to meet his eyes. "Are you under some misapprehension that I do not speak English, Master Talent?"

The broad planes of his cheeks colored as his eyes narrowed. She did not give him a chance to respond. "I understood every word you've stated thus far, ridiculous drivel that it was." Her skirts brushed the tips of his battered boots as their glares clashed and warred. "As you stated, we are partners. Which means equals. And if you want me to cease 'managing you,' as you call it, then I suggest you learn to keep your temper under control. Now would be a fine time to start, thank you."

His mouth opened, the glitter in his eyes growing dangerous, but she held up a hand. "Save yourself the trouble of shouting again. I am through speaking with you."

She gathered her skirts and turned toward the exit. But she paused and looked over her shoulder at him. "Unless you'd like to tell me what has you so upset over the idea of interviewing the archbishop?"

For she had to wonder if this little outburst was his attempt at diversion. As if he read her suspicion, his jaw snapped shut with an audible click. Oh, but his nostrils flared, his close-cropped hair sticking out wildly.

"No?" she said when he merely stood there, baring his teeth at her like a madman. She shrugged. "Then we shall be conducting that interview."

She took one step farther, when his terse response lashed out. "We are *not.*"

"We *are.*"

Jack would have liked to say that his instinct for trouble had always been well honed. Unfortunately, his education in that arena had been painful and hard-earned. But earn it he had, and thus he knew he ought to have listened to his instinct and stayed away this day. Pierce worked for the bloody Archbishop of Canterbury? Jesus, this was a cock-up. This doppelgänger killer knew too much. Jack's underbelly was exposed, revealing a wound that had never truly stopped bleeding.

He was aware he'd been an ass of the first order to Chase. He had not been able to control it. Bloody, bloody arch-bloody-bishop. An old rage boiled to the surface, one that cried out for release, to tear into something. Jack gritted his teeth as he walked alongside her. She was too quick by half. Something, in normal circumstances, he'd appreciate. Save he had little recourse when she dug her heels in, nor did he know how he was to conceal certain facts without getting caught.

They had walked halfway down the road when a runner caught up with them and ordered their immediate return to headquarters. Wilde wanted to meet with them.

Thankfully, Wilde cut straight to business as soon as they arrived in his dark and dreary office.

"Lord Darby called on me this morning."

"Really," Jack drawled, "I'm surprised. I'd have thought him fast asleep given his proclivities." He'd had to watch the bloody bastard go at it for hours the other night. Shifter stamina was an impressive thing. Regretfully so, at times.

He could all but feel Chase squirm beside him. Good. He was in a foul mood. And she made up the greater half of it.

Wilde's mouth pitched to the side, an odd half-twitch. Sitting calm and tall in his chair at the head of the table, he merely rested his hands upon the glossy surface and continued. "He appears to find Mistress Honeychurch and Master Evans preferable escorts and has requested that you, Master Talent and Mistress Chase, be taken off guard duty rotation. In short"—Wilde's cool, black gaze bore into them—"he wants nothing further to do with you."

"I suggest you tell him to piss off." Frankly, Jack was glad to be rid of Darby. He knew that path led to a dead end and had not been looking forward to tonight's guard. But the request was a slight against him, and Chase. God knew Chase didn't deserve it.

Wilde's brows rose. "Oh, certainly. I shall ignore the fact that he donates hundreds of thousands of pounds to SOS operations and tell the earl to 'piss off' because his reasonable demand has sent my regulator into a fit of pique."

Chase's skirts rustled. Jack caught a flash of wine satin before jerking his attention back to Wilde. Jack crossed one leg over the other. "I was under the impression that our organization looked beyond money and title."

"Are you also under the impression that our employees work for free?" Wilde inquired smoothly. "For that can be arranged."

He was about to retort, but Chase's smooth voice cut in. "I agree with my partner. Kowtowing to a man solely because he pays the bills is folly."

Damn, but Jack liked her too well. Just as he'd feared he would. Lust was one thing. It burned off quickly. "Like" was decidedly dicey. "Like" could grow, lead to other unfortunate "L"-words that did not bear thinking of. Of course there were words to offer a fine distraction, such as "lick," "linger," "luxuriate," or the more-obscure-but-rife-with-possibilities "lingua."

Jack ran his lingua along the backs of his teeth, then promptly bit down on it to focus. "Lummox" was another word he would do well to remember. "It is badly done of the SOS," he added, just to dig in, because there was something fun about joining with Chase.

Wilde's pale skin grew ruddy, the pinch about his mouth more pronounced, but it all eased in a blink. "Lord Darby will still be watched. Just not by the two of you." Wilde shook his head, looking weary and slightly bemused. "I don't know what you did to annoy him, Master Talent—"

"I merely talked to him."

"Apparently," Wilde murmured, "that is enough to annoy anyone."

A gurgling sound came from somewhere in Chase's vicinity. Jack refused to look.

Wilde stood, meeting over, discussion done. "Do not pin your focus on something you cannot change." He smiled briefly. "Pieces shift on the board. It is the end game that counts."

As though she'd been waiting for it, Chase took the moment to speak up. "I've heard from the Archbishop of Canterbury's staff."

Jack went utterly cold. Slowly he turned toward her. Chase's cameo-smooth skin glowed in the dingy office light as she looked up at Wilde. Perfectly composed. As though she weren't driving a stake under his chin. Traitor! Outmaneuvering miss. Through a hollow tunnel of sound he heard her. "The Archbishop of Canterbury has agreed to meet with us. This afternoon, in fact."

Bloody fucking hell.

He might have cursed out loud, for Wilde and Chase both turned with twin expressions of surprise mixed with censure. Jack cleared his throat. "Do either of you honestly believe that the Archbishop of Canterbury is murdering shifters?"

He was surprised he could speak at all, given that his heart was thundering in his throat and his insides had turned watery. He could not go back there. He could not. The ringing in his ears grew louder. "He is one of the most powerful men in the realm. Nor is he likely to even believe in supernaturals, much less know of their existence."

"That is hardly the point," said Chase. "He might have information, however innocuous it might seem on the surface. Never mind the fact that, as investigators, it is our duty to leave no stone unturned."

"How very diligent of you," Jack muttered. But he was trapped. Wilde was studying him as though he were a particularly interesting insect, and Chase was just waiting for him to further object. He did not doubt she had a store of volleys waiting to be lobbed back at him.

"It is a delicate situation," Wilde said. "No, he does not know of our kind. Nor will he." The fact was so implicit that Wilde did not bother phrasing it as a threat. "But since he has agreed to speak with you both, so you shall."

Chapter Twenty

❧〰✦〰❧

He was in a nightmare of his own making. Jack had never felt that truth more keenly than now, when bloody Mary Chase had marched them into Lambeth Palace, never mind his protests that this was all for naught. After giving him the brisk order to "go the bloody hell home if you're so against it," she'd ignored him.

The very idea of sending Chase in here alone curdled his insides. Cold sweat dripped down his spine and tickled the backs of his ears as they were led into a murky drawing room. The last time he'd paid the palace a visit, he'd been huddled on the stone-cold floor of the crypts, hugging that dank ground as if it were his salvation. Looking back, he could not fathom why he'd had the faith to seek sanctuary here. Nothing in his young life ought to have given him that hope. Yet he'd come. And John Michael Talent had been destroyed that dark day.

The very proper footman closed the door behind them, effectively entombing them in the drawing room. Damn it, but he couldn't breathe in here. The room was too dark, the heavy velvet curtains drawn almost closed, a silly practice to protect the furniture and artwork. What good was art when one couldn't see it?

Chase moved idly about the room, a rustle of satin and crinoline. She'd dressed to perfection for this meeting, the wine-colored satin of her gown stunning yet restrained. The gown offered little in the way of adornment, simply a wide band of pleating around the hem and the edges of her gathered overskirt. A nice trick to convey humility, save that the clean lines of her bodice merely emphasized her graceful curves and made a man long to linger.

The darkness here muted the golden brown of her hair, so prettily coiled at the back of her head, and turned her creamy skin a shade of unnatural white. She appeared a painting just then, only alive by the virtue of her glittering gaze.

In some sick way, he was glad for her presence. It did not make a lick of sense, but when she was near, the world was real. Not some strange play that he viewed from afar. And that gave him a certain strength. If he could face this, he could face anything. Because of her.

"Chase." He did not know why her name slipped from his lips, or what he would even say now that he'd called for her attention.

He stiffened further when her lazy gaze settled on him. "What is it?"

Yes, Jack, what is so important that you had to call out to her? Furious heat worked over his skin, and he struggled not to squirm like a lad. Clearing his throat, he blurted out the first thing that came to mind. "Would you like to talk about it?"

She stared back at him as though he'd gone mad. She'd be right, he thought bitterly.

"About what?" she asked, her smooth brow wrinkling. "Your vile temper of late? Which is really saying something, I should add."

Well, he'd walked into that one. "No, I—"

"Your little act of reciprocity by reconnaissance?" One delicate brow lifted a fraction as her golden eyes pinned him. He had wondered what she thought of his watching over her. And whether she'd mention it. The devil had clearly crept into Jack, for he'd been unable to resist going to her home and making sure she was safe and well. Nor had he moved when he'd seen her coming to the window. Madman that he was, he'd wanted her to see him. Wanted to know what she'd do. Nothing, it seemed.

It did not help matters that Chase had cooled on him. She'd retreated straight back into that thick shell of hers where he meant precisely nothing, and anything he said was met with a bland reply.

"Actually," he ground out, "I was referring to the other night." Christ, his collar was strangling him. "Look, Chase, the things I said about you and Lucien, I—"

"Here?" she hissed, her eyes suddenly sparking. "You want to discuss that here? Now?"

"I was simply going to—"

"For pity's sake," she snapped. "I used him too!" She took a quelling breath, a slow rise of her breast before letting it go. "I used Lucien to keep others away. I don't know much of men, and what interaction I've had . . . well"—her slim shoulders lifted—"it has not endeared me to them." The thick bronze fans of her lashes swept down, hiding her eyes, and she said no more.

Ugly, twisting guilt hit Jack straight in his heart. "I'm sorry. That was all I was going to say." He'd been jealous. And guilty. A bad combination.

Her wide brow wrinkled. "Sorry?"

"For the way I've treated you." His hands clenched. "It was badly done, and I've no excuse." None that he wanted to give, at any rate. "But there are good men, Chase. One day, you shall…" God, would the floor please open up and swallow him? "…You'll find one who treats you as you deserve." He wanted it to be him. So badly his chest hurt.

Chase ducked her head, her lips soft and beguiling. "I know there are good men in the world, Talent." She looked at him then, looked right into him, and he swore he bled inside. "Such as Ian Ranulf."

Right.

"When I saw how he treated Daisy, I knew it was time for me to leave Lucien and our false front. I knew it was time for me to search for something more."

It struck him like a stone: Mary Chase was looking for someone to love. The very idea of her linked to another, of seeing them day in and day out, made him perversely cold. He'd leave London when that happened. Leave bloody Europe.

She looked so forlorn just then. Every word he'd ever said crushed down upon him. Regret was his constant companion, but never more so than now.

"Chase." He hesitated, then said what he must. "You accused me of thinking you'd be better off dead. I have never believed that. Never." His chest swelled, rising up as if his whole body protested the very idea. Her wide, stunned gaze crashed over him as he finished his thought. "We are partners now. Should it come down to the choice between my life and yours, I will sacrifice mine. Without question."

Her lips parted, a shocked circle of pink. "But why?"

"Because yours holds all the promise that mine lost

long ago." And because he'd die anyway should she be lost to this world.

Happiness bloomed over her face, so utterly lovely and glowing that he did not know what to do with himself. She looked at him as if he'd just become her knight with banners flying. As if she was seeing him anew, or perhaps for the first time.

Jack was caught in that look, the net drawing tight around him. His whole body answered, boiling with persistent want. It rushed about him, a violent tumult that set his equilibrium rolling. Words filled his head: *Yes, yes, thank God you finally see me.* And *No, no, I am not what you think. I am not that hero.*

He could not speak. He could not move, caught as he was. Before he could stop it, two images of her were before him: a lovely woman in the full blush of health and a crushed and bleeding wretch upon a wet pavement. They crashed over him with brutal force. He almost staggered.

She would not forgive him if she really knew what he and his friends had done.

He could not live with her. He could not live without her. Jack knew he was being selfish, but there it was. And so he drove the wedge in deeper, reminding her of all the reasons she should go on seeing him as just a man. One she'd be better off disliking.

He turned away from her, an abrupt cut she'd feel. When he spoke, his voice was decidedly cool. He would have congratulated himself for it, save that self-loathing got in the way. "It was foolish to come here. I know you like to think of yourself as an investigator, Chase. But you really have no notion of what you are doing."

He could almost feel the joy gust out of her, deflating like the last gasp of an aeronautical balloon.

"My, but you like to flog the dead horse, Talent." Her voice was once more that cold, crisp sliver of ice that had defined their arguments of old.

Jack let the frost of her ire numb him further. "And you are a dog with a bone."

"What is it about this meeting that has you so out of sorts?"

"Out of sorts," he muttered. Now that he'd picked a fight with Chase, his fear returned tenfold. "I merely protest the waste of time."

Jack thrust his fists deep within the wells of his pockets. The shaking within him grew, his heart thrumming against his throat. He reminded himself that he'd gained a foot and a half of height and nearly five stone of weight since that black day. He'd gone from ignorant boy to bitter man. Perhaps he wouldn't be recognized.

Mary watched Talent's shoulders hunch and the wall he erected against the world come back up. Her mind had gone foggy. Die? For *her*. Was there anyone she'd be willing to die for? When she'd fought so hard for the right to live?

Damn him.

No matter where she looked, where she went, Jack Talent was lurking in the shadows of her mind. There was something about him that made her want to learn more, pry open his protective casing and see what made him tick. Mary feared she would never understand him. He set her world upside down and inside out. And he made her ashamed. She'd been looking for signs of his guilt, *wanting* to find them at some points. The man who would die for her.

Mary turned from the sight of him and glanced at the ornate porcelain wall clock, depicting Adam's downfall in the Garden of Eden. The minute hand pointed between Eve's pale breast and the golden apple resting on her outstretched palm. "Nearly a quarter hour has passed," she murmured, annoyed at waiting. Annoyed at Talent.

"They'll keep us waiting for twenty minutes at the least." Tension coiled about Talent like a snake, but his tone was subdued, almost resigned now on the heels of his former snappishness.

"How do you know?" Mary did not want to stay in this place any longer than necessary. Gilt furnishings and silk-lined walls spoke of luxury. The rough-hewn floorboards beneath the priceless Holbein carpet spoke of humility. But past all the declaratives so carefully orchestrated throughout the room, an air of quiet menace lurked. Or perhaps she was simply being fanciful.

Talent glanced at her, his features stark. "Standard procedure." His lip curled in an ugly smile. "My guess would be that it forces one to think on their sins."

As soon as the words had left his lips the dark humor in his expression deflated, and he abruptly turned to inspect the drawn curtains. "No doubt we are to fall upon our knees and beg for forgiveness the moment he enters."

"I've yet to encounter a soul capable of casting that first stone," she said smartly.

He gave a snort of dry amusement, so soft she almost missed it. His fluctuating mood disturbed Mary. Strangely, she felt as though she needed to remain here for Talent's sake, as if he needed that small protection.

They stood apart, each lost in thoughts as time dragged along with a loud *tick, tick, tick* that had Mary's neck tensing further and further.

"How is it that you know the standard procedure for the palace?" she blurted out when she could take no more.

Talent pivoted on one heel. His thick brows slowly lifted, as if he found her slightly daft. Or perhaps he merely searched for a reasonable response when there was none. She wouldn't get to know, for his hand came up in the age-old gesture for silence, though she hadn't said a word.

"He's coming." Talent's expression went utterly devoid of emotion.

A moment later she heard the footsteps. And Talent grew even more withdrawn, his skin the color of death. The massive double doors opened, and Mr. Antony Goring, Archbishop of Canterbury, walked in.

Mary wasn't certain what she'd expected, but the man who entered was not it. Tall and lean, he walked with command. A thick shock of snow-white hair swept back from a high brow. There was something about his large, square jaw and strong blunt nose, and when he set his eyes on her, that sense of having seen him before grew. While his hair was white, his brows remained brown and framed dark eyes that snapped with cunning intelligence.

It was only when he drew near and took her hand did she realize that his eyes were not brown but a deep forest green, surrounded by thick lashes. "Oh," she exclaimed, struck by their singular hue.

He smiled kindly. "That is not the usual response I receive when meeting guests, but quite lovely all the same."

Mary flushed to her toes. She hadn't meant to say a thing. But those eyes struck a chord within her, and her instincts clamored for her to think clearly and stop fiddling about with niceties.

The archbishop straightened, a smile still hovering about his lips. "Ah, but it is far too dark in this room, is it not?" He reached out to a small lamp resting upon a side table. With a click, bright white light illuminated the space around them. The archbishop beamed. "An incandescent lamp. Isn't it glorious? I do so love modern advancements. It is my mission to see the whole of the palace wired for electricity within the year."

A surprising and extravagant expense to say the least. But Mary merely murmured her agreement and let him guide her to a seat. She glanced at Talent, who stood hovering in the shadows, his face white and his teeth bared. The archbishop noticed her attention straying and followed it.

The archbishop's benign expression crashed, revealing one of disgusted horror. Another second and it shifted to icy cold disdain. It happened within a blink of the eye, yet Mary took it all in and noted a similar change overcome Talent. Only his expression went from careful blankness to utter rage.

His green eyes glowed with it, the square hinge of his jaw bulging as if he ground his teeth together.

A terrible tension thickened the air as the two men glared at each other. Talent was bigger, pure brawn, and topped the other man by five inches, but facing off, she could see the similarities in their features, cut from the same model, only Talent's was harder, his life experience having given him a rough edge.

"You dare return here." The archbishop's tone was pure frost.

Talent cocked his head and regarded him. It was almost indolent the way he took his time, but there was no mistaking the way he held his body in tight readiness. "I did not think you'd recognize me."

The archbishop's lip curled. "You've the look of her."

The coldness in his eyes grew frigid. "Her male counter-part. A grotesque version of all that was good and true."

Talent took a hard step in his direction before halting. His fists curled, the corner of one eye twitching. "You ought to know depravity when you see it." His voice was almost controlled, almost normal. "Having practiced it before."

"Enough!" The archbishop smacked an open palm against his thigh. "Get out, spawn. Go back to the dark-ness from which you came."

"Stop." Mary could hear no more. Both men flinched as though they'd forgotten she was there. She tried for a reasonable tone. "Surely we can all calm—"

"Miss," interrupted the archbishop, "I am going to assume you know not with what you've come in contact. However, I implore you to come with me. For your safety."

"Mr. Talent is not a thing," she said incredulously.

A growl rumbled in Talent's chest at that moment. Mary stepped closer to him, but kept her gaze upon the archbishop, who looked at her with false patience. "Your Grace, I do not understand what lies between you and my partner, but surely—"

"What lies between His *Grace* and me," Talent cut in sharply, "is murder."

The archbishop went livid red. "Murder is the killing of a human. Otherwise it is simply a necessary extermination."

Talent sprang with a roar, tackling the elder man and crashing to the floor with him.

"Talent!" She hurried over, her heavy, voluminous skirts hampering her progress. Any moment now guards would come. His life would be ruined.

But Talent was past hearing. He hauled the archbishop up, and the man's head bobbled, even as fervent prayers rattled from his pale lips. " 'He cast upon them the fierceness of his anger, wrath, and indignation, and trouble, by sending evil angels among them.' "

"Prayer will not help you," Talent shouted over him.

" 'He made a way to his anger; he spared not their soul from death, but gave their life over to the pestilence.' "

Talent bared his teeth, his fists curling into the man's cassock. "You were supposed to help. You were supposed to save us all. You destroyed my family—" His voice broke.

"No, you did. With your unnaturalness." Spittle flew as the archbishop snarled up at him. "You killed your mother. Your father—"

"Why stop there?" Talent snapped. "Perhaps you'd like to see how I exterminate?"

Long claws began to grow from his fingertips, his teeth dropping to fangs. Mary did not know what he'd become, nor did she care. She rushed headlong to him. "Talent. Stop this." He did not take notice of her.

Neither did the archbishop, who glared up at Talent, defiant, but so very fragile and human when compared to Talent's raw strength. "Do your worst. My soul is pure."

A bark of cold laughter rang out, and Talent's claws grew. A shimmer wavered over his form, his control breaking into a shift. "We shall see."

Chapter Twenty-One

~~~~~

Mary moved as through a fog. She was barely aware of leaving that dark, dreadful room. Talent had been ready to slice into the archbishop. It was only when she'd cupped his cheek that he'd stopped, springing backward at the contact, his eyes wild upon her and without a hint of recognition. His broad chest had heaved on a fast pant. And then his gaze had cleared, and he'd given a vicious curse and fled.

Guards came, a commotion broke out around her, shouts and accusations abounded. She moved through them, and no one stopped her. As she left, the battered archbishop had called for silence, telling his staff to go about as they had been. Odd. But she did not care what prompted his incongruous actions. Her mind was on Jack Talent.

Mary's ears buzzed, and her bones hummed. One thought consumed her: he'd die for her.

Jack Talent's fierce declaration clamored about in Mary's head like the ringing of bells as she rushed from the palace, still hampered by her damned skirts and too-tight corset. A fierce need welled up within her breast. To touch him, to wrap her arms about his big, strong body and give it shelter, to tell him that he too had promise; he just didn't see it.

She found him by the high brick wall that surrounded the palace. He faced away from her, leaning against the wall, forearms braced upon it as if to hold himself up. The broad expanse of his back heaved with each quick breath he took. She hurried forward just as he struck the wall, bits of red brick flying up from the force of his fist.

"Talent!"

He did not heed but kept punishing the wall, pounding brick into fine red dust. Blood sprayed from his knuckles. Mary grabbed his arm, her touch halting him so quickly that she swung forward into him.

Talent bared his teeth, and small fangs gleamed, his eyes wild. Sweat pebbled the pale skin along his temples, and his bloodied hands shook. "Do not!"

He stalked away, only to turn about and stride the other way. A man caged within his mind. "Leave me," he ground out. "I cannot..."

She took a step closer to him. He was a wild thing now, his fingers opening and closing into fists, the whites of his eyes growing redder. "Talent."

"Just go!"

"No."

He stopped his pacing and simply stared as though he couldn't quite understand her resistance. His stillness was an illusion, for he vibrated, his nostrils flaring as he breathed in hard pants. Mary edged closer and lowered her voice. "Talk to me."

He shook his head before running his hand through his hair to clutch the short ends and hold them tight, his muscles bunching and his body trembling.

She licked her dry lips. "Like it or not, I am your partner. I will not leave you. Not like this." She feared he'd be well and truly lost if she did. Mary knew that level of rage and fear. It took hold of a soul and shook it to its core. It sucked a person down into nightmares and blackness.

He cursed, rocking a bit where he stood, and turned away from her as if he couldn't bear the sight of her. Slowly, as if approaching a cornered and injured animal, she eased forward. He stiffened at her approach, his head shaking back in forth in negation. Mary ignored it. "Take my hand." She held it out, waiting.

He did not answer. And she came closer, enough to scent his sweat and fear. Enough to see the clenching of his jaw and the blood oozing over his knuckles.

"Jack," she whispered.

The sound of his name appeared to stir him, but still he would not move.

"Come with me." Knowing patience was needed, she simply stood close to him, her hand out and open. Moving as if half-frozen, Talent's hand descended from where it had been pulling at his hair. The touch of his hand against hers was such a relief that she almost closed her eyes in thanks. Careful of his wounds, she closed her fingers over his. Immediately he responded, clasping their hands together in a comfortable hold.

Quietly she led him out of the courtyard and then into the waiting carriage. He did not try to pull away as they moved down the streets, nor did he speak. They simply sat side by side, linked by their hands.

The coach rocked in time with Jack's heaving innards. He stared at the filth littered upon the hack's floor. A button lay there, cracked on one edge. His skin pricked with cold sweat, but at his side was warmth. Mary. She held on to him. She hadn't left, damn her. As much as he wanted to let her go, jump from the coach, and run away until he could catch a normal breath, he held on to her too.

Thankfully, she did not speak as they made their way to God knew where. But the questions would be coming. She always wanted to know more. He couldn't give her what she wanted. Hell, he refused to think about it a second longer. Memories were acid to his insides.

Black rage hovered at the edges of his sight. Hell's bells, just seeing that bastard. He flinched. His soul screamed for justice. Go back. Finish him. A soft touch stayed his jerking movements, her thumb brushing over his split knuckles. Jack took a shallow breath. Stupid, stupid, stupid. He should not have gone today, and bollocks to his pride.

The coach rolled to a stop, and Mary descended before he could make himself move to assist her. They were at the end of a small, crooked lane. An older pocket of London, so very dark, with squat wooden houses leaning against each other for support. Hard-packed dirt competed with broken cobbles, and in grimy windows, shadows moved.

Despite the gloom, Mary's step was lively. She tugged him along, and he realized that she once again had caught up his hand in hers. The embrace felt good, as if he should settle in and stay there.

Mary led them to an ancient, Tudor-style house, its windows comprised of dark bottle glass and heavy lead lattices. The battered wood-and-iron door swung open with ease. He blinked, his eyes adjusting to the dimness, the heady scent of roasting meat making his mouth water even as the smoky interior had his eyes stinging.

It was a tavern, though the patrons appeared to be more

interested in eating than drinking. Several tables were filled, men and, surprisingly, women hunched over their meals while conversing in low tones. Heavy green bottles of wine sat on many a table, though a barmaid wove through the crowd, distributing pints of ale as she went. At the far end of the room, a large fire roared in the massive stone hearth. An older woman worked at a grill set up over the fire, and the hiss of sizzling meat grew higher as she flipped thick steaks. Jack swallowed hard at the scent it gave off. Even soul-sick, he yearned for a bite.

A few nodded to Mary in greeting as she towed Jack along to a dark corner table. Deftly she removed her cloak and hat, hanging them upon a hook. His flesh jumped as she smoothed her hands over his chest and eased his coat away. Her touch was fleeting, perfunctory, and still his heart banged against his ribs and his body grew greedy for more, even as she turned to hang his coat, even as she guided him into a chair and then took her own.

"What is this place?" His throat was raw, his words coming out rough yet weak. He did not like to be around others. It made him twitchy. But the feel of the place soothed. The murmur of voices—content and constant—and the scent of meat in the air settled him in small ways.

A lamp illuminated the table and bathed Mary's features with golden light. "Safe." She glanced around, and he did too. There was something about the patrons. They all appeared fairly young, healthy, attractive. He sat up straighter, becoming aware of the soft whirring sound that filled the room. Hearts. Many clockwork hearts. GIM.

Jack gave a small start of surprise. GIM did not, to his knowledge, congregate en masse. Like shifters, they were solitary creatures. And as objects of suspicion, they tended to keep to the shadows of the underworld. Jack slid his gaze away as a few men glared at him. He wouldn't cause trouble for Mary. Not here.

Not when she was looking at him with expectation. Her eyes gleamed like polished topaz. "Our refuge." She signaled to the barmaid. "And home to some of the best food in the city." She grinned, and his breath caught. "Likely because the cook is French."

"I'm not hungry," he muttered.

She treated that as the lie it was and ordered them supper when the barmaid arrived. Jack took the opportunity to watch the two men sitting at the opposite wall as they tuned their fiddles. The gentle strains of the instruments relaxed him further.

They did not speak, and when the barmaid set down two platters of sizzling beefsteaks, they ate their meals. Oddly, the silence was not uncomfortable. Mary appeared in no hurry and seemed to enjoy her food. As for Jack, with each bite of the juicy grilled meat, a bit more warmth spread through him. A flagon of wine appeared before him, and he poured for Chase before helping himself. Slowly his shoulders eased, and the jitters that wracked his body quieted.

"Will you tell me now?"

Her voice cut through their shared silence. He took his time finishing his bite. It did not ease the hard thump of his heart against his ribs, or the way his fingers suddenly went cold. Nor could he avoid her indefinitely. Nastiness might have put her off, but she'd stayed with him, had given him comfort.

Gripping his cutlery as though it were a lifeline, Jack finally lifted his head to face her.

Talent slowly chewed his food, as if considering how to answer without giving too much away. In perfect honesty, she'd expected him to snap at her, divert her somehow, but he simply took a sip of wine and then set his glass down. "Not here." He glanced at the crowd around them, and the flickering lamplight played with his rough-hewn features, making them loom larger than life one moment and then shrink away the next.

His gaze snapped back to hers. "Will you come somewhere with me?"

"Anywhere you want." How frightening to realize that despite her fears, and their old history, she'd spoken the absolute truth: she would follow him anywhere.

They did not speak as he led them to St. Paul's. Deep below the cathedral was a hidden door beneath the crypts that led to SOS headquarters; thus regulators had access to St. Paul's at all hours. Not that the Church knew of this, but it proved useful on occasion.

In the blue twilight, the cathedral rose up around them, the space at once reverent yet haunting. They'd learned the art of walking without being detected, and thus only the soft pattern of her breath made a sound. He guided her to the north tower and the Geometric Staircase. A work of genius, the stone staircase hugged the cylindrical limestone tower's wall, suspended without visible supports. It was a thing of beauty, swirling above like a nautilus. Their steps chuffed as they ascended, the black latticed handrail cold beneath Mary's hand.

At her elbow Talent's agitation was palpable, a twitching, buzzing energy that affected her heart rate. She'd seen the capitulation in his eyes. He would tell her his truth, and she found herself fearing the answers.

They exited onto the triforium, an elegant balcony that overlooked the cathedral's main chapel.

"I come here sometimes," he said after a moment, his

voice a soft echo off the limestone. As if it choked him, he wrenched off his cravat and collar and tossed them to the side before taking a big breath. Then he leaned his forearms against the rail and stared at the floor below. "No matter how I have avoided it, my upbringing has infected me." He frowned down at his clenched hands. "And I find this place soothing."

A lump rose in her throat. "It is a good place to think. And my mother never brought us to church."

He made a sound of dry amusement. Then his body tightened even further. "He is my uncle."

"The archbishop?" It was only due to years of training that she kept her voice modulated, yet she had seen the resemblance between them. And the man had called Talent "spawn."

His upper lip twitched with a sneer. "The very one." He gave her a measured look. "You understand that shifters start the change at the end of their first decade?"

"Yes."

He glanced back at her, his eyes nearly black and glittering with rage. "You've no idea. One moment you are a normal child. And then comes the pain. So intense that you scream and writhe on the floor. You don't understand. You've never felt this sort of agony." His nostrils flared. "The next moment you're running on four legs, not knowing how you got that way, or what you even are. You think perhaps it's a dream.

"A child doesn't think about such things in terms of madness or possession. He simply wants help. For his mother and father to comfort him. Wake him from the dream."

The corner of his lip curled as he studied the cathedral floor below. "My father almost killed me the first time. I'd turned into a panther. One moment I was studying a picture book about the exotic animals of the Orient. The next I'm crashing about the house, running from my father's shotgun." The bitter smile upon his face grew. "He winged me. Here." He pointed to his left shoulder. "And then, when I was bleeding on the ground, I turned back. It was not...pleasant, my parents' reaction."

All sound faded down to the pumping of her heart and the low rumble of his voice. "They thought I was possessed." A choked snort broke from him. "I do not blame them. I would too."

Perhaps, Mary thought, clutching her hands together beneath the shelter of her cloak. But she understood the pain in his voice. Logic was very well and good, but it meant nothing in the face of a parent's betrayal. When those who ought to protect turned against you, the wound left behind did not easily heal. For years she had bled from such wounds.

Gently as she could, she asked the question burning within her. "There wasn't another shifter in your family?" She wasn't sure how else to phrase the question, but the fact remained that no supernatural springs from the sea, fully formed in a clamshell.

"I don't know. If there was one, he or she certainly didn't make it known. All I can tell you is that I looked like..." A small, bitter hiss left him. "You heard that bastard. I've the look of my mum." His lips compressed, and for a long moment he said nothing. "After it happened, my parents thought I might be a changeling, the devil's child left in place of theirs. Likely that's true."

Talent studied his large fists resting on the carved limestone, and his voice grew detached. "My mother insisted we seek out her brother for help. The Archbishop of Canterbury." Emerald-green eyes were suddenly upon her. "The bloody saint of the family. My only hope."

Silence descended, and Mary fought not to reach out to him. He wouldn't want that. Regardless, her hand trembled with the need. Talent's agitation and pain unsettled her far more deeply than she would have liked to admit.

"Years," he ground out. "Whippings, kneeling on rice, endless praying. Years." A growl rumbled in his throat. Fangs touched the smooth curve of his bottom lip. He shivered, then blinked. On a breath, he was calmer. Ice-cold now. "She killed herself."

When he didn't say anything more, Mary found her own voice, a cracked and painful thing. "Your mother?"

A quick nod. "She'd failed, you see. To take the devil from me. When Father found her..." His lashes swept down. "He beat me to within an inch of my life. Shot me point-blank. Then he turned his gun on himself."

A gurgling sound filled the air. Mary realized it was her own cry.

Talent did not seem to notice. "Didn't realize a simple bullet wouldn't keep me down."

"How old?" Her heart spun and pumped with painful force.

He met her gaze, and his was dead. "Thirteen."

Jack. She didn't say a word. She would not do that to him.

"And when I went to that...bastard for help." His fangs erupted again, his irises going wide and animalistic. "He shot me too. Called me Satan's spawn. Had them toss me into an alley."

Wild eyes flashed in the dimness, Talent's fists opening and closing as he struggled, his breath hissing between clenched teeth. Mary's soul cried for him. Then, with a sigh, he sank to the ground and rested his arms upon his knees. His head pressed into his forearms.

"I can't stand living in my own skin some days," he said, not moving. "The nightmares. I close my eyes and I'm staked to a wall...Shit, Chase." A violent shiver wracked his body.

"I thought"—she licked her lips—"I thought that Lena destroyed them."

A bitter snort rang out. "And then left me hanging there? Hardly. I was Lena's guest for all of one day. Her little minions took my blood, polite as you please, and went about their business. Then the Nex came."

His jaw worked as if he was trying to find the words. When they came, they were stilted and rough. "They played her, letting her think she was in control of her *pets*. And they...Well, they used me right thoroughly, didn't they?"

Quietly she sank down next to him, but she didn't touch him. She knew that sick, dark feeling. And when it came, the physical touch of another could make her snap. He said nothing more. He did not even move, but merely sat frozen.

"Are you the Bishop of Charing Cross?"

He flinched, and Mary pressed on. "The time for secrets has passed. If we are to remain partners, I need to know." It made perfect sense that an agent as skilled as Talent hadn't yet solved this case and that he wouldn't want her on it.

Talent's lips flattened, then he destroyed her last bit of hope. "Yes."

Mary sucked in a sharp breath. He heard it and angled his head toward the sound, but did not face her. "Or I was." Talent squeezed his fingers over his eyes. "In the beginning. But the shifters, I did not kill them. Nor have I harmed any innocents."

"Why did you do it?" Mary suspected, but she needed to hear it from him.

The sound of his harsh breathing filled the silence, and his shoulders trembled. "They were the ones, Mary. I cannot live knowing that they do."

Mary cursed those beings to hell for the torture.

He glared up at the arched ceiling high above. "I've lost myself," he whispered. "And don't know how to get it back."

"You are coming back." Her voice was cracked and too loud. Mary swallowed and spoke again. "You are not a mindless killer."

"But I want to be." The confession was soft. Talent ran his thumb along the claws that had formed on his hand. "If I'm mindless, then I won't remember."

They sat quiet for a long moment. Then he stirred, a small movement that brought their shoulders into contact. The hard muscles along his arm flexed, then eased.

Leaning against her, Talent rested his back against the railing and stared ahead. He took a long breath. "I hate that it was you who found me." His whisper was so raw that it scraped against her skin. "Hate that you saw me that way."

"I know," she whispered back. She hated it too, though not for his reasons.

Blinking rapidly, Mary leaned into him just a bit more, giving him her heat, shoring him up. Talent eased into the touch on a breath. "I see you and..." He pressed his lips together for one sharp moment. "I remember."

"Jack." Heartbroken, she let her head fall to his strong shoulder. Talent went stone-still then, and on a sigh, rested his head against hers.

For a long moment, they simply sat in the cold peace of the church.

"You came for me," he said on a sudden breath. "I thought I'd hang there forever. But you came. Even though..." His chest hitched. "I'd done nothing to deserve your rescue. I'd always been an utter ass to you." The hopeless bafflement in his voice pained her anew, as if he could not fathom the idea that she would help *him*.

Mary plucked at a fold on her skirt. "When I realized they had you"—she squeezed her eyes tight to fight the prickling heat of tears—"it was my fault."

"What?" He turned his head, but she refused to lift hers. She couldn't look at him. "A demon took my blood, disguised himself as me to get to you. I ought to have been more vigilant. I ought to have suspected."

His chest lifted and fell with a sigh. "Hell. I didn't realize you thought that way."

"How could I not?" Even now guilt crushed her chest.

"Because it's stupid."

Mary's head shot up, but his big hand gently eased it back down. "You might as well blame the inspector and Mrs. Lane for bringing us into that situation, if that's your thinking. We both understood the danger when we sailed with them."

She couldn't argue when he spoke so sensibly. Even if her soul still protested.

"Let it go, Merrily."

"Don't call me that." She said it more out of habit than annoyance, for his tone was not derogatory but affectionate.

A pregnant pause swelled between them, and then his soft voice closed the distance. "But that is how I think of you. Gliding over cool, still waters. A life of dreams and sweet merrymaking."

His words pierced her, breaking into her clockwork heart and setting it off rhythm. Beside her he tensed and awkwardly cleared his throat. "So," he said after a moment, "you helped me due to misguided guilt."

"No." Mary turned her head a fraction, just enough that her cheek touched the rough wool of his coat sleeve. Talent's scent surrounded her, what was once an irritant now grounding her in ways she didn't want to examine. "We might have been enemies, but you are not a bad man. I could never leave you to such a fate."

"Are we enemies still?" The quiet query held a mix of caution and hope.

A nerve twitched at the base of her throat. Were they enemies? They'd been at odds for so long. For reasons she didn't fully understand. Yet she could not keep away from him. Here they sat, curled into each other, and it felt... good. Her lids grew heavy, as if she could sink into sleep, sink into him. She wanted to be here with him more than anywhere else. "No."

He let go of a long breath, as if he'd been holding it. "You saved me, Mary. *You.*"

With dreamlike slowness she eased away and turned toward him. His head was bent, his expression a mixture of confusion and wariness, as if he thought she might leave. Their gazes met.

A visible ripple went through him. "Merrily."

Then she saw what he'd only given her a glimpse of before. Need. So stark and pure that the hard marble beneath her seemed to dip and sway. A surge of something fierce went through her body. The strong column of his throat worked on a swallow, and his words came out raw. "I didn't want to feel this."

That she knew precisely what "this" was made her

want to cry and to laugh at the same moment. "Neither did I."

He'd laid himself bare. She kept that knowledge close to her heart, and when she touched him, she did so gently, her fingertips skimming along his strong jaw. He held himself tight as new bed ropes, but his breath left in a small exhalation as her fingers slid into his soft hair to cradle his skull.

The wool of his coat whispered as he moved. His big hands cupped her cheeks as if she were blown sugar. Inches away, he stared at her, his gaze a living thing that thickened the air and sent heat and trepidation skittering along her needy flesh. His gaze lowered to her mouth. Such power in a look, the way it made her lips feel fuller, softer. And he responded, making a small sound as he came closer, his breath light and quick, his lids at half-mast. "Do you know what it's like to have what you want most in the world constantly in front of you," he whispered, "and never dare take it?"

Oh, yes, she knew. How well she knew that sweet ache. And she'd been a fool to ignore it. "If you never dare," she said, "how will you know you are truly alive?"

His mouth trembled, a flit of a smile. And then his expression grew intent. He would kiss her now. She wanted it so badly that she shook inside. And yet...

Mary tensed. Instantly Jack paused, his gaze flicking up to hers. The hot, languid air about them cooled and stilled as he pulled back. Mary wrapped a hand around his wrist, keeping him there. She took a shaking breath, the quivering feeling within her making her stomach ache. "I don't... That is, I've seen it done, of course. But I gather seeing and doing are altogether..." She winced, searching his face and wanting him to understand. "I don't know how to kiss."

He blinked once. His brows knitted. She knew what he was thinking: Impossible. Mary grimaced. Awareness of him washed over her, of the heat of his body and his strength. Of the fact that, until this moment, they'd never faced each other in complete honesty. Her voice came out too rough. "What need had I to kiss a man? Why, when I never wanted..." She trailed off, her face flaming.

The furrow deepened between Jack's eyes.

"I don't want to make hash of it," she said, so low she barely heard it herself.

Light came into his eyes. Again the air changed. His power surrounded her, not threatening, but hot and heavy, like a welcome cover against the cold. His thumb whispered over the trembling corner of her mouth, and the touch lit along her skin. When he spoke, his voice was a soft rumble tempered by tenderness.

"A kiss," he said, "is a conversation." Easing closer, he continued to speak as he caressed her cheeks with featherlight strokes of his thumbs. "A first kiss"—his lips neared hers—"is an introduction."

And then his mouth brushed against hers. The contact sparked, sharp and bright like lightning. Yet his lips were soft, unexpectedly so. Her breath caught the same instant his did.

Against her mouth he whispered, "That was hello."

His breath mingled with hers as he waited, his lips so close she could feel their warmth. For a moment she simply breathed him in, growing heady on the scent of him and the tight anticipation gathering in her belly. Then she understood. Nerves fluttering, she brushed her lips across his as he had done. Again his breath hitched as if he too felt that same spark, that hot need.

Her eyes drifted closed, and his voice poured over her

like warm cream. "This is 'I'm Jack.'" Another brush of his lips, but slower now, clinging at the last touch.

She liked that one better. The tightness within her spread down her thighs and up to her breasts. Mary tilted her head slightly as he had done and repeated his kiss, soft, slow. *I'm Mary.*

Over too soon.

From under lowered lashes, dark-green eyes gleamed at her, and the corners of Jack's wicked mouth curved in a slight smile. He held that look as he came back for her, holding her where he wanted. "This"—a gentle nip at her bottom lip—"is"—a nibble on her top lip—"'Pleased to make your acquaintance.'" Another soft nuzzle, his mouth moving along hers in a languorous glide.

So very lovely. Her breath grew sharp and pained. She wanted to fall against him, grind her lips into his, so violent was her need. She held herself in check and gently, slowly followed his lead. Jack made a sound against her mouth. She eased her grip and slid her hand to his neck. A tremor rent along the muscles there, his skin dry and hot. Beneath her touch his pulse raced.

His fingers threaded into her hair as he came at her again with the same steady deliberation, exploring her as she explored him. Their breathing grew unsteady and fast. Mary clung to him, her head growing light. One muscled arm wrapped around her waist, and he drew her across his thighs. Her breasts pressed against his chest, and she felt small, fragile, safe.

Jack's heavy pant mingled with hers as he rasped, "This is 'I want you.'" His kiss deepened. The warm, slick tip of his tongue glided along the edges of her lips, coaxing them open. Mary shivered. She'd never felt the like, as though his tongue touched more than her mouth, as though it licked at the tips of her breasts, down her spine, between her legs. Whimpering, she opened her mouth wider, her fingers clutching the hard swell of his shoulder.

He responded with a low groan, his tongue delving deeper, sliding and coaxing. And she ignited. Her chin bumped his in her greedy haste to kiss him. Mary twined her tongue with his, learning his taste, loving the way he trembled under her touch, and he surged against her, all desperation and heat. *I want you. How I want you.* He'd been her enemy, teased and taunted her, made her blind with rage. And he kissed her as if she were the only thing in existence. As if she *were* his existence. And it was perfect.

Her world tilted, and then she was sinking onto the cold, hard floor. His warm, dense chest pressed against her, and his hot, clever mouth fed upon hers. She was dizzy again, her whole body trembling, her breath too short. Her breasts ached, and her skin burned. She could do nothing more than hold on to him as her old world crumbled about her.

"Jack." She needed more.

His hand was at her hip, the other one under her head, holding her to him. The lines of his face were severe, almost harsh in the blue shadows. The look in his eyes was pained. "I want you." His lips shaped the words against her. "But I need you more."

Blind need had her clawing at his shoulders, holding him as if he'd pull away. Her hands grasped his short, shorn locks, then lost purchase as he kissed his way along her check, down to the tender juncture of her shoulder.

Something in him must have eased a bit, for he suddenly gentled. Soft lips pressed against her skin, scattering shivers down her spine. His breath gusted warm and humid into the well of her neck. "Slowly," he said as if speaking to himself. "I can go slowly."

He leaned against her, his fingers opening and closing on her hip as if he fought with the impulse to let her go. "You deserve slow care." Another shudder wracked him. "*We* deserve it."

Mary wound her arms about his back and held him. "Slow, fast, as long as it is with you, Jack." She'd never given proper voice to it, but the words were out, and she knew the truth. For better or worse, Jack Talent was the only man she'd ever wanted. And she feared that he was the only man she'd ever want again.

He lifted his head, his eyes dark and glittering. He studied her for a brief moment, and then he kissed her. It was no longer frantic, but something altogether different. Something *more*. The tender claim behind it was a kick to her heart, and some small part of her feared it would stop altogether if he were to leave her just then. But he didn't. He merely kissed her again. It was no introduction, this kiss. He was telling her something new, something she couldn't quite understand. But she felt it.

"It was always you, Mary," he said. "From the moment we met, it was you."

Chapter Twenty-Two

Kissing Mary Chase. Mary Chase beneath him, soft, fragrant, and pliant. In his arms. How had it happened? Jack's head reeled, and his thoughts scattered. It might have been a dream. But no. His dreams of her had never felt this good. Her taste was not light and sweet as he'd imagined, but dark and smoky, rich and complex. She was whisky and chocolate. Goddamn but he shook like a lad as he tucked her lithe body close and kissed her gorgeous, luscious mouth.

That she'd wanted his kiss, when she hadn't wanted any other, lit him with joy and lust until he scarcely functioned. She had no idea what it meant to him. For the truth was, he'd only kissed one other woman in his life, and she'd been paid by Ian to do it. Ian, who had declared that all men needed to be taught how to please women, and that a good tup would set him to rights. While Jack had enjoyed his lesson, it had never felt right, knowing that his partner had been bought and paid for. Then he'd met Mary. And he hadn't wanted any other.

Mary. She was his flavor, the only taste he wanted to indulge. His body was heavy and tender. Pleasure washed over him in a hot, rolling wave as he feasted on her mouth, slowly. So slowly that he ached. Sweat bloomed on his skin, making him shiver again. His fingertips glided along her fragile jaw as he licked her upper lip. He didn't allow his hands to explore lower. It would be over too soon that way. He'd fought this for so long. Now he planned to drown in her and enjoy every moment.

She made a little sound of contentment every time he slid his tongue into her warm mouth. And his cock throbbed in response. He lost track of time, forgot where he was, as they lay in a languid, heated cocoon of their own making, simply kissing, as if it were the only thing in the world. Even so, his fingers soon found their way to the clasp of her cloak. The grey wool slid open, revealing a lining of shimmering bronze silk. He smiled against her mouth.

"Why are you smiling?" A whisky voice to go with her whisky mouth. Like liquor, it went straight to his head.

"Because I am happy." Wholly, incandescently. He kissed her again, lingering. "Because you cannot resist this small luxury." He touched the cool silk. "You crave it."

Her wide eyes crinkled at the corners. "Just as you do."

Yes. Because they were more alike than either of them had known. And she cared. She'd come for him on that dark day, not out of guilt or duty but because she cared. Oftentimes he'd been tempted to ask what her motives had been, but base cowardliness had stayed his tongue. Now he knew. It felled him, made him want things he had no business wanting.

He burrowed against her neck, inhaling her fragrance. "This spot," he whispered against her skin. "I've dreamed of this spot. Of kissing it"—he kissed her there, and she shuddered—"of licking it"—his tongue slid over silken skin—"sucking…." His breath came on hard and fast, his grip upon her growing tighter.

Mary moaned, arching against him. He shivered, laving that heated spot. "God, I want to bite you here, Chase."

Her gentle laugh vibrated against his mouth. "Do you know, Jack Talent, I think I've wanted you to bite me there for some time." Her voice lowered to utter softness. "I think I've always wanted it."

Then she touched him, a small caress of his jaw as if he meant something to her, as if she could protect him with that simple hold. Jack lifted his head. Her eyes gleamed gold and bronze. Wide open.

His throat closed up, heat prickling behind his lids. A sharp blade of emotion scraped over his skin, down into his heart where it pierced deep. At that moment she owned him. She altered him, from blood to vein, to bone and sinew and flesh, reshaping what once had been into something new—hers. He was hers now. Irrevocably.

It did not terrify him as he'd long thought it would. It made him feel strong, larger and more infinite. He had a purpose now. And he had a home. Her. Always. Her.

He kissed her. Frantic. Deep. She knew the core of him, past all his blundering and foolishness. So bloody well. The feeling crescendoed. A perfect moment of clarity and peace. And then it crashed down around him, so painful and raw that he squeezed his eyes shut. Because she might own him, but he would never own her.

Gritting his teeth, he pulled back. His body protested, his arms moving too slowly, and his heart trying to pound free. "I can't." Just saying it cut into his throat. So he said it again. "I cannot do this to you."

*   *   *

At first Mary thought she'd misheard Jack. She was almost certain of it. Save he rolled away from her and sat up, bending his knees and putting his head in his hands.

"I am the one, Mary."

Instantly she went cold, her chest seizing. "You... you're killing the shifters?"

He wrenched around to look at her over his shoulder, his brows drawn. "What?" Confusion melted, but he appeared more pained, his eyes red beneath those scowling brows. "No. Not... Hell."

Jack stood and turned. She could only gape at his tall form looming over her. Strong. And glorious. He destroyed her concentration.

As if realizing this as well, Jack muttered a curse and stepped away, his movements graceful and lithe. He was beautiful. And he was distressed, all those lovely, dense muscles along his fine frame twitching as he moved.

Turning back to her, he stopped, his expression broken and helpless. He made a furtive gesture toward her but halted.

"Jack." She caught hold of her skirts and stood as well. "Tell me what pains you."

His chest lifted on a sigh. And then he turned to stone before her. Cold, distant Jack Talent was back. That more than anything else terrified her.

"Mary. The night you died. I was there."

"What? No." No, he wasn't one of the men who had hurt her. She remembered each leering face. They'd been older. Good God, had he shifted into another identity? He couldn't possibly have. She'd killed them all. She struggled to breathe.

"I killed you, Mary." His voice was deadwood. "I was driving the gin wagon."

Her scattered thoughts stopped. Jack's haunted eyes stared back at her. "Me, Will, and another named Nicky. We'd stolen the wagon from a London gang. We...we worked for the Nex, Mary."

She flinched. He'd worked for the Nex.

His mouth flattened. "I was driving the wagon, urging the horses faster. You ran out of nowhere."

Before her lay the gaping maw of the alleyway. Her feet slapped over the cobbles, wet and cold, as she raced for it, for safety. She'd lost a shoe. Cold air hit her skin. Lamplight blinded her. The clatter of horses. She bobbled, her ankle twisting. And then the wagon racing down the lane.

Oh, but Mary didn't want to remember that. Or what came moments later. A flash of wide, terrified eyes. A boy's. The big, brown length of a horse's snout. And then the hit. So hard she didn't feel a thing at first. Just a jumble of sounds. And then the pain. Bright and blinding. She'd hoped she would feel peace. It had been so far from that. There had been nothing but regret.

"I didn't stop," Jack said. "Not for a half block. Couldn't get the horses under control." He looked away, the tendons along his neck standing at attention. "Nicky said to keep going, but you were lying there." Jack ducked his head, and his lashes hid his eyes. "I knew what I'd done. I knew that if I left you there..." He bit his lip. "I was a liar, a thug. But I'd never killed a person."

"How old were you?" She was surprised at the calm in her voice. Inside she was numb.

Perhaps so was he. His eyes were dry, clear, and direct when he looked up. "Fourteen."

"And you—" She fisted her overskirt, her palms cold and clammy. "You recognized me? It was but an instant.

When, Jack? When did you realize I was the one you'd run over?"

She didn't want to know.

"Mary." He stopped and started again, resigned. "Lucien's barge."

She flinched, the blow striking her in the center of her breastbone. Slowly she gathered her cloak and wrapped it around her. Clutching it like a shield, she approached him. He stood perfectly still, his eyes on her face as she came to him.

"All this time." She stopped before him. "From the moment you recognized me"—for she could remember that moment too, the way he'd suddenly grown cold and distant—"I thought it was because of how Lucien and I were together." Her teeth clicked. "You made me think that," she ground out. "Made me feel like a whore."

His gaze was impassive, as if he were merely listening. As if he weren't even there.

She got closer, and her voice dropped. "When it was never that."

"Oh, I hated seeing him touch you." His retort was a soft whip. "Never doubt that."

So cold. So very Talent.

"But that isn't why you recoiled," she snapped. "No. All this time, all these years of strife. It was out of guilt! For killing me."

"Yes."

Her hand met his face with a ringing slap. He didn't flinch. But she did. He broke her heart.

"I would have forgiven you, Jack." She stepped away from him. "Isn't that ironic? I would have done it in an instant. You were a boy. A stupid, ignorant boy. And I ran into you, really." She laughed low and ugly before tossing a glare over her shoulder, back at his pale, implacable face. "What I cannot forgive is that you held your own guilt over me. For *years*. You made me feel as though I were in the wrong. Deliberately."

"Yes." Weaker now. A ghost of a whisper. Pitiless. Hollow.

"Good God, I was so very wrong about you," she said. "I thought you were redeemable, that there was hope for you."

"No, there was never any hope for me," he said. "Now you understand. There is only ugliness inside of me."

Though her insides were shaking, she drew herself up and pretended that he hadn't just run her over anew. "You don't even care who you hurt."

She got all the way to the stairs before he answered. "That is the only thing I do care about now. More than you'll ever know."

But it was too late. And he didn't try to stop her.

Chapter Twenty-Three

Holly's new laboratory was a frigid cellar with low, arched ceilings that seemed to press down upon her. Stone and grit scuffed beneath her boots whenever she took a step, and the cold permeated her bones. She shivered once again, drawing her heavy smock-coat closer, and the shackles around her wrists rattled. Holly ignored them. If she thought about how she was chained to the wall... She took a bracing breath. *Calm. Keep your wits, girl.*

That rotter Talent had at least thought to provide ample light, by way of hundreds of candles in the three thick iron rings that hung from the ceiling.

"Quite adequate for the fifteenth century," she muttered under her breath as she bent over the worktable and studied the infernal device she'd just created. Holly had never been accused of being ignorant. This electric prod that bastard had forced her to create, she knew exactly what the device would do to any GIM who felt the business end of the thing. And it made her ill.

Talent and Mary's dislike of each other was well

known. Regulators were taking bets as to who would do the other in first. All in good fun, of course. As much as people tended to stay clear of Talent and his foul moods, no one truly thought he'd harm Mary.

Holly's throat burned when she thought of him turning that weapon against Mary now. And Holly would be an accomplice. She wanted to scream, rage against the iron bars at the cellar door. Those iron bars clattered now, and she nearly jumped out of her skin.

The man she knew as Jack Talent walked in, only the moment he came closer, she realized it wasn't him at all. He had the look of Talent, true, similar eyes and build, but he'd shifted again, revealing a face pitted with decay. He wore no shirt, only rough trousers, and his torso was as ravaged as his face. The true horror, however, was the center of his chest, where, beneath the exposed bones of his sternum and ribs, a shriveled and blackened heart beat weakly.

A ringing sounded in Holly's ears, her head going both heavy and light.

"The lovely Miss Evernight," he said with an evil smile, making the pockets of puckered raw flesh ooze pus. "Hard at work, I see. Excellent."

The ringing grew louder, and her limbs numbed. "Who—who are you?"

"I am pleased you asked, my dear. You may call me Master."

Something dangled in his hand and dripped upon the floor. He moved, holding his hand up higher as if allowing her to get a better look. Holly was sorry when she did. Several clockwork hearts, still attached to arteries, dangled in his grip. Blood oozed from golden gears, and a drop landed on the ground with a splat. "I have another assignment for you."

*   *   *

Jack stood before the glossy black door to Mary's flat. The large stone of regret that lay in his chest seemed to grow, pushing against his ribs and making each breath he took a painful effort. For a long moment, he simply stared, noting the fine striations the painter's brush had left in the lacquer and the tiny rust spots at the edge of the brass NO.6 that hung on the door.

For years they had tried to make him beg, to plead for forgiveness. He could all but feel those long-ago grains of rice boring once more into his knees, and the shafts of agony driving through his flesh. Jack had never begged. Not even when they'd nearly killed him.

He swallowed hard, willing himself to move, to speak. This was different. This was necessary. He could do this. Because he had to. His hand shook only a little as he lifted it and knocked on the unforgiving iron-plated door. The sound echoed in the empty hall. Nothing stirred.

Blood rushed through his ears as he waited. But silence crushed down on his shoulders, and the stone within him grew heavier still. Jack cleared his throat, the sound over-loud to his senses.

"Mary." He cleared his throat again. "Mary, open the door."

Sweat bloomed over his skin as sharp pricks of sensation crawled down his neck. The memory of another door, the dark chasm of a hall at his back, threatened. His childish voice haunted him. *"Mama, please."* Rough hands grasped his upper arms, yanking him back. And the door receding as they tugged him away. *Don't you be bothering the mistress anymore, boy.*

Jack blinked, forcing his focus on Mary's door. "Mary." His fist slammed into the door, shaking it now. "Let me in. I made hash of it this morning. I should have explained." He could smell her. He smashed his fist against the thick iron.

The empty hall pressed in upon him, his blows on the door rattling and mocking. "I know you're there. I know . . ." Jack's chest heaved as he braced his forearms on the door. "I can hear you." Her heart ticked and whirred. So loudly it might have been right on the other side. "I can feel you, Mary." His throat worked painfully, his mouth too dry. "I've always felt you . . ." His breath came out in a hard pant, his forehead pressing into the hard surface. "I always have. From the first."

Still nothing. Only her scent and the feel of her vibrating around his soul. He traced a scar in the door as he spoke past the tightness in his throat. "I was a bastard. Worse than that. A despicable idiot. An ass." He ground his forehead into the door until it hurt. "Whatever you want to call me, I agree." His hands flattened on the cool lacquer. "I know I ought to slink away like the dog that I am. But I can't. I . . . shit." He ground his teeth and closed his eyes. It ought to be easy, saying the truth. It ought to be a balm to his soul. It wasn't. It hurt like hell. "I need you. I don't remotely deserve you but . . ."

He couldn't say any more. No matter how much he wanted to, his mouth didn't seem to obey. Wincing, he clenched his fists and tried again. "Mary. Please. Let me in. Let me protect you. Or provide some comfort. I know you are hurting. I can feel that too."

She did not come. Something black, and hot, and sick welled within him. He tasted blood. His breath seared his throat. "Goddamn it! Open the bloody door, Mary!" His fists slammed into it. Again and again. The blows echoed around him. "I am not leaving, do you hear? I'm not going!"

Two dents formed beneath his fists, and the thick iron creaked ominously. But still she did not come. Jack shoved off and paced, raking his fingers against his skull. His vision blurred, and on a curse, he slumped against the wall. "I don't know what to do to make it better," he said to no one in particular. God knew Mary didn't seem to be listening. "I don't know what to do, all right?" It was a shout now, directed to the implacable door. His Adam's apple bobbed as he looked up at the sooty hall lamp. "I've never known. I tried to stay away and make you hate me. Because it seemed better." A short, bitter laugh left him. "It's not. God, it's not."

He blinked down at his battered knuckles. "It's tearing me apart," he said quietly. "Every day, for four years, I've felt like half a man. Small. Unfinished." He sighed. "No, that's not right." His fingers curled, digging into his knees. "The night I left you on those wet cobbles, I lost my soul. I left it with you, tarnished thing that it is." His head was unbearably heavy, and he rested it against his forearms, drawing himself up tight. "Every time I looked at you, I knew it. That I had become what they accused me of being. Soulless."

He ought to go. She wasn't going to come out. Yet he had no place to go. He knew that now. There was no longer any place to hide from himself. Or the knowledge that she was his happiness, his purpose. She had cracked him open, rent him in two. And the exposure was an agony he could not live with.

"I don't know what to do." He wasn't sure if he actually spoke the words that clattered about in his head. His blood and uneven breathing roared in his ears, drowning everything else out. He didn't know how long he sat there, but a sense of emptiness eventually stole upon him, and he realized that she was no longer in her flat. She'd slipped out some other way, leaving him behind.

The tiny ticking of Director Wilde's pocket watch filled the silence. Mary sat with her back so straight she feared it might crack and stared at the rough surface of the meeting room wall. Someone, at some point in time, had covered the hewn stone with a thick layer of pale yellow paint. Combined with the lumpy texture of the wall, it called to mind bile.

Her hands rested, unnaturally heavy upon the folds of her drab wool skirt. She did not shake. She did not feel. It was better that way.

The chair beneath Wilde's frame creaked as he sat up. "Where the devil is Master Talent?" he burst out.

She swallowed once. "I do not know." Nor did she want to. The idea of facing him, hearing his voice, had her fingers going cold and her chest constricting. She was a coward, slipping out of her back exit, leaving Jack behind. His pain, so raw and exposed, had nearly destroyed her. But she hadn't been able to face him. He'd opened up an old wound, and his secrets had torn into ones that she'd kept too. Ones she did not want to speak.

"He's twenty minutes late," Wilde groused before pinning a hard stare on her. "Have you any progress to report, Mistress Chase?"

"No." Her pulse thrummed an insistent *tell him, tell him, tell him* against her throat. And what would she even say? *Jack Talent is the Bishop. He's a killer, and a liar, and it is all I can do not to rise from this chair and go to him*.

Cold sweat trickled down her spine as Wilde's eyes bored into her and his mouth turned down at the corners.

He broke their stare off with a *harrumph*. "You are a fount of information this morning, Mistress Chase."

A surge of irritation and discomfort had her back trembling, but she didn't cower.

Wilde's chair creaked as he leaned forward. "This case is charging downhill. I've been informed that Lord Darby has gone missing, which means yet another shifter may be dead."

"I—"

"The bodies of the regulators assigned to watch over him were found in the mews behind his home," he went on in heated fervor. "Mistress Evernight is still missing. The Archbishop of bloody Canterbury has sent a complaint to the Queen, stating that Jack Talent attacked him." At this he paused to expel a hard breath. "And I have to wonder … what the bloody hell is going on?"

Before Mary had the chance to reply, the door opened. Her entire body lurched within her skin. But it was merely Director James, who poked her head in and took a look around. The woman's thin face grew pinched, and her words came out clipped and cold. "A word, if you please, Wilde."

"I am conducting a meeting, James."

"I realize, and if it weren't urgent, I would not have interrupted." Her dark brows rose as if to add, "now would I?"

Wilde sighed. "My apologies." He glanced at Mary. "Give us a moment, Mistress Chase."

"Of course." On wooden limbs she rose and passed Director James, aware of the woman's cool eyes upon her.

"And if Master Talent decides to grace us with his presence," called Wilde as she left, "do let us know."

It would be the very first thing on her mind, Mary

thought bitterly. Once out in the dim stone corridor, she paused and released a sigh. "Bloody hell."

The end of the hall opened to the common rooms. The chatter of her coworkers echoed along the walls, a happy sound that somehow managed to depress her. Not wanting to meet another person, she moved toward the small alcove just ahead, where Wilde liked to make delinquent regulators wait before he served punishment.

She'd reached the alcove when a hand whipped out and grabbed her arm. In a blur she was against the wall, and then he was on her. For she knew it was he. His scent and the feel of his body was as familiar as instinct now. Jack. All around her. The warm press of his chest, the hard bracket of his arms on either side of her shoulders. Protest ended with his mouth fitting to hers. Not a kiss but a method of silencing. She pushed against his mouth with hers, trying to buck him off. He was a mountain of strength and will.

He sucked in a breath, and then tilted his head, adjusting the angle of his attack. Everything became soft, melting heat, his lips nuzzling, nipping, claiming, as if nothing else mattered but here and now. And she was defenseless against it, her mind spinning and her body humming. The rough tips of his fingers found the hinges of her jaw, and he coaxed open her mouth to let him in. Before she could protest, he swooped down, kissing her fiercely, not making a sound as he surged into her.

Mary shuddered. Unable to move, only to feel. They were too exposed. Laughter and conversation echoed against stone, the sound of footfalls that could be coming from any direction tightened her skin. Her fingers dug into the crisp lawn shirt on either side of his trim waist, and he grunted, a near-soundless exhalation of air. His grip upon her grew more secure.

They were chest to chest, Jack's heartbeat matching her own heart's mad rhythm. His hot breath mixed with hers as he drew away just enough to come at her again, plundering with soft, steady intent. And she took it, letting that slick, warm tongue invade and tangle with hers until her body grew fevered-hot and needy.

Someone beyond called out to a friend, the sound overly loud and plucking at her nerves. As if fearing her escape, Jack leaned farther into her, and the thick length of his cock bunted into the softness of her belly. Damn her black soul, she wanted to open her legs and guide him inside where he'd fill her emptiness. The very idea had her whimpering.

"Shh," he whispered into her mouth, his fingertips tracing down her neck, an eruption of shivers breaking out in his wake. "Shh. Just once more." He kissed her again, hot, silent, and deep. The wet glide of his tongue traced her upper lip, then licked inside her mouth. She shivered, her nipples hard and pained against her bodice. As if he felt it, he sighed into her. "Mary. You won't talk to me, and I can't think of any other way to show you."

Tears prickled behind her lids. How very much she wanted to tell him that it did not matter what he'd done. She wanted him. She would always want him. At the cost of her pride. Her movements were sluggish, her body protesting her will, but she turned aside, breaking his kiss. He did not move away. Nor did she have it in her to push him off.

They leaned into each other, her fingers still tangled in his shirt, and his lips brushing against her temple with every soft exhalation he took. Warm fingertips pressed into the sensitive skin of her neck, holding there as if to feel her pulse. His body shaking, he burrowed his nose into her hair, as though seeking comfort. "Tell me how to make amends."

Mary swallowed, her throat moving against his touch. "You—I cannot—"

"I should have honored you from the first moment we met. I know that now." His thumb caressed her neck, an awkward touch as though he fought against it. "Because I wanted to. So very badly. You are my world, even when I didn't want you to be."

His world? He'd turned her world into a dark fog. He pierced her heart and made that rusty device feel tender and soft. And sad. Unbearably so. "You have to let me go." She did not think she could stand another moment of his regret. Not now.

His fingers tensed, biting into her skin. "You might as well ask me to cut off a limb." His mouth touched her brow. "Honor, logic, whatever it is that good men have, is lost to me when I am with you. You're mine, and I am yours. You kissed me and everything changed."

Mary's skin flushed. "You kissed *me* and—"

"Only because you didn't know how." Tenderness colored his words and heated his breath. Of course he would make mention of that. His lips grazed her jaw. "You're an exceptionally quick study, however."

She would not smile. Nor would she yield. Mary turned her head. "I cannot ignore what you've done."

"And I cannot go back to pretending that you aren't my everything. I don't want to."

She pushed at his chest to no avail: he held her fast. She released a breath and spoke into the warm hollow at his throat. "But I don't want you."

His broad chest gave an abrupt jerk as if she'd thrust a

spike into him. Ye gods, she'd become so very proficient at lying.

"I deserved that," he muttered, still not letting go. "But I didn't expect it to hurt so much."

"This is merely lust talking," she said sharply. "Leave me be and it will die down."

A hard, bitter laugh escaped him. "Lust, is it?" He turned his head and pressed his lips against the crest of her cheek. "Mary Chase, I want to tup you. Hard and slow and all week long. I want to so badly that my cods ache and my heart hurts. But considering that I've felt the same way for going on four years and have managed to survive, I think it's bloody well safe to say this isn't about lust."

Just down the corridor, a door opened, and Wilde's voice drifted out. "Yes, Minerva, I understand perfectly. Did she say where Father was?"

Slowly Jack pulled back, and it felt as though he'd taken away her one support. Cold hit her chest, and she struggled to remain standing. His eyes met hers, and the devastation in his gaze slashed like a blade. She faced him head on, refusing to soften. She was not in the wrong. He'd done this to them. As if he heard her thoughts, his expression tightened, and his golden skin faded to pale cream.

Wilde's voice came again, so normal-sounding compared to the pain that rose between Mary and Jack. "No, I'll handle it," he said within his office. "Please let me know when he returns."

Jack glanced in that direction, then back to her.

"I can't forgive and forget, Jack," she whispered.

Dark shadows danced over his pained features. Without another word he turned from her and moved away at the blurring speed of a supernatural in his prime.

A moment later Wilde appeared, his frown concerned. "Was that Talent?"

She could only stare at the now-empty corridor, her body frozen.

Wilde shook his head as if annoyed, then cut to the chase. "There's been an incident."

"The Bishop?" she managed.

"I'm not certain." His gaze dimmed, going cold. "But I think you ought to see it."

Chapter Twenty-Four

———— ❧ ❧ ————

It took a great deal of effort for a supernatural to become foxed, but Jack was going to give it a proper go. Hunched over a table in the coffeehouse where he'd first dined with Mary, he wrapped his hands around a flagon of cheap whisky and took another great swallow. It burned going down and tasted like hell. But the pleasant numbing sensation that followed could not be argued with.

Oblivion was welcome. He'd tried to explain, and she had ignored it. Told her that she was his world. And she hadn't turned a hair. What else was he to do? A raw curse broke from him, and a few people turned their heads. Jack gave one fellow a good glare. But his attention was diverted as a young lady glided toward him. Her effortless walk reminded him of Mary's, though it was not as refined. No one eased through a space quite as well as Mary. The ethereal look of the woman, with her crystalline green eyes, announced her as a GIM before he even heard the telltale clicking of her heart. Jack vaguely recognized her as one of the new SOS recruits, though the style in which she wore her hair spoke of a generation five decades past. Odd, how some of the immortals held on to the fashions of their youth.

Her gaze settled over him with all the warmth of winter ice. "Master Talent." Disdain tainted her low voice. "Getting fuddled, are we?"

"Hitting the benzine, if you want to be precise about it." He took another fiery drink and ignored the chit. But she did not move on. With a sigh he slammed down his mug. "Mistress Tottie, I presume?"

She gave a little sniff of acknowledgement.

"Well," he prompted, "what do you want? As you can see, I'm busy."

"Lucien Stone requests your presence without delay."

"Does he? I'd best be running along then." Jack made no move to rise but picked at a nail. Fucking Stone. The day Jack answered his summons...

The GIM before him huffed. "Mistress Chase is already headed to him," she said.

Jack lurched up from the table, and Tottie sneered as if she had expected his reaction. "They are at our tavern." A quiver took hold of her mouth. Rage. He knew the emotion well. "I believe you know the place."

"I do."

Her nostrils flared, and accusation ran high in her eyes. Jack frowned. What was she about? It was then that he truly took note of her greying pallor and the tremor in her hands. Not just rage, but fear as well.

Jack stepped into her space and tried to ignore the increase in his heart rate, and the worry. "What the fuck happened?"

She lifted her chin. "Best you *run along* and find out, Talent." Then she turned and flounced away without a backward glance.

It took him too long to find the damn tavern. His memory of driving to the place the last time was faulty at best, and his current agitation was high. He growled low in his throat, his vision going hazy for a moment. When he finally reached the tavern, he wrenched open the door, and the hinges screeched in protest. One step over the threshold and he halted in shock. In his building temper, he hadn't scented death, which was saying a lot considering the overwhelming stench that slapped his senses now. Blood splattered the walls, and bodies lay strewn about like rag dolls dropped in mid-play.

Instantly Jack went on full alert. Almost as quickly he found her standing in the midst of the destruction, her glowing gaze focused on him. Despite the carnage, something deep inside him eased. She was well. And furious. Whether at him or the situation, he could not tell. Nor did he care. She was well.

They stared at each other in silence. Defiance ran through Jack's veins. She might no longer want him, but he wasn't going away. Oh, he'd keep his distance if that's what she needed. But he was still her partner, whether she liked it or not.

A slight movement at her side had him tensing. Lucien Stone glared back at him.

"What happened?" Jack snapped. His breathing was too fast: the mere thought of Mary walking into this death house made him want to break things. Not much left to break.

Lucien glanced at the carnage around him, and rage flared in his eyes before he dampened it. "Did you do this?

Jack's control broke. "The fuck I did!" He took a step in the GIM's direction. "Do not dare accuse me of this."

Lucien watched with cool detachment. That didn't

mean he was unaffected. The dandy's face was pale and drawn. "As I understand it, you were the only outsider who knew of its location."

"And every damned GIM in London."

One dark brow rose in cold contempt. "You think one of my kind did this to their own?"

"Worse things have happened."

"And Mercer." Lucien studied Jack carefully. "He knew. I believe he was your informant, Mary?"

Mary nodded shortly before turning her gaze back to the room, the corners of her eyes tight and pained.

"Mercer?" Jack's insides cooled even as his rage threatened to ignite once more.

Lucien gave a small, humorless smile. "I believe he accused you of being this Bishop of Charing Cross." He tossed a chin in the direction of a body. Mercer lay on the floor. Or what was left of him, which was not much.

Jack took a step closer to Mary, his flesh rippling. The urge to shift loomed high, wild, and hot. "You think I am capable of this?"

Her expression was smooth as porcelain, her eyes glowing, but then she blinked and her slim shoulders slumped. "Of course I don't."

Jack's brittle spine relaxed. He gave her a curt nod.

"Nor did I, particularly," said Lucien. "But one has to ask." He waved a tired hand around the bloody room. "Look at them," he said. "Tell us what you see."

Jack drew back and glanced around. Each victim's shirt was torn open, a cross burned into each one's flesh, and their hearts had been ripped from their bodies. The smell underlay the lingering scent of roasting meat that had burnt down on the doused grill. Leaving the mechanical Mistress Chase behind, he went to one of the bodies.

The poor bloke stared up at him in silent accusation, and Jack's stomach knotted. A gaping wound lay the man's throat open to the spine. Frowning, Jack bent closer.

"The spine isn't severed."

Stone arrived, and Jack stepped away to let him see. A moment later Mary stood by his side. It was all Jack could do not to grab her and haul her into his arms. Where she'd be safe. But she didn't pay him an ounce of attention. Her skirts rustled as she bent over the dead GIM and plucked a piece of paper that stuck out of his front coat pocket.

" 'They are dead, they shall not live; they are deceased, they shall not rise: therefore hast thou visited and destroyed them, and made all their memory to perish,' " she read aloud.

A slow shiver ran through Jack's body. Was it coincidence or bad timing that this had occurred after he'd given the fiend his blood? The bastard had known Mercer, and from the torture that had been inflicted on the demon, it was safe to say he might have divulged the location of this place.

"Well, the message is a bit more blunt this time," she said.

He turned abruptly to face her, and Mary's gaze was steady on him. "A Bible quote was found in the area where Holly Evernight disappeared."

"Why did you not tell me?"

Her lips pressed together for a moment. "It slipped my mind."

Jack snorted. "The demon we found at Pierce's house had a verse on him too." When Mary gave him a reproachful look, he smiled without humor. "Slipped my mind."

Before she could reply, Jack moved to another victim. Blood had sprayed from this one's wound, wild and deep

red. The old violinist. He'd clawed at the wood floor trying to escape. Saliva filled Jack's mouth, and he looked
away. "When did you find them?"

"Less than an hour past." Stone's celadon gaze moved
to the body of a woman, and his mouth tightened. "Someone will pay for this."

"One can hope." Plenty got away with murder and
more. Not bothering to see Stone's reaction, Jack went to
the old woman hunched by the stove. Burn marks marred
her forearms from her struggle with her attacker. Blackening blood pooled beneath her.

Jack straightened. "We have three human victims bled
out and a roomful of GIM, cause of death unknown."

"What do you mean?" Lucien asked.

"I mean"—he pointed at a body next to him—"their
throats were cut, and their hearts torn out. But it was done
after death. Look at them. They hardly bled in comparison to the others. And they didn't fight. They're lying
where they fell. Look at the humans, they fought."

Understanding slowly dawned on Lucien's face. Jack
wondered if, in the shock of finding so many of their
kind murdered, Mary and Lucien hadn't fully studied the
crime scene. Only thought to accuse. Again, the shivering
urge to go animal lit over his body.

"Do you honestly think one man could take on an
entire room of supernaturals and kill them all?" He
wanted to spit, it was so absurd.

"Somebody did," Stone murmured, his expression
thoughtful as he stroked a hand over a young woman's
head. The gesture struck Jack; Ian looked at his lads in the
same manner. These GIM were Lucien's responsibility.
Some of the anger went out of Jack.

"Without a massive fight on his hands?" Jack shook

his head slowly. "Something killed them before they even understood the danger."

Stone cursed as he looked at one young lad. "Took their hearts with him."

"The killer doused the fire," Lucien observed quietly as he looked at the black scorch marks that flared up two walls.

"Because he wanted us to see what he'd done," Jack said.

Almost idly, Stone ran a finger along the edge of a table, where one victim slumped back in his seat. Jack walked over to him. "He's taken some victims with him." Jack pointed to the table. "This has been set for two, yet one remains." A quick glance around confirmed more empty table settings. "Two, three, four," he counted, growing dread spreading through him as he did. "There were more people dining in here than there are victims."

Stone uttered a blue curse. "I do believe you are correct."

"Jack." Mary's call from the back of the tavern had him hurrying to her.

He stopped short. The body was crucified to the wall, much as he had been in those dark days. Naked and sagging against the iron spikes that held him fast was Anthony Goring, Archbishop of Canterbury. His throat had been cut, allowing blood to pour over his body in a grim wash of crimson.

"Bloody hell," Jack whispered, coming closer.

A strange pang knocked Jack's chest and made his breath hitch. He didn't understand it. For most of his life, Goring had been the source of his greatest fears, and his deepest anger. But now he felt something close to sorrow.

"Jack." Mary touched his arm, a hesitant gesture. "Are you all right?"

Was he? Jack studied his uncle's body. So thin. The grey skin wrinkled and sagged a bit. Looking up at his uncle's lifeless eyes now, he only saw frailty and a waste of life.

"Yes," he said, realizing that he meant it. The memories of this man no longer had the ability to hurt him. In truth, they hadn't had that power for quite some time. Jack no longer wanted revenge. He wanted peace. He wanted what he'd experienced in Mary's arms before he'd gone and mucked everything up. It was all he needed.

"This wasn't just a message to the GIM," Mary said by his side.

Turning with a grunt, Jack walked away from the body, and she followed. "He's playing with us," he said as he reached Stone once more.

Jack forced himself to look at Mary. It hurt to do it. Hell, being in the same room hurt. When he spoke to her, his voice was hard. "Whatever you feel about me, you aren't safe. No GIM is right now. Let me protect you."

Mary's lashes lowered, her creamy cheeks pale. "I shall take proper precautions."

Stone turned away as if to give them privacy, but not before Jack saw the satisfaction in his eyes. And Jack's teeth met with an audible click. God, but he wanted to rip the man's cods off and feed them to him. "With him?"

Mary's lithe frame moved in a flash, her palms smacking into the center of his chest with enough force to capture the whole of his attention. "Don't you dare!" she snapped, her eyes glowing pure gold. "Never again! Do you hear?" Her palms connected with his chest with another loud smack. "Never again will you sneer or imply something untoward between Lucien and me."

"Mary—"

Jack's outstretched hand was slapped away.

"Do not 'Mary' me." She brushed a lock of her hair back from her face as she advanced on him. "You seem to be suffering under a misunderstanding. My life is not your concern. If I go back to Lucien's barge and swive him senseless, it is none of your concern."

Jack wanted to howl. The muscles along his back burned, and he feared those strange leathery wings would soon break through. "Stop." It was more of a plea than anything. Fangs were growing in his mouth. Soon he would be smashing things. "Please."

All at once her expression turned somber and tired. "You say you wanted me from the first, that I was your world. Then where were you all these years?"

Right here. Watching you. Needing you. Dying a little more every day.

"When I needed a friend," she went on, "a kind word, a bit of support? It was Lucien who provided that. Where were you?"

Blood pooled in Jack's mouth, and he forced his fangs to recede. It took all he had not to look at Lucien, not to point his finger and shout the truth of her dear Lucien's culpability in this. That bloody blackmailing bastard might have spoken up, but he didn't.

Mary glared up at Jack, hurt and anger twisting her lovely features. And it twisted his heart. He couldn't do it. He would not hurt her further. If she believed Lucien was the only good and trustworthy man in her world, then he'd leave her that comfort. Even if it tore him apart.

When he did not answer, she made a soft, scoffing noise. "As I thought. You say you are sorry. But that isn't a cure-all." Her lip trembled. "Actions count too."

The ground beneath him seemed to sway. He held steady by will alone.

She took a deep breath, as if bracing herself. "It is finished, Jack. Just ... go."

Humiliating heat swept over him. Stone's presence, Mary's disappointment in him. The heat flared to pain. It was over, then. And he'd lost. "As you wish."

Jack sat in a darkened corner of the cathedral. A slow ache washed over him, as though he'd been in battle.

"I'd have thought this would be the last place you'd go to hide."

Jack nearly bolted out of his skin. In the dark calm of the cathedral, he ought to have heard anyone approach. Steeling himself, he turned toward the sound and found the same bastard who'd toppled the freight car on Mary. His hands fisted tight. "I ought to rip your head off where you stand."

The man laughed. "And yet you took what I offered. You went after Mercer."

Ugly memories slid through Jack. "I did not finish him."

"Weak."

Slowly Jack stood. "You are the one who came after me, begging."

A low snarl snapped through the darkness, and a set of red eyes gleamed. "You wish to play the game of begging?"

That was one thing Jack had never done. Not even when he had wanted to die with every breath he took. He wasn't about to start now.

The man's bootheels clicked against the marble as he took two steps closer. Again came the cold bunting of an unnatural fog. It drifted from the man's long, bulky cloak, seeping out from his sleeves and collar, billowing down around his legs. Jack had never seen the like. The faint scent of cold stone and rot rode on that fog, so like that of their surroundings that it wasn't any wonder Jack hadn't noticed his arrival.

"You could be free from this quest for vengeance, by ending it." He cocked his head, those cold, slightly off eyes gliding over Jack in a way that made his blood congeal within his veins. "You could have the world in your hands."

Silky words slid through the dark. "Join me."

Jack shook his head. He'd had the world in his hands. For one shining moment. And then he'd ruined it. "Not interested. I'm not playing that game. Not with you. I gave you blood. I won't give any more."

"Tell me, what did you think of my latest work?"

Jack lunged, lashing out. His claws scraped against unyielding stone. On the other side of the room now, the man danced back, laughing. His smile glittered with white fangs. Holding his gaze, the man lifted his arm, and his hand caught the light of the moon, the gun he held glinting. "Predictable, Jack."

Jack laughed. "A bloody gun? You think that will stop me?"

"Iron bullets are fairly painful, are they not?"

"They will hurt like the devil," he admitted. "And so will my claws going through your neck, for I won't stop until it's torn from your head."

The gun did not waver. "Have you not considered that I might have associates?"

Steps sounded, and two figures dressed in hooded cassocks appeared.

Regardless, Jack's arms twitched. Everything in him said to finish this, tear the bastard's head off. But he might fail, leaving Mary unprotected. Whatever the fiend was, he had speed and agility. His companions were not particularly large, nor could he see their faces, but when dealing with the supernatural, he could be up against unlimited power and not know until it was too late.

"I see reason has finally drifted into your thick skull." He grinned at Jack and suddenly, with a shimmer, he was Jack.

Fuck. Jack snarled, stepping forward. The man laughed. "Don't like that face much, do you?"

He stared at Jack with something akin to mad pride. A strange look that had Jack's blood running cold. "You don't even know how perfect you are," the bastard said. "I need more blood."

"No."

Jack's own face scowled back at him, but the man didn't say a word. And then understanding cleared Jack's mind. "You can't take it," he said in wonder. "You cannot take my blood without my permission."

Before Jack could question or protest, the man flew forward and smashed into him. The hit crushed the bones of his shoulder and cracked his ribs. Sharp pain exploded through Jack's body as he slumped down the wall. The power behind the hit was like nothing he'd ever felt. He hadn't time to defend himself before hands hauled him up and iron was punching into his chest.

Jack roared, his back bowing from the pain. Another stake slammed into his shoulder, pinning him against the limestone wall of the church. Maddened, he strained against the stakes holding him, not caring if it tore him in half. He would not be imprisoned again. A stake speared his gut. Jack retched, vomit and blood spilling over his front. Teeth chattering, he slumped. There was too much iron in him now, sapping his strength.

Dimly he heard a chuckle and forced his head up. A cold finger touched his face. "I might not be able to take your blood. But there are other things I can take from you," said the man. "Make no mistake." His face twisted into a frown. "But I rather think you'll want to hear what I have to say before you decide to deny me."

Before him, his tormentor shimmered again, and when he reformed, Jack convulsed against the iron spikes. His uncle, Anthony Goring, the Archbishop of Canterbury, reached out and gently stroked his cheek.

"Hello again, John Michael."

"You mad fuck—"

"That really ought to be 'Your Grace, you mad fuck,' " the man interrupted with a shrug. "However, since we're family, I'll allow it." He grinned again. Though he wore the face of Jack's uncle, open sores ravaged his face. His skin was sunken and rotting, giving off a putrid stink. "What? No kind words for your uncle?"

When Jack sneered, he laughed. "There's gratitude for you. I was under the impression that you hated your uncle. Now he is gone."

"Forgive me if don't believe that was your motive in killing him," Jack ground out.

"Ah, well, you are correct there. For it occurred to me that your uncle held a position of extreme power. It would be a waste not to use it." A gleam lit the bastard's eyes, and Jack strained against the iron. Not a chance in hell was he letting this madman assume the identity of the archbishop. His influence would be too great, for he would have the ear of the Queen, and the people.

"Bit stupid of you," Jack said past the pain in his gut, "to spill Goring's blood, demon. That glamour won't last for long without it."

"I don't need blood to shift, ignorant boy. Nor am I a demon. I'm something more." The man let his robes fall open. Blackening flesh hung on his bones. And in the center of his chest, a massive hole gaped, a raw and ugly wound. Beyond the bone, gristle, and muscle, a pathetic and shriveled heart barely pumped. "I am fallen. I am Amaros."

A fallen angel. Bloody perfect.

Amaros closed his robe. "I am decaying. But you are going to help me fix that."

"Don't see how." Jack gave a wry look down at his gut, where a thick shaft of iron stuck out of him. It was agony, but he was damned if he'd let that show. "I'm a bit hung up at the moment."

The sores along Amaros's neck gaped as he tilted his head and looked Jack over as though he were a piece of prime meat on a hook. "I'm rotting away. Unable to die, only to live in agony. For a millennium I've wasted away. And then I tasted you, Jack." Cold fingers raked Jack's cheek, and he flinched, much to Amaros's delight. "Slowly I began to heal. Imagine my happiness when I thought that the blood of a shifter could heal me. But it was only you. Your gloriously rich blood. It can heal me."

Through his pain Jack choked out a laugh. "Right. It's done a bang-up job."

A blow set Jack's teeth rattling and blood pooling in his mouth. With an exaggerated sigh, Amaros leaned against the spike in Jack's gut. Jack gnashed his teeth to hold in a scream. Amaros didn't miss the reaction, however, and sighed. "It doesn't have to be like this. We can help each other."

"Your idea of help," Jack ground out through shallow breaths, "is a little lacking, mate."

"But I have been helping. I was the one, you realize. Who took you."

The fact that this putrid thing had been his main tormentor made Jack's skin crawl.

"And yet when I might have tormented you further," Amaros went on, "I set you free from your captivity."

"Set me free?" Jack laughed. "I was saved, you deluded prat."

Slowly Amaros shook his head, as if Jack were daft. "I suppose it never occurred to you just why Mary Chase was able to waltz into that barge and rescue you? Without a fight? Without one guard left to watch over you?"

Jack swallowed against the thick lump in his throat. Bloody hell, but it made sense. "Why let me go?"

"Because your blood was weakened by the iron needed to hold you captive. I needed you to heal, to grow strong." He grinned his off-kilter grin again. "But then I discovered what you are."

"Oh?" Jack coughed, a loose and rattling sound deep within his chest. Christ, that spike hurt. "And what am I?"

"You are one of the Nephilim. The offspring of an angel and a human."

Jack stilled. "You're bamming me."

"I do not know what that means." Amaros's eyes gleamed darkly. "Have you not paused to wonder why it is that you sprout wings when roused?"

"I am a shifter." Jack knew he was being stubborn. Even so, he suddenly felt overset.

Amaros uttered an annoyed snort. "Shifters, angels, and Nephilim can change appearance at will and are weakened by iron. And Nephilim do not show their true selves until they reach full maturity, which, by the look of you, did not happen until this year."

Jack was twenty-six, but it was true, he had only just grown into his full strength. And he'd never sprouted wings until now. "I don't believe it," Jack said.

"Neither did I at first. Your kind is rare. Before you, one had not been born in two millennia." Amaros's expression turned earnest, save for the mad light in his eyes. "Shrouded in myth. Even for the supernaturals. Only the fallen truly know your kind."

"My kind." Jack sneered. "And you've decided to tell me this out of the goodness of your heart."

"No. To whet your appetite. I can give you something that you've always wanted. Your heritage. The name of your true family."

Jack's heartbeat thundered in his ears, but he remained silent.

"You think I don't see the hunger in your eyes?" Amaros whispered. "You, the lost boy that no one wanted. You want to know, want to belong somewhere. Even if you deny it with every breath."

There was a part of Jack that thirsted for what Amaros was offering. For too long he'd wandered, not belonging anywhere.

The fallen's gaze grew soft, inviting trust. "I gave you the names of your tormentors, did I not? Give me what I want, and I will give you that knowledge."

Jack looked into the fallen's eyes and saw an abyss. It would never end. The bargaining. The bartering of his pride.

That the fallen seemed to believe his offer would negate all that had been done to Jack caused a bone-deep rage to rise to the surface. He bit down hard on his battered lip, and blood filled his mouth with a metallic flavor. And though a small, cold part of him shouted not to do it,

Jack spit the blood into the fallen's face. "That's all you'll get from me."

It pebbled over Amaros's raw cheeks and dripped off the tip of his nose. Far from being annoyed, he closed his eyes and inhaled, his nostrils flaring. "Then we are at an impasse. Or perhaps not." Amaros's teeth flashed in a sick grin. "Mary Chase."

Jack did not let a single muscle on his face move. Amaros would make him pay for Mary. And it would hurt. Jack's heart thundered hard enough to feel in his throat. "You can't touch her, and I'll cut my own throat and bleed out before I let you get one drop." His chest heaved, the movement tearing his flesh, and warm blood trickled over his skin. An all-too-familiar sensation.

The fallen was silent, watching him with cool eyes. "You saw what I did to those GIM." He glanced at his cohorts. Jack had forgotten they were there. The two robed figures stepped closer. "It took only a moment to kill every last one of them."

Jack strained against the spikes, wanting to lash out, but they held fast and he sagged.

"Let him down," Amaros said.

Being pulled off the iron was as bad as being impaled. Jack slumped to the floor, his blood pumping out of him even as his flesh closed. Amaros stood over him. "Choose, John Michael. Your blood, or the safety of every GIM in London." The GIM, not only Mary but Daisy, and by extension everyone Jack loved.

With a swirl of his black cloak, Amaros turned to go. "Trafalgar Square. One hour. Otherwise I'll start with Mary Chase."

Chapter Twenty-Five

Dread. It had been his companion for years. Constancy did not diminish its power. No, it merely made it grow. How strange then, that on the eve of seeing all his fears come to fruition, dread had lost its power over him. Jack was numb—no, not numb—he merely ached so badly that it blocked all other feeling out and made his limbs thick and heavy.

Mary. Her name bloomed in his mind without his permission. And a thick twist of discomfort went through his chest. He'd never believed in love. Never allowed himself to truly feel it. Not for his family—though he cared for them with a protectiveness that was fierce. And to have someone to call his own? Someone who claimed him as hers? Never had he believed in that. Because if he couldn't love himself, how could he expect another to love him in return?

Ah, but the folly in trying to curb one's emotions. It couldn't be done. It was a joke, a lesson in futility. No matter how many mind games one played, emotion, need, *love* had an insidious way of seeping in. And while Jack did not know how to love, he knew with painful clarity how it felt to be in love. Agonizing.

He did not know what to do about that, but knew where he had to go.

The butler let Jack into the library and closed the door. Jack stopped at the threshold as the two men within turned in unison to look at him. What a sight they made, each man occupying a deep leather armchair set up before the cheery fire. The light set an orange-gold cast to everything, turning one set of eyes aqua blue and the other to pale ice. And sprawling upon the chest of the blond man, like a lumpy sack of potatoes, lay the youngest male in the room, his tuft of baby hair a lick of flame against his father's fine tweed coat, now covered in drool.

"Don't you two make the cozy couple," Jack murmured.

Ian Ranulf grinned, his canines gleaming bright. But his voice came out whisper-soft. "If you wake this child, Jack Talent, I shall have your hide."

Jack moved on quiet feet to claim a spot on the ottoman just between the two men. "I wouldn't dare," he said, keeping his voice low. "I've heard the little pisser screech too many times." Ellis Lane was as vocal, if not more so, as his mum and aunts. A right charming devil, he was.

Winston Lane let out a small sigh as his head rested against the high back of his chair. "I do not even remember what an entire night's sleep feels like anymore."

With infinite care Jack reached out and laid his fingers on the curve of Ellis's nappy-padded bum.

You want to know, want to belong somewhere.

Something inside him warmed and eased. Not enough, but it felt all right. "I take it Poppy is resting now?" Slowly he gave Ellis a tender stroke, all the while aware of Ian's attention and the hopefulness of it. Jack's iced-over heart gave a kick of regret.

"Mmm," agreed Lane. "I shall shortly join her, now that my little songbird here is truly sleeping." His keen gaze darted between Jack and Ian, who sat quiet in his chair. The awkward heaviness of the room increased significantly. "In fact," Lane said, standing in one graceful move, "I think I shall do so now." Holding a big hand against his child's small body, he glanced down at Jack. "Good to see you, Jack."

Lane left them, and though it was his house, he never questioned Jack's visit. As if he knew perfectly well that Jack wasn't here to see him.

Jack rested his arms upon his knees and stared at the dancing flames, Ian's silent presence like a heavy hand upon his back. He wanted to speak but found his voice had fled.

"How did you know I was here?" Ian's soft query cracked out like a whip between them.

Jack straightened. "Daisy said you and Lane like to play chess at this hour." The board lay in play just beside Jack. And it looked as if Ian was losing.

Noting the direction of Jack's gaze, Ian made a snort of annoyance. "It's a bloody nightmare in the making. The ignominy of it. I have to defend my honor. But I swear, young Ellis is giving the bastard tips. I think it might be in the form of baby babble code."

Jack's mouth twitched, but the dull, heavy ache returned. "I've made mistakes."

At his side Ian stirred, coming forward. "We all do."

"No. Not like this." Staring into the fire, he told Ian everything, of his ties with Will and the Nex, of trading blood for information, and of what he'd done to Mary. Just saying it was like regurgitating shredded glass.

Jack's confession ended in ringing silence. The fire snapped as a log broke, and then Ian sighed. "Fuck me." A soft curse for the damned. But no condemnation, no mention of his idiocy, just "I take it Miss Chase was rather—"

"As she ought to be," Jack finished dully. He stared down at his clenched fists. "Deep down I knew that if I treated her badly enough, I'd ruin any hope of her forgiveness. I pushed her away." Jack closed his eyes. Hell, he excelled at pushing people away. "It wasn't fear that she'd find out. I knew I didn't deserve her."

Ian snorted, a wry sound. "I've yet to meet a man head over heels in love who believes himself worthy of his lady."

Jack tried to smile but couldn't. "I deserved what I've got. And Chase has made it quite clear that she wants nothing more to do with me." His knuckles turned white. "At any rate, I'm not here for advice. I will fix what I can, however I can." The image of submitting to Amaros loomed to the fore, and it took a moment to master his voice. "I'm here because...I needed someone to talk to. And you are that person." Jack shut his mouth and blinked.

Ian cleared his throat, a brusque, sharp sound. "Well. Good." He cleared it again. "I am glad. That you did, I mean." He eyed Jack and then spoke just as gruffly. "You're a man now."

"And I wasn't before?" Jack quipped.

"No, you were a pup trying to snarl his way past fear. Now you know better. And I'm bloody proud of you, ye wee bugger."

Hell. Jack lurched up, his heart throbbing in his throat and his eyes far too hot. He made to go but halted and looked down at Ian, who sat frozen in his chair. Neither man looked directly at the other, each choosing some point in the vicinity of the other's chin or shoulder. Jack had been an ass. He'd known it. And Ian had never censured him, because he knew exactly why. Suddenly it wasn't humiliating. It was a gift.

Jack reached out and clamped a hand upon Ian's shoulder, an ungainly move but necessary. Then he bent down and placed a kiss upon the top of his head. *"Tha gaol agam ort, Athair." I love you, Father.*

Ian sucked in a sharp breath, and his hand whipped up to grasp Jack's wrist in a grip so tight Jack's bones bent. They both stayed like that, Jack's hand wound into the fabric of Ian's shirt, and Ian with a death grip on Jack's wrist. Then, as if by silent agreement, they both let go.

Jack turned and walked away, a bit lighter and a bit shaken.

"Jack."

He halted to find Ian standing in front of his chair, his eyes burning and bright. "I'm here for you," Ian said. "Always. You understand that?"

Jack's chest constricted, dull pain giving way to sharp. He might never see Ian again. Not like this. Not if fate played its current hand. It was his turn to clear his throat. "That's why I came."

A woman was in the parlor chair, sitting by the empty hearth and waiting. Mary sighted her the moment she entered her flat. In the next breath, she had her baton in hand.

"I heard that," said the woman, her voice crystal-clear in the darkness. "You needn't bother with weapons. I have no interest in hurting you."

Mary kept a light hold on her baton as she moved farther into the room. "All the same, I'll be leaving it in hand." Keeping her eyes on her guest, Mary lit the lamp by the door. Soft golden light illuminated the small space.

The woman blinked once at the sudden glow. She was beautiful, in a sharp sort of way: narrow face, cold amber eyes, black hair. Her dress was highly fashionable, an indigo taffeta trimmed with crimson piping. Pale, elegant hands rested calmly in her lap.

Just as Mary inspected her guest, she was treated to the same once-over. The woman's full lips curved in a satisfied smile. "You know, they said you were lovely. I do not think they did you justice. You have the face of an angel."

"And the temper of the devil," Mary warned lightly, as if her insides weren't still trembling.

A soft laugh. "Don't we all?"

Mary took a step closer. She let her senses expand, scanning for hidden threats while keeping her eyes on the woman. "Who are 'they'?"

"My associates." The woman inclined her head, a graceful nod toward the small settee before her. "Do sit down."

"How gracious of you to play hostess in my own home." Mary made her way over to the next lamp and turned it up. The corners of the woman's eyes crinkled.

"Sanguis?" Mary asked her. Sanguis demons were notorious for their dislike of bright light.

The woman's eyes narrowed further. "Clever girl."

"The girl grew up long ago." Mary stopped and regarded her visitor. "State your business." She needed this woman out of her home before she completely lost her composure. She'd told Jack they were finished. It had hurt to hurt him. *You might as well ask me to cut off a limb.* That was precisely what it felt like. When had he become an essential part of her?

The woman shifted forward, a deliberate and calm movement designed to invite trust, and Mary set herself back on guard.

"Since we know each other's intimate makeup," the woman said, "ought we not exchange names?" Pale lips curled again. "I am Miss Ada Moore."

Mary leaned a hip against the arm of her settee, just as deliberately stating that she did not trust Miss Moore an inch. "I shall assume you know my name, Miss Moore. Your business, please."

Moore rested her hands back in her lap, as proper as any governess. "I am here to make you an offer, and give a warning." Her tone was soft yet clipped. "I work for the Nex." She smiled a little. "I see by your expression that you have a decidedly prejudicial view of my organization."

Decidedly. Mary worked day and night to run them to ground. "You can't have expected otherwise." Against the folds of her skirts, Mary eased her grip on her weapon, getting more comfortable with it.

Cool amber eyes turned hard and pure black. "It would be a mistake to attack me, Miss Chase."

"And it would be a mistake to underestimate me."

"Understood. Sit. We can talk."

Mary remained standing. "What is your offer?"

"You have a traitor in your midst," she said. "Your amiable partner to be exact."

"Talent?" Mary's blood stilled. "I do not believe you." True, Jack had just admitted to seeking revenge on demons. He'd even admitted to belonging to the Nex when he was younger. But had he ever truly left? She thought of Poppy's concern, and rather feared it would be quite easy to accuse Jack Talent of the ultimate betrayal now. *Jack*. Another spear of pain went through her.

"Such loyalty." Moore snorted. "For a man who has been notoriously scornful of you?" Moore's head tilted, sending the small curls of her fringe slanting over her brow. "How interesting."

Mary forced herself not to react. "You have proof?"

A gleeful light glowed in Ada Moore's eyes. "That is a given. You do realize that he is the Bishop of Charing Cross."

"Yes."

It was almost amusing to witness the shock running over Moore's face.

"Well, that is enlightening," Moore murmured at last.

"If the Nex has known, why haven't you killed him?" The question coated her tongue with bitterness and turned her stomach, but she need to understand. "Why come to me now?"

"The situation is delicate. He is killing our agents, and he must be made accountable." Moore's expression grew pinched, and her hands clenched in her lap. "However, he is also under the protection of one of our top counselors. This counselor is not under Nex control. He does what he wants. And, at the moment, he wants Talent alive, regardless of our concerns. They are working together for their own selfish ends."

"And you cannot go over this man's head?" Mary asked incredulously.

Moore grimaced. "He is not one we want to upset."

"So you want me to take Talent out of the equation? And thus spare you the trouble of gaining this man's wrath?" Mary laughed. "Pardon me if I don't jump at the opportunity."

"We do not want you to kill him. We want you to talk him out of his present course of action."

Again Mary laughed. "Why on earth do you believe I would do such a thing? Or that he would even listen? He might just as well kill me for what I know, if you are telling the truth."

Moore smiled like the toad that had snared the fly. "Because you love him. Just as he loves you."

Love? Jack's taste was still in her mouth, his touch, his tender words, all of it was a ghost in Mary's head, haunting her. For one precious moment, Mary had begun to believe in love. Then Jack Talent had pulled the rug out from beneath her feet.

"Come now, Miss Chase, it is written all over your skin."

Mary focused on her present predicament. "You are grasping at straws. You have picked the wrong one. I have wanted to bring Talent down for four years. In fact, the way I feel about him right now, you'd do better asking me to kill him for you."

Moore shrugged. "Then you get to play the part of good little regulator and turn him in. Or kill him. It matters not to me."

"If Mr. Talent loves me as you say," and how it hurt to utter those words, "you could achieve the same result by simply threatening my life." Mary didn't want to give them ideas, but they had to have contemplated as much. She needed further information.

"That approach would only serve to exacerbate the situation," said Moore. "This is quite simple. You shall either agree and talk him out of it." Because if Mary was lying and she did love Jack, she would do anything to save him from ruin. And Moore's smug expression said as much. "Or," she continued, "you solve our problem for us. Regardless, we get what we want without any culpability."

There were threads here going far beyond Mary's ken. Her mind raced forward. "There is still the matter that you offer no proof of Mr. Talent's wrongdoing. You understand, I have no reason to trust your word."

Moore rose and swept her trailing skirts out of the way. "Come with me and you shall see your proof."

Chapter Twenty-Six

———— ✦~~✦ ————

Deep in the darkest part of the shadows, Mary stood. A light rain had begun an hour ago, only to turn into a downpour. Now, despite her thick black cloak, her skin was damp and cold. No matter. She did not move, but watched and waited. Concentrating on her breathing kept her still, and, every few minutes, lifting one and then the other foot just a fraction kept her circulation flowing and her muscles alert. She feared it would be a long wait this night. Sensible humans were tucked up in taverns, sitting out the rain by drinking and carousing. And because their prey was inside, the scum that fed on them were tucked up as well. Waiting.

It seemed everyone waited.

Water ran along her icy cheeks, beaded in her lashes, and clung to her lips. She did not move. He would not come. She knew it in her bones. It was only a matter of time and patience to prove Moore mistaken. Before her lay Trafalgar Square, abandoned save for a few industrious rats, picking away at refuse that was scattered about.

Residual light from the city cast an eerie blue-green glow along the glistening pavers and against wet brick buildings.

"Soon," whispered Moore at her side. "Soon he will come."

Mary quelled the urge to flee. She'd spied on Jack once before and had vowed never to do it again. Yet here she was. A twinge went through her body, and she almost turned away when she felt him. Not in a touch, but in the way the energy in the air shifted. Few would ever understand that the world was filled with frequencies of energy. Constant vibrations buffeted her spirit, and each being had a unique feel. Jack Talent's was now more familiar to her than any.

He approached from the east, his movements slow but steady. Darkness cloaked him, and she was too far away and too hidden to see his expression. Everything in her froze as he drew nearer. Would he sense her as she did him? Scent her? However he did not look left or right, but simply moved toward Nelson's Column.

Cold metal touched Mary's clenched fingers, and she flinched before she realized that Moore was trying to hand her something. A small pair of binoculars. Moore's voice was but a breath at her ear. "Watch."

Heart cranking so slowly that her veins hurt, Mary eased the binoculars to her eyes. Talent's face loomed large and clear. Pain and weariness lined his features. His once bright eyes were dead hollows.

Another figure moved out of the shadows and headed toward Talent. Talent's entire frame stiffened, his expression wiped clean. The man stopped too close, his body leaning in.

Mary's stomach clenched, her grip on the binoculars

bruising. No words were exchanged, the man merely waited, the whole of his attention on Talent. Talent hesitated, his shoulders lifting on a deep breath; then he pulled back his undone collar, exposing the tender column of his throat.

A dizzying wave of nausea hit Mary so hard that she swallowed convulsively. He wouldn't. He couldn't. He'd die before giving up his blood. But he stood still, his gaze burning into the other man. A low laugh rolled over the square, evil and smug all at once, and then the man leaned in, blocking Mary's view of Talent's face. But not enough for her to miss the way Talent's body seized, or how his head fell to the side, his fist clenched and bone-white against his black topcoat.

Or the way the man embraced him, pulling him closer. Like a lover.

The Nex had held him, used and stolen that which ought to be his right to give. Why would he give more? Because he would do anything to get revenge.

The pain in Mary's heart grew unbearable as she watched the men separate. The stranger staggered back, his eyes glassy with gluttonous satisfaction. Then he glanced down at his hands and grinned. Words were exchanged, the man's delivered with a satisfied smile and Jack's with an angry scowl. And then Jack walked away, his head bent as he lurched out of the square. Both men soon faded from sight. An icy wind swept over her a second later, so cutting it burned her eyes.

"Poor girl, how you shiver." A gentle hand stroked the back of her head and warm breasts pushed against Mary's arm. "And for a man so undeserving."

Moore's breath limned her skin, her taunt burning as she whispered into Mary's ear. "No better than a whore, really." A soft laugh left her. "Not that I can truly condemn our man for taking what is offered. Talent's blood is so very delicious." Cool lips brushed Mary's temple. "Hot from his flesh."

Tears gathered in Mary's eyes, distorting the shapes of the square. Later she would let them fall. But not now. "And did you take it?" She turned, and Moore's lips were so close to her that she breathed in each exhalation. Mary did not back away. "Fresh from his flesh?"

The woman's lashes lowered as she studied Mary's lips. "Oh, yes. Many times." Her mouth curled into a smile, and their bottom lips touched. "In many ways—"

Mary's move was swift. A strangled gurgle left Moore's lips as she jerked and lashed like a fish on a hook. Mary held her close, not letting her get away, clutching tight to the wooden stake she'd thrust under the woman's chin. Blood bubbled from Moore's mouth, hot splashes hitting Mary's face. She did not let go but stared into Moore's eyes as the light in them began to fade.

"It is too bad, really," Mary whispered against Moore's cheek, "that you will not be able to tell them how I shall do the same to anyone else who has touched him." And then she punched the stake straight through the woman's brain and let the body fall. Because Jack could not live in a world where they existed, and now, neither could she.

Chapter Twenty-Seven

~~~~~~~~~~~~~~~~~~~~~~

Mary was still shaking as she made her way across the square. The National Gallery held the closest secret entrance to SOS headquarters that her muddled brain could remember.

She'd killed. And though she'd do it again, her soul quaked from the recoil of that violent act.

The rain died, leaving only bitter cold and an icy road beneath her feet as the gallery building loomed over her. Mary trudged onward, barely feeling her limbs move. Vengeance. She understood it. She'd craved it once too. As for his? The image of him crucified to the wall of that hellish room, his blood running in crimson rivers down his body to be collected and used. His broken and bruised body. She been the one to hold him up, desperate to relieve the strain on those iron spikes they'd driven through his flesh. She'd been the one to see his eyes, haunted and agonized, when he'd roused, when he'd realized someone was there with him. In that moment she'd known what they'd done to him, for his eyes reflected the same fear and horror that she'd felt one dark summer night when her innocence was robbed.

Her blood curdled when she remembered what Jack Talent had endured.

A choked sound of defeat and dark humor tore from her breast. He'd die for her, but she would kill for him. For Jack Talent, a bloody bounder, rude, mercurial, amusing, loyal, and hers, whether she wanted him or not.

"You shouldn't have come here."

Mary gave a start as the very man she'd been thinking of appeared in front of her, as if materializing from the ether.

"Jack."

He stared down at her, his eyes as cold as the wind, and a shiver of trepidation ran down her spine. His words had finally sunk in. She'd been watching him. He knew. And he was not happy. None of that was responsible for the fear creeping over her skin. It was menace and hate frosting over his expression. She'd never seen hate in Jack's eyes. Nor heard it flat and lifeless in his voice.

"Jack, I realize this—"

His backhanded blow smashed into her cheek, and she tumbled to the ground, her knees slamming into the rough pavers. Her mouth worked soundlessly, bitter, thick blood welling up over her tongue and between her teeth. Black spots danced before her gaze, her gloved hands trembling as she tried to rise. He'd hit her. He'd hit her.

"Jack." It was a whisper between blood and despair.

Pain exploded through her as his booted foot connected with her stomach. Mary flew back. Her brain jostled within her skull when she landed. A sob broke from her. She needed to get up. He'd kill her. Yet she could hardly think past the unbearable hurt of his betrayal.

And then he was there, grabbing her roughly by the front of her bodice, his long fingers digging into the flesh of her breasts. He grinned then, a horrible version of his usual one. "Say good night, Miss Mary."

He held something in his hand, a baton or club. She could not get a good look. White-hot lightning tore through her, and her body bucked in agony. She screamed just before everything went black.

Think of nothing. Think of nothing. It did not work. Jack's body convulsed as he remembered the feel of Amaros's arms wrapped tighter around him, pulling him closer. God, God. But Jack no longer believed in God. Or anything. Not when Amaros's wet mouth had attached to his neck, sucking out great gulps of Jack's blood. Not when he had smelled the rot of Amaros's body and felt the bones along the man's flank and arm.

Above him the grey rain fell over his cold skin to blend with the tears that leaked out of his burning eyes. He wanted to die.

But he would not. Because she needed to live. *Mary.* Just thinking her name sent a balm through him. Her gentle smile, that reluctant gesture that needed to be coaxed out to play. And when he saw it, it felt as though he'd received a rare gift. The way she never backed down, not from him, not from anything. Steel and silk, glowing eyes and fragrant hair. Mary. Even if she was never to be his, she was worth the sacrifice.

Amaros's parting volley haunted him. "It was a pleasure, Jack. If ever you want another go, I'm more than happy to entertain you."

Jack's stomach pitched. *Mary. Think of Mary.* Amaros had what he wanted: Jack's blood had healed him. It was over now. But even as the square faded from sight, Jack knew it was never going to be over.

The thought had barely registered when a scream crackled through the night. He halted, his skin icing over. He didn't understand how—he'd never even heard her scream before—but he knew it was Mary.

Terror made him clumsy as he spun around and raced back. At the foot of the fountains Mary convulsed upon the ground, whips of lightning sparking over her as she flopped about. And the form of a man, holding her down.

"No!" Jack shouted.

The devil hovering over Mary lifted his head. Jack froze. The face that stared back at him was his own. A deep voice, smooth with a slight hitch to it, floated over to him. His own voice. Taunting. "Not very careful of you," Amaros said, "letting her follow. And who do you suppose she believed killed her?"

A roar ripped out of Jack, tearing at his throat with its intensity. "You promised to leave her alone."

"I lied." Amaros, now healed and strong on Jack's blood, took his true form and a pair of black feathered wings sprouted from his back. "Come and get me then."

Jack flew over the pavers, his feet pounding hard as Amaros simply waited. White teeth gleamed in a ghoulish grin that had Jack leaping the last few feet. He slammed into the fiend with everything he had.

The impact reverberated through his bones and rattled his skull. Both men smashed into the base of the fountain, and then Jack smashed his fist into that grinning face. Amaros laughed, blood running between his teeth, and then he attacked.

Blows rained down. White pain took hold of Jack. Blood blurred his vision. Jack's counterattack was just as vicious. The bones in his hand snapped from the force of his punches.

The devil got his foot under Jack and kicked him off. Jack flew back before landing on his feet. Claws extended as he snarled. He didn't know what he'd become, only that it equaled his rage. Muscles stretched and swelled, white fur erupted over his skin. The change healing him, giving him strength.

Amaros was changing too. His body morphed into a wolf. A *were*.

Jack glanced at Mary's prone form. She wasn't moving. Her heart wasn't pumping. Terror lit through him like a fuse. This needed to end now. Jack did not fully shift. Not yet. He charged as a man. Claws raked his side. Amaros grinned in victory. Bollocks to that. He grunted and then shifted in a burst of anger.

Amaros's eyes widened as Jack loomed over him in the form of a polar bear. Good enough for Jack. His roar echoed through the square. One swat of his massive paw had Amaros flying through the air and landing with a splash in the fountain. Jack followed, his bulk fine with the wet. His massive jaws clamped onto Amaros's neck, ready to shake the life from him. But he met with air. Growling, he swung his head, searching for his prey, but Amaros had become shadows and fog, escaping on the wind.

Jack took one lumbering step to follow, but halted. Mary. In an instant he was himself again, naked and scrambling out of the fountain.

She lay as pale as death, and so bloody still. He bit his trembling lips hard as his shaking hands traveled over her body. Nothing. Aside from the bruises on her face, there was no grievous injury, no massive blood loss. Cursing, he pressed an ear to her chest. Not a sound.

Water dripped from his hair and splattered onto her face. Viciously he tore at his skin, and when the blood welled, he pressed his gaping wrist against her mouth. She did not move. Whatever had been done to her, his blood could not fix it. She'd left him.

"Merrily." It was a sob. He sucked in a breath, touched her hair. No, he was not bloody losing her. He hauled her up and held on tight. He needed help. And there was only one man who could provide it.

Chapter Twenty-Eight

❦

Too long. Jack did not want to think about how much time had passed since Mary's heart had last pumped. Shit, piss, and fuck. How long could a GIM survive this way? Panic surged. His muscles burned from running and now from paddling the small skiff he'd nicked from an irate wharfman. Mary lolled about in the bottom of the little boat, unmoving, not breathing.

"Shit!" He plunged the oars in as fast as he could.

Lucien's barge loomed up before him.

"Oy!" he shouted toward it. "Stone! Get out here now."

The skiff slammed into the side of the barge just as Lucien's scowling face appeared over the rail. His expression swiftly changed to alarm. "Her heart isn't running," Lucien accused. "What the devil did you do to her?"

Jack didn't pause to explain, nor did he give a pig's shit when Lucien raised a brow at his nakedness as he threw Mary over his shoulder and hurried up the rickety rope ladder hanging on the side of the barge.

"Fix her." He practically threw Mary into Lucien's arms, making the GIM stagger. "Now!"

Lucien took off, Jack following on limbs that wobbled.

"How long?" Lucien barked, kicking open the door to his cabin.

Jack did not want to think of the time it had taken for him to run along the Victoria Embankment with Mary in his arms, nor the hellish race across the Thames.

"Too bloody long. Hell. Nearly half an hour." His vision blurred. Impossible to come back from that.

Lucien's lips pinched. "Christ."

Jack blinked hard as Lucien set Mary on a massive bed and began to tear at her clothes. The bodice ripped down the middle, and with it her underclothes and corset. Honey-tipped breasts bobbled at the rough movement. Jack sucked in a sharp breath. Countless times he'd imagined what she looked like beneath her clothes. He didn't want to find out this way. Something twisted inside him, fear, helplessness, and rage. He tamped it down and focused. Between those perfect breasts were interlocking teeth of gold that formed a sort of track the length of a handspan. The entrance to her clockwork heart.

Jack hated her vulnerability. Hated that Lucien looked upon her too.

But when the GIM began to feel along Mary's long neck and then her belly with thorough hands, Jack snarled. He grabbed Lucien's arm. "What the fuck do you think you're doing?"

Lucien wrenched free with surprising ease. "I don't have time for tantrums, shifter." He bared his teeth as he glared. "I need to find her key."

"Key? What bloody key?" Mary's torso was smooth, too pale, and showed no trace of wearing a key.

"To restart her heart. She's no longer under my command so I don't have it anymore." With that, Lucien went back to touching Mary, tracing the neat little half-moon that was her navel as he muttered. "It ought to be here. We all wear it close."

Jack gnashed his teeth at the sight of Stone touching her with impunity. The desire to throw him across the room made Jack's muscles quiver. But he could not. Mary needed the fucking GIM. Jack ran his hands through his shorn hair and locked his fingers behind his head to quell the temptation to strike.

Lucien paused for a moment, then laughed. His fingers went to the tawny peaks of her nipples, and Jack nearly howled. But the bastard stopped with a grin. "Cheeky girl," he said fondly to Mary before turning back to Jack. "Got it."

Jack stilled. "What? It's on her…" Heat coursed through his body as, with a gentle curl of his finger, the GIM lifted something from the tip of Mary's left nipple. A crystal key glinted in the lamplight. Hanging from a piercing. Like that, Jack's cock leapt to attention.

"Shit," he muttered, realizing that he was naked.

Lucien gave him a quick look and sneered. "Christ, man, get some clothes out of my bureau before I am ill."

Face burning, Jack did as bidden, keeping an eye on Stone while throwing on a too-small shirt and trousers.

More precious seconds were wasted as Lucien struggled to free the tiny key from the nearly invisible hoop that attached it to Mary's nipple. Once it was free, Lucien ran his fingertips along the golden path between Mary's breasts. He stopped at a small section and slipped the key into a tiny keyhole.

"You might not want to look," Lucien murmured.

Bollocks to that. Jack moved forward and grabbed Mary's hand. It was ice-cold and corpse-stiff.

Lucien turned the key. Immediately a series of clicks went off, sounding over-loud in the room. The golden tracks separated, parting Mary's flesh as well. Blood welled, and then an ivory length of bone appeared.

Jack had seen a number of things in his time. Had even helped Ian repair the inspector after Lane had fought the soul thief Isley. They had not prepared him for this sight. His head went light.

Mary's sternum creaked, and then, as if they were merely gates, her ribs began to open.

"Christ almighty." Jack swallowed hard. Through the blood and gore lay her heart, a miracle that appeared much like a human heart in shape, save it was made of gold. Thick valves attached to the arteries were of gold as well. A glass window dominated the center of the heart, showing the inside where cogs and gears sat unmoving. Just above the window was another keyhole. Lucien slid in Mary's crystal key and turned it counterclockwise. Blue-white light flashed from the key and traveled in cracking licks of electric current along the arteries surrounding her heart.

Slowly the cogs and gears began to move. A whirling tick-tock filled the silence. The most gorgeous sound in the world. The light increased, the currents zapping outward.

Mary's body jolted, her back bowing. Lucien moved to hold her shoulders down, but Jack was quicker. He grasped her as gently as he could but had to firm his grip as she writhed.

Lucien leaned on her hips, holding her in place as her ribs closed.

"The key," Jack protested.

Lucien's gaze remained on Mary. "Patience."

Before their eyes, her chest sealed shut. A deep breath lifted her breast, and then, with a shudder of her slight frame, the crystal key was expelled from the tiny slot in the golden teeth that held her chest closed.

Jack grabbed it, lest it fall, and Lucien quirked a brow. Jack ignored him and pocketed the key. Hell if he was letting Lucien touch Mary's breasts again. The bloom of health was spreading along Mary's skin. Jack's shoulders slumped, and he took what felt like his first real breath in over an hour. All he wanted to do was let his head fall to her breast and hold her tight. But she'd be waking soon.

Letting her go was hard. But he did, and with careful hands pulled the ragged edges of her chemise over her nakedness. "She'll believe that I did this," he said to Lucien.

Surprisingly, the GIM did not ask if it was true. Instead he studied Jack with those unnerving light-green eyes. "Then it's best if you stay." Lucien gave a pointed look to Jack's stance.

Jack hadn't realized it, but he was poised for flight, his arse already halfway off the bed. He plunked back down, and Lucien grinned outright. "That way she won't have to hunt you down before she tears you apart."

Jack sneered, but at that moment Mary's eyes snapped open. Her golden gaze focused on him in terror and rage. He opened his mouth to explain, but she lurched forward. Slim hands slapped against his chest. A jolt struck him hard, resounding though his flesh and bones before hooking onto his soul with such ferocity that he felt as though it'd be ripped to shreds. Then the world simply stopped.

Jack hit the floor with a hearty thud and lay there, prone. Mary did not know how long she'd been out, only that her body was sluggish and cold. And it was that bastard's fault. He'd hit her, hurt her. The memory of white light flashing before her gaze confused her. He'd done something more to her. With a growl she surged forward, wanting to finish him. His soul had been in her hands for one moment before the man sitting beside Mary had separated them. Struggling to move, she realized that the same man now held her back from leaping on Jack and delivering the killing blow.

"Hold, Mary. Hold!"

Lucien. She stopped, looking around with wild fear. Lucien's room. How?

His breath was on her cheek, the familiar scent of him calming yet confusing her more. Why was she here?

"He's down," Lucien said. "Now let him live, for pity's sake." There was laughter in his voice, and she wrenched free to glare at him.

She did not expect to see the quiet fear in Lucien's eyes. "He saved you." Lucien glanced at Jack on the floor. "Your heart had completely stopped. You would have died if he hadn't brought you here."

"He did this to me," she rasped. A draft shivered over her skin, and she looked down to see her breasts bared. Blushing, she yanked her torn chemise closed. Although Lucien wouldn't care; he'd never so much as bothered to look at her undressed.

Proving her point, Lucien kept his eyes on her face, studying in his unblinking way, plotting, most likely. "He said you'd believe that."

"How can I not?" she snapped. "He attacked me."

A rough, deep voice answered her. "It was not me."

Mary froze at the sound of Jack's voice coming from below. A groan rang from his broad chest as he heaved to sit. Rubbing his head and glaring at her in weariness, Jack continued to speak. "You pack a devil of a punch, angel."

Clutching her chemise tighter, she drew her legs under her, getting farther away from the edge of the bed, and from him. Logically, she could understand that if Jack had brought her to Lucien, he could not be the one who had hurt her. Viscerally, however, her body only remembered the utter betrayal of seeing him grin as he struck her. Jack eyed the movement and snorted. She expected one of his snide comments but he merely looked at her, his body so still that she wondered if she'd addled him with her attack.

With a sigh he leaned back on his hands as if too weak to do anything further. "He took on my appearance." Jack's dark brows met. "Likely to unnerve you, and hurt me."

His expression grew stark, and a tremor racked his frame. "I thought I'd lost..." With a scowl, his mouth snapped shut, and he leapt to his feet. Such a graceful move, and one that had her flinching, despite herself. The scowl grew when he saw her reaction. "What happened?"

Mary glanced at Lucien. "A moment, if you please."

"But of course, *chère*." He gave her a small bow. "See me before you leave, eh?"

Jack sniffed as if something foul had been shoved under his nose, and he eyed Lucien as the man made his way out. As soon as the door clicked shut, he turned his attention back to Mary.

Awkward silence choked the air between them. Mary crossed her arms over her breasts, and Jack's gaze stayed purposely away from her undressed state. An action that only served to emphasize it. Gathering her strength, she slowly stood, wobbling a bit as sensation rushed back into her legs.

He made an abortive move to help, but she held him off with a warning look. Jack snapped back into his guarded stance, his eyes wary as she made her way to Lucien's wardrobe and helped herself to a dressing gown. Aware that her familiarity with Lucien's room and his things only served to exacerbate the long-standing strain between her and Jack, she quickly tied the robe and assumed a professional manner.

"He looked just like you." Obvious, and it sounded too much like an accusation, but she was struggling to get past the horror that she'd felt when she'd thought Jack had hit her. Part of her wanted to go to him now and simply feel his skin, just to reassure herself. She didn't need to, though. His eyes, those lovely green eyes that shone like holly in the mellow glow of the room, were proof enough.

"Yes," he said.

She took a breath. "That is why he got to me. I wasn't expecting the attack."

"I am so sorry, Mary." His brow furrowed as he ran a tired hand along the back of his thick neck, and his shirt strained against his bicep. For the first time, Mary took in his odd attire, the too-tight shirt and too-short pants. Lucien's clothes. Her lips twitched. Following her gaze, he swore under his breath. "I shifted to fight the bastard," he said. "I'd have killed him if I could. For touching you."

"You've no reason to be sorry, you know. It wasn't you who attacked me." She could acknowledge the truth now that her head had cleared. His eyes had been wrong, his voice missing the essential ingredient that made him Jack.

He shrugged absently, as if he disagreed but would let it go, then glanced at her, his gaze sharp. "Why were you there?"

Mary nibbled on her bottom lip, considering.

"Chase." A warning.

"An agent from the Nex was in my house when I came home tonight."

He swallowed several times before sighing. He did not appear to find the notion threatening. If anything, he appeared resigned.

"If the SOS were to find out that you were Nex, you'd be banished, Jack." And his family would be devastated.

His fists curled and pressed into his narrow hips as he stared blindly at the corner of the room.

"Worse," she said, "is that you've declared war on the Nex, and they have taken up the gauntlet."

Jack's expression grew fierce, lit from within by anger and frustration. "Good. There are more of them out there. The ones who... Hell."

Any regrets she'd held about killing Moore fled. "You're giving that man your blood. Why?"

Pale now, he stood before her, unable or unwilling to move, or answer.

"What goes on between you?"

Jack ran a hand over his face. "Will Thorne is an agent for the Nex. As a favor to me, he supplied me with the names. But he could only go so far. That night at the railroads, the man we chased offered me the rest of the names in exchange for blood." Jack's cheeks went dull red, and he wouldn't meet her eyes. "I'm stuck in it now. I've been stuck since he gave me the name of another who'd..." His lips pressed together. "Mercer Dawn."

"Mercer?" Mary straightened. "Jack, his body was in that restaurant."

Jack grew still and watchful. "I didn't place it there. Hell, I wanted to kill Mercer," he said. "I almost did a few nights ago. Then I couldn't."

"Why not?" she asked quietly.

His dark eyes were haunted. "It was close, so bloody close," he whispered. "Then I thought of Ian, of Daisy, of how they call me their family. And I thought of…" He turned away. "How could I keep facing…everybody, knowing what I've done?"

For the first time in her life, she felt impossibly old. "Are you going to use those ill-gotten names now?"

He scrubbed his face again, but did not answer her.

"Why do you continue to give that man your blood?"

His Adam's apple bobbed on a swallow.

"Jack," she insisted when he would not look at her. "What hold does he have over you?"

He glared at her then. "I cannot stop this, Mary, so do not ask me to."

On a sigh, Mary pressed the tips of her fingers against her sore eyes. "The first thing I did after becoming a GIM was to hunt down each piece of filth who raped me." At Jack's harsh breath, she let her hand fall. "I gutted them. And each time, I returned home and threw up until there was nothing left inside of me. It was as if they raped me all over again." A hard, choked laugh left her. "You've thought me a cold fish, a heartless creature."

"No—"

"You were right. I am. I've spent a decade learning to feel nothing."

Jack's crestfallen face gave her pause, but she had to finish. "I looked the other way for you, and will keep on looking, because I *know*, Jack. I've been there too." He made to speak, and she lifted a hand. "Just as I know that if you keep this course, there will be nothing left inside of you either."

Haunted eyes of dark green searched her face, and

when he spoke, it was in a clear, quiet voice. "It's too late to stop that, angel."

"Jack." Her vision misted, and she blinked hard. "If you have any care for . . . well, for the people who love you, end your association with that man."

His mouth tilted, but it was far from a smile. "And who might those people be?"

She wanted to let what he'd done to her go, but the years of strife between them, the wasted years of petty insults that were all for nothing, swelled within her. And her jaw locked, refusing to open.

Which was clearly answer enough for Jack. "Right." Ducking his head, he strode across the room.

Mary's nerves leapt as he came near, but he merely walked past her.

"Where are you going?" Her voice was woebegone, and she cursed herself for a fool.

He halted at the door. His knuckles whitened as he clutched the doorframe, but he did not face her. "Home. You need rest."

"I do not. I am fine." Lie. Nothing felt fine. He'd turned her world on its ear.

He gave a half-laugh. "Well, then I need mine." His fingers spread over the glossy wood. "I—" He drew in a stiff breath, and it seemed as though he would go, but he hesitated. His eyes, when he turned to her, burned with emotion that left her oddly breathless. Jack's low voice rolled over her. "I'm glad you are well, Chase."

Chase. As if they had gone back to the beginning.

Chapter Twenty-Nine

———❦～❦———

This time, when Jack stormed into Will's lair, the bastard was ready for him. He had barely opened the door when a fist slammed into his face. Jack staggered back into the open doorframe.

Will grinned at him through a red haze. Grunting, Jack glanced at Will's fist. "You bloody fuck. Throwing punches with iron knuckles?" He launched forward, catching Will about the neck. They slammed down, splintering a wood chair on impact. Jack's fist smashed into Will's smug face. Twice.

Will merely laughed through the blood. Then he jabbed Jack in the gut. It sent a raw shard of agony straight down Jack's spine. With a snarl he grabbed Will's head and bashed his forehead into Will's thin nose. The bony protuberance crunched, metallic scented blood pouring out. Jack leapt back, distancing himself before he did the man further violence.

His chest sawed up and down, anger and the fight still coursing through him. Will lurched to a sitting position and yanked a handkerchief out of his pocket. A crack rang out as he reset his nose and then glared up at Jack. "Jesus, Jack, you're a pain in my arse."

"Rather thought you'd say *nose*." Jack was tempted to hit it again. Years of experience had taught him the nose was a man's true weak spot. And Will's aristocratic snout made an excellent target.

One shining black eye narrowed behind a hank of limp pale hair. "Rotter." Will hauled himself up and righted one of the remaining chairs before sitting in it, his long legs sprawled. Wiping the blood away, he smiled grimly. "I simply wanted to slow you down before *you* threw another knife at me."

"I never threw gold, nor Christ's-thorn," Jack pointed out bitterly. They were two materials that sanguis demons found intolerable, as they would burn through the demon's system and cause great pain, even death if used properly. Just as iron did to a shifter. Jack rubbed his jaw gingerly. "A low move, Will."

Will shrugged. "Never claimed to be a saint." He tossed the bloody linen on the table. "What is it now?"

"The Nex led Chase to my rendezvous point tonight. Have you sold me downriver, Thorne?" Jack took a step closer, the need to shift shimmering over his too-tight skin. "Because I assure you, it won't go well for you from here on out."

Will, unaware or uncaring of the danger, laughed lightly. " 'Downriver'? You sound like Lucien Stone."

That stopped him. Jack cocked his head and studied his old friend. "What do you know of Stone?"

Will slouched, looping an arm over the back of his chair. "Who doesn't know Stone? Do not let his little lazy effeminate charade fool you. He's infamous. A killer."

Icy eyes pinned him. "And you've always underestimated him. I do wonder what he thinks of you toying about with his former pet."

How little Will knew. Jack had never underestimated that conniving bastard. He'd never been allowed the luxury.

But Lucien had been correct in one thing. Jack was no good for Mary. He'd failed to protect her tonight, and had exposed her to Amaros.

Jack's teeth met with an audible click as he stared down at Will. "Why have the Nex involved Chase? What do you want with her?" Though he could guess. The thought was a cold ballast stone in his gut.

Will's cocksure demeanor vanished. "Jack, you should know, my superiors have not involved me in this. I believe they find our former connection to be a weakness." It hurt Will to admit, that was clear.

Crossing his arms in front of him, Jack stood firm and pretended that his heart weren't trying to pound out of his ribs. When would it end? This feeling of disgust? The need to tear free from his own flesh? Few things mattered to him anymore. But Mary did.

He looked at his old friend. "Will, I am asking. What the devil do you know?"

With an unsteady hand, Will raked back his long white hair. "Hell, I don't know much." He frowned up at Jack. "I do know that there's been rumblings about the threat of a high-up member going rogue. Whoever he is, he's got enough power to have the superiors very worried. And earlier this evening, one of our agents, Ada Moore, was found dead in Trafalgar Square. We thought it might have been you, but she was stabbed with a Christ's-thorn stake."

If Jack hadn't been well trained, he would have sagged against the wall.

"I've read Ada's file, Jack." Will's voice dropped. "Didn't realize that she was one of the ones who..."

Jesus. A strange, happy ache surged into something sharp and cutting, wonderful yet at the same time terrible. Mary had killed for him. He remembered the slight wince and darkness that had clouded Mary's eyes when she spoke of the Nex agent. Moore had been the agent who brought her to the square.

He cleared his throat, struggling to think of something to say, but all he wanted to do was return to Stone's barge and... he didn't know what he'd do. Jack did not deserve her. But he wanted to.

After dressing in one of her older gowns, Mary found Lucien in the dining room. Like a true pirate, Lucien liked to conduct business there while lording over his feasts. She suspected the man had been starved as a form of torture at one point, for he loved nothing better than to glut himself on food. Not that it would affect his form in the least. Perhaps that was why as well, she mused, as she found him sitting at the head of the table, his booted feet resting comfortably upon the arm of a neighboring chair. There was something quite decadent about being able to indulge as one wished without fear of consequences.

"I agree with Jack Talent's sentiments," Lucien said as she approached. "I am greatly pleased that you are still with us, my dear."

"I do not believe that was Mr. Talent's precise sentiment." She leaned over Lucien and gave his cheek a light peck. "However, I thank you." She straightened, and Lucien gave her hand a fond squeeze. He loved to touch, and since she knew she'd given him a scare, she allowed it.

"I think you underestimate Mr. Talent's depth of feeling," Lucien added.

So many offerings on the table. Rolls and loaves of bread, a platter of cold meats and cheeses, cakes and biscuits, a tureen of what appeared to be hominy grits— Lucien's favorite. Mary shuddered and moved on.

His voice went soft. "You can always come back. I do miss you, you know."

He'd been the one to offer her the choice, and they had been good friends for twelve years, confidants. Remembering it now brought a lump to her throat. "I miss you too." She smiled wryly. "Some of the time."

He scoffed. "Oh, well, flatter a man, will you?"

"That would be gilding the lily, Lucien." She grinned, then sobered. "I don't want to come back. Nor should I. I left for your sake as much as I did for mine."

"I don't know what you mean." He looked away, petulant to the last.

"You are one hundred and twenty years old—one hundred and fifty, if you count your first life—"

"Again with the flattery," he muttered.

She leveled him a look. "And yet you've hidden behind my skirts like a lad in short pants for a decade." Mary lowered her voice, coaxing now, because she knew it was a tender spot with him. "We do not live within society, Lucien. You might have a life, not a perfect one, granted. But—"

"Hidden and subversive nonetheless, eh?" he said with a humorless laugh. "That is not how I want to live, *mon amie.*"

Sadness and frustration crashed within her. Lucien

would never be able to live free and open. He desired men, not women. Even if the underworld did not condemn him, should any hint of improper relations reach human society, he could be imprisoned.

"Nor does it matter," he said quietly. "That part of me is better off dead." An old hurt Lucien never spoke of. He was silent for a moment, and she could almost see the cogs working in his mind. A rare contemplative look passed over his features, and, as though he'd reached a decision, he straightened his shoulders and looked up at her. "Your Mr. Talent believes we are lovers. He has for some time now."

A childish parry if ever Mary heard one. She glared at Lucien sidelong. But the bastard merely smiled. "He is not *my* Mr. Talent."

"Whatever you say, pet."

Pet. That's how he'd always thought of her. Despite missing his wry company, she was glad to be out from under Lucien's thumb.

Lucien grunted in apparent amusement over her pointed silence, but made no further comment on the sticky subject of Jack Talent. "Physically you are well, but are you happy, love?" He had been gracious about letting her go, but his tone implied that he second-guessed the move.

To her horror, tears welled in her eyes. She blinked them away, but the damage was done. He'd seen. "Mary?"

"I have not been happy for some time, Lucien." She forced a smile, though it hurt to do it. "Do you want to hear the strangest bit?"

"Yes," he whispered, his eyes searching her face as though he was seeing her anew.

"Until last night, I was closer to happy than I'd been in years." A little laugh broke from her.

Her old friend grimaced, his hand going to his chest to rub it absently. He was silent for a long moment before he sighed, a real one, not the dramatic bit of nonsense he used to convey his displeasure or boredom. Tired eyes stared back at Mary. "I know what he did, pet."

Slowly, Mary turned to fully face him. "How?"

"There isn't much I do not know about my own people, *chère*."

"Do not hedge with me, Lucien. Why are you telling me this now?"

To his credit he did not shy away from her. "That day on the barge when you first met Talent, I followed him and threatened to expose his prior involvement with the Nex to Ian if he didn't make certain to stay away from you."

Wind knocked from her soul, Mary slumped against the high back of a chair. "He never said."

"No. But it is the truth."

"Why?" she whispered.

"I was jealous."

"Pardon?" She hadn't heard him correctly. Surely.

Lucien visibly winced. "I saw the way you looked at each other. He wanted you." His green gaze turned soft, sad. "And you wanted him."

A hard lump filled Mary's throat, and she looked away. That day. She remembered it with knife-sharp clarity. And it hurt. "I thought..." She grimaced, not wanting to say the words. "He seemed different, sweet." A half-laugh broke from her. The very idea of Talent being sweet. "But I was wrong. Talent spent the good part of four years looking down his nose at me as if I were river scum."

"Because I walked in that room and deliberately made him think you were my plaything," Lucien said in a low, rasping voice. He wouldn't look at her now.

"Lucien..." She cleared her throat, but that only made it ache more. "I never resented acting the part of your lover." He'd given her a new life and protected her in so many ways that she had wanted to do the same for him. Lucien's machinations had never truly hurt her because they'd both known precisely what they were doing.

Frowning, Lucien shook his head. "It was one thing to play that part when we were working, but that was not why I did so then. And deep down you know it. Admit it, you resent me now because of it."

She did. Mary closed her eyes and tried to breathe. Oh, God, she did. She'd wanted to kill Lucien that day. And she'd wanted to kill Jack Talent for believing the worst of her every day since.

Lucien studied her face and sighed again. "Ah, *mon amour*, I did you such a wrong." His booted feet hit the floor with a thunk as he rested his arms upon the table. "I do not think I realized how great until just now."

He looked up at her, his jade eyes imploring. "I knew he would take you from me. And I would be alone. I ought to have let him, *chère*. You deserved happiness, something real. I'm so very sorry for that, Mary. I miscalculated. Badly."

Emotion welled up within Mary, and she quelled it with a vicious clench of her jaw. "You berate yourself too harshly. Did you give him instruction as to how he ought to treat me?"

"Well, no—"

"I did not think you did." Mary picked up a silver spoon, not knowing what she was doing, only that her hands shook. "And now he says that he needs me, doesn't want to let me go." She laughed. "Can you imagine?"

"Yes."

The spoon landed with a loud clang. "I confess, I am a novice to love, but I cannot believe one should feel this..." She punched her chest, where the deep ache would not go away. "This agony. Should one?"

"Ah, *mon amie*, you are asking the wrong man. The brief glimpse I've had of love was a vision of pure hell."

Mary winced, sorry that she'd broken open that tender subject. But she could not refrain from adding, "The only thing I know for certain is that, until I allowed him certain liberties, he was content to treat me with scorn." Until she said the words, she hadn't fully realized how much it burned her pride. And how angry she was at Jack.

Lucien looked as though he would argue, and Mary cut him off. "Please." It was a rasp, desperate and pained. She blinked hard, refusing to look at her old friend.

He was silent for a moment, then he leaned back in his seat, once more insolent and undemanding. "Very well. Tell me what happened tonight, *chère*."

Mary turned away, inspecting a lovely cornucopia of fruit spilling down the center of the table. "It was vicious, brutal." She swallowed hard. "He drew a weapon." Her nail edged a groove in the mahogany. "It appeared to be like a baton, with two spikes on the end. But when he touched me with it"—on a sigh, she faced Lucien again—"a bolt of pure electricity coursed through me, then I knew no more."

Lucien wiped a hand over his face. "Damnation." They both knew what electricity could do to their hearts. "So"—Lucien idly tapped one toe against the edge of the table—"we now know what killed those GIM."

Mary wandered over to the table and selected an apple before going to the window to peer out. "And then there is Talent, who is in danger of being driven over the edge by what has happened to him." Mary could confide that much, because Lucien knew. The blasted man knew everything, it seemed.

"As much as I dislike the prig," Lucien said quietly, "revenge is not always the loss of sanity, but sometimes its very balm. And if that is what all of this Bishop mess is about, then devil take the SOS and the Nex, leave it be and let the boy have at it."

She glanced down at the apple in her hand. "I killed tonight, Lucien."

The chair he sat upon creaked. "Tell me." The command was so soft that she almost did not hear it.

Her nail broke through the bright red apple skin with a little pop. "A Nex agent. She was one of them. Who hurt him." Mary blinked rapidly. "I know what you're thinking."

"What am I thinking, *chère*?"

That I've fallen for him. Her eyes burned but no tears came. "That I was foolish to risk so much for a man such as he. I cannot explain it well, only that I know he's damaged, but he is not destroyed. You see revenge as a balm." Mary shook her head, still looking at the apple. "It is a toxin. He has a family who loves him. Should he fall, they will be destroyed too." She took a deep, shuddering breath. "What is one more kill to me? I am already dead inside."

"No, Mary." Lucien lurched forward. "You are not dead. And you are loved too. *I* love you." He stabbed a thumb at his chest as he glared at her.

Of course he did. Lucien had never hidden the fact. But the love of a friend, while comforting, was not enough anymore. It did not soothe the restless discomfort that pushed against her chest or quell the loneliness that seemed to grow within her each passing day.

Her smile was wobbly. "I love you too. At any rate, I merely meant that avenging the crime against Talent hurts me less than it hurts him. Moreover, it felt good to do this thing for him."

That had been the strangest part. For the past two years, Mary had believed that the SOS would fill the dark void that held residence within her chest. And while it helped, she hadn't felt as strong and as right as when she'd plunged the stake into Ada Moore. What did that make her?

Her voice was subdued when she spoke again. "But now I find myself wondering if I should quit the SOS. I am a regulator, Lucien. It is my duty to uphold the very rules I broke."

Lucien's mouth twisted. "Rules rarely take into account the stickiness of life."

"You always were a nonconformist," she said weakly. Instinct and logic warred within. Right now logic was screaming that she was a fool and to end this madness and let Jack Talent dig his own grave.

They fell into quiet. Outside, the weather slowly rolled in, and below, the Thames dulled to pewter. Mary took a deep bite of the apple, relishing the way her teeth sank into the flesh and the crisp snap of the fruit giving way. Tart-sweet flavor filled her mouth as she crunched.

From behind her came Lucien's snort of disgust. "That is one thing I shall not miss."

She turned to find him pinched-faced and glaring at the apple in her hand.

"Lord above, woman, the way you go at those things. You're worse than a cow with her cud." He waved a lazy hand toward the silver cutting knife resting by the fruit platter. "Has it never occurred to you to cut your fruit like a civilized person?"

She almost laughed but took the pleasure out on the apple. He winced at her exaggerated bite. And she smiled, her mouth full of fruit. "If the way I eat apples bothers you so greatly," she said around the apple, which made Lucien sneer, "then why provide me with them all of these years?" It had been the one gift from him that she'd truly valued above all others, for it spoke to her pleasure rather than his vanity.

Lucien sighed. "My dear girl, it was all I could do not to ban them from the household." His brilliant eyes twinkled with wry amusement. "Do you honestly believe I'd provide you with the means for your disgusting habit? I thought you placed the order for those things."

The apple stuck in her throat, aching and burning as she forced it down with a hard swallow. It took her a moment to speak, but when she did, her voice came out rough yet weak. "You did not send gifts to my rooms? Leave fruits at my doorstep?" The week she moved out of his barge, she had received her first basket. They'd kept coming, once a week without fail. Mary had taken it as a sign of Lucien's approval of her final step to living her own life.

A stillness settled over the room. Lucien tilted his head slightly as he studied her. Contemplation made his voice smooth and low. "No."

The half-eaten apple grew heavy in her hand. "Nor figs in winter? Strawberries in the spring? Or plums and cherries in the summer?"

A small smile crept over his mouth. "No, no, and no."

Mary blinked at him, unable to say a word more. A strange bitter flavor coated her tongue. Years, she'd received those gifts of fruit. She thought of the other small gifts, the ones that upon reflection did not fit with Lucien's grand gestures. The thick mackintosh overcoat the year it rained incessantly, the fine set of steel quill nibs that showed up when she broke one of hers, a flagon of spiced wine on Christmas day. For years, at least four...

Dizzy, she leaned against the wall, her arm pressing against the cool window. "But..."

Lucien's voice held a hint of teasing as he softly sang, "Somebody has an admirer." He leaned farther back in his chair and laced his hands over his stomach. "Now who could it be?" His toe tapped faster now. "Oh, surely not that angry shifter who nearly tore my head off when I went searching for your key?" He tutted, but his eyes held Mary's. "After all, he has hated you for all these years."

The apple fell from Mary's fingers and hit the floor with a juicy thwack. Whatever else Lucien said fell on deaf ears as she stalked out of the room.

Chapter Thirty

⟡⟡⟡

If the light glowing in his bedroom window was any indication, Jack was still awake. Which was preferable, for despite her turmoil, Mary hadn't the heart to creep up on him while he slept. Jack was proud, but had not stopped the staff at Ranulf House from gossiping about his vocal nightmares. In hindsight, that more than anything was the likely reason for his decampment to a home of his own.

In cowardly fashion she hovered by the gatepost, silently cursing her unmoving feet. Everything would change if she went into his house. She knew it on a visceral level. What she did not know was if she wanted the change. Nor if she'd be welcome, after the way she'd tossed his declarations back in his face.

"Only one way to know, you ninny." Taking a deep breath, Mary let herself in through the back door and made her way up the stairs. Darkness steeped the house in tones of blue and black, and the only sound came from the hall clock ticking and the countermeasure of her heart clicking. She did not attempt to be quiet, nor did she stomp about with her displeasure. He'd scent her coming at any rate, probably had been aware of her a block out. Even so, her breath was stilted, and her heart whirred faster as she carefully mounted each riser.

A sliver of golden light marked his door. No movement from beyond it. Only stillness and Jack Talent waiting. Even though she yearned to, she did not pause at the threshold but boldly put her hand on the doorknob and opened it.

Most people read in a chair. Not so for Jack. No, he sat, tucked up in the middle of his pasha's bed, saffron silk pillows piled behind his head, a blue velvet duvet over his lap. Clearly he read there often, for a small table and reading lamp were set up just next to the bed. Lamplight cast his skin in honey gold.

That glorious torso of his was once more unveiled. Lovely, sculpted, built for strength and endurance. Her body tightened, and her lungs seized. It had been one thing to see him when she thought him unaware. It was quite another to face him in the flesh. And he was looking at her, as if he too knew the significance.

Her lips parted, but no sound came. It was not resentment that darkened his eyes, but a hint of fearful resignation, as though he waited for the ax to fall. Yet beneath it all, something simmered like yearning, only stronger. It was that need, so carefully tamped down and controlled, and so much like hers, that tugged at her soul. She couldn't think. Couldn't do anything more than take a step farther into the room.

Talent's body went perceptibly harder, his muscles bunching, yet his hands remained still upon the book in his lap. Her hands, however, shook as she lifted the apple from her pocket and presented it.

"I brought you a gift." Her voice was a stranger's, breathless and quick.

He did not look at the apple. His attention was riveted on her. Oh, but his guilt was evident in the small tic at the side of his expressive mouth. The silence between them stretched. It took everything she had within her not to move closer to him. He compelled her, made her want to... she didn't quite know, only that she feared the feeling and craved it in equal measure.

"Why?" she asked, when he did not speak.

His throat moved on an audible swallow. "I wanted... Lucien never took proper care of your needs. Neither did you. Somebody had to." It appeared he would say no more, but then his words came, awkward and rough. "And you said you craved apples."

Her ears rang. One flippant remark, a small desire of hers, and he'd taken it to heart. Somehow she ended up at the side of the bed. Up close his skin appeared velvety smooth. Dark brown hairs gathered just below his navel and trailed down his tight belly, and a pale swath of bare hip, peeking out from the duvet, caught her attention before she looked away.

His pulse beat visibly against the little hollow at his throat. A silver chain dangled about his neck, glinting in the light. She'd never seen it before.

"Why?" she asked again.

"To make up for what might have been." His hand lifted as if he'd touch hers, but then it dropped, his fingers curling in the cover. "In a different world, I might have tried to make you mine from the first." His thick whisper lanced her clockwork heart and had her breath quickening as he continued. "In a different world, I might have deserved you."

Then he moved. The warmth of his fingers made her flesh jump, but she did not pull away as his forest-green eyes burned into hers. "I might have met you that long-ago day in Lucien's parlor, and instead of running away"—the rough pad of his thumb brushed over her knuckles—"I might have told you how utterly and completely you captivated me."

Her knees gave out, and she sank to the bed, her thigh brushing against his. They were face-to-face, close enough that she might touch him. That he might touch her. Neither of them moved. But the connection of their linked hands held her in place.

Her voice, when she found it, shook. "You merely had to show your true self to me, and I might have been captivated too."

A sad smile tipped his lips. Slowly, as if giving her every chance to move away, his hand lifted. Warm fingertips brushed her cheek, and her lids fluttered under the sensation. "Ah, Merrily, you assume this is my true self?" He traced down her jaw and lingered at her throat where her skin was the most sensitive. A tentative touch, as if he wasn't certain how he'd be received. "Even now I hide from you."

She leaned in, allowing herself the small pleasure of touching him, just on the corded length of his forearm. It turned to steel beneath her palm, and she applied firmer pressure, reveling in the illicit contact. "Then show me, Jack. Show me who you are."

A challenge. He never could resist one. Even now his lips firmed, and his blunt chin lifted a touch. His fingers wrapped around her throat, not hurting, simply holding her. He studied her. A large part of her rallied to hide from him, don a mask of indifference as she'd always done. She ignored it and let him see her. And his eyes widened a touch, his lips parting.

Her voice broke the silence. "Show me who you are, Jack."

He squeezed his eyes shut, as if cursing himself. The air about him shimmered, his form blurring. It happened in a blink, and then he reformed.

Mary's breath hitched. He was still Jack. Save for the scars. The cross caught her attention first. No bigger than the span of her hand, the nearly faded mark was a white ghost against the gentle rise of his left pectoral muscle.

"My uncle did that one," Jack said. "To remind me of my profane nature. Hurt like the devil."

His lips curled on a wry smile but Mary could not return it. She thought of all the demons similarly branded, and of a young boy being cruelly tortured. Something of her thoughts must have played on her face, for his mouth turned down and his voice lowered. "They..." He cleared his throat. "They had a particular fascination with that scar. Some of them took to calling me their acolyte." Jack's mouth snapped shut with a click of his teeth, his high cheeks going ruddy. "I wanted there to be no doubt who was coming for them."

Slowly she nodded, her throat thick and her eyes burning. The cross was not his only scar. Her gaze wandered over them. Not simple scars, but cruel marks blackened and carved into his flesh. Thick swirls and symbols. Demon signs. She remembered them, dripping with blood as he hung on the iron spikes.

"They rubbed ash and iron dust into them." Jack's voice was dispassionate, dull now. "Makes it permanent."

Mary's throat closed. Bastards. Jack did not move as

she reached out to touch one, but she stilled at the last moment. "But the marks are different."

"What?" It was a shocked whisper.

She met his eyes. "I remember them. Each one." She would never forget. And the symbols were not the same.

A smothered sound left him. "Found a demon scribe. He changed the symbols. Carved new ones from the old." His jaw clenched. "I'll not be bound by those bastards."

"No." She touched him then, resting her hand against his chest where his heart thudded beneath. His skin was warm and smooth, the scars not raised but more like a tattoo.

A small furrow worked between his brows as he searched her face. She remained silent, not knowing what to say, or what he needed. When he spoke, his deep voice ended their stalemate. "I don't like to see them."

Mary's chest squeezed. He thought she needed an explanation for why he hid them. She pressed her hand more securely to his firm chest. But Jack didn't appear to notice. His scowl grew. "I don't want to remember." He looked at her as though he believed she'd find him lacking for such a confession.

"Does it tax you to hide them?" she asked softly.

"It's as easy as breathing."

"Then don't stop. Hide them now if it eases you." She couldn't see him hurting.

He blinked, and beneath her hand, his chest rose on a slow breath. "No. I want you to see me." A small shiver ran over his skin. He leaned toward her, the bedclothes rustling as he moved. "I want you to know all of me."

And because she understood him with perfect clarity in that moment, she let her gaze move over him, learning every imperfection. His face was slightly different too. A bump along the bridge of his nose, a thick scar bisecting his left brow and another faint one on his stubborn chin. He noticed her inspection of him. "Poker to the head, age eleven. Blow to the jaw, age twelve. A few beatings in between." His lashes swept down. "I did not heal as well when I was younger."

She cupped his face. Immediately he closed his eyes and leaned into her touch, his whole body relaxing on a sigh. It spoke of trust. And she realized that he'd already given his to her. She had yet to do the same. Her fingers pressed into his skin. "Jack, I have something to tell you." Because he should know all of her too.

His eyes opened, brilliant green and beautiful. "You can tell me anything, Merrily. You ought to know that by now."

She was here. Jack could hardly believe it, but he wasn't letting go. Fuck pride. Fuck staying away. He wasn't going to leave her anymore. He'd stay by her side, or die trying.

"Talk to me, love."

She licked her lips, a quick dart of her pink tongue. "You did not end my mortal life."

He frowned. "As much as I hate to belabor the point, I'm afraid I did."

"No. I…" Her hand slid from his cheek. "I ran in front of the wagon. I wanted to die."

The very thought of her trying to kill herself—He cupped the back of her neck with both hands, holding her steady, holding himself steady. "What?"

"I ought to have told you. Only I was ashamed. I *am* ashamed. Do you understand? Adam doesn't grant life to those who toss theirs away." She paled. "But he didn't know. I never offered the truth. I took that secret and burrowed it deep into the darkest pit of my soul. Until your confession."

"Mary—"

"If a GIM were to find out what I'd done, I'd be banished. I wanted to tell you, but after the way you treated me, I was afraid to trust." She searched his face. "The worst of it is that, had you known, all these years of miscommunication, of you feeling soulless, might never have been."

Her eyes glowed like polished topaz and filled with tears. His hand shook so violently that when he wiped at the tear trickling down her cheek, he only succeeded in smearing it about with his thumb.

"Don't cry," he whispered. Anything but that. "Not over my feelings. I'm not worth it."

She caught him by the wrist, staying his clumsy efforts. The simple feel of her fingers on his skin gave him the strength to move. Jack pressed his forehead against hers and just breathed, taking in the scent of her, that warm, sweet fragrance that felt of home and hope.

"I don't want to live without you," he said, cracking, pleading. He did not care. "That is my truth."

Her slim fingers curled about his forearms. "You hurt me, Jack." She was close enough that he heard her swallow. "For so long."

"I'm sorry." Pathetically small and useless words.

Soft breath caressed his face. "So I tried to hurt you in return. But it only made my pain deepen. I suspect it was the same for you."

She did not know the half of it. But he shook his head slightly. Words burned as they worked their way out. "Your pain is mine." His fingers tightened on her. "Infinitely."

You deserve better than me. You deserve someone who can make you happy.

"That's where you went terribly wrong," Mary said softly. "You make me happy."

He hadn't known he'd spoken aloud. Jack stared at her, not knowing what to say. So he kissed her. Not hard. Not frantically. But in the way he'd always wanted to: as if she were his. Mary opened to him, her warm tongue sliding into his mouth.

Together they fell back onto the bed. He slid between her open legs, rocking his stiff cock against the barrier of skirts and sheet, gritting his teeth when pleasure and want punched through him with the force of a freighter.

A little sigh escaped her, and her fingers drifted down his face, along his throat, raising the tiny hairs upon his skin as they went. She stilled as she reached the chain about his neck. Her finger hooked it and lifted. It had taken him a few moments to figure out that the key turned invisible to the eye when worn against the skin. Only by pulling it away could one see it.

A smile played about her lips. "My key."

The chain was too short for him to see the key now, but he could almost feel it dangling just above his skin. "I wanted to keep it safe for you."

Her legs twined farther around his as she gazed up at him. "That you did." The color deepened upon her cheeks, and she licked her kiss-plumped lips. He watched, his cock twitching, his pulse picking back up. Her voice grew almost shy, save for the huskiness underneath it all. "Will you put it back on me?"

Jack swallowed. Hard. Beyond the roaring of his ears and the tightness of his skin, he felt the chain around his neck loosen and slither free, and then she was holding her key. An offering.

Everything grew silent, save the sound of their breathing

and the thundering of his heart. His focus narrowed to the rise and fall of her chest and the row of toggles fronting her regulator's tunic. It was a simple linen one, the sort they wore when practicing combat. The natural shape of her beneath the cloth made it clear she was not constrained by a corset. Anticipation made his words thick. "Were you expecting a fight?"

A small smile tilted her lips. "Perhaps." Her gaze grew dark. "Or perhaps I did not favor too many impediments during our *discussion*."

His breath caught. "Practical girl." It was said lightly, but the knowledge she'd given made him shake, every bit of him, save his fingers. They were steady and determined as he pulled each toggle tight, then released it with a tiny click. With each button set free, his blood grew hotter. Her eyes followed his progress, and her sweet lips parted, drawing in short gasps of air.

The tips of her fingers, so lightly holding his biceps as he worked, seared his skin. At last her tunic was spread open, revealing the tissue-thin ivory chemise beneath. Gently he touched the smooth skin just below her collarbones, and her breath hitched, that fine skin prickling with gooseflesh. His breathing grew labored, his mouth dry, as he worked the little pearl buttons free, and when he finished with the last one, he opened his prize.

He'd seen her before. But not like this. Not when she was arching her back ever so slightly, lifting her luscious breasts up like an offering. Not when he could touch her.

So he did. Light and careful, as he ran a finger along the edge of the golden teeth guarding her heart. "Does it hurt?" he whispered. He needed to know that first.

"No." A tiny tremor lit over her skin. "It feels... wonderful."

He stroked the other edge, gently, smiling as he did it. He hadn't expected to smile with her. Not this way. Happiness bloomed warm and tender beneath his ribs. His fingers drifted down, tracing under one breast. They were small breasts, firm yet delicate like the rest of her. The honeyed caps of her nipples pointed upward, just begging a man to suck.

Well then. Jack swooped down and drew a silken tip in deep. Mary cried out, her lithe body bowing into him. He smiled around her sweet nipple, then caught the hard hoop of her piercing with the tip of his tongue and worried it.

"Jack!" She grabbed his shoulders. Her nails biting into his flesh were a sharp pleasure.

Slowly he pulled back, holding on to his prize as he went, until the tip was freed, glistening in the light, and the little crystal hoop stood at attention. "I had to prepare it." Unable to help himself, he gave the stiff nipple a flick with the end of his tongue before looking up at her flushed face. "Give me your key."

Lightly panting and hand shaking, she handed him the key. His fingers were too large and clumsy for the task, fumbling with the effort to remain calm as he unhooked the hoop and slid the tiny key into place. By the time he finished, they were both trembling, a sheen of sweat covering their skins.

Resting a hand upon her stomach, Jack smiled down at his handiwork. "That has got to be the most erotic sight I've ever beheld." Idly he touched the small key, moving it back and forth and loving the way she instantly writhed against his finger, as if seeking more.

"Sensitive, are you?" God, but she made him burn. Before she could answer, he leaned in and kissed her nipple. And again, because once was not enough. And she whimpered beneath him, her arms closing ranks around his neck, holding him there. Jack closed his eyes, shuddering as he gave in to the heady sensation of simply letting go with her. Heat washed over him as he suckled her. His teeth clicked against the key, and he bit down and gave it a tug.

"Sweet God, that feels so..." Mary groaned, her fingers grasping the short ends of his hair. He tugged it again, twisting a bit. And she jerked, a moan tearing from her. "Don't stop, Jack."

Palming her other breast, he gave her what they both wanted, tormenting her with his mouth as his fingers plucked at her other nipple. Lust drew him in circles, making him dizzy.

"I *can't* stop touching you." He kissed his way back up her body, finding that tender spot on her neck as his hands roamed over satin-smooth skin. "I don't want to."

She roamed too, finding sensitive patches and secret hollows of pleasure along his body. Kissing a line across his cheeks, along his jaw. Her hips lifted, pressing against his. An invitation. Jack pulled back, his chest working against hers.

"Let me see all of you, Mary. I want to. So badly." Instinct shouted that he take, plunder. But enough had been taken from both of them. Her tremulous smile and small nod were his reward. He undid the ties of her skirts, fighting impatience, and then slid them down her slim hips. His mouth went dry. She was everything he'd ever wanted, and things he'd never even known he needed.

Gently curved, slender limbs rose up to meet a dark-gold triangle of curls and a small glimpse of sly pink. Her buttery skin prickled, a light shiver working over her. Uncertainty creased the corners of her wide eyes and tightened her mouth. Jack couldn't bear that.

The first touch of his hand upon the soft skin of her thigh nearly undid him. Slowly he caressed her, and his skin tingled as if he were the one being caressed. "Ah, Merrily," he whispered. "I've no words. Not the proper ones to do your loveliness justice."

"Nor I for you, Jack Talent." Her hand eased over his arm, a light, heady touch that drove him insane. Her lips curled. "I suppose we shall have to muddle through."

But she deserved words. She deserved to know that she was cherished. His hand glided to the subtle swell of her hip. "Show yourself to me, love." His voice was as rough as splintered wood.

Her pale thighs trembled as she spread them. Her sex, glistening coral pink, was plump with desire. For him. Mary Chase wanted him. She was waiting for him, her gaze not shy but hot and impatient.

He prolonged the moment, taking his time to reach out for her. And when he ran a finger down her slick center, she bucked, a little helpless gurgle filling her throat. But she opened her legs wider, canting her hips. For him.

He found himself panting, his body quaking with lust. "God, just to be able to touch you." Slowly he circled her sex, watching her writhe. "Do you know what that does to me?" He pushed a finger into her tight quim, and her lips parted on a wordless cry. Jack eased out and plunged in again, his throat closing, making his words raw. "Have you any idea?"

Mary licked her lips, her sweet breasts heaving as she struggled. "I've a good guess."

She snuggled close, pressing her side against his, so much smaller than him, and yet the difference somehow made *him* feel fragile. Her fingers trailed over his chest, pausing at his nipple to circle it. He groaned but she drifted further down, to his aching cock, that somehow was still half hidden beneath the rumpled sheet, all but his head. That was peeking out, begging, really, for attention. Her lids lowered in somnolent perusal as her voice darkened. "Let me touch you, and we shall compare."

The linen slithered over him, caressing before the cool air hit. It only inflamed his ardor.

"Glorious." Her warm hand ran over his flesh, and he sighed.

Tentative and exploratory at first, her touch soon grew more assured. And then it turned almost reverent, as though she loved the feel of him as much as he loved the feel of her touch. Resting his forehead against hers, he simply breathed her in and caressed her sex, keeping time with her strokes. Their breath mingled and steamed.

"Do you know how long I've wanted you here?" he said against her open lips. "How many times I've pictured you in my bed?"

Her lashes fluttered down, her mouth soft and exploring, making his head spin. "I wanted it to be me. When you were pleasuring yourself. I wanted to be the one touching you."

"I wanted it to be you too," he rasped. "So much so it hurt." God, had it hurt.

One slim hand held on to his shoulder, the other hand stroking, pulling. He was silent, his eyes closed, just feeling. Feeling her hand love his flesh, explore it with bolder touches. Stroking.

Hands stroking. Always so gentle at first. Coercing, teasing. Cold sliced through him, twisting his guts. No, not now. Not *here*. And still he shuddered sickly, his mouth watering with nausea. His hands left her, found the sheet, and gripped tight. *No. Not with her.*

She knew, had to have felt his panic, for she stopped, her hand sliding to his hip. Hell, he hated the relief that coursed through him when she let go.

"Jack?"

He took a shaking breath and faced her. Concern was there, and understanding. He could not stand seeing himself reflected in her gold gaze.

The steady warmth of her palm at his hip seeped into his bones as she spoke. "I don't have to touch you."

"I want you to touch me." His voice broke, weak and pathetic thing that he was. He sucked in another breath. "I need you to touch me. It's...I closed my eyes and—" Hell. He didn't want to say it.

But she knew. Of course she knew. She saw far too much of him. "Look at me, Jack."

He could never refuse her.

She was beautiful. She'd always been lovely, but affection and tenderness transformed her into the most beautiful woman he'd ever see. Their gazes locked as her hand wrapped once more around him, giving him a little squeeze. Blood rushed back to his cock. It swelled and filled her hand as if it belonged there.

She stroked him, a long, assured glide. He grunted, his balls drawing up tight and his body going hot. Her eyes watched him. "Feels good?"

"Yes. God, yes." His breath fractured.

Another stroke, down, then up, her thumb gliding over his swollen head. He grunted, arching into the touch.

She kept at it, steady, deliberate. "Look at what I'm doing to you, Jack."

The sight of her slim, elegant hand wrapped around him, her skin so pale against his ruddy flesh, had him shivering, swelling harder.

"This is us, Jack," she said as she worked him. "You and I, this is what we create."

A choked, broken sound left him, and he burrowed his head in the crook of her neck. "Mary. Mary." His arms wrapped around her, pulling her closer. His body felt like cold stone, save where she touched him. Dully, his heart thudded against his ribs. "For however long you'll have me, Mary. Whatever it takes."

He wasn't coherent, he knew. Yet she understood. Her breathy, tender reply felled him. "I suppose I'll be keeping you then, Jack Talent."

Her slim arm wrapped about his waist, and the soft mounds of her breasts pressed into his side. Lightly she traced a finger down the groove that divided his abdomen, the touch making him shiver.

"Why?" he croaked. When she first arrived, he'd expected her to rail at him about the apples, perhaps chastise him for violating her privacy, then go on her way, leaving him alone.

"Because, Jack Talent, I can no more live without you than you can without me."

A shuddering breath left him, and he pulled her closer, tucking her half under him. "I don't understand."

"You always think too much, Jack." Her voice was low, her fingers still exploring, gently soothing him. "Did you honestly believe that I wouldn't find you worthy?"

Jack drew back to look down at her. He tried to speak and failed. Because she knew him, knew how broken he was. Shame over his cowardliness hit him. All this time he'd been afraid to confess to her, but in truth, it wasn't simply the confession, it was the belief that she wouldn't have him regardless.

"It's all right," she said again, then placed a small,

light kiss on his chest. "Broken or whole, I will always want you."

A choked breath burst from him, and he fell over her, his face burrowing against her soft breasts as he clutched her hips. "I love you." He wound his arms about her, crushing her surely. He couldn't let go. "I love you. Always. Constantly. Completely. With everything—" And then he could speak no more.

Mary wrapped her arms about Jack's broad shoulders and held him as he held her. She could not help but marvel at how good he felt in her arms, his solid strength against her, surrounding her with his warmth.

"I hate the way I treated you." His voice was muffled and raw against her skin. "I'll regret it until my dying day."

She knew he could not quite understand why she'd forgiven him. Just as she knew most people would wonder the same. They did not know what she did. Her hand smoothed over his close-cropped hair, so silky yet rough on the upstroke. On the outside Jack Talent was tarnished and battered, but underneath he was sterling. Not even Jack truly understood this. But she would help him see it.

"Hush now," she whispered. "Be at ease." Because she knew that he needed the words too. He needed to know he was protected.

For her whole life, she'd thought of men in terms of force. Blunt instruments that asserted their will and strength. Jack was that, more so than most. But she had never truly realized a man's vulnerability, that a man might need comfort and tenderness. In truth, a man was like crystal, all hard, cool surfaces and solid strength, yet so easily broken if mishandled.

They were twined together, Jack's thigh between her

legs, her arms wrapped about his shoulder and around his waist, his arms doing the same. Though it did not feel sexual, not at that moment. It felt peaceful. And she could not help but think of them as two strings, wound up tight to become rope, and stronger for it.

Because she'd been the one to give comfort, Jack's head rested on her shoulder, a warm weight there now. Gradually she became aware of each soft breath he took, blooming across her breasts. Her nipples tightened against the tickling caresses, and she arched into the sensation, a small furtive motion that she could not resist.

Awareness shuddered through Jack, obvious in the way his muscles tensed and his breath grew unsteady. Slowly his big, roughened palm skimmed along her hip up to her waist. He held it there, his fingers just stroking, sending little shivers of pleasure through her. Jack's hand stopped just beneath her breast, his fingers spread to cup her.

They were just her breasts, but when he looked at them, they became something more. Beautiful, erotic. They grew heavy, aching under his gaze, and a languid rush of heat coursed through her, the slick place between her legs clenching with delicious anticipation and need.

Even so, she couldn't resist another tease. "They're small."

He lifted his head, and his gaze darted from her breasts to her eyes and back again, as though he couldn't keep from staring. The corner of his mouth quirked. "They are."

She frowned, and he grinned with wicked intent. "Perhaps I can take the whole of one in my mouth." Without warning he ducked his head and sucked her in deep, pulling nipple and flesh into his warm mouth as if he'd devour her.

A strangled sound tore from her. She arched up into him, jerking with each hot, wet tug. Her fingers dug into the sheets and she held on. "Jack!"

He smiled around her flesh before drawing away. "Close." He kissed the under-curve of her breast. "But not quite all of it."

She panted up at him. "You'll kill me."

"Then we'll die together." His breath brushed over her damp flesh as he nuzzled her nipple, then her collarbone. Mary shivered. His mouth found the spot at the base of her neck. His spot. He kissed it as the warm wall of his chest brushed against hers. "But not yet."

Then he proceeded to destroy her by increments, his mouth everywhere, slow, wet kisses that discovered her secrets, warm hands coasting over her skin. And all the while whispering his love for her, how she made him burn, how she drove him mad, as if she were the one doing the destroying. And she sank into the feel of him surrounding her, her own hands and mouth charting the swells and valleys of his body.

Jack's mouth met hers, his kiss melting and reshaping her lips, as he slid between her legs. They were flesh to flesh, from chest to thigh, his hard strength to her soft endurance. He cupped her jaw as he tilted his head and kissed her again, and again. "Mary," he whispered. "Let me?"

Emotion clogged her throat. "I am yours."

His head lifted, and his dark-green eyes went wide, his nostrils flaring. For a moment she feared he would stay that way, silent, staring as if he'd gone somewhere far away. Then his breath left in a sigh. Like relief. Like a first breath. "Mary mine." His voice rolled over the words, as if trying them out for size.

Before she could answer, he canted his hips, a slight adjustment, and his thick crown was at her opening, a hot encroachment that held the attention of every cell within her body. She craved that intrusion with a strength that had her thighs shaking. Yet at the crest of that want came the memory of the last time she'd been invaded. The pain and degradation. She did not want that foul business tainting this act. If Jack could move past his darkness, so could she.

He knew her so well that he paused as if sensing her conflicting thoughts. A bead of sweat trickled down his temple. Braced above her, the muscles along his shoulders and arms twitched with restraint, but his eyes held hers, gentleness and understanding there. He eased back and then touched her temple, tenderly brushing back a lock of damp hair. "Is it because I'm on top of you?"

She gave a brusque nod, her throat closing painfully. In the silence he studied her. "You like it when I crowd you against a wall, though, don't you?" It was a decadent whisper, filled with promise, and she shivered. Of course he knew she did. He'd scented her desire.

And, as if he scented it once more, a slow, playful smile pulled at his mouth. "Come." Lightly he tugged at her hand, drawing her from the bed with a rustle of the covers. Mary was momentarily dumbfounded as he unfolded his long length and the firelight glowed upon his skin. He was massive, a study of flat, hard planes, long vistas of undulating muscle, networks of tight sinews. And his hot gaze roamed over her as though he might soon gobble her up.

Slowly he backed her up until her shoulders met the cool wall. Eyes on her, he leaned in, bracing his arms on either side of her, surrounding her with his warmth and power. She didn't know why it was so, but she did not feel pinned but bolstered, protected. It shamed her that she had panicked before. "Jack, you don't need to do this. We can lie down."

"Shh." Softly, he kissed her cheek. Then the other one. Moving with great care, he kissed his way down her neck, each tender press of his lips sending a little punch of heat into her flesh. His mouth found her nipple and gave it an open-mouthed kiss, lingering only long enough to make her arch off the wall before he moved on to the other one. *Tease.*

Mary closed her eyes, her breathing growing light and agitated as he knelt before her and his big hands closed over the swells of her hips. He leaned against her for a moment, his mouth against her breast, his breath warm and damp over her skin. And then he sat back on his heels, and his lips glided over her navel, brushing past her hipbone, his teeth gently grazing.

She knew where he was headed and what he wanted. Her sex throbbed with the knowledge. The sight of him before her, his dark head against her pale skin, nearly undid her. His hand eased down her thigh and beneath her knee. And she moved with him, languid and dazed, lifting her leg to hook over his shoulder. Exposed.

His expression was fierce as he looked at her, his chest rising and falling with greater urgency, and then he glanced up and their eyes met. He held her gaze as he leaned forward and licked her with the flat of his tongue. Slow and lazy. A strangled cry left her, and her legs wobbled. His grip tightened, his eyes on her as he did it again.

Pleasure rolled through her so hot and strong that her body tensed, her nipples tightening with a painful throb. "Jack."

Green eyes glinted as he reached out and flicked her swollen bud with the tip of his tongue. A featherlight touch. Maddening. She canted her hips, chasing his touch, but he backed away, not giving her the satisfaction.

His breath against her wetness almost felt cool, and his voice grew rough. "I want to be in here, Mary." His tongue probed her opening, dipping in just enough to make her quake. "Do you want me here?"

Mary panted, her throat burning. "Yes." *Now.*

Smiling, the fiend kissed her, hot and deep. A reward. One that shot through her body. "Jack!"

He held her still, one hot, rough palm upon her belly and the other at her hip, pinning her, supporting her. Trusting that he had her, she sagged against the silk-lined wall.

"Bloody hell, that feels good," she rasped. An understatement. Pleasure overwhelmed her. And she wanted more.

He grinned, slow and wide. "If we do it correctly, it will all feel good, love." His smile faded, replaced by a look of hot intent. "Show yourself to me." Taking her hand in his, he guided it down to her sex.

Oh, but he was wicked. Her breath came out in a pant, and her hand shook as she complied and opened the folds of her sex for his delectation. He growled low in approval. "Beautiful. You are beautiful, angel." Then he kissed the center of her, a tender, reverent gesture that made her heart stutter and pulled a strangled sound from her throat.

His lashes fluttered, his expression languid as he kissed her in earnest, nipping, licking, and sucking, his tongue sliding over her fingers and along her slick flesh. And it was too much. Too much sensation. The wet sound of his mouth on her, the small, greedy noises he made, and the way he wholeheartedly came at her, as though she were his last meal. It was messy, real. Life. She could not hide from it. She no longer wanted to. All these years. She hadn't realized it could be like this. She didn't feel shamed or used. But adored.

Her skin flared hot, then cold, her nipples aching so badly that she grasped one breast and gave the distended tip a sharp tug. A bone-deep shake began at her hip, spreading outward.

Gently he slipped a finger into her, touching a spot that had her quaking. She moaned, wanting to get away from his marauding mouth and probing finger, yet wanting to get closer.

He heard the sound and glanced up, his eyes gleaming bright in the lamplight. "Oh no," he said roughly. "The first time, we come together."

She whimpered, so close to completion that she throbbed. But he was already moving, licking his way back up her heated skin, rising above her. And when he fully stood, her legs were locked around his trim waist and his hands were cupping her bottom. And he smiled, tenderly if not a bit unsteadily.

"This is me." He pushed in, slow, thick, filling her, not an invasion but a joining with her. At last. "And you."

He rocked his hips, going in a bit deeper, and they both shivered. "This is us." Then it was his gaze that faltered, a look of pleasure mixed with pain making his brows furrow. A low groan tore from him as he seated himself to the hilt. His body twitched as he began to pant, holding himself still. For her.

"Look at us, Merrily."

And she did, where she was stretched wide, and he pulled back, a long, easy glide, the breadth of his thick cock glistening and ruddy. He thrust inside her, disappearing from sight. He filled her up, wide, dense, and complete.

Beneath her heavy lids, she looked at him. He was as undone as she, his eyes hot, his lips parted. She took advantage, capturing his mouth to kiss him, and her breasts slid against his damp chest. He responded immediately, the kiss turning rough, delicious. Her legs eased further open, cradling him as he thrust into her, a steady, strong movement that she savored.

Her body arched, pleasure and heat breaking in a garbled cry. "Jack"—she sucked in a breath—"I need..." She shivered, heat licking her skin, her body trembling.

"Tell me, love." He nipped her shoulder, his breath fast but light as if he were restraining himself with effort. "Anything."

"Don't hold back." She cupped his cheek and stared into his eyes. "Give me everything." She needed it now, to feel him wild and free against her, to feel wild and free herself.

A low growl sounded in his throat as understanding lit in his eyes. Biting down on her neck, he turned them so that he leaned against the wall and she was balanced on his hips. Gripping her bottom hard, he lifted her high, nearly pulling her off him, and then slammed her back down, brutal and perfect. His expression intent, his muscles bulged as he worked her on his cock, moving her how he willed and controlling the pace. Mary clutched his shoulders, her nails digging in, and squeezed her inner walls.

"More," she ground out. "More."

On a curse Jack lurched forward. His elbow hit a vase, and it went tumbling with a crash. They stumbled back, her world tilting, before she landed on the bed, Jack still inside her and controlling the fall. "Yes?" he asked, wanting to know if she was all right. She managed a nod, touching his cheek in gratitude, and then he was thrusting hard and fast, deep grunts rumbling in his chest as he pumped. And the tight, relentless heat coiled within her again, demanding more.

"Harder," she rasped. She wanted him to break her, reform her into something new. And he complied, rising up on his arms for better leverage, rutting against her in a way that was dirty, decadent, and unhinged. Everything that she wanted.

"Fuck, Mary." He groaned, his backside tightening as he flexed into her. "Oh, fuck you feel so good."

Her hipbones ached from the force of his body slamming into them, her sex burning from the friction. Pleasure grew within her, swelling outward until she shook. And she clutched Jack's shoulders like a lifeline, her body tensing against his. "I…can't…I want…" She couldn't think, could barely breathe.

"Let it go," he whispered against her cheek. "Let yourself go, love."

As if his words were a reprieve, the thing she'd been waiting for, the pleasure within her peaked. And then she fractured, coming so hard and fast that she sank her teeth into the meaty juncture of his shoulder.

At her bite, his entire body seized before a violent shudder wracked him, his brows furrowing tight as he bared his teeth on a wordless cry. The tendons stuck out on his neck, and his head canted as if reacting to a blow. It was glorious. The sight sent an unexpected tide of sensation through her once more. She strained against him, sore and pulsing as he filled her with warmth.

And then they both collapsed. For a moment Jack simply panted, his body half slung on top of her, then he gathered her close and tucked her snugly against his side. "I knew we'd be like that together," he whispered on an unsteady breath.

Mary stretched against him, luxuriating in the soreness along her limbs and the feel of him still deep inside her. "Had I known," she said, running a hand over his sweaty back, "I'd have insisted we shag the moment we met."

He grunted, and she squeezed the hard swell of his shoulder. "Jack," she whispered. "Let's do it again. Now."

Surprise rippled through him, which did delicious things to his muscles. And as if answering her, his cock twitched against her sex, growing thick once more. He eased himself up to peer down at her, and a wide, cocksure grin erupted over his mouth. She'd never seen that particular smile, but she liked it.

"Again?" His voice was a rumbling rasp. And that lovely grin grew wider, and his cock pulsed. A light laugh left him. "Oh, angel, just let anyone bloody try and stop me."

Chapter Thirty-One

One more adjustment and it would be finished. Closing her eyes, Holly ran her hand over the heart, feeling for any weak spots in the design. Her fingertips reached an area that felt dark and unsteady. There. Taking a breath, she let her power go. The metal heated to searing hot, but did not burn her. Concentrating on what she wanted the device to do, Holly held on. The metal quivered, then rearranged itself. Another moment and her invention was cool once more. And complete.

Holly opened her eyes and picked her creation up. Despite her disgust with this place, pride in what she'd accomplished surged forth. It was a thing of beauty, developed using a wax casting method, backbreaking hours of work, and the power no one else knew she wielded.

At her elbow was the working diary of her predecessor. The mere thought that another had been here before her filled Holly with icy terror. But his notes fascinated. The man, Pierce, had been a clockmaker. At first he'd attempted to create new hearts, but when they failed he'd tried his hand at repairing stolen GIM hearts.

With a shiver Holly remembered the ruined remains of Mr. Pierce and the damaged clockwork heart she'd taken from his corpse to examine. Though his notes did not say, Holly did not think he had volunteered to have the very heart he'd fixed placed in his chest.

Would the same fate be forced upon her? Tentatively she lifted the heart a little higher. It glowed in the low light, a pale sheen that appeared silver, but was platinum. Rare and incredibly strong, platinum had the distinction of being the one metal that supernatural bodies did not adversely react to.

That had been the key. That bastard was putting steel or gold hearts into shifters and sanguis. Both metals poisoned their victims, creating a change that was catastrophic. As if gaining a mind of its own, the metal would take over the body, weaving its way into the fabric of the immortal's flesh, causing intense pain, mental instability, and, eventually, a complete body failure.

The endless line of failures had not pleased the madman holding her here. Peace in this hell only came when Master—how she hated that name—had consumed a few drops of the glimmering blood from the vial he kept close to him at all times. To his glee, one drink had closed a few of the smaller sores on his face. Talent's blood, if his rantings were to be believed.

Holly had hoped that would be the end of it, but she'd been ordered to create a heart that worked. Her guts cramped at the thought. Because if she didn't find a way, she was dead.

Holly had put all her skill into the creation, for she realized that success would ultimately destroy him. Holly simply needed to make a heart that would work. Once Master put one into himself, she would use the electric prod against him and stop his heart. Not a very strong plan, granted, but it was all she had.

The door to her cell slammed open, and a man strode in. With shining hair, firm skin, and a gleam in his eye, her captor fairly beamed at her. Rising from his back were a pair of wings covered with glossy black feathers. One dropped to the floor as he came forward.

"Happy day, Miss Evernight," he said. "My body is whole once more." He gave a wry little laugh. He glanced at the platinum heart on her worktable. "Is that it?"

"Yes."

"It is marvelous." Gently he touched the smooth arch of the heart's outer surface, and Holly had the mad urge to snatch it from him. But she held still as he lifted the device up to the light. "Platinum, is it?"

Holly knew he wanted an explanation. He always wanted to hear her methods. "I believe previous failures were due to the type of metal used. Platinum ought to be benign to immortals."

"You are a diamond of the first water, Miss Evernight."

And you are a disgusting coward. I'd like nothing better than to ram my screwdriver into your eye.

"You made two of them?" he asked, grinning wide.

Because the coward wouldn't attempt to use it on himself before trying it out on another. Which was a pity, since she'd hoped he'd take a chance on this one and replace his own heart with it. Despite this, her curiosity compelled her to ask, "If you are healed, then why bother with these hearts?"

Gently, he fingered the curve of the heart. "So that I may never be vulnerable again."

Holly would be quite satisfied to watch him die. "This is the first. The second should take a day."

He frowned slightly, his eyes gleaming silver-white for an instant. But then he waved an idle hand. "Very well." He set the heart down and clapped his hands, the sound booming unnaturally loud.

A hunched figure walked in, pushing a screeching trolley before him. She ignored him in favor of the man strapped to the top. The large male, dressed only in trousers, thrashed against the golden bands that held him down. White hair fell in tangles around a sharp face, and dark-blond brows arched over eyes that flickered from ice to coal. He was beautiful. And completely helpless. A demon, if gold could hold him fast. Sanguis, if the needle-sharp fangs dropping down over the gag around his mouth were to be believed. Bloodsucker. Beautiful, but vile.

But when Master stroked the demon's cheek with the loving care she'd just shown her inventions, as if he too were looking at a creation, nausea rolled up Holly's throat, and she swallowed hard. She knew that look, and what would come of it.

"Mr. Thorne here has been telling tales to those who should not hear them."

Thorne bucked, and the gold bands cut into his lean torso. Dark rivulets of blood ran over his dusky, ivory skin. He snarled against his gag, the corners of his mouth turning white.

Walking over to a worktable set off to the side of the room, Master picked up a long, ivory-handled bone saw.

Thorne grew unnaturally still, his now-black eyes tracking the movement.

Slowly, and with great theatricality, the sick winged bastard let the steel blade catch the light as he turned toward Thorne, whose chest begin to lift and fall in rapid motion. Thorne's gaze clashed with hers, and his eyes widened, a desperate plea shimmering in them. Her insides pitched. She couldn't look away. Nor could she save him.

God. God. God.

"Shall we try our newest creation?" Master asked softly.

Holly jerked to her feet, the chains about her wrists and ankles clattering. "Stop! We haven't chloroform." She couldn't stop the surgery, but she could ease the poor man's pain.

Master simply grinned. "Not to worry, it will not affect the procedure."

Holly swayed. A cold sweat broke out over her clammy skin. Master reached the table, and Thorne went wild, bucking so hard that the trolley rocked.

"Come now, Mr. Thorne," said Master. "I am giving you a gift. Blood such as you've never tasted, a bit of my power." For their *benevolent* Master had imbued each of his crawlers with the ability to dissipate into shadow at will. That none of them survived long enough to truly appreciate it wasn't his concern. "Should you survive, you will possess a body stronger than you could imagine."

Thorne was unimpressed and continued to fight his bonds.

"Ingrate," snarled Master, and while the silent guard held Thorne steady, another took a metal tube attached to a funnel and shoved it into the corner of Throne's mouth. Jack Talent's blood emptied out of the glass vial and went down Thorne's resisting throat.

Master wasted no more time. He made the first cut. Thorne's shout broke around his gag.

Holly bolted, her mind blank and her blood ice-cold. The chains held her back, and she crashed to the ground.

Above her Thorne thrashed, his raw bellows echoing in the stone chamber.

Sobbing, Holly curled into a ball and tried to block out the sound. But Master glanced back at her, and a vicious gleam lit his eyes. "Get her up here," he snarled to the guard. And then he grinned once more. "Come, Miss Evernight, and see your creation be born."

Struggling was useless, and too soon she had a personal view of the carnage. She gave a great dry heave but her stomach was empty. Thorne's agonized gaze lit on her, and a murderous rage burned bright there before Master carved deeper into him; then he was screaming, the veins on his neck standing out as he threw his head back. The guard held her there as Master did his gruesome work. And the scent of terror and hopelessness filled the cell.

Mary woke at the break of dawn to find Jack sleeping beside her, his face half-mashed into the pillow, his hair adorably mussed. With his lips soft and parted and his cheek scrunched up by his eye, he appeared a boy, if one discounted the masculine sprawl of his body, half-hidden beneath the sheets. Her gaze followed the light and the way it touched his skin. The smooth arc of his back raced down, then swooped up to the hard swells of his buttocks, just peeking out from the linen.

As if feeling her admiration, he stirred, giving a little grunt, and turned onto his back, the move pulling the sheets farther down. Oh, my, but that was a lovely sight. She could not help herself. Her hand fell to the taut hardness of his belly and began to caress it, loving the contrast between silky smooth skin and the rough trail of hairs that led the way down.

His cock rose before he did. When it lay thick and

heavy against her hand, his eyes opened, long, dark lashes surrounding irises the color of evergreen on a winter's day. His gaze focused on her, and a smile lit over his features. Little lines fanned out from his gorgeous eyes, his brows tilting on an upward slant, his wide mouth curling up, flashing even white teeth.

Mary's breath caught. With shaking fingers she touched one of the brackets emphasizing that grin of his. "Ah, now, Jack Talent," she said with quiet awe, "when you smile, your soul shines through." Her palm settled on his warm cheek. "And it is utterly beautiful to me."

His smile wavered, his eyes clouding with something like shock and discomfort. "Christ"—he laughed lightly—"that ought to be my line, Merrily, not yours."

In a blink she was under him and he was sinking into her with a deep, smooth glide that took her breath, his body warm and loose-limbed from sleep. "Are you sore?" he murmured.

"Yes." A delicious, decadent ache.

His mouth quirked, but he didn't stop moving within her. "I'll be gentle." He kissed the sensitive spot on her neck. "But thorough."

Shivers of heat licked up her sides as his hands skimmed along them, up over her breasts, her arms, until he found her hands. Their fingers linked, and he held them tight. He'd trapped her, leaving her unable to do anything but feel. Jack in her, around her, filling her. Each withdrawal had her whimpering in protest. Each surge back in made her groan. And so slow that she couldn't stand it.

"Feel good?" he asked, giving her back the words she'd asked him before.

"Yes." She shuddered. "God, yes. But"—she licked her

lips—"I want to move." Her flesh was on fire, her muscles trembling in protest.

His smile was sweet, and evil. "I know, love." He kept her pinned, his thick heaviness moving in and out just enough to torment. And the pressure within, the shuddering pleasure, increased. She struggled against it, and he caught her lower lip, suckling it, his slick tongue slipping into her mouth like a tease. She licked back, wanting to feel the hot sleekness of him, but he edged away and gave her a soft, chaste kiss instead. "I know."

"Jack," she growled. He was driving her mad. And he knew it, chuckling, his pace never faltering. Mary stretched, having nowhere to go. Her body wasn't hers. It had become a needy, hot, pulsing thing. "*Jack.*" She licked the salty smooth skin along his collarbone, loving the way he shivered. It wasn't enough. She wondered if it ever would be. "God, I want you."

His smile was lopsided and wry, even as his eyes lit up. "Just so you're aware, you're having me." He moved with a little grunt. "Right now, in fact."

She laughed softly even as that greedy need grew stronger. "You move, you bloody breathe"—she spread her legs wider, trying to take him deeper—"and I want you more. I want to bite you, do you a violence."

"Christ, Chase." He thrust hard and firm, his lips parted on a ragged breath. "Christ. You destroy me."

That dark, hot feeling surged again, and she turned her head and sank her teeth into the hard swell of his bicep. And he lost himself in her. Just as she wanted him to do.

This time, when she came, it was a quiet shiver that rippled over her body, her cheek pressed against his. They stayed that way for a moment, Jack a heavy, wonderful weight and her arms holding him as close as she could. "You *are* beautiful, you know," she said.

He snorted softly. "I've always thought you were a bit touched in the head, angel."

But she could hear the cautious happiness hiding behind his quip.

"That is because you don't see your true self. But I do." She smiled. "You cannot hide from me."

Again the joy within him peeked out, but his voice was low and somber when he spoke. "That is because you own me heart and soul, Mary mine. You always have."

Her own heart felt like a thing made not of metal but of spun glass, fragile and light. Her thumb traced the corner of his mouth, noting the way it stretched upward, despite his disquiet, as if her touch made him happy.

"I love you, Jack."

He did not blink, not even when she kissed his mouth with infinite care. But she felt the rapid rise and fall of his chest. She kissed him again, tenderly because she knew he was unhinged just then. "I love you heart and soul."

He was pale when he settled back, his eyes wide and searching. "Say it again."

"I love you." It was an easy thing to say. Keeping it back would have been harder, for she felt it with her whole being.

His hands wrapped around her forearms, and he dragged her up, laying her over his wide chest, where she could feel his heart pound. "I hear the words," he said slowly, "only I can't believe them."

"Can't believe that I love you? Or that anyone could?"

His lashes lowered. "They didn't. My parents. They saw the true me and deemed me unworthy to live."

Her fingers stroked along his scalp, then rested on his cheek. Jack leaned into the touch on a sigh.

"They were your childhood," she said. "But they aren't your family. You know who your real family is. One day you'll know how much you are loved. You'll feel it."

Chapter Thirty-Two

———— ❧ ❧ ————

How the crisp linen envelope with an SOS seal ended up on Jack's bare chest hours later was a mystery. One he could not do anything about, for whoever had left it was long gone by the time Jack woke and found the thing. Easing out of bed, he left a sleeping Mary, fragrant and warm with the intoxicating scent of sex and sleep, to read it.

The message was simple, a time, place, and request that Jack arrive alone scrawled with a fanciful hand. An elaborate *A* was the only signature. Jack, having learned a thing or two from the men in his life, all of whom loved headstrong women, woke Mary and showed it to her. Last night he'd told her everything he knew of Amaros, and of his being a Nephil, which still unsettled him. Upon hearing that Jack was part angel, Mary had grinned wide. "Your dulcet nature ought to have been the first clue."

"Ha!" Jack had murmured against her neck; his hands were busy elsewhere. "You are truly hilarious. A comic bard."

"And to think you call me the angel." She'd chuckled, a warm, contented sound that went straight to his heart. Her hands ran over his back. "My winged wonder—Ack!"

Mary Chase, Jack discovered, was ticklish. And they'd said no more for quite some time.

Now, resting on one elbow, Mary read the note. Sunlight shone in her hair, picking up glints of gold, bronze, and amber. "I do not like it," she said when she'd finished.

"Nor I," he said. "But I think I ought to go."

"I am going to follow," she said.

Jack smiled and leaned forward to kiss her soft lips. Happiness was a strange sensation. It filled him up until his body was tender yet strong. Fancy that. God, he'd had it so very wrong when he accused Ian of being weak with love. At this moment he felt infinite and invincible. And he felt afraid. For the world would not go away simply because they wanted it to. His hand smoothed down the satin dip of her waist before holding fast. "I did not doubt that for a moment."

And so they went, Mary's spirit drifting above him like a guardian angel. When they reached St. Paul's, she disappeared, taking another route up so that he might arrive utterly alone. But he knew she'd be close. And it was a comfort he had not expected.

Trouble, Mary thought as she followed Jack up to the Golden Gallery, a viewing platform at the top of St. Paul's dome. Though she was currently without a body, apprehension weighed her spirit down. The city sprawled out beneath her. It reminded her of a flea circus with tiny little figures darting to and fro, miniature wagons and carriages rolling here and there. There were times when Mary could watch the city for hours. Not think, not feel, just watch the world move on. Today was not one of those days.

The wind whistled, and beside her Jack hunched in his coat as he glanced about.

The air stirred again and became heavy with a presence. Whatever it was had power. Immense power.

On a snarl Jack spun around and faced whatever had arrived. Mary hovered above him, not able to help, which annoyed her greatly. More so when the strange presence showed himself.

"Who the bloody hell are you?" Jack demanded.

The man who stood before them was of a similar height and build to Jack, his features stamped with the strong lines of a Roman coin. But that was where all trace of humanity ended. His skin was silver-white, translucent yet not, as if he were made of cut crystal. Even his hair, which curled about his temples, was brilliant silver. Most unnerving of all were the shimmering white wings that made two graceful arcs from behind his broad shoulders. The man let them look their fill, then smiled. A genuine gesture that seemed almost fond. "Master Talent." His crystalline gaze shot to Mary. "Mistress Chase." It was a voice so rich in timber that it shivered with power. "I am Augustus."

"Doesn't quite help me out, mate," Jack snapped, his fists clenching. Mary knew him well enough now to understand that his protective instincts had been roused the moment Augustus spotted her.

However, Augustus's friendly smile grew. His form shimmered, and he became a dark-haired, dark-eyed man who might have been an Italian. "In one life," the man went on, "I was known as Marcus Augustus, Roman soldier and reprobate." He shrugged, looking almost sheepish.

"I lost all memory of myself for a while back then. However, I believe you'd best know me as Mr. Augustus Maximus." That strange, almost beguiling smile returned. "After all, we are both members of the same society."

"I don't know any regulator by that name," Jack said with a scowl.

"No, I don't suppose you would, as I am not a regulator." He took a small step forward. "My dear Poppy Lane calls me Father."

Not Poppy's father, but Father.

Jack gave a start. "You're Father?" The enigmatic founder and head of the SOS.

He made a neat bow. "The very one."

"Where have you been?"

A good question. According to Poppy, he disappeared for long stretches at a time.

"Here and There," Father said. "There are three main planes of existence for my kind. Here, There, and Nowhere, which is the place your kind calls Hell. I might further explain it to you one day, but for now I'd rather discuss you."

"And why would you do that?" Jack asked.

"Because we are blood."

At this Jack straightened. And Mary eased closer. Something deep within said to trust this man. But that wouldn't stop her from keeping up her guard.

"All angels are what you might consider blood relatives. My true name is Ramiel. Though I'd rather you call me Augustus. It feels fitting somehow when I am Here," he mused.

Jack gave Mary a quick glance. "A Watcher," he said. "One of the fallen angels."

"We did not fall," said Augustus. "We arrived. To be with man." The corners of his eyes crinkled. "A rather good choice, if you ask me. But it is true that all of the so-called fallen are cursed in one manner or another."

Though Mary was not in her flesh, a shiver seemed to run through her spirit. She'd thought angels would be something less than human, something terrifying and menacing. Wrath of God and all that. But this man, he was more human than any supernatural Mary had ever come across. Every nuance of emotion expressed itself on his face and shone brightly in his now-dark eyes.

"I know your sire," he said to Jack in a voice laced with gentleness.

Jack tensed, and Mary knew he loathed to show any hint that he cared. But he did. The child in him would. Even if the man had accepted his past. "I've heard that claim before. Forgive me if I do not jump to plead for the answer."

Augustus shook his head slightly. "From Amaros, the cursed one. He is troubled."

"An understatement."

Augustus leaned against the iron balustrade. "For a fallen, it is quite easy to discern who your father is. For there is only one angel who has the gift of true healing. Raphael."

Jack laughed then, an uncomfortable and incredulous sound. "Raphael? He's a bloody archangel, not a fallen."

"Debatable," said Augustus with a small smile. "Regardless, there are only two beings in existence that possess healing blood. Raphael. And you."

Jack's lids lowered, his lashes hiding his eyes. But his shoulders tensed, and Mary rested her hand there. He would only feel the chill of her spirit, but even so he leaned closer as if he needed that contact. "What is he like?" Jack asked softly.

"He is impetuous. Full of life. Creating you was a mistake on Raphael's part." Augustus noticed Jack's scowl and smiled. "A mistake in that he lay with Angela Talent, a woman who had no notion of what he was. He never took into account how fragile her mind might be."

Augustus looked off, the fine lines around his eyes deepening. "We've been around longer than you can imagine. Living so long has not deadened us, but made us susceptible to emotions. Oftentimes we react without thinking things through." He glanced back, his eyes wry and amused. "In truth, we do not like to think about things too deeply. Not any longer. Nor do we pay attention to this world as we ought.

"At any rate," Augustus continued, "Raphael is no longer Here—"

"But There?"

"Yes," Augustus said with a broad smile. "We all have our crosses to bear. Raphael's is that he can no longer travel Here. My curse is that I can only be Here for a short period of time." A shadow of sorrow darkened his eyes. "With each passing year, that period of grace grows smaller."

"And why are you using your moment Here to speak with me?"

"In an indirect way, I am the one who has caused the problem."

"Forgive me," Jack said with a politeness he clearly did not feel, "but you're not explaining yourself very well."

Mary wanted to be annoyed as well, but the goodwill flowing off the angel could not be denied. She liked him. Instinctively.

"Poppy often tells me the same," Augustus murmured. "It is simply this. Two years ago, Winston Lane was attacked by Death. I intervened and brought him to Benjamin Archer." A strange look of pride lit the angel's features for a moment, then was gone.

"Death, thus cheated, prompted another, Apep, to break free from Nowhere or what you call Hell," Augustus explained with a wave of his hand. "A rift was opened, and many who had been consigned to hell used the opportunity to escape, including Amaros. The Nex gained power and strength in those new allies."

Augustus's mouth turned down. "While I do not regret saving Winston Lane's life, I regret the unforeseen effects of that action. The least I can do is give you knowledge to defend yourself. When Amaros took your blood, he thought himself cured. Unfortunately, it was a temporary stay of execution. He needs a constant diet of your blood to remain as he is. As your healing blood is a gift, you must freely give it to him for it to have full potency."

Deep within Mary's soul, something stilled and then went on alert. She could see the end, a dark shadow on the horizon, and it was she who stood between Jack and that chasm.

Yes. You understand.

Augustus's voice was clear in her mind. She glanced back at him, but he gave no indication that he'd spoken.

"He won't get any more from me," Jack said flatly. "Let him die."

"Do you honestly believe that once he realizes your blood did not permanently cure him that he will not come after you?" Augustus shook his head sadly. "While his mind might be muddled by madness, he is not without intelligence. Expect him to return soon. And his rage will be great."

"And so will mine," Jack retorted.

Augustus's gentle expression turned solemn. "I know what you are planning, Jack. And it is not the answer to your troubles."

But you have the answer, do you not, Mistress Chase? A flicker of his gaze toward her.

Her spirit stretched wide, then collapsed tight. Did she? Her mind raced. No answers came.

Wholly ignorant of their exchange, Jack stood straighter, his hands at the ready. "What am I planning, then?"

If the threat in his voice bothered Augustus, it didn't show. "That you will kill him." He smiled slightly. "It is what I would do to anyone who threatened my beloved."

"A good guess." Jack rolled his tight shoulders. "And the right one."

"It will not work." Augustus sighed, and the air upon the platform grew warm and tinged with the scent of a summer storm. Augustus's expression grew grim. "If I could, I'd kill Amaros myself. But a fallen is forbidden to kill his kind."

Mary drifted closer to Augustus. A queer sort of anticipation surged through her being. As if the answer was just bumping along the edges of her mind.

"Which is why Amaros is now cursed," Augustus said. "Long ago, in a fit of rage, he killed another fallen and has been rotting away ever since."

Jack frowned. "I am half fallen. Can I kill him? Or will I too be cursed?"

Dark, ancient eyes held his. "You will be cursed just as he is. To destroy his soul is to destroy your own. That is our way."

"Hell." Jack pinched the bridge of his nose.

Can I kill him in Jack's stead? Mary asked Augustus.

"Miss Chase has asked me if she could destroy Amaros in your stead."

Jack lurched up from where he'd been leaning. "Absolutely not." He glared at Mary as she glared back in defiance.

"No other immortal has ever killed a fallen," Augustus said. "They are too physically strong to destroy. Ironically, one needs the strength of a fallen, or Nephil, to do the deed."

The weight of Augustus's words sank like a stone.

Then why tell me that I have the answer?

Sometimes the answer is not in the physical, but in the spirit.

Beside her Jack suddenly flinched as if a realization had come fast upon him. "But if Amaros is already cursed, then..."

"He can destroy you," Augustus finished. "Without doing himself further damage."

His curse is soul-deep. You understand the soul, do you not, Miss Chase?

And suddenly Mary did. She knew precisely what needed to be done. It was risky. And Jack would never agree to it.

Mary looked at Augustus. *This is why you haven't spoken of this aloud, isn't it?*

Would you rather I had? Augustus's response was wry, yet tinged with sadness. Because he too knew the risks. She could feel his concern for her like a warm hand upon her shoulder.

"Then I shall offer him free use of my blood," Jack said.

His freedom.

"I see no other recourse," Augustus answered sedately.

No! It was a shout in Mary's mind. *Never*. She would not let Jack become Amaros's blood whore. She would not see him go back to that dark place of hell and despair. Offering himself to the being who'd held and tortured him.

As if hearing her very thoughts, Augustus glanced at Mary. *Then you know what must be done.*

Jack ran a tired hand over his face and turned away to stare out over the city. "Then I shall do what I must."

To protect those he loved, Jack would do anything. And so would Mary.

"Two squared is four. Three squared is nine. Four squared is sixteen." Holly hugged herself tight, rocking slightly as she continued to count. The words burned against her throat. "Five squared is five-and-twenty..." Numbers. Sensible, reliable numbers. They would not harm her.

Her accommodations had changed. No more laboratory. Only the icy, dank hole of her cell. There were others here, rows of black cells that held the damned. She could not see them, but she could hear them. Moans, curses, weeping.

She could almost bear the sounds of their misery. But not those of the demon who occupied the cell with her.

A violent wave of nausea ran through her when she glanced to his side of the space. Lying upon a hard pallet and still strapped down by chains of gold, he shook along the whole of his lean body as he stared blankly up at the ceiling. His teeth were clenched and bared, and white fangs cut into his bottom lip until blood rolled along his chin and pooled at his neck. Holly doubted that he was aware. He simply shook as if nothing would ever again warm him.

His muscled torso shone pale, nearly luminous in the dimness, an uncomfortable contrast to the purple bruises mottling his chest and the ugly, ragged scar that ran down his sternum. Thick, awkward stitches held his skin closed, puckering his once-smooth flesh and sticking up like thorns in a briar patch.

The memory of witnessing his heart being ripped from his chest to be replaced with a clockwork one would haunt Holly for the rest of her days. She couldn't stand to look at him now. Nor could she stand to look away. If she looked away he might die. Alone. She couldn't allow that. Not when it was her invention clicking away in his chest.

Holly pressed her knees harder into her breast and let the numbers flow through her mind. *Six squared is six-and-thirty. Seven squared is nine-and-forty.*

A long, agonized groan tore from her cellmate's lips, and his body bowed off of the pallet, restrained from falling by the chain across his shoulders and thighs. As if hit, he slammed back down and began to thrash and groan.

A childish urge to cover her ears had her arms twitching. But she crawled to his side.

"It's..." She extended a hand to touch him, then stopped when he bucked again. "It's all right." Feeble words. He didn't hear them anyway. Unfocused eyes stared wide. His mouth hung open as if locked in a scream, but no sound came. Sweat rolled down his temples and pebbled on his torso.

Would he die? Was his body rejecting the heart? She could not tell. But something was changing. From the edges of his wound, little rivers of shining platinum began to creep along his skin. No, not along, but *through* his skin.

"Oh, no." Her platinum heart was a failure after all. Holly watched in horror as the gleaming metal rapidly spread outward like the root system of a tree. Up over his chest and down his side it went. And all the while he thrashed, as if it was agony.

Heedless of the danger, she reached out and touched his shoulder. So cold and clammy with sweat and shaking violently. But she smoothed her hand down his arm in a slow, gentle caress. Strangely, the metal's progress stopped. But not on the other side. Platinum twined and writhed down his left arm and twisted along his fingers. The demon clenched his fist and sobbed. A trickle of blood leaked from the corner of one eye.

The sight sent a ripple of disgust along her skin. She hailed from a family of logical inventors, yet some deep-seated part of them maintained a vigilant Irish suspicion of blood drinkers. *Dearg-due, Abhartach.* Reviled creatures who lusted for blood. Ungodly fiends. As soon as the thought entered her head, shame chased it out.

Holly touched his cheek, and he leaned into it with a whimper.

"There now, big man," she whispered, as she covered him with her blanket. "You're not alone." With a hand that shook, she ran her fingers over his brow and through his damp hair. The white strands clung to her hand like spider silk but the demon calmed. No, his name was Thorne. He was not some nameless demon. But Thorne.

His eyes were closed now, long bronze lashes lying against unnaturally pale cheeks.

"You are not alone, Mr. Thorne."

At the sound of his name, his eyes flew open. No longer simply black as onyx, a starburst pattern of luminous platinum radiated around his pupils. His head turned toward her, but not a flicker of recognition or sense lay in his strangely beautiful eyes.

Holly opened her mouth to say something, anything that might offer some comfort, but a massive bellow rang out, echoing off the stone walls.

"Evernight!"

She jumped back, her bottom hitting the floor, just as the door to the main cellar smashed open.

Master surged in on a tide of rage. Open sores and great gaping wounds once again held dominion over his flesh. Holly cowered as he strode forward, seething and growling. His wild gaze landed on her, and she knew she was dead.

While Mary went home to reconnect with her body—and Jack had no doubt she was desperate to give him a thorough tongue-lashing—Jack went to Thorne's house. He'd put his friend at risk for selfish reasons, and though they worked on opposite sides, it did not sit well with his conscience. Thorne needed to know with what they were dealing. A mad fallen was a menace to all. The Nex was insane to think it could control Amaros.

But the moment he stepped up to Thorne's town house, Jack's skin prickled along his neck. All appeared quiet, but a thick fug of dark power hung over the air around the place. The broken door lock did not ease his worry. Slowly Jack entered the main hall, taking in the destruction and the carnage of slaughtered help.

Sliding out a knife, more for a sense of security than for actual protection, Jack made his way down to Thorne's subterranean lair. More destruction. Blood splattered the walls; the furniture was broken down to kindling.

Regret sucked at Jack's gut as he made his way home to Mary. For Thorne alone he yearned to kill Amaros. So great was his ire that it took him a moment to realize something was wrong as he entered Mary's flat. It was too quiet, and her scent was not strong enough. As though she was gone. Then he spied the message written in blood upon the blue-lacquered wall. Jack's knees hit the floor, his head going light, his limbs ice-cold. And then came the rage, powerful and welcome, and running like lightning through his veins.

If you want her, come and get her.

Chapter Thirty-Three

———◦◦◦⦁◦◦◦———

Having her body stolen was certainly a new experience. Mary had returned home only to find it gone. Fortunately, a GIM could always locate her body. Unfortunately, she knew quite well that she would not like where it was. And she was correct. Following the pull of her physical flesh, Mary soon found herself in the cellars beneath Lambeth Palace. Gold torchlight flickered off moldering, damp stones.

She kept to the upper shadows, where the ceiling curved low and rough. She glided over a number of well-armed guards, each of whom wore a Nex tattoo upon his left hand and a tattoo of a chain about his neck—a blood-bonded slave. Mary wondered if any of them wanted to fight their servitude. Mary also wondered exactly how Amaros had discovered her home, until she entered an underground chamber and spied Tottie O'Brien seated at a table covered with food and drink. Tottie, who had claimed to see Jack abduct Holly Evernight. Tottie, who had access to Poppy's files. Tottie, who would live in a world of regret as soon as Mary got her hands on her.

But for now Mary hovered. Her body lay on a blood-encrusted trolley. Not a pleasant sight. Nor was that of Amaros bending over her. Augustus had been correct, the fallen was rotting again. His robe gaped and revealed his cursed flesh. A faint, almost sweet stench emanated from him. But the power radiating from him belied his decrepit appearance.

Grabbing hold of her bodice, Amaros tore it in two. Mary supposed she ought to feel humiliation upon seeing her body exposed. Anger came instead.

"Quite lovely, no?" he said to no one in particular, but Tottie answered quickly enough.

"If you're going to shag an empty body, tell me now, and I shall leave you to it." Her pert nose wrinkled in disgust.

"It will not be empty for long." With brutal efficiency he reached down and ripped the key to Mary's heart off her nipple. Blood welled from the torn tip, and Mary gave a mental wince. That would hurt when she came back to herself. And he now had the means to stop her heart.

"I'll do worse," Amaros said to the room. "I can last all night." He turned, and with unerring accuracy focused on her. "Fallen see spirits, Miss Chase. Now get back in this body, before I have at it."

It was a chilling thing to face him. She knew he'd make her suffer before he was through with her. But she couldn't hover like a coward. Gathering her courage, she dove into her flesh. It hurt, just as she'd suspected, her breast burning with pain. But she did not let it show as she rose and pulled the ragged edges of her bodice back together.

"So glad you could join us." Amaros inclined his head with a smirk.

Mary slid a hand along her thigh and felt the throwing knives still strapped there. "The pleasure is all yours." Curling her legs up on the trolley, she turned to face him and, in the same movement, slipped a hand into the hidden opening of her skirt. Her fingers grasped the knife's hilt.

Amaros gave her an amused look. "Are you planning to use that weapon on me?"

"No." It would be useless against him. But against others? In a smooth glide of movement, she pulled the knife free and threw. It hissed through the air and landed with a juicy thud deep within Tottie's eye socket. Tottie screamed, her body arching against the pain.

"Traitorous bitch," Mary snapped as Tottie flailed about, and Amaros laughed with delight. Mary ignored him and watched Tottie. While GIM could heal, they could not regrow limbs or eyes. "Think on your deceit every time you look in the mirror."

"You are a savage little thing," Amaros said with a wide, insane grin. He snapped his fingers, and a pair of guards took hold of the still-screaming Tottie and dragged her out. When she was gone and her cries had faded, he turned back to Mary. "I do believe we shall get on well, Miss Chase."

"While we wait for Jack to come to my rescue?" She suffered from no illusion as to why she was here.

"Yes." All humor left his face, and he bared his teeth in a grimace. "Have you not seen?" He waved a hand over his body, gesturing to the sores. "It appears that I am not healed after all."

In a violent blur of motion, Amaros grabbed a goblet from the table and flung it against the far wall. The pewter exploded upon impact, sending thick shards of metal across the room. He kicked a heavy wooden chair over and stalked toward her. "I want my body restored! And that little bastard is going to give his blood to me. I am going to suck on him until he begs for mercy."

And Jack would let him. Mary knew it to her core. He couldn't kill Amaros, or he'd be cursed to the same fate. But he'd do it for her. Well, Mary thought, she wasn't going to let him. There was one game she knew how to play quite well.

"I would like a new gown," she said calmly.

Amaros visibly paused, frowning at her as if she were touched in the head. But then he gave her a patient smile. "Of course. No need to sit in discomfort."

"Very kind of you," she murmured, all the while letting her full GIM nature free. Beguilement, seduction. It swirled in the air and throbbed in her skin. She knew she'd gone luminous, and that her eyes softly glowed.

Interest lit in the fallen's gaze. As she'd known it would. Good, let him want her. A man led by his cock was a man who did not use his brain.

"Now what are you planning, Miss Chase?" Amaros drawled.

To kill you. "I have a proposition for you."

"Oh?" He loomed over her, his rage a seething mass of dark energy that affected her heart's rhythm. "Other than a nice long fuck, what can you possibly give me?"

Ignoring the flutter of anxiety within, Mary moved with languid grace to the table to pick up a goblet. Slowly she poured a glass of wine and raised it to her lips, Amaros tracking every move. Holding his gaze with hers, she let the glass play along the curve of her bottom lip, noting the way his own lips parted and his body tightened.

"A better existence."

He paused, his mouth turning down. "Pardon?"

"One that doesn't leave you beholden to another's blood." She said it calmly, but Mary knew her ploy could turn down a wrong lane in an instant. But it couldn't be helped. Jack needed her. She glanced at the table. "Might we discuss it?"

Amaros smiled, the very picture of geniality and good breeding. A veritable wolf in sheep's clothing. "By all means. Please, do have a seat." His black robes gave his movements a flowing quality as he gestured to an empty chair.

Once Mary sat, he righted his overturned chair and followed suit.

"Jack's blood heals you," she said. "But it does not last, nor will it restore your heart."

Amaros's eyes narrowed in impatience. "The Evernight girl has made me a new heart. It will work."

"It will turn you into a shadow crawler, decaying ever still, dependent on blood to stay whole. But I can make you a ghost in the machine. A true GIM, born from magic, pure and restored."

Suspicion clouded his eyes. "How is this so? Only Adam is known to have such power."

In an effort to hide her clammy hands, Mary adjusted her skirts. "It was a gift bestowed upon me by Adam."

"And why would he do such a thing?"

"That is my business."

Amaros's nostrils flared before he got his temper under control. "I think you had better prove your claim, Miss Chase, for I remain wary."

"Before we go any further, if I agree to this pact, then you agree to leave Jack Talent alone. You must swear to never pursue him for blood or harm him in any manner."

A moue of resistance marred Amaros's face. It was clear that he did not fancy this part of the bargain. A calculating look came into Amaros's eye, and Mary decided to nip it in the bud. "This gift can only work of my free will. It cannot be made under duress." She held his dubious gaze with one of cool authority, as if she weren't lying through her teeth; she had no idea how the gift worked, or if it even would.

The corner of his eye twitched, and he offered her a tight nod. "Very well. I agree. I shall not pursue Jack Talent for his blood, or seek to harm him. Easily done," he added, "if you can do what you say you can."

"A blood vow, Amaros. I believe fallen are just as beholden to those as sanguis, yes?" It was said that the fallen had given birth to the sanguis line, hence they both had a taste for blood. Once a vow was made, he could not go back on it or his soul would crack. An irrevocable break that would leave him senseless.

He did not flinch from her demand. "Blood oath it is. Dependent upon your ability to turn me into a GIM."

"Then we have an agreement."

Silver flared in his eyes at the words and that slightly off, tilted smile returned. "Not just yet. I'd have assurances as well, Miss Chase."

Her heart slowed. "Which are?"

"What is to say that you will stay loyal to me? What is to say this isn't a trap?"

Right. Mary smiled, her eyes glowing with the light of the GIM and all the persuasion it afforded. "Because I love Jack Talent. I would die to protect him." It was the truth. And if it came to that, then so be it.

"Not good enough."

A movement by her side gave her only enough time to

steel herself, then a guard was there, holding an electric prod against her side. Mary stilled. She remembered the pain of that prod. "Not very hospitable of you."

"Apologies," Amaros said.

"Nor is it a good way to get what you want," she added.

"I'd rather kill you and risk becoming a crawler than be betrayed, my dear." His smile was a parody of a kindly gentleman's.

"Then what do you suggest?" she asked, as if her heart weren't stalled within her breast.

"I give you my bond, and you give me yours."

Mary did not like the lascivious look in his eyes, yet her voice came out smooth. "I'm afraid a blood bond won't work on me."

"No," he said, "but a slave bond will."

Bound to do as he willed. She'd never be able to harm him. Worse, once bound she could not leave her body in spirit form unless he willed it so. Her mouth went dry. She'd be his slave for the entirety of his life or hers. Mary took a steadying breath. She had no other choice. She knew perfectly well that if she backed out he'd kill her anyway. That truth was written in the steadiness of his gaze and the small but smug smile playing around his lips.

She needed to believe that when Jack came for her, he would understand enough to do what was required. Together they were strong enough to defeat the fallen. She knew it within her soul. And it gave her the courage to forge ahead.

"All right," she said, with a calm she did not feel.

Again came the mad gleam in the fallen's eyes and the disturbing smile of triumph. "Then let us perform the bond and complete our bargain."

A knife appeared in his hand, the move so quick she didn't see it. He sliced through his palm and then hers, the burn of the cut but a blink in her mind before he grasped hands with hers and held tight. As their blood mingled, Amaros gave his bond.

"Now," he said when he'd finished, "give me yours."

The words tasted like filth in her mouth. "By this blood, I am your slave."

Instantly something snaked around her neck, coiling tight and choking off her air. She struggled for a breath, and then the tightness eased, until it felt as though she simply wore a collar. Which she did. Unable to resist, Mary touched her tender neck. It was smooth, but sensation rippled beneath her skin.

Her hand shook as she let it fall.

"Lovely," Amaros breathed as he fingered the hollow of her neck.

Mary's skin crawled. More so when he leaned in, his lids lowering with lazy intent.

"Let us see how well this bond truly works." His tongue ran over the tip of one fang. "Kiss me."

The demand punched through her like a fist, and she could not stop from leaning forward and putting her lips to his. A sob of despair stuck in her throat.

"Mmm, like you mean it," he said, as his hand slid inside her torn bodice.

Go numb. Do not think. Numbness was not so easily achieved as before. As his thick tongue filled her mouth, she felt the humiliation of the act down to her soul.

Jack walked into the ancient crypt alone, his footsteps making a hollow sound against the stone. Not a soul moved out of the shadows to stop him. He was, after all, expected. To plead for Mary's life in exchange for his. But Jack was not so naive as to think either of them was walking out of this hell unscathed. Jack would plead, and Amaros would taunt and torture. Their mutual hate was too deeply rooted for any other outcome.

Physical torture Jack could take. Hell, he'd prefer it. But Amaros would know that as well. What Jack could not stand was the thought of Mary being harmed. His love for her crippled him here.

Only hours ago he'd been swimming in her sweet scent, drowning in her tight heat. Hours. The difference between dawn and dusk.

"Piss and shit." He halted, unable to take another step. How could he be strong and still keep her safe?

He couldn't. The realization surged through him. He had to rely on her strength to get her through. He had to believe in her. Just as she believed in him.

Following her scent, Jack ended up before a pair of massive metal doors. Iron. Lovely. On either side stood a guard. They did not look at him, but immediately opened the doors.

A vast underground hall spread out before him and, in the flickering light of torches, sat a court of demons. Raptors and sanguis. His skin crawled. They eyed him with greedy intent as he strode forward.

Sitting at the far end, like a puffed-up king, was Amaros. And he was no longer an injured fallen. He was a GIM, his golden clockwork heart proudly displayed behind the glass window in his torso. Glowing with health and vigor, his GIM eyes gleamed topaz like Mary's. How the bloody hell had he managed it? But Jack knew. And it drained the blood from his head.

Mary. She was at Amaros's side. Jack had expected it,

but not to see her in a blood-red gown whose bodice was so low that the swells of her breasts spilled over. But that was not what curdled Jack's blood. It was the chain tattoo around her throat.

A bonded slave. What had she done?

The floor beneath his feet seemed to sway as he forced himself closer. That chain tattooed about her neck... Blood pooled in his mouth as he bit down hard to keep from shouting.

But Amaros knew too well how it affected Jack, and he draped a lazy arm around her slim shoulders, his fingers dangling just above her breasts. Mary stared at Jack, her eyes haunted and her skin pale. No longer could she pretend indifference, and the knowledge broke his heart.

Jack stopped before them. "I've come to offer myself in her stead."

"Mmm," murmured Amaros as he began to idly stroke Mary's shoulder. "Well, that is a problem, for you see, I do not need you anymore." His fangs flashed. "And I am rather enjoying my new pet. Perhaps I'll let my court use her too."

Bile burned up Jack's throat. He wanted to scream, to lunge and kill the bastard. But he had Mary in his grip. Her gaze burned as though she willed Jack to understand something. But she wouldn't speak. Likely couldn't.

Claws dug into Jack's fists.

Jack took a slow look around the room. He knew these fiends. They'd been party to his greatest humiliation. They'd been Nex. But if Will was correct, they were no longer.

"You've broken from the Nex," he said to Amaros.

"I was never with the Nex." Amaros waved an idle hand. "I used them. Never think otherwise."

"And yet you have recruited their agents." Jack glanced pointedly at them. "The Nex will not simply let that go. Once Nex, always Nex. Isn't that what they say?"

A soft grumble went around the room.

"They will come at you with everything they've got." Jack said. "I give you free use of my blood. You may no longer need to restore your health, but it still has power."

"So you would join my merry band? To cut ties with your new little family? With the SOS that you hold so dear?"

"They will understand," Jack said quietly, as though sweat were not pouring down his back, as though the sight of Mary being debased did not drive him to one breath away from insane rage.

"What makes you believe you are even worthy of their regard?" Amaros sneered. "A thief, a killer, a sullen boy who hates the whole world."

All of it was true. At one time or another he'd pushed away everyone and everything that mattered to him. He could be a right bastard, and knew full well when he was acting the part. Was he worthy? He glanced at Mary. A fleeting look. He didn't need it, really. Every inch of her was committed to his memory. She'd live there until the end of time.

"She loves me," he said.

"What?"

Jack's conviction made him strong. "Because that woman loves me. Because my family, my *true* family, loves me. That is why I am worthy. Because *they* are the most worthy, brave, loyal people I know. And if they see something in me that is worth loving, despite my many flaws, then that is all the proof I need." He took a step closer. "It is *all* I need."

He was loved. And it wasn't going to be taken away.

"She is my slave." Amaros grinned. "Any loving Miss Chase shall be doing will be with me."

Jack laughed without humor. "Bloody hell, I never thought I'd see the day a fallen was led about by his cock."

Amaros leaned forward in his chair. "You're here because of your cock, boy."

"No, I'm here because of love. Do you love her?"

Amaros snorted.

"I did not believe so," Jack said. "So now I'm wondering why you hesitate to take my blood. Tell me, Amaros, are you afraid that it will harm your new GIM body?"

"A nice ploy, my boy." Amaros leaned back in his chair and hauled Mary closer. "However, since you insist on taunting, I believe we can accommodate your desire to give up your blood. Call your sacrifice a gesture of good faith. Then I shall consider the matter."

Jack stood still as two raptors approached him. One female and one male. They hummed in appreciation as they drew near. The first touch crawled over his skin. He kept his gaze upon Mary.

"I remember you," said the male. A cold tongue touched Jack's ear, and he flinched. "Do you remember me?"

Nausea rolled within him. "Yes." Too well.

A little laugh rumbled in his ear. Then those vile lips were on his neck. He did not cry out as fangs broke his skin and the taut pulls began. He kept his attention on Mary. For her he could endure anything. But he had underestimated his resolve in one fatal way.

Amaros's hand dug beneath Mary's bodice. And Jack's world went red.

Chapter Thirty-Four

~~~~~~

The moment the fallen touched her, Mary knew what would happen. But she hadn't expected the ferocity of Jack's response. His nostrils flared wide and, in the next instant, he burst free of his tormentors with a roar of sheer rage. His bloodstained shirt fluttered to the floor as a pair of massive black wings appeared on his back with a crisp snap.

There was a moment's silence and then chaos as Jack ripped into the demons with fangs and claws. None of them had a chance. They were paper dolls in his hands, torn asunder in a blur of fury.

Beside her, Amaros simply laughed as the blood flowed and the demons scrambled to get away.

She had to get to Jack, tell him what needed to be done. And then she needed to die. She'd known that the minute she'd made her bargain. Unfortunately, since she was a slave, there was only one way to get close to Jack. Mary eyed Amaros. Arrogance had been the downfall of many a better male than this one. Mary would use it now, and pray that he took the bait.

"He'll be coming for you," she said to him. God, she wanted to claw the fallen's eyes out, slice into him the way Jack was cutting through those who'd tormented him.

"Oh yes," Amaros said with another chuckle. "And I'll suck him dry and eat his marrow."

"You promised not to harm him." *Tell me to do it. Make me suffer.* She knew Amaros was cruel enough to consider pitting Mary against Jack. He only needed a little motivation.

A sly smile twisted over his face. "I may have neglected to tell you, my dear, but blood bonds will not hold me, for I am already mortally cursed."

Her hopes plummeted for an instant. Then she changed her course, trying again. Whatever it took, she would get to Jack.

"He did this for me." She glanced down, letting a tear fall. With wide eyes she looked up at him, even as she struggled to evade his touch, which only inflamed him. His grip grew painful, and she flinched again. "Please," she begged in a breathy voice. "Please stop this. I cannot bear it. I will do anything."

"You will do anything regardless."

As if he heard them, Jack's wild gaze focused on them, and he bared his teeth in a snarl. Gone was any trace of the man she knew and loved. He was pure rage now. And when he stalked toward them, his massive fists curled tight.

Still smiling, Amaros let her go and stood, predictable in his arrogance. "You can't kill me, boy. But I am happy to play."

They crashed into each other with a loud smack and tumbled to the ground. And Mary waited for the perfect moment to strike.

*   *   *

Jack relished the pain of Amaros's hit. His body absorbed it and then he lashed out, smashing into the fallen's face with all his strength. Bones snapped and blood sprayed. He did not wait but hit again, aiming for the fragile glass window that protected the fallen's heart. But Amaros was quick and countered with an uppercut. Jack's head snapped back, blood filling his mouth. He swallowed it down and whirled, jabbing Amaros's exposed ribs, hearing them crack, before he ducked under an oncoming blow.

Not fast enough. Amaros caught his arm and, in one move, broke it at the elbow. Jack bellowed, pain slicing through him. His useless arm flopped down, and the fallen's eyes shone bright with victory. Jack lashed back, realizing that it was his wing he'd used. The massive appendage caught Amaros on the head, and he staggered. Jack used the moment to bring his knee up. Hard. Into the fallen's bollocks. A low move, but he didn't care for shit about honor. Destroy or die trying. That was all that mattered now. Not a bloody curse. Mary's freedom meant more than any suffering he'd face.

The fallen crumbled, and Jack launched himself onto him, grabbing hold of one glossy feathered wing and pulling with all his might. A meaty, tearing sound filled his ears as Amaros screamed and the fallen's wing ripped free. Hot blood sprayed Jack's face as he landed a sharp kick to Amaros's jaw.

"Jack!"

Mary's shout halted him. She was striding toward him, something metal in her hand, her face a mask of determination. "Stop."

Stop? Not bloody likely. Something deep within told him that the loss of the fallen's wings would be fatal.

On the floor Amaros stirred as though trying to shift. Or fade away.

"Attempting to turn into shadow?" Jack taunted, for he remembered that cowardly trick from the fountain in the square. "I think your new GIM nature ended that power." Maybe it hadn't. Jack wasn't waiting to find out. He growled, reaching for the fallen's other wing.

But the hard press of cold metal and Mary's arm wrapped about his neck had him freezing.

"I needed you to fight him so that I could get close to you," she said against his ear. "But I will not let you kill him."

He balked, not understanding, until he caught her gaze. She'd only be able to come near in defense of Amaros. All the more reason to destroy the fallen. She was not going to be enslaved a moment longer.

Heart thundering and blood boiling, he glared down at Amaros. "Let me go, Mary. I *will* finish him."

"No. Not when it means seeing you become what he is."

The curse? He didn't care. Not if it meant Mary was a slave to this bastard.

The moment he moved, she tensed, pressing the metal more firmly under his chin. "Do not make me hurt you, Jack."

On the ground Amaros lay panting. His color had turned an ugly white, his skin sweating and blotchy as his blood ran blue-crimson over the stone floor. But Jack could see that spark of vitality still within him. He would heal. Unless Jack tore the other wing off and beheaded the bastard. The truth of it was a whisper in his head. He would obey it now. For only he had the strength to do it.

The fallen's eyes held this knowledge, and the realization that Jack had no hesitation. Amaros lifted his gaze to Mary. "Kill him."

Chapter Thirty-Five

———◆◆◆———

At his back Mary went stiff, drawing in a sharp breath. Jack knew she'd be compelled to act or suffer. And his heart squeezed tight.

"Now," Amaros rasped as his lids began to flutter closed.

Jack turned, capturing Mary in his arms, and her wide, pained eyes looked up at him. If Mary did not kill Jack she would die in agony for disobeying her master.

"Do what you must," he whispered, holding her steady as her heart clicked away at a frantic pace. He could see her struggling to disobey and the wash of pain that accompanied her defiance. "Do it, angel."

But she shook her head abruptly. "Kill me," she managed in a gasp. The length of metal she'd been holding found its way into his hand, and he realized it was the electric prod that had stopped her heart before. "Hurry."

No! "I will not."

She touched his cheek, and her fingers curled as if she wanted to rake his flesh. Mary gritted her teeth. "Trust me, Jack. I will end this."

His throat tightened, the pain in his chest branching out along with a sick sense of dread. "I cannot."

Her body twitched, her mouth growing tight and pained. "This is the only way. Jack . . ." She shuddered, her hands coming up and around his neck as if to choke him. "Please."

"Mary, love, I can't."

With a gasp of pain, she grabbed his wrist and forced the prod upward, determination making her stronger than he. His vision blurred. He could not hurt her, take her life. What if she didn't come back? He couldn't live.

Beneath them Amaros was stirring, trying to rise, his mouth moving as if to speak. Another order from him and Mary would likely break. Sweat dotted her brow, and her body convulsed. "Together, Jack," she whispered, "we are stronger than you know."

Trust. He had to believe in it. In her. Stifling a sob, he held her tight. Tight enough that his arms would never forget the feel of her body. "I love you," he whispered. *Come back to me.* And then he pressed the button.

Electricity surged through Mary's body with razor-sharp pain. Her heart slammed to a halt, and she fell to the floor just as Jack roared. Free. She was finally free of Amaros's bond and command. All her focus went to him. Being both GIM and fallen, he could see her clearly. His eyes widened as she rushed toward him. Finally she had him where she wanted him.

"You may have owned my body," she said. "But I own your spirit."

He heard every word and scrambled back on the floor. *The creator giveth life, and the creator taketh away.*

She reached for him. Amaros's soul was black and yellow, a muddy slime. Horrid and foul. And it was bound to her immediately. Blackness and terror surrounded her, Amaros's soul tainting hers with each moment they were connected. And then she tugged the fallen into hell.

The moment Jack saw Mary's spirit merge with Amaros's, he understood perfect terror. Her clean, bright soul was turning black, becoming diseased with the fallen's evil. Above him Amaros's soul thrashed, desperate to return to his body. And yet she stayed connected. For them.

She mouthed the words "I love you" and then, as if a light had been doused, Amaros's spirit simply vanished. And so did Mary's.

"Mary!"

But she was gone, disappeared as though she'd never been. She'd taken Amaros's soul, which meant Jack could destroy his body without fear of being cursed.

With all his strength Jack lunged, his claws slicing through Amaros's neck in one swipe. Jack ripped the fallen's remaining wing off with one pull, just as the severed head toppled to the floor.

Cursing, he leapt over Amaros's body and ran toward her prone form. "Mary!"

She'd return now. She had to. But her body was cold when Jack gathered her up. "Merrily. God. Come back." Tears blurred his vision as he stroked a hand over her cheek. Her wide golden eyes were open and void of life. Viciously he ripped open her bodice and went for her key. But it was gone.

"Shit!" He eased her down and scrambled back to Amaros's body. He had to have taken Mary's key.

Already the fallen's blood was disintegrating. Foul

clumps of flesh stuck to Jack's fingers and he tore about, trying to find the key. His vision blurred, his movements too frantic.

"Shit, shit, shit." Taking a breath, he forced himself to think, to go slowly. "He'd have worn it or risked losing it," Jack muttered to himself. Jack reached for the stump of the fallen's neck, and his pulse leapt. Dangling from a black cord lay the key to Mary's heart.

Too much time was wasted reaching her again, inserting the key, and turning it. Sweating and shaking, Jack sat back as the heart began to start, and her body closed. But nothing else happened.

"Mary." He gave her a gentle shake, but she remained silent and staring. Her eyes void of life. "Merrily, wake up. Wake up."

Still nothing.

"Fuck." Tearing at his flesh, Jack held his wrist over her parted lips. Blood poured into her mouth, but it merely ran over her lips and down her cheek. She was gone.

He'd destroyed everyone who had hurt him. And it meant nothing. Not without her.

Mary. She'd died for him.

Chapter Thirty-Six

❦

She was in Nowhere. Mary would rather call it Hell. Attached as she was to Amaros's soul, she had known she would be dragged with him. It was not a physical place, but one of spirit. No fields of ice or lakes of fire. There was simply sensation and reflection. Every deed, experience, regret, every small secret part of her soul reflected back at her. She felt it all magnified to such a degree that her soul yearned to shatter, if only to end the overwhelming barrage of emotions.

Hell indeed. But for Amaros it was agony.

The instant they entered Nowhere, his terror and suffering rippled through her like the recoil of a gun. But while Hell wanted him, began to feed on his soul with greedy pulls, it seemed to know this was not Mary's place. Their souls divided once more. And she was cast out of Nowhere.

With dizzying speed she hurtled through the dark void and then slammed into her body with so much force that she lurched upward.

Air rushed into her lungs on a great gasp. Her eyes focused. Jack Talent scowled down at her.

And wasn't that a lovely sight.

His blazing green gaze traveled over her face, and then, with a sob, he hauled her close. "Piss and shit and buggering, bloody, fucking hell, Mary. Don't you *ever* scare me like that again."

He buried his face in her hair as his thick arms tightened around her, and his ribald litany continued.

She snuggled in closer, letting him curse, letting him pet and kiss her. Because Jack Talent, in all his imperfect glory, made her perfectly happy.

Something stirred from without. Holly could feel it as much as she heard it. So could her fellow prisoners. The quick, clipped sound of the approaching footsteps sounded nothing like those of her jailers. And though every inch of her was battered, she hauled herself to her feet and pressed her face to the bars of her cell, straining to see what she could.

Across the way a pair of dark, glittering eyes peered out from behind thick glass. Watching. Waiting.

Holly looked away. At her side Thorne lay still and quiet. Too quiet. Were it not for the slow, even breaths he took every few seconds, she'd have believed he was dead.

At the turn of the lock upon the outer doors, her icy fingers gripped the bars tighter.

As if flowing on a wave, the sound of her fellow prisoners beginning to move filled the cellar. Locks clattered, a man's murmur of reassurance following. A giddy sort of hope grew within Holly. And then he was there. Jack Talent. Holly reared back, her nerves destroyed.

"Easy now," he said softly. "You're safe." As if he

knew exactly how frayed and open she felt. He glanced at Thorne and horror darkened his face. Uttering a ripe curse, he opened the door and hurried to him.

Then Mary Chase appeared. On a sob Holly flew into her friend's arms, and Mary held her fast.

"It's all over now, dearest."

Mary and Holly went to help with Thorne when a commotion broke out in the cell across the way. A violent darkness swarmed there, and the unsuspecting man who'd been opening the glass cell leapt back with a yelp as a hundred spiders scurried past and out the door.

Chapter Thirty-Seven

Mary woke to find the space next to her empty. Cool, rumpled sheets told her that Jack had been gone for some time. Pushing her hair back from her face, she sat up, and the sound of crinkling paper alerted her to his note.

In true Jack Talent fashion, it was brief, though the words were surprisingly formal.

> I apologize for my absence. I had to see about a matter of great importance. Would you do me the honor of meeting me at headquarters at four o'clock?
>
> Yours,
> J

Mary let the note fall to the bed. What matter was so very important that he could not wake her?

Her curiosity stirred higher when, having dressed and ventured downstairs, she encountered Jack's day housekeeper, who brought her a fine breakfast and news that Mr. Talent had sent for a few of Mary's gowns in order that she be properly attired. Indeed?

She was still perturbed, hours later, when she arrived at headquarters wearing her best day dress—for Jack had only selected her most formal gowns—a sleek creation with a pale-bronze silk bodice and overskirt and a rippling underskirt of deep, luscious wine satin.

Her trepidation only heightened when Inspector Lane met her instead of Jack. Where was the blasted man?

Her instincts screamed that something was afoot.

"Mistress Chase," said Lane, "you look lovely." He offered her his arm. "If you would come with me?" His blue-grey eyes twinkled. "And before you ask, I'm not at liberty to divulge any information. Master Talent's orders."

"Since when do you take orders from Jack?" she asked, as they made their way up a narrow spiral staircase.

Lane grinned, and the scars along his face wrinkled. "Since he asked me to return a well-earned favor."

Without another word he led her through Holly Evernight's laboratory. The lofty space was abandoned and too quiet, and the click of her heels echoed against the marble.

With the bearing of a duke's son, Lane stopped at a pair of massive doors hung on rollers, and pushed one wide.

Sunlight poured through the glass ceiling and bathed Holly's dirigible with brilliant white winter light. Standing at the prow, his form just visible behind the wide glass windows, was Jack.

Mary began to smile, her heart whirring just a bit faster.

Seeing her, he moved away from the window and emerged a moment later to deftly descend the dirigible's ladder. Mary barely noticed Inspector Lane stepping away. Her attention was on the man walking toward her.

And then Jack was there. Neither of them spoke, Mary because he'd struck her dumb. The man who stood before her was the Jack Talent of old, impeccably dressed and groomed, so very stiff with formality, and yet he was also the Jack she'd become close to, large and vibrating with strength and energy. He was utterly gorgeous.

He wore a charcoal-grey morning suit that hugged the broad strokes of his torso like a second skin. The cutaway coat emphasized his strong thighs and long legs, encased in dove-grey trousers. A smoky-green silk tie was knotted beneath his pristine white collar, the contrasting hues emphasizing the color of his eyes and the golden tone of his skin.

"Well, look at you," she finally managed.

A tinge of color washed over his broad cheeks. "It was past time." His voice was subdued, almost hesitant, and Mary wondered again what he was about this day.

Jack took another step, then planted his feet and linked his hands behind him. Such a stiff pose, yet his eyes roamed over her with a kind of hunger that made her flush. Why wouldn't he embrace her? He stood as though he were afraid of her, but looked at her as if she were the only person in the room. Mary did not know what to make of this change. Nor did she know how to act in the face of it.

"You are beautiful," he blurted out, then took a deep breath. "Truly."

"Thank you." It almost came out as a question because she still could not fathom what reason he had to be nervous.

Gently, as though she might break, he took her hand, engulfing it in his big, warm one. "Come for a ride with me?"

A flush of pleasure washed through her. "Up? In the air?"

He grinned, that brilliant, glorious grin that made her knees weak every time she saw it. "That is the idea." He tugged her forward.

Excitement mounted as Mary climbed the ladder into the dirigible's cabin. Smelling of polished wood and motor oil, the cabin gleamed in the sunlight. It was an open space with large windows on three sides. A group of armchairs had been bolted to either side of the cabin floor, each chair facing a window. To the fore, a wall cut the pilot's booth off from the main cabin, and the door to it lay closed.

"Do you know how to pilot this thing?" she asked Jack, who stepped in beside her.

"No need to." Jack reached out and grabbed a brass cone that came out of the wall. He spun a small lever next to it, and the air crackled with sound. "All set back here, Charlie," he said into the cone.

Before she could question, a great shudder ran through the craft as the engines roared to life. The cabin vibrated, and Mary took a step nearer to Jack. Laughing softly, he cradled her close and drew her to the window. "Look," he whispered. Below, Inspector Lane was now at the control box. He fiddled with the dials and knobs, and a loud clattering followed.

Mary and Jack craned their necks to see the massive iron chain dangling from the hangar wall start to move. Far above them the glass-paneled roof pulled back.

Jack's lips grazed her ear. "Off we go."

The craft lurched, and Jack braced them. Mary's insides dipped. She clutched Jack tighter and looked out.

"Scared?" he whispered, a note of concern in his eyes.

"No." Mary grinned. "Thrilled."

They laughed together as the airship rose, up, up, up. London seemed to sink away, falling farther and farther below. A lovely illusion. And beneath her feet, the wondrous ship swayed and surged, a thrilling combination of power and buoyancy.

"You said you wanted to know how it felt to fly," Jack said to her as the craft turned east and billowy clouds, pierced by sunbeams, rolled past.

"Jack..." She cupped his cheek. "It is perfect."

A flush worked across his skin, and his lashes lowered. Strangely bashful, he studied the floor before him. "Your scent," he said abruptly. "Your voice. Your humor. Your kindness." He glanced at her, then away. "Your smile." Taking a short breath, he faced her, his shoulders back and square. "In that order."

Mary blinked at him. "I'm sorry?"

His flush grew. "Damn..." Jack's mouth firmed. "Those are the things I first fell in love with about you. When we met that night on Lucien's barge."

"Oh...well." A lovely warmth spread over her skin as she stared up at him.

"But what captured my heart"—he swallowed quickly, his eyes not quite meeting hers—"what stole my soul, was your mind. That sharp, twisted, utterly lovely mind."

He looked at her then, brows raised a bit, his expression soft. "I didn't want you to think it was merely physical, you see."

She did see, and the warmth in her bloomed bright. He opened his mouth to speak but she beat him to it.

"Am I not allowed to give my list as well?"

"Oh. Yes. Of course." Jack shifted his weight, bringing his hands back before him like a pupil facing a headmaster.

Mary's lips wanted to twitch, but she kept her expression neutral. "The impeccable cut of your suit. Your gorgeous eyes." He flushed at that. "Your voice, smooth as cream sherry. Your wit. And your smile, like the sun on the sea."

Jack cleared his throat, a gruff male sound that made her smile.

"But what captured my heart, stole my soul, was the dark, twisted, ridiculously blunt"—he scowled, though humor lit his eyes—"wonderfully loyal man inside that delicious package."

"Mary..." He took her hand and led her to a chair. As she sat he made that nervous sound again, his skin ruddy against his white collar. When he sat in the chair opposite her, his spine was stiff. Behind him, framed by the windows, endless blue sky opened up. Large blocks of sunlight drifted across the floor and landed upon his shoulders. Hints of bronze glinted in his dark hair as he bent his head and stared at his hands. "The thing is, we're not like other people."

She nodded, still at sea with this whole strange conversation.

"We'll live forever," he went on, his color high and his voice growing increasingly strained. "Societal laws don't truly touch us." Jack's head jerked to the side as if he found his collar too tight. "You and I... we might go on just as we are now, and be content."

Mary's heart clicked. What was he trying to say? But before she could ask, he was moving. Her breath caught as he knelt before her, taking her hands in his own. His fingers were ice-cold and trembling along with his voice. "The thing is," he whispered, keeping his eyes on their hands, "while I'll have you any way you let me, for however long as I can, I want—"

He took an audible breath and then raised his gaze to hers, and Mary's throat closed. The whole of his soul was reflected in the green depths of his eyes. Utterly, perfectly beautiful.

"I want the pomp and circumstance. I want to vow before our friends and family that I shall love and protect you. I want the world to know that you are mine and I am yours. So then..." He licked his lips and quickly hurried on. "Mary Chase, would you do me the great honor of becoming my wife? I know that I'm not—"

She grabbed hold of him and kissed him silent.

"Yes," she said against his lips. "Yes to all of it."

And he fell into the kiss, his mouth desperate, his tense body letting go with a shudder.

"Thank God," he breathed, then kissed her again, quick, loving kisses that had her laughing. But he soon jerked back. "Damn it..." Jack let her go and fumbled about in his coat. "I knew I'd get it wrong." His ears grew red as he pulled a gold ring from his pocket.

"Now, I've heard that women fancy diamonds, and I'll go back and get you one if you desire it, but..." He shook his head a little, his brows furrowing as he took her hand in his. "I saw this ring and thought, 'That is us.'"

Mary bent forward to see, and when she did, a happy laugh broke from her. Coiled around each other to form a ring were two stylized golden snakes, their little heads tucked close to form the ring's face. Prince Albert had given Queen Victoria something similar. Snakes for immortality and eternal love. "It's perfect," she whispered.

Slowly, and with a bit of difficulty, for his hands shook, Jack slipped the ring onto her finger. The light caught it, and the tiny emerald and topaz stones that made up the respective snakes' eyes flared. Another wave of giddy laughter surged through Mary, and she wrapped her arms around Jack.

He pulled her close, rising and then settling back on the chair with her in his lap. The cabin dipped and swayed as the airship changed course. And Mary's heart felt buoyant. Together they watched London roll away, all dark shadows and hard angles. Ahead of them lay an expanse of green with the blue sliver of the English Channel just beyond.

"It's all right, then?" Jack asked after a moment.

Still worried. Dear man. She glanced down at the little gold snakes on her finger. Cold-blooded creatures whom most thought unable to love. And yet there they were, coiled about each other in perfect contentment. Stronger together than apart.

"It is us, Jack. To a T." Mary cupped his cheeks. "I love you." She kissed his nose. His chin. "I love you, John Michael Talent." She kissed his mouth. "I love you, Jack."

He let go of a long breath. "Don't ever stop." He kissed her back, softly lingering.

"Never."

Jack's hands slid to her shoulder blades, holding her against him. "Don't ever stop telling me," he demanded softly against her mouth. "Tell me today, and tomorrow, and all the days after."

She sighed into him, taking his breath, giving him hers. "You'll grow weary of hearing it."

His hand eased down her back. "You'll have to test the theory and see." Then he flipped her, so quickly and easily that she could only squeak before she was on the chair and he was blanketing her with his body. She loved the size of him and that he could move her about as he willed.

"And what of me?" she asked, wrapping herself around him. "Am I not to receive such verbal admiration?"

Smiling, he kissed her. "That and more. I'll tell you until you think it your name." His lips found her neck. "And every look I give you will say the same: I love you. Wholly. Utterly. Completely."

She chuckled, nuzzling closer. "But those words mean the same thing."

"Precisely. That I love you." He raised his head to glare at her, though not very effectively. "Stop trying to distract me, Chase. I have an objective here."

"Which is?" A silly question. She could feel his objective rather insistently nudging her thigh.

A low, pleased growl rumbled in his throat as she shifted her leg, and he nipped her shoulder. "Demonstrative proof."

Epilogue

~~~☙~~~

He died. He remembered that clearly. Died in pain and degradation, his body taken and torn asunder. He remembered the pain, how the jagged blade had carved into his chest, and how they'd ripped his heart out and replaced it with one of metal. Strange that the pain hadn't left him. He'd fancied that once dead, one would feel no pain. Apparently that was not to be. *You're in it now, mate.* Unending agony that he couldn't get away from, couldn't catch his breath between.

Should he be able to breathe if he was dead? He stopped to think about this and realized he didn't know his name. Didn't know who he was or what he'd been. Panic surged, and he tried to focus. But there was only that heart, so heavy and unwelcome, clicking and whirring within his breast. And blackness. All-encompassing. *Black. Pitch. Tar. Raven. Wings . . .*

Words bounced about in his mind like water over a rocky path. *Focus.* He would remember. And when he did, the one who had hurt him would pay.

Jet. Sable. Ebony. Night . . .

His eyes snapped open. "Evernight."

Once the flames are ignited,

they will burn for eternity.

Please turn this page for an excerpt

from the first Darkest London novel,

Firelight

Firelight

―――――――――❦～❦―――――――――

Getting married was a happy dream that had filled Miranda's girlhood thoughts and promptly left as she grew older. She well knew the face that looked back from the mirror each morning. She was not foolish enough to pretend that she was without beauty. Vanity may be a sin but so was lying. She was fair of face and form, though she knew many a girl who looked better.

However, as a woman without fortune or title, she received few offers of marriage. The most consistent offers came in the form of teasing shouts from market vendors when she walked to Covent Garden each Saturday morning. How then, she thought as Daisy pinned white roses in her hair the following morning, had it come to this?

Perhaps it was a dream. The woman in the mirror didn't look at all like her. She was too pale. Her pink gown, one of many provided by Lord Archer's money, ruffled and frothed around her like a confectionary. Miranda turned away with disdain. It was the image of an innocent and a maiden. She was neither. And yet *he* had come for her. Why?

She did not believe Father's nonsense about him wanting her for her beauty. There were plenty of pretty daughters of utterly bankrupt, thus desperate, nobles for a wealthy man to choose from. What, then, did he want? *What has the world come to when men such as he are permitted to roam the streets…* Perspiration bloomed along her upper lip. And yet Lord Archer did not know precisely what he was acquiring when he took Miranda as his bride, did he?

To create fire by mere thought. It was the stuff of myth. She had discovered the talent quite by accident. And had burned through her share of disasters. Father and Mother had forbidden anyone to ever speak of it and, more to the point, for Miranda to ever use her talent again. Poppy had simply disappeared in the library to search for an explanation; she never found one. Only Daisy had been impressed, though quite put out that she did not possess a similar unearthly talent. As for herself, the question always remained: Was she a monster? Both beauty and beast rolled into one unstable force? Despite her desire to know, there was the greater fear of putting the question to anyone and seeing them turn away as Martin had. So she kept it inside. She would not tell her husband to be, no. But she took comfort in the notion that she was not without defenses.

Poppy and Daisy's mutual disregard for Father kept them at a distance as Father hovered by her elbow, guarding all possible attempts to escape. Their chatter was no more than a din, Father's hand upon her arm a ghost, as they made their way to the small family chapel by the river.

Reverend Spradling met them at the door. The brackets around his fleshy mouth cut deep as his eyes slid from Miranda to Father. "Lord Archer is..." He tilted his head and pulled at the cassock hugging his bulging neck. "He is waiting in the vestry."

"Grand," said Father with an inane smile.

"He wants to talk to Miss Ellis in private," the reverend interrupted as Father tried to walk through the doorway. "I told him it was inappropriate but he was most insistent."

The two men turned to Miranda. So now her opinion mattered, did it? She might have laughed, only she feared it would come out as a sob.

"Very well." She gathered her skirts. Her fingers had turned to ice long before, and the ruffles slid from her grasp. She took a firmer hold. "I won't be but a moment."

Slowly, she walked toward the vestry door looming before her. She would finally face the man who would be her husband, the man who sent brutes to hospital and caused women to swoon with terror.

He stood erect as a soldier at the far end of the little stone room. Women, she thought, letting her gaze sweep over him, could be utterly ridiculous.

She closed the door and waited for him to speak.

"You came." He could not fully stamp out the surprise in his deep voice.

"Yes."

He was tall and very large, though there wasn't a spare ounce of fat discernible over his entire form. The largeness of appearance came from the breadth of his shoulders, the muscles that his charcoal gray morning suit—no matter how finely tailored—could not completely hide and the long length of his strong legs encased in gray woolen trousers. It was not the elegant, thin frame of a refined man, but the brute and efficient form of a dock-worker. In short, Lord Archer possessed the sort of virile body that would catch many a lady's eye and hold it—were it not for one unavoidable fact.

She lifted her eyes to his face, or where it ought to be. Carved with a Mona Lisa smile upon its lips, a black hard mask like one might wear at Carnival stared back. Beneath the mask, his entire head was covered in tight black silk, offering not a bit of skin to view. The perversity of his costume unnerved, but she was hardly willing to swoon.

"I thought it best," he said after letting her study him, "that you enter into this union with full understanding." Black-gloved fingers ran over the silver handle of the walking stick he held. "As you are to be my wife, it would be foolish of me to try to keep my appearance from you."

He spoke with such equanimity that she could only gaze in amazement. A memory flickered before her eyes like a flame caught in a draft, a vision of a different man, in a different place. A man who also hid in shadows, whose gloriously strong body had haunted her dreams for months afterward, made her want things she hadn't the name for back then, things that made her skin heat on many a cold night. It had shamed her, the way she had coveted the dark stranger. But it could not have been Lord Archer. The stranger had a voice like shadows, rasping and weak, not like Lord Archer's strong, deep rumble.

"Look sharp, Miss Ellis!" The walking stick slammed on the stone floor with a crack, and she jumped. "Do you still intend to proceed?" he asked with more calm.

She stepped forward, and the man went rigid. "Who are you? An actor of some sort?" Her temper swelled like fire to air. "Is this some joke Father has concocted to bedevil me, because let me tell you—"

"I am Lord Benjamin Archer," he said with such acidity that she halted. His eyes flashed from behind the mask. "And it is no joke I play." The hand on the walking stick tightened. "Though there are days I wish it to be just that."

"Why do you wear that mask?"

"Asks the woman whose beauty might as well be a mask."

"*Pardon me?*"

The immobile black mask simply stared back, floating like a terrible effigy over broad shoulders.

"What is beauty or ugliness but a false front that prompts man to make assumptions rather than delving deeper. Look at you." His hand gestured toward her face. "Not a flaw or distortion of line to mar that perfect beauty. I have seen your face before, miss. Michelangelo sculpted it from cold marble three hundred years ago, his divine hand creating what men would adore." He took a step closer. "Tell me, Miss Ellis, do you not use that beauty as a shield, keeping the world at bay so that no one will know your true nature?"

"Bastard," she spat when she could find her voice. She had been beaten once or twice, forced to steal and lie, but no one had left her so utterly raw.

"I am that as well. Better you know it now."

She gathered up her train, but the heavy masses of slippery fabric evaded her grip. "I came of my own free will but will not abide cruel remarks made at my expense," she said, finally collecting herself. "Good-bye, Lord Archer."

He moved, but stopped himself as though he feared coming too close. A small gurgle died in his throat. "What will it take?"

The tightly controlled urgency in his voice made her turn back.

"If you find my character and appearance so very distasteful," she said through her teeth, "then why ask for my hand?"

His dark head jerked a fraction. "I am the last of my family line," he said with less confidence. "Though I have love for Queen and Country, I do not desire to see my ancestral lands swallowed up by the crown. I need a wife."

The idea that she would procreate with the man hadn't entered her mind. It seemed unimaginable.

"Why not court one of your nobles?" she asked through dry lips.

He lifted his chin a fraction. "There are not many fathers who would give their marketable daughters up to a man such as me."

It irked her that his words made her chest tighten in regret.

Lord Archer tilted his head and assessed her with all the warmth of a man eyeing horseflesh for purchase. "Your appearance may matter little to me but when the time comes for my heir to enter into society, your stunning looks will help a great deal to facilitate him."

She could not fault the sensibility of his plan. Even so...

"Why do you wear that mask?" she asked again.

The mask stared back.

"Are you ill? Have you some sort of sensitivity to light upon your skin?" she prompted.

"Sensitivity to light," he uttered and then gave a short laugh of derision. He lifted his head. "I am deformed." That the confession hurt his pride did not escape her. "It was an accident. Long ago."

She nodded stupidly.

"I realize my appearance is far from ideal to an attractive young lady in search of a husband. On the other hand, I can provide a lifestyle of wealth and comfort..." He trailed off as though pained by his own speech and then shifted his weight. "Well, Miss Ellis? What say you? This is between us now. Whatever your decision, your father may keep what little funds he hasn't managed to squander without fear of retribution from me."

"And if I say no? What will you do? Is there another girl you might ask?" She shouldn't care really, but her basic curiosity could not be quelled.

He flinched, a tiny movement, but on him it seemed as obvious as if he'd been struck by a blow.

"No. It has to be you." He sucked in a sharp breath and straightened like a soldier. "To speak plainly, there is no other option left to me. As to what will I do should you say no, I will continue to live alone. In short, I need you. Your help, that is. Should you grant it, Miss Ellis, you shall want for nothing."

The man in the black mask seemed to stand alone, apart from everything. Miranda knew loneliness when she saw it. Her mind drifted over another memory, one hard repressed. One of herself standing in the very same corner of the vestry, watching as Martin cut their engagement and walked away. And it had hurt. God, it had hurt. So much so that the idea of doing it to another made her queasy.

Lord Archer had shown his weakness, given her a chance to cut their agreement. He'd given her power over him. The man was clearly intelligent enough to have done so with purpose. A chance at equality was unexpected.

Still, none of that might have mattered. Foolish was the

woman who gave away her freedom out of sympathy. No, it was not sympathy or the hope of power that prompted a decision; she felt something when in the presence of this strange man, a tingling thrill that played over her belly, the sense of rapid forward motion though her body stood still. It was a feeling long dormant, one gleaned from taking a sword in hand, swaggering through dark alleys when all proper girls were in their beds. It was adventure. Lord Archer, with his black countenance and rich voice, offered a sense of adventure, a dare. She could do nothing short of picking up that gauntlet, or regret it for the rest of her days. Perhaps, then, she could help them both. The idea of helping rather than destroying filled her with a certain lightness of heart.

Miranda collected the blasted train that threatened to trip her and straightened. "We have kept my father and sisters waiting long enough, Lord Archer." She paused at the door to wait for him. "Shall we go?"

THE DISH

Where Authors Give You the Inside Scoop

From the desk of Jaime Rush

Dear Reader,

DRAGON AWAKENED and the world of the Hidden started very simply, as most story ideas do. I saw this sexy guy with an elaborate dragon tattoo down his back. But much to my surprise, the "tattoo" changed his very cellular structure, turning him into a full-fledged Dragon. I usually get a character in some situation that begs me to open the writer's "What if!" box. And this man/ Dragon was the most intriguing character yet. I had a lot of questions, as you can imagine. *Who are you? Why are you? And will you play with me?* This is the really fun part of writing for me: exploring all the possibilities. I got tantalizing bits and pieces. I knew he was commanding, controlling, and a warrior. And his name was Cyntag, Cyn for short.

   Then the heroine made an appearance, and she in no way seemed to fit with him. She was, in the early version, a suffer-no-fools server in a rough bar. And very human. I knew her name was Ruby. (I love when their names come easily like that. Normally I have to troll through lists and phone books to find just the right one.) The television show *American Restoration* inspired a new profession for Ruby, who was desperately holding on to the resto yard she inherited from her mother. I knew Ruby was raised by her uncle after being orphaned, and he'd created a book about a fairy-tale world just for her.

But I was still stumped by how these completely different people fit together. Until I got the scene where Ruby finds her uncle pinned to the wall by a supernatural weapon, and the name he utters on his dying breath: Cyntag.

Ah, that's how they're connected. [Hands rubbing together in anticipation.] Then the scene where she confronts him rolled through my mind like a movie. Hot-headed, passionate Ruby and the cool, mysterious Cyn, who reveals that he is part of a Hidden world of Dragons, magick, Elementals, and danger. And so is she. Suddenly, her uncle's bedtime stories, filled with Dragon princes and evil sorcerers, become very dangerously real. As does the chemistry that sparks between Ruby and Cyn.

I loved creating the Hidden, which exists alongside modern-day Miami. Talk about opening the "What if?" box! I found lots of goodies inside: descendants of gods and fallen angels, demons, politics, dissension, and all the delicious complications that come from having magical humans and other beings trapped within one geographical area. And a ton of questions that needed to be answered. It was quite the undertaking, but all of it a fun challenge.

We all have an imagination. Mine has always contained murder, mayhem, romance, and magic. Feel free to wander through the madness of my mind any time. A good start begins at my website, www.jaimerush.com, or that of my romantic suspense alter-ego, www.tinawainscott.com.

Jaime Rush

♥ ♥ ♥ ♥ ♥ ♥ ♥ ♥ ♥ ♥ ♥ ♥ ♥ ♥

From the desk of Kristen Ashley

Dear Reader,

I often get asked which of my books or characters are my favorites. This is an impossible question to answer and I usually answer with something like, "The ones I'm with."

See, every time I write a book, I lose myself in the world I'm creating so completely, I usually do nothing but sit at my computer—from morning until night—immersed in the characters and stories. I so love being with them and want to see what happens next, I can't tear myself away. In fact, I now have to plan my life and make sure everything that needs to get done, gets done; everyone whom I need to connect with, I connect with; because for the coming weeks, I'll check out and struggle to get the laundry done!

Back in the day, regularly, I often didn't finish books, mostly because I didn't want to say good-bye. And this is one reason why my characters cross over in different series, just so I can spend time with them.

Although I absolutely "love the ones I'm with," I will say that only twice did I end a book and feel such longing and loss that I found it difficult to get over. This happened with *At Peace* and also, and maybe especially, with LAW MAN.

I have contemplated why my emotion after completing these books ran so deep. And the answer I've come up with is that I so thoroughly enjoyed spending time with heroes who didn't simply fall in love with their heroines. They fell in love with and built families with their heroines.

In the case of LAW MAN, Mara's young cousins, Bud and Billie, badly needed a family. They needed to be protected and loved. They needed to feel safe. They needed role models and an education. As any child does. And further, they deserved it. Loyal and loving, I felt those two kids in my soul.

So when Mitch Lawson entered their lives through Mara, and he led Mara to realizations about herself, at the same time providing all these things to Bud and Billie and building a family, I was so deep in that, stuck in the honey of creating a home and a cocoon of love for two really good (albeit fictional) kids, I didn't want to surface.

I remember standing at the sink doing dishes after putting the finishing touches on that book and being near tears, because I so desperately wanted to spend the next weeks (months, years?) writing every detail in the lives of Mitch, Mara, Bud, and Billie. Bud making the baseball team. Billie going to prom. Mitch giving Bud "the talk" and giving Billie's friends the stink-eye. Scraped knees. Broken hearts. Homework. Christmases. Thanksgivings. I wanted to be a fly on the wall for it all, seeing how Mitch and Mara took Bud's and Billie's precarious beginnings on this Earth and gave them stability and affection, taught them trust, and showed them what love means.

Even now, when I reread LAW MAN, the beginning of the epilogue makes my heart start to get heavy. Because I know it's almost done.

And I don't want it to be.

Kristen Ashley

♥   ♥   ♥   ♥   ♥

From the desk of Kristen Callihan

Dear Reader,

In SHADOWDANCE, heroine Mary Chase asks hero Jack Talent what it's like to fly. After all, Jack, who has the ability to shift into any creature, including a raven in *Moonglow*, has cause to know. He tells her that it is lovely.

I have to agree. When I was fifteen, I read Judith Krantz's *Till We Meet Again*. The story features a heroine named Frederique who loves to fly more than anything on Earth. Set in the 1940s, Freddy eventually gets to fly for the Women's Auxiliary Ferrying Squadron in Britain. I cannot tell you how cool I found this. The idea of women not only risking their lives for their country but being able to do so in a job usually reserved for men was inspiring.

So, of course, I had to learn how to fly. Luckily, my dad had been a navigator in the Air Force, which made him much more sympathetic to my cause. He gave me flying lessons as a sixteenth birthday present.

I still remember the first day I walked out onto that small airfield in rural Maryland. It was a few miles from Andrews Air Force Base, where massive cargo planes rode heavy in the sky while fighter jets zipped past. But my little plane was a Cessna 152, a tiny thing with an overhead wing, two seats, and one propeller to keep us aloft.

The sun was shining, the sky cornflower blue, and the air redolent with the sharp smell of aviation gas and motor oil. I was in heaven. Here I was, sixteen, barely legal to drive a car, and I was going to take a plane up in the sky. Sitting in the close, warm cockpit with my instructor,

I went through my checklist with single-minded determination and then powered my little plane up. I wasn't nervous; I was humming with anticipation.

Being in a single-engine prop is a sensory experience. The engine buzzes so loud that you need headphones to hear your instructor. The cockpit vibrates, and you feel each and every bump through the seat of your pants as you taxi right to the runway.

It only takes about sixty miles per hour to achieve liftoff, but the sensation of suddenly going weightless put my heart in my throat. I let out a giddy laugh as the ground dropped away and the sky rushed to meet me. It was one of the best experiences of my life.

And all because I read a book.

Now that I am an author, I think of the power in my hands, to transport readers to another life and perhaps inspire someone to try something new. And while Mary and Jack do not take off in a plane—they live in 1885, after all—there might be a dirigible in their future.

From the desk of Anna Sullivan

Dear Reader,

I grew up in a big family—eight brothers and sisters—so you can imagine how crowded and noisy, quarrelsome and fun it was. We all have different distinct personalities, of course, and it made for some interesting moments. Add in a couple of dogs, friends in and out, and, well, you get the picture.

I was the shy kid taking it all in, not watching from the sidelines, but often content to sit on them with a good book in my hands. Sometimes I'd climb a big old elm tree behind our house, cradle safely in the branches, and lose myself in another world while the wind rustled in the leaves and the tree creaked and swayed.

Looking back, it's no wonder how I ended up a writer, and it's not hard to understand why my stories seem to need a village to come to life. For me, the journey always starts with the voices of the hero and heroine talking incessantly in my head, but what fun would they have without a whole cast of characters to light up their world?

The people of Windfall Island are a big, extended family, one where all the relatives are eccentric and none of them are kept out of sight. No, they bring the crazy right out and put it on display. They're gossip-obsessed, contentious, and just as apt to pick your pocket as save your life—always with a wink and a smile.

Maggie Solomon didn't grow up there, but the Windfallers took her in, gave her a home, made her part of their large, boisterous family when her own parents turned their backs on her. So when Dex Keegan shows up, trying to enlist her help without revealing his secrets, she's not about to pitch in just because she finds him...tempting. Being as suspicious and standoffish as the rest of the Windfallers, Maggie won't cooperate until she knows why Dex is there, and what he wants.

What he wants, Dex realizes almost immediately, is Maggie Solomon. Sure, she's hard-headed, sharp-tongued, and infuriatingly resistant to his charms, but she appeals to him on every level. There must be something perverse, he decides, about a man who keeps coming back for more when a woman rejects him. He enjoys their verbal sparring, though, and one kiss is all it takes for him to know he won't stop until she surrenders.

But Maggie can't give in until he tells her the truth, and it's even more incredible—and potentially explosive to the Windfall community—than she ever could have imagined.

There's an eighty-year-old mystery to solve, a huge inheritance at stake, and a villain who's willing to kill to keep the secret, and the money, from ever seeing the light of day.

The Windfallers would love for you to join them as they watch Dex and Maggie fall in love—despite themselves—and begin the journey to find a truth that's been waiting decades for those with enough heart and courage to reveal.

I really had a great time telling Dex and Maggie's story, and I hope you enjoy reading about them, and all the characters of my first Windfall Island novel.

Happy reading,

Anna Sullivan

www.AnnaSulivanBooks.com
Twitter @ASullivanBooks
Facebook.com/AnnaSullivanBooks